TEMPTATIONS OF THE PAST

Temptations of the Past

Julia Åberg

Copyright © 2024 by Julia Åberg

All rights reserved.

No part of this publication may be reproduced, distributed, or transmitted in any form or by any means, including photocopying, recording, or other electronic or mechanical methods, without the prior written permission of the publisher, except as permitted by Swedish copyright law. For permission requests, contact Julia Åberg, info@juliaabergauthor.com.

ISBN: 978-91-989700-0-5 (Paperback)
ISBN: 978-91-989700-1-2 (Hardback)
ISBN: 978-91-989700-2-9 (Ebook)

The story, all names, characters, and incidents portrayed in this production are fictitious. No identification with actual persons (living or deceased), places, buildings, and products is intended or should be inferred.

Book Cover by MiblArt
Illustrations and Interior Formatting by Mariska Maas (Rubre Art)

1st edition 2024

*To everyone who still peeks inside old
wardrobes in hopes of finding Narnia*

The tears of the Creator fell
Not in sorrow but love
Love for life and death
Love for the future and the past

The tears turned into a pond
The pond turned into a lake
And from that lake rose the first angel

CHAPTER ONE

DYING TRULY WAS AN inconvenience.
It didn't matter how many times it happened; she could never get used to the all-consuming fear that filled her, the devastation of drawing ones final breath.

Trying to still her hammering heart, she looked out at the scene that had sparked the wave of panic triggering this particular memory.

The nightclub was a battlefield. The dance floor a sea of bodies moving and swaying to the beat of the music. Or perhaps it was more like a mating ritual, less deadly but just as primal. Either way, Eliana Whitmore did not belong there.

She could feel the pump of the bass in her bones as the thumping music filled the room. The despair of dying still clung to her like a wet blanket, but she forced out even breaths and acknowledged the pain and fear as she let it pass through her. She had learned long ago that fighting the memories only made them worse.

The club before her was packed with people, the dim light casting shadows over the crowd grinding against each other on the small dance floor, the air thick and heavy. Sweat, perfume and alcohol mingled in the air, making it harder to draw in full breathes to control the emotions racing though her. A DJ's music blasted from a small dais next to the bar, the wall behind it lined with bottles from floor to ceiling. People were crowding there, trying to get a drink.

"Are you sure that's a dress, Ellie?"

No, Ellie wanted to say, *it's not.* She fought hard to keep from tugging at the hem of the black lace, still taking deep breaths to steady herself. If it had been up to her, she would have worn jeans, but apparently that wasn't an option.

"Yes, I'm sure, Lucas. It's more of a dress than most girls are wearing, and you don't seem to mind those dresses," Ellie shouted to be heard over the music at the guy next to her.

Before he could stop himself, Lucas swept the room with hungry eyes. He knew he'd been caught when he met Ellie's knowing glare. "Yeah well, most girls aren't you. I mean, you're totally hot and everything, but you're my friend. I don't like guys looking at you like..."

He trailed off and Ellie couldn't help but smirk. "Like you look at girls? You know, they're someone's friend too, right?"

Lucas' grin said it all and Ellie knew there was no point arguing. He deserved someone so much better than the girls he dragged home, but no amount of telling him helped and Ellie had long since given up.

Finally, the last shadows of fear and anger dying always filled her with left her and Ellie looked back out over the dance floor.

Just breathe, she thought as she tried to relax enough to avoid triggering round two. *It's just a club.*

She let her eyes sweep the room again, but this time she was trying to spot Jen's red dress.

"Tell me again why we're here?" Lucas said into Ellie's ear to be heard over the music. "I mean, other than the obvious reason of me hooking up with girls wearing even more non-existing dresses than yours."

He brushed against Ellie's black curls, no doubt messing up Jen's handiwork. He looked different tonight. His blond hair wasn't its usual mess but a perfect tangle of locks. His golden strands made his light blue eyes shine. His angular face was scanning the room, his nose scrunching as if he smelled something bad.

"We are supporting Jen," Ellie said sternly. "Have you done something different with your hair?"

Lucas lifted his right hand towards his hair as if to grab it but stopped himself halfway. Instead, he rolled his eyes.

"Isabelle did it. She hid my t-shirts as well, all of them. Like I'm a baby. Sometimes I swear she was adopted. No sister of mine would ever be so cruel."

That would explain it.

"I don't know if not wanting you to leave the house in shirts with offensive prints on them is cruel, Lucas."

"My shirts aren't offensive. They're awesome and you know it. Besides, you should know she has added you to her list of the greatest fashion failures of all time."

Ellie couldn't help but wince. She already had Jen who wanted to burn her entire closet, she really didn't need someone else pointing out that jeans and plain t-shirts did nothing for her supposed curves.

"Anyway, why are we supporting Jen?" Lucas asked.

Ellie sighed. She fixed her gaze on Lucas and took a deep breath. "Because she is our friend."

"Oh, okay."

Ellie turned back towards the dance floor, but Lucas clearly wasn't done.

"And we are friends with Jen because?"

"*Lucas.*"

"*Ellie.*"

Ellie rolled her eyes at him.

"What? I thought we were doing the whole saying your name with a stern expression thing. No? Okay, my bad."

Ellie couldn't help but smile.

She had met Lucas on her first day at UCLA. He was in her history class and had tried hitting on her. After failing miserably, which Ellie later learned he did most of the time, they had become friends. He was actually a really sweet guy, but he didn't allow many people to see it. Jen most certainly did not.

Lucas' voice cut through the pulsating music, a sharp contrast to the neon-lit chaos around them.

"Look, Ellie!" he shouted, leaning close to her ear, "I know you've been friends since you were kids, but seriously, she's nothing like you."

Ellie's gaze swept the crowded dance floor. Jen – vibrant, wild, and utterly unlike her – was lost in the sea of bodies. They were polar opposites. Jen reveled in the nightclub's frenzy, while Ellie preferred the quiet corners of libraries. Jen's social circle was vast; Ellie's was a solitary island.

But none of that mattered. The day they both received acceptance letters from UCLA remained etched in Ellie's memory – the shared joy, the escape from Bellingham's perpetual gloom. Of course, Jen's parents could write tuition checks without flinching, while Ellie scoured scholarship applications, her foster care history a stark reminder of financial limitations.

And yet, Jen sat with her, huddled over coffee-stained scholarship forms. Ellie could almost taste the bitterness of the fifth cup. "We don't leave, remember," Jen had declared, determination in her eyes.

Ellie smiled at the memory, her heart swelling.

She spotted Jen's black hair, a beacon in the crowd framed by a daring red dress. Without hesitation, she tugged Lucas along, parting the dancers like a ship through stormy waves. Jen stood near the bar, engrossed in conversation with a guy. Their eyes met before Ellie reached her, and in that shared glance, years of friendship spoke louder than any nightclub beat.

"Ellie!" she cried and waved.

Ellie smiled and pushed past the last grinding couple.

"Jen! This is amazing," Ellie said in her ear while hugging her.

"You really think so? We were lucky to get DJ Nat, she's really big in the house scene right now."

Jen's almond shaped brown eyes were dashing around the room, no doubt trying to judge whether or not people were enjoying themselves.

Ellie caught her face between her hands, forcing Jen to look at her. "It's great."

Jen smiled and seemed to calm down at least a little. But her smile disappeared just as fast as she looked over Ellie's shoulder and spotted Lucas.

"Great, you brought the dud," she said, and Ellie prayed Lucas hadn't heard Jen over the music.

"Did you say stud? Aw, thank you Jen. That means a lot and it is lovely to see you, too. I see your party-planning business is picking up."

No such luck.

Jen narrowed her eyes at Lucas. "I am *not* a party-planner."

Lucas held up his hand in mock surrender with a grin Ellie recognized all too well.

Please don't make it any worse, Ellie silently prayed to whoever might be listening.

"You're right. I'm sorry, 'club organizer.'" Ellie saw Jen's eyes darken but Lucas seemed determined to dig an even deeper hole for himself. "You know, Jen, the fact that jellyfish have survived for 650 million years despite not having a brain is *really* good news for you."

"Oh, bite me, Lucas."

Lucas winked, seemingly pleased with himself. "I'm getting a drink. Later!"

After Lucas left them, Jen turned her attention back to Ellie and shook her head. "Anyway, Ellie, this is Andrew. Andrew, this is Ellie."

The guy standing next to Jen gave Ellie a curt nod before turning back to his friends who huddled the other side of him.

Nice to meet you, too.

"He seems... nice, Jen. And the club is awesome." *It just sent me into a slight panic attack resulting in a near death experience but you know, other than that,* she added quietly to herself. Because really, it wasn't Jen's fault big crowds sometimes had that effect on Ellie.

Thankfully, Jen didn't seem to notice the hesitation.

"I know, right?" Jen smiled and a mischievous grin lit her face before she rather harshly, pushed Ellie out onto the dance floor. "Now, come on, let's dance."

Ellie didn't put up much of a fight. While she wouldn't have attended a place like Club Rouge had Jen not been in charge of the event there, she secretly loved every chance to dance, so she quickly lost herself to the rhythm. She would never tell Jen that though. Ellie would be dragged along to every club in town if she knew.

Jen disappeared with Andrew not long after, getting swallowed by the crowd and carried away from Ellie, but she didn't mind much. In truth, she didn't particularly care for a partner to dance. And besides, Jen looked happy, and if there was one thing Ellie wanted it was that.

Then the world around Ellie changed. *The club with its flashing lights disappeared and a grand hall with soft music filtering through air surrounded her. A light blue gown swirled gracefully around her legs as Ellie spun a laughing woman close to her.*

Then it was gone, and Club Rouge blared around her again.

Ellie didn't miss a beat as she danced. It was not the first time the memory of the ballroom had pressed on her mind, and in contrast with the previous all-consuming fear of dying, this memory always filled her with peace.

Ellie swayed to the beat, lost in the nightclub's kaleidoscope of lights. The music pulsed through her veins, urging her toward the dance floor's edge. She couldn't explain the pull, but it tugged at her like an invisible thread.

A hand, warm and insistent, landed at the small of her back. Ellie startled, heart leaping, but she didn't turn around or move away; instead, she leaned into the touch, allowing it to guide her movements. The hand slid to her hip, another joining it. Their bodies synced, a wordless rhythm.

Ellie liked to dance, but not with people she didn't know. Especially not with guys who mistook the dance floor for a free pass to grope. Yet, she remained rooted, the man's arm encircling her waist. His touch felt both familiar and safe, like a half-remembered dream.

His muscles flexed against her spine, and the air thickened. Ellie's heartbeat raced, nerves sparking. Alien emotions swirled – a cocktail of desire, fear, and vulnerability; she felt like she was drowning in sensations, desperate for air.

Then, with a gasp, she broke free. Shame washed over her as she stumbled forward, pushing through the crowd. She didn't glance back, even when the man's voice trailed after her. Each step away eased her breathing. She needed to get out of there.

The memories of another life that was not her own were a part of her. She'd had them for as long as she could remember and she often found solace in them, a part of her father's world still with her. But this, this was all her and that scared her.

Her head had started to pound, and her emotions were running wild. She felt happy, sad, angry and most of all *hot*. Not paying attention to where she was going, Ellie stumbled into a couple who were trying to eat each other's faces. At once, Ellie's knees weakened with desire and all the air left her lungs, her heartbeat quickening and warmth rushing through her lower abdomen. Now well beyond panicked, she pushed past the couple and went in search of Jen.

Fortunately, she didn't have to look for long. Jen's red dress really stood out, even in this crowd. Ellie made her way over.

"I have to go," Ellie rasped quickly.

"What? You can't leave now," Jen whined, her eyes pleading.

"I'm sorry but I have to study for this big test on Monday, and I have a really bad headache."

It wasn't a complete lie. Ellie's head still pounded and there *was* a test. Jen didn't need to know Ellie could probably pass it in her sleep.

Jen looked like she was about to argue but Andrew leaned in and said something in her ear. Jen giggled and then gave Ellie a quick hug. "Okay, be safe and don't wait up."

Ellie nodded. "I'll be fine. Have a good night, and you be safe, too!"

She turned to find Lucas, but he was gone. Ellie groaned. The headache was getting worse by the minute and all she really wanted to do was get out of there. She couldn't even imagine the humiliation of running into that guy again. Having no idea what he looked like, she didn't even know what to hide from.

But Ellie couldn't just leave without telling Lucas. After all, it was Ellie who had dragged him there with her, not wanting to go alone. The least she could do was let him know she was leaving.

Ellie made her way through the dancing crowd when a man

blocked her path. Ellie panicked – what if it was him? She stubbornly focused her eyes on the floor, apologized and sneaked around him, but when she looked up, he stood a few feet ahead of her again.

It was definitely *not* the same guy. The man wore a pair of dark leather pants and a loose white shirt, which was weird even for this club. Light cascaded from him in waves, illuminating his every feature. He towered above the unknowing crowd and his muscles could be seen through the thin fabric of his shirt. His olive skin made Ellie believe he hadn't spent a minute out of the sun in his entire life, and his dark green eyes were full of intensity. There was something familiar about him that Ellie couldn't place. It was more a feeling than the man.

But what made her sure it was not the man she'd danced with was the fact that the man in front of her was more or less see-through.

He stood motionless, eyes locked onto Ellie, his dark crown of shoulder length hair floating around his carved face. Ellie's head pounded even more, and she looked around to see if anyone else witnessed the man before her, but everyone around her were dancing like before. When Ellie looked at the man again, a girl passed straight through him.

Ellie spun on her heels and bumped straight into Lucas.

"Ellie, are you okay? You look like you've seen a ghost," Lucas yelled, concern in his eyes.

"Do you see him?" Ellie yelled back frantic.

Lucas looked over her shoulder, confused. "See who?"

"Him." Ellie turned to point but the man was gone. She darted her eyes across the room, but he was nowhere to be found.

Lucas looked at her in real alarm now. "Are you sure you're okay?"

Ellie shook her head, trying to clear it. "Yes, I'm fine. It's just been a weird night and I have a really bad headache. I'm gonna head home."

"Oh, do you want me to walk you?" Lucas asked. Ellie didn't miss the disappointment in his voice nor the quick glance towards the bar. A pretty blonde stood there, and she was exactly Lucas' type – female. He wasn't very picky.

But Lucas could be very protective, and Ellie could practically see the internal struggle: go with Ellie or stay and hit on the blonde. Ellie decided to put him out his misery.

"No, I'll walk back. The fresh air might do me some good," Ellie said and looked over at the bar again. "I think the blonde at the bar smiled at you. You should go over there."

Lucas' eyes were eager as he responded. "Okay, yeah? Great, because I have this new line I've been dying to try out. Listen, 'Are you made of copper and tellurium? Because you are *cute*.' Awesome right?"

Ellie wanted to tell him to just be himself, but he was already pushing his way toward the bar.

Ellie didn't go after him but instead pushed herself free of the crowd.

THE BLACKNESS EMBRACED HIM with its nothingness, almost giving the comfort of an old friend. He had long ago lost count on how long he'd been drifting between life and death. It might have been weeks or decades. When you were left with nothing but your mistakes, time ceased to matter. And he had made mistakes. Too many.

Her face filled his mind like it always did. The crinkle at the corner of her brown eyes as she smiled, her long black hair that fell down her back, every detail of her forever etched in his mind. Then her eyes turned pained, and her hair matted with sweat.

He let his mind drift to his other mistakes.

A light pierced the dark and its embrace shattered. Then he saw her. She stood in a sea of bodies looking straight at him. Her black hair fell down her back in the same way it always had, but her eyes were green, not brown, and they held only fear.

No, she was gone. There was nothing he could do to change that. But he would correct his second mistake and then the Creator might grant him his final rest.

CHAPTER
TWO

THE COOL NIGHT AIR enveloped Ellie, easing the worst of her headache and dissipating some of the confusing emotions that had plagued her.

Outside Club Rouge, the line still snaked along the sidewalk, and despite everything, Ellie felt genuine happiness for Jen. No one else believed Jen could ever make it into UCLA, but Ellie knew her better than anyone. Jen projected a carefully curated image to the world – parties, boys, and not a single care in the world, but Ellie knew the other sides of her friend as well.

As Ellie walked, she pulled her jacket tighter around her, shielding herself from the cool autumn wind that tugged at her hair. The throb in her head still persisted slightly, a reminder of the night's unusual weirdness, and that was saying a lot coming from her.

She had left the bustling clubbing district behind and found herself halfway to campus. The apartment buildings loomed on either side of the street, their windows dark and silent. The few people she encountered moved with heads down, hurrying through the night.

As Ellie strolled along the dimly lit street, a passing car momentarily disrupted the quiet. She glanced back to the other side of the road when she spotted him – the same man from the club. He stood motionless, his gaze fixed on her. Slowly, deliberately, he raised his arm, pointing directly at Ellie. Before she could comprehend what was happening, pain surged through her body, doubling her over. It felt as though the very air had been knocked out of her lungs, leaving her gasping for breath.

The man was from her memories, or he *felt* like her memories yet he didn't. He felt like a fragment of her past, yet somehow more tangible, less ephemeral. The memories were her father's, or so she guessed. They usually showed her glimpses of a different world full of wonder, but not once had she questioned their authenticity; they were as vivid as her own heartbeat. She had tried to ignore them and block them out – not because she didn't believe them, but because it hurt too much to not know.

Why had he abandoned her on Earth, adrift and alone, with nothing but these fleeting recollections from a life that wasn't truly hers? The ache of not knowing gnawed at her, leaving her with more questions than answers. With time, she'd been left with no choice but to accept she would probably never know.

But the man in front of her was real, not a shadow from another life. And the pain was most certainly her own.

Ellie lurched away when a hand touched her back. A woman stood beside her. Her mouth moved and Ellie realized she'd said something, but Ellie simply glanced at the place the man had stood, but he was gone.

"Are you alright?" the woman asked again kindly.

Ellie tried to get her breathing back to normal, but it didn't help she could *feel* the woman's concern.

Actually, she could feel everything.

The sadness of the girl on the other side of the street, the fear of the old lady clutching her purse a few feet away, the pain of the man with a limp who turned the corner. Ellie lived it all. It felt as though a darkness was gnawing at the very core of her being, devouring her very essence.

Deeper and deeper she fell, and just like at the club, she was drowning in an ocean of emotions. Ellie sensed the woman's gaze intensify along with her worry and at once, she fell deeper. In that moment, she managed to stumble away, assuring the stranger she was fine. Ellie quickly made her way off the street and turned into an alley that swallowed her. She sank to the ground, her limbs trembling.

Desperate, Ellie drew in a lungful of air, attempting to steady herself. But her breaths emerged as short gasps, erratic and insufficient.

This is ridiculous, Ellie thought. The harder she struggled, the deeper she sank, but she stubbornly kept fighting against whatever pulled her down.

As the last piece of strength left her body, a light, pure and unwavering, pierced the darkness that surrounded her. Then came another and another until Ellie found herself bathed in their luminance. And then everything went black.

SOMETHING WET LIGHTLY TOUCHED her cheek when she woke again.

Ellie fluttered open her eyes and winced at the pain throbbing in her temples. The world spun as she slowly rolled onto her back, the rough pavement cool against her skin. She closed her eyes again as her mind struggled to catch up. What the hell had just happened?

TEMPTATIONS OF THE PAST

As she lay there, trying to regain her composure, a pressure weighed down on her chest. Confused, Ellie cracked one eyelid open and was met by a pair of icy blue eyes.

The puppy tipped its head to the side with an amused look in its eyes. Before Ellie could react, the puppy closed the distance between them. Its pink tongue darted out, leaving a wet trail from her chin to her forehead. Ellie blinked, stunned. The dog gave her one last glance before springing off her chest.

Ellie slowly sat up, cradling her sore head in her hands. She looked at the dog, utterly at a loss as to why it was there, then scanned the dimly lit alley that was covered in graffiti, wondering what *she* was doing there.

The puppy met Ellie's stare with one of its own before it nonchalantly started to lick its paw. The fluffy bundle of pristine white looked more like a living snowball than a dog. Its fur, as soft as freshly fallen snow, obscured any discernible features. No collar adorned its neck, no tag to hint at an owner. It was as if the puppy had materialized out of thin air.

Ellie's lips curved into a gentle smile as she leaned closer. The puppy's eyes met hers, and she whispered, almost conspiratorially, "Where did you come from, little one?"

Glancing around the alley once more, Ellie couldn't remember much of what happened for her to end up there, except pain and panic. Who had that man been and what on earth had he done to her?

Ellie instinctively reached for her hair, intending to sweep it away from her face, but as her hand grazed her ear, she noticed a sticky warmth clinging to her skin. She froze, her heart skipping a beat. When she looked down at her palm, her breath caught in her throat.

Blood.

Crimson and vivid against her pale skin, it stained her fingertips. Ellie did her best to wipe it off with the sleeve of her jacket and stood.

Her dress was covered in a layer of dirt, and Ellie cursed under her breath. She would have to clean it before Jen ever saw the dress or she would never hear the end of it. The puppy watched her straighten the fabric and dust herself off the best she could.

Ellie's head throbbed, a relentless ache that echoed through her skull. But amidst the pain, there was a strong relief of only finding herself there.

This must be a new memory, she mused. There was always a different experience each time a new memory surfaced, and clearly this one had decided to appear as a shot of adrenaline straight to her brain. She pushed the small voice that said she hadn't had a new memory in years and that they never hurt to the back of her mind. Ellie didn't want to dwell on the implications. She wasn't sure she could deal with anymore weird in her life.

A sudden ray of sunlight pierced the alley, catching her eye. Ellie squinted upward, her vision adjusting to the brightness. The sun was rising, casting long shadows across the pavement.

How long was I out?

She pushed herself up, wincing as her sore muscles protested. She grabbed her purse from the ground and pulled out her phone. She hoped Jen had spent the night with Andrew, but when she entered her password, several notifications glared back at her. Five missed calls and four texts from Jen, and three messages from Lucas. Apparently, the blonde in the bar had fallen for his charms and Lucas was kindly letting Ellie know he was the master of the universe. Ellie rolled her eyes as she scrolled though the texts.

Jen's texts were first filled with concern, but the last one was some cryptic stuff about how she 'understood' and that Ellie should enjoy herself.

As Ellie made to leave, the puppy barked, echoing through the eerie silence of the alley. She turned and locked her gaze onto the puppy. Its eyes, those soulful, pleading orbs, held her captive. For the first time, Ellie truly understood the expression 'puppy eyes.' She couldn't leave it there, but animals weren't allowed in the dorms. Ellie wavered between compassion and reason for several minutes before she finally surrendered.

"Fine," she whispered, her voice carrying promises and uncertainty. "You can come, but only for tonight."

The puppy wagged its tail and bounded up to her, licking at her bare legs. Ellie laughed and they stepped out onto the street, the sun's warmth enveloping them. Ellie glanced down at her newfound friend.

"You owe me," she teased, and the puppy tilted its head, as if understanding every word.

SMUGGLING THE PUPPY INTO the building wasn't the daunting task Ellie had thought it would be. They only passed two people, neither of whom spared them more than a glance. As quietly as possible, Ellie slid her key into the lock.

Ellie's bleary eyes adjusted to the familiar room; its contours etched into her memory. Jen's half a riot of chaos, Ellie's a haven of simplicity.

Jen's side resembled a hurricane's aftermath. Clothes lay strewn like casualties of a fashion war. Posters adorned the walls, but they weren't mere posters; they were shrines to unattainable heartthrobs – the kind of guys who could make a girl forget her own name. Their smoldering gazes and whispered promises lingered in the air.

And then there was Jen's bedspread – a pink explosion of frills and lace, now crumpled at the foot of her bed.

Ellie's half of the room stood in stark contrast. Some might call it boring, but she preferred the term *uncomplicated*. Her bedspread was a serene sea of muted blues, a canvas for dreamless nights. Why would one wish to dream at night when your waking hours were more than enough to screw with you head? No posters adorned her walls – no brooding eyes or promises of eternal love.

Plain and uncomplicated. Ellie couldn't help but grin at the irony. Maybe uncomplicated wasn't the best word to describe her anymore, but a girl could dream, right?

The room was just as she left it and the familiarity of it almost made her doubt the last few hours had even happened.

Nothing happened, she reminded herself. Just a new memory.

Jen lay sprawled in her bed, one arm flung over her eyes and the sheets tangled by her feet. The shear baby-doll she called her nightgown exposed enough for Ellie to avert her eyes. She sighed and shuffled towards her own bed. Her heavy eyes demanded sleep, but the puppy seemed to have other plans.

It jumped up onto Jen's bed, causing her to jerk awake. Ellie cringed, trying to keep still – perhaps Jen wouldn't see her and go back to sleep. But even if Jen hadn't seen Ellie, she definitely saw the dog on her bed, especially when it licked her face with great vigor.

"Ellie! I see you over there. What the hell is this?"

"A puppy," Ellie said, deciding truth with as few details as possible was the best way to go.

"Yes, thank you. I can see it's a puppy. I am asking why it is in my bed." Jen pushed the puppy down onto the floor and scrambled out of bed. At least she didn't seem to notice her ruined dress.

"I found it on the streets. I couldn't just leave it there. I'll try to find its home tomorrow, I promise."

Jen, still groggy with sleep, seemed to accept her explanation, but then her eyes snapped back to Ellie's. "And why were you on the streets? You left hours before me but when you didn't pick up your phone, I assumed you'd gone home with that guy."

Ellie filled with alarm; Jen had seen him? "You... you saw him?"

"Everyone saw you; you were practically having sex right there on the dance floor." Ellie flushed a bright red. Oh, that guy. She had forgotten about that guy.

She managed to stammer out an answer. "No, I just went for a long walk and lost track of time." Jen was about to argue, but Ellie hurriedly added, "and what about you? I thought you'd be with Andrew?"

"Don't talk to me about Andrew," Jen said, and Ellie thanked her lucky star Jen had the attention span of a goldfish. She had no idea how she would have explained what had actually happened had she been forced to.

"He and his friends were such jerks. They got wasted and tried to start a fight, so I had them thrown out."

Ellie blinked a few times. "You can have people thrown out?"

"Of course, and no guy was about to ruin my night."

"Are you okay?" Ellie asked.

Jen usually didn't introduce guys to her if she didn't really like them, and the way she'd been talking about Andrew the last few weeks had led Ellie to believe she *really* liked him. But Jen waved her worries away.

"Yeah, he was just being an ass. I'll talk to him tomorrow and remind him I am the best thing that has happened to him and show him the bracelet he can buy to make it up to me."

With that, Jen went back to her bed and crawled under the covers.

Ellie let out the breath she'd been holding and skimmed out of her dress and into the t-shirt she slept in. The puppy lay at the foot of her bed, fast asleep with its head tucked under its tail. Ellie didn't have it in her to push it away, so instead, she slipped under the covers and closed her eyes.

"Ellie?" Jen's voice was muffled as she spoke.

"Mhm?"

"The dog goes tomorrow."

Ellie smiled a little. "I promise."
"And Ellie?"
"Yes?"
"You're paying for dry cleaning."
Shit.

ELLIE DID AS PROMISED the next day and went down to the library to print some flyers. She put a photo of the puppy, who was a Siberian husky according to a quick internet search, in the center of the flyer, then added her phone number underneath so the owner could contact her about picking it up. She stuck the flyers mainly around the streets near the alley, but she put a few up around campus as well, just to be sure.

But no one called.

When a week had passed, Jen finally succumbed and allowed him to stay. The puppy was quite charming when he chose to be, even melting Jen's heart.

That left only the small problem of the housing regulations. No pets, except small fish, were allowed in the dorms and Ellie didn't think they would believe the puppy was her service animal. She was in deep thought when Lucas spoke beside her.

"Don't you think hot chocolate would like to be called beautiful, just once?"

Ellie blinked in confusion.

"Never mind, what are you thinking so hard about?"

They were at a café on campus, sitting at a small table in the back where the clatter from the counter wasn't quite as loud. "I was just thinking about the puppy. I don't want to put him in a shelter, but I just don't see how I can keep him."

"You've had him for a week. If no one has noticed by now, I doubt they will. Besides," Lucas continued, looking down at the puppy, who lay under the table. "I get the feeling that if he doesn't want them to see him, they won't. I swear there is something strange about that dog."

Ellie looked down at the puppy who was currently licking his more private parts and laughed, waving Lucas' concerns away.

But as the days passed, Ellie began to wonder whether or not Lucas had been right after all. Ellie and the puppy had been coming back from a walk when she literally ran into the hall monitor, but she had simply steadied Ellie, asked if she was okay and walked on. After that, Ellie stopped worrying and the puppy took permanent residence in her dorm.

Both Jen and Lucas kept pestering her about naming him, but Ellie didn't feel like any one name suited him, so instead, she settled for Puppy.

CHAPTER THREE

Sunlight filtered through the leaves, dappling the grass below. She sat in the soft glade as a little girl, the dew-kissed blades tickling her bare feet. The world felt both familiar and strange.

"I really don't think you should eat all of those nuts." Eliana lay in the grass at eye-level with the mouse in front of her.

Why not? Do you think I'm getting fat? Because that's the whole point! The annoyed tone in the mouse's voice rang in her mind. Mice, they could be so touchy.

The brown mouse finished with the last nut and scurried out of the clearing, disappearing through the trees. Eliana rolled onto her back, watching the clouds pass by. The basket full of berries stood beside her in the grass, forgotten for the time being.

Then, with a blink, Eliana found herself walking through the forest, the basket still in her hand. She glanced to her right, knowing that the wolves were watching their new pups play by their cave a few feet away from where she stood. It wouldn't take long to stop by and say hi. Who would even know?

Eliana took the right turn and continued to walk. After only a couple of minutes, the wolves' cave came into view, and she giggled as the pups jumped on her.

"Hi, did you miss me?"

Their wagging tails and barks of joy told her more than words ever could. They were still too young to talk to her the way older animals could. The pups needed to learn how to sort through their thoughts first. At the moment, their minds were a jumble of sensations, instincts, and fleeting impressions, nothing coherent enough for Ellie to grasp.

They love you; you always give them that weird food. They say they like it. *A big gray wolf walked up beside Eliana while the pups were busy sniffing at her pockets. That's where she usually had the dog treats she would bring for them. Not today though.*

I've told you a thousand times, Moonclaw, it's not weird food, it's dog treats. You know, candy, but for dogs. *The wolf named Moonclaw made a sound that reminded Eliana of a snort.*

Wolves don't have candy, we have food.

Then the wolves faded away like a whisper on the wind.

This was usually when Ellie woke up but instead, she walked up a path. She was no longer a little girl, but herself.

As she approached the path's end, a small house materialized before her. Its wooden walls exuded warmth, and the red door stood as a silent invitation. Beneath the windows, flowers bloomed – a kaleidoscope of colors, each petal a fragment of her past.

And then realization dawned on her. This was not the human world. It was the world from her memories. The moment the thought flew through her mind she knew she was right. It felt right. *Some part* of Ellie had always believed her father had left her in the human world to keep her safe, but looking at the house in front of her, she realized it wasn't a mere dwelling; it was her sanctuary. The walls held echoes of laughter, whispered secrets, and the promise of belonging. Ellie had been safe here.

In front of the house stood two figures. Ellie walked up to them, but before she could speak, the woman caught her in fierce hug. "Mom, relax. I'm home now."

The woman who had raised her as her own drew back and wiped tears from her eyes. The sad smile on her face and the serious look in her father's eyes made Ellie wary.

"What's going on?" she asked when something at her father's feet caught her eye. "Why is my bag here?"

"I'm so sorry, Eliana, they've found you. You have to leave, now. A man is waiting for you by the river. He will keep you safe."

Ellie's head spun, questions colliding like storm clouds. How had they discovered her? Her vision blurred, and she stood rooted in place, caught between fear and disbelief.

"Eliana, listen to me," the man's voice pleaded. "We knew this day might come. There has always been the chance that whatever protection your father put on you before he left you with us wouldn't hold them off forever."

Ellie looked into the kind eyes of the man she knew and loved as her father. The one who had sheltered and loved her, who had held her through nightmares and believed in her dreams.

"He's not my father, you are." The voice held all of the determination of a six-year-old and Ellie fought the tears that were threatening to fall. "I don't want to leave you."

"Eliana, look at me. Look at me." It was her mother. "You know we have always loved you as our own daughter and we always will. But it is not your destiny to die here today. So now I need you to run, do you hear me? You run and don't look back."

"But you have to come with me, you will –"

"We have to stay here to give you as much time as possible." Her father looked over Ellie's shoulder and swore. "They are almost here. Now, run!"

Tears were streaming down 18-year-old Ellie's cheeks as she picked up the bag and slung it over her slender shoulder. As she went to hug her mother goodbye, something broke through the trees. Her father immediately pushed Ellie behind himself and his wife.

"Hand over the girl. There is no need for you to die here today." The man's cool voice sent shills down Ellie's spine.

Her father turned his head towards Ellie and told her to run one last time before he turned back to face the man again. "You will not lay a hand on her."

Whatever was said after that, Ellie didn't hear. The dream moved her away from the scene and towards the trees. But before she could reach the tree line, she smashed into something hard and unyielding. Hands grabbed her arms hard, and she looked up to a beautiful but cold face. Ellie thought she heard her mother cry out something, but she wasn't sure. She twisted in the man's grip, but it was useless, the girl in the dream was only six-years-old and fighting a grown man. Ellie could feel the fear of the little girl and she thrashed, desperately trying to free herself.

Then something gray at the corner of her eye caught Ellie's attention. Before she had time to react, Moonclaw flew out from between the trees and latched his jaws around the man's throat. The man screamed and let go of Ellie, his hands desperately trying to pull Moonclaw off him. This time there was no mistaking her mother's cry.

"ELIANA, RUN!"

She ran.

ELLIE SHOT FROM THE bed with a gasp. Puppy sat at the foot of her bed looking at her, an unreadable expression in his eyes. The dream was still vividly real in Ellie's mind, except it didn't feel like a dream at all but a memory. And not a *memory,* but a real memory. A fragment of her past, a piece she'd believed lost in the labyrinth of time. Ellie's childhood had been a blur – a tumble of foster homes, faces, and fractured stability. The trauma of constant upheaval had cast a fog over her earliest years. Whenever that small voice of reason whispered, *you should remember something,* she'd told it to shut up. The pain of forgetting was easier to bear than the weight of what might lie hidden.

"It took you long enough. I hope they are not overestimating your powers."

The voice made Ellie jump and she looked around the room. The same man Ellie had first seen in the club and then on the street stood in the corner of the room. He moved towards the bed and Ellie scrambled up against the headboard. Seeing him up close, Ellie noticed a wilderness in him she couldn't place.

Ellie opened her mouth to speak but no sound left her throat.

"Not here, child," the man's voice sliced through the room, and he gestured toward the opposite side.

Ellie's gaze darted to Jen in her bed. She willed Jen awake, silently pleading for her eyes to flutter open, but Jen remained lost in dreams.

Before Ellie could process anything else, a brilliant light erupted, consuming the room. It was as if the very walls dissolved, leaving only luminescence. A sudden force took hold of her and pulled her out into nothingness, dragging her through a maze of light. With a thump, Ellie landed in damp grass.

The dorm was gone and in its place was a forest. Or to be more exact, a clearing in a forest. Lines of trees closed it off from the rest of the world in a wide circle. Morning dew covered every strand of grass and spring flowers were slowly waking from their long slumber.

Ellie could hear water purling from a small pond on her right, water rippling down from a large rock. It was beautiful.

The man sat down in the middle of the meadow. At once, the flowers around him were in full bloom and animals were emerging from the forest around them, settling down near him. Ellie watched in awe as birds landed on his shoulders, twittering happily.

"Please, sit."

His voice startled her out of her trance. At a loss of anything else to do, Ellie slumped down, startling some of the deer to her left. A few whispered words from the man and they settled back into feasting on the moist grass.

"Who... who are you?" Ellie's voice shook but she was glad when words left her mouth.

The man looked up and shooed the birds away with a gentleness that surprised Ellie. "I am Hayyel. I was assigned to your protection when I lived. It seems the Creator didn't end the task after my death."

Ellie only stared.

"Close your mouth, Eliana, a lady does not gape like a guppy."

Ellie's mouth snapped shut, but not for long. "What do you want with me?"

"The spell that was put on you when you were a child is disappearing and your powers are awakening. I am here to teach you how to control them." Hayyel's words flowed effortlessly, as if they were the most natural thing in the world.

It wasn't. "What spell, what powers?"

"Have you never experienced something you couldn't explain? Felt emotions not yours?"

Ellie immediately thought of the night at the club. Oh, and the constant stream of memories not her own came to mind.

"Ah, I can see you have. Well, that is your power, to feel and control emotions. You are an Empath, Eliana"

Ellie looked at him with a blank expression. "Oh, okay. Of course. Well, if you don't mind, I am going to wake up now. So, it was nice meeting you, but I hope I never see you again."

Ellie closed her eyes hard and willed herself to wake up.

"Eliana, what are you doing?"

"Hush, I'm concentrating."

But nothing happened. Ellie opened one eye. She was still in the meadow.

"This is not a dream, Eliana. Now pay attention!" Hayyel's words sliced through the air, demanding her focus.

Ellie obeyed, opening both eyes to meet his unwavering gaze.

"Your mother was human," he continued, each syllable a revelation. "She died giving birth to you. Your father, knowing your life was in peril, used his powers to conceal you with a couple sworn to protect you – like me. Your father was not human."

Ellie's heart raced. Everything in her mind willed her to turn away from this, that once she passed this line there was no going back. But the desire to unlock her past had always simmered within her like a relentless flame.

"My parents died in a car accident." Obviously, Ellie knew that was a lie and it sounded bleak even in her own ears, but she desperately clung to the illusion.

"That is what you were told, but it is not the truth," Hayyel said with conviction, and it was all it took for the lie to crumble like brittle paper.

The dream – no, the memory – she'd just had screamed in her mind. And although she knew she should go back, the will to know was too strong. "If my father wasn't human, what was he?"

Hayyel unblinking gaze held hers. "Your father was an angel."

A what? Ellie's mind whirled, grappling with the revelation. He was a *what? But then that would mean... that I am an angel, too?* Her head spun, and her vision blurred. The people in her visions – those elusive memories – had always felt otherworldly. Yet she'd never allowed herself to dwell on what they truly were. Now, nausea clawed at her, and she fought to remain conscious.

"He – he was an angel?" Ellie squeaked out. "As in an actual angel?"

Hayyel looked at her, his eyes unreadable. "That would depend on what you think an angel is."

Well, if that wasn't cryptic, Ellie didn't know what was. She sighed and her temper flared, a piercing clarity through the fogginess that clouded her mind.

"Wings, halo, just kicking it up among the clouds..." she said in a dry voice.

Hayyel did not look amused.

"Then the answer is no, he was not what you think an angel is."

Silence.

Ellie threw her hands up in surrender. She was beyond the point of no return now. "Please enlighten me then, oh great master, on what a real angel is."

Hayyel gave her a stern look but thankfully decided to answer. "An angel is a magical being. They serve no God and they do not live up among the clouds as you so eloquently put it. They are the Protectors of this world and everything in it." Hayyel paused and searched her eyes for something, actually looking slightly concerned. "Do you want me to continue, you look pale?"

She didn't trust her voice enough to speak, so Ellie settled for a nod.

"Before time itself, there was our Creator. She spent hundreds of your human years creating our world, giving it life. For a while, she sat back and watched her creation, relishing in its beauty, but she soon felt selfish for not sharing it with someone other than the animals. That was when she created the first angel, Michael. You have never seen anything more beautiful than he. For a time, they continued to enjoy this paradise, living in harmony with nature. But Michael longed for others of his kind and soon the rest of the First Four were born. The Archangels, Michael, Raphael, Gabriel and Uriel.

"As the Creator continued to fill the world with life, she created more angels to protect it. These angels had different gifts and were divided into orders, protectors of all things living in the Creator's world. The first four were charged with protecting the angels.

"Men were not created, they evolved as your learned ones say. So were many other species but none more important than man. They looked like the angels and as time passed, the angels saw their intelligence grow. The First Four understood they would need to create more angels to both look after and control this growing species. The Creator blessed the angels with the ability to reproduce and the first angel was born."

Okay. Nothing to be alarmed about. Just an almighty creator who created the world. Ellie had always known she wasn't all human, why not half angel?

Hayyel continued, seemly unaware of Ellie's internal struggle. "I am sure you recognize some of what I am telling you. Angels have fallen into myth here in the human realm, but they are still very much real. There is a veil that divides their two worlds now, angels reside in one, humans in the other."

"But wait. I always thought my father's world was destroyed, and that is why he left me here."

She remembered the first time she'd glimpsed the memory of a dead, burning world. It had offered strange comfort – the belief that her father had abandoned her due to some catastrophic event. As a child, she'd spun fanciful tales about him, but reality had a way of shattering illusions. Still, that burning world remained – an ember of hope that her father had fought to save her.

Then another part of what Hayyel had said registered. "And if my mother was human and my father an angel and they were supposed to live in separate realms, how the hell am I here?"

"Your father left you in the human realm not because of the destruction of the angels' home but because it was impossible for you to stay there and live."

Hayyel only answered the questions he wanted to and simply ignore anything else, something that was causing Ellie to quickly lose her temper again. "Why couldn't I live there? And what about my mom?"

Hayyel looked at Ellie and a sudden sadness washed over his eyes, but it was gone so fast Ellie almost thought she imagined it.

"Your mother died giving birth to you and that is all I can say. Please do not speak of this again. Your father tried to hide you in his realm, but he soon understood you could never be safe there."

Despite the fact that Ellie had lived without her parents all her life, a small piece of her heart still broke for her mother. A mother she had never known and never would.

"The Archangels have forsaken the duty bestowed upon them by the Creator. They no longer look to protect life but to conquer it. Anyone in their way is either enslaved or killed. The angels are living in fear."

"But I'm sure there a lot of other children in danger there," Ellie said, confused, gently closing the door to the corner of her heart where she put her mother. "What is so special about me?"

"You are the Empath."

The way he said left an uneasy feeling in the pit of Ellie's stomach. Not *an* Empath but *the* Empath. Suddenly, Ellie wasn't sure she wanted to know anything else.

"What do you want from me?" she said, a slight tremor in her voice.

There were other questions burning at the back of her mind, but Ellie wasn't sure she would like the answers, so she pushed them back.

"You need to learn how to control your powers. If left untamed, they can hurt both you and people close to you."

"But I'm just me, just Ellie." Whoever that was. Before, it was the orphan girl with glints of memories of a lost world. Now apparently, she was half angel and Empath belonging to a lost world that was very much still there.

"I cannot force this choice upon you, it is one you yourself must make. But your powers will grow, and I cannot promise that the veil separating our worlds will keep you safe any longer."

Ellie opened her mouth and closed it. What could she possibly say?

Hayyel saved her from having to answer that question. "Do not decide now. Your Guardian will bring you back when you have made a decision."

Ellie was exhausted and her voice was tired when she asked, "I have a guardian?"

"Yes, and here he is. He will take you back."

Ellie looked behind her and saw Puppy walking up to her. By this point she was too tired to care.

She followed Puppy and entered the blazing light again.

CHAPTER FOUR

The sun caressed Ellie's skin as she lay in the grass with Puppy beside her.

The small park, hidden from the world's hustle, had become her sanctuary. Day by day, she sought solace there beneath a sprawling oak tree that created the perfect balance between dappled sunlight and cool shade.

Ellie looked at Puppy and sighed. A week had passed since her encounter with Hayyel yet doubt still gnawed at her. Aside from the walk from the meadow, Puppy had behaved like any normal puppy would, but Ellie watched his every move with suspicion.

Then abruptly, the park vanished and the realm of the angels appeared.

The world burned. Before, Ellie had always focused on the flames, but she looked more closely now. The flames licked at the trees as they devoured the forest until there was nothing left. A world covered in ashes. Normally, the memory let go of her at this point but not this time. Instead, it took her deeper.

Walking through the burnt field, something caught her eye. A small green plant pushed through the blackness, standing defiant against the darkness.

Then she was back at the park.

The world might have burnt but it had not died. There was something there, something refusing to give up.

Ellie groaned and pinched her eyes closed. What did all of this mean? Somehow it had been easier to think everything in her memories was just that, memories. But now she couldn't help but wonder about her father's people, the angels, and their obvious suffering.

The Empath.

With a sigh, Ellie opened her eyes. A mother and her child playing by the pond caught her attention, and suddenly Ellie wondered what emotions they were experiencing. Hayyel had revealed that her powers allowed her to sense and control others' emotions, but how?

She sat up, fixing her gaze on the scene, attempting to feel anything.

At first, nothing happened, and Ellie scoffed at her own silliness. But then, like a spark in the dark, an emotion flickered within her – a pure, unbridled joy only a child could know. She quickly averted her gaze. *What am I doing?*

Ellie sat back in the grass. She couldn't deny the sudden rush she felt. A strange power surged through her, making her feel like she could do anything. A small smile graced her lips as the mother and child moved farther away, disappearing from view.

She glanced at her watch. *Crap.* She was late – again. Ellie hurried to gather her books and belongings and then ran from the park. Dr. Garner would not appreciate it if she was late again to his class on ancient Greek mythology.

You would think there wouldn't be any rush in this particular subject seeing as history was rather unlikely to change, but when Lucas had pointed that out to Dr. Garner, well, let's just say he had *not* agreed.

Ellie loved to study – it was what she was good at – but she seemed to have some sort of disease making it impossible for her to be on time. Ellie didn't know what it was. She could be ready an hour before class began and yet, she always barely made it. Today proved to be no exception.

Flushed and out of breath, Ellie ran through the almost empty corridors. She glanced at her watch again and saw she had three minutes to spare when she finally reached the doors. With Puppy by her side and a triumphant smile, Ellie pushed the doors open and entered the room. It was empty.

Why was the room empty?

Ellie went back out to check the room number. She had accidentally gone to the wrong room before and those were the most awkward two hours of her life.

Today, however, Ellie was sure she was at the right room after double and triple checking, but there was no one there. Ellie looked at her phone, about to call Lucas when it started ringing. "Lucas, where are you?"

"I am at the library, where we decided to meet and study because class was canceled, remember?" Lucas replied, sounding amused.

This was not the first time he had suffered from her time-management problems. He was right of course. Ellie vaguely remembered the conversation, but her mind had been otherwise occupied lately.

"Shit, you're right, sorry," she said. "I'll be there in like two minutes, three tops." Ellie hurried towards the library and tried to shoo Puppy away once they reached the building, but he walked right past her and into the library.

No one even looked at him as he took his place under the table where Lucas was waiting. She didn't have time to question his strange behavior and instead hurried through the bookshelves.

"I'm so sorry," Ellie said as she sat down opposite Lucas, but he waved her off.

"No worries, you allowed me some quality time with my favorite person."

Ellie looked around, confused, and Lucas smirked.

"Me, of course. You know, on average there are seven people in the world that look like you, and to them I would just like to say, you are welcome."

Ellie rolled her eyes and opened her books, but she couldn't concentrate. She couldn't shake the feeling of both fear and excitement she had felt in the park.

She looked over at Lucas. He wore one of his usual t-shirts today; apparently Isabelle had taken pity on him and given them back. This one had a print that said, 'Why be rude when you can be nude?' His hair was its usual mess as well and kept falling in his eyes while he read.

"You take religion, right?"

Lucas looked up from his books, a little startled. "Yeah, a total snooze fest, I would not recommend it."

"What do you know about angels?"

"Not a lot, it's not bible school," Lucas said.

He was about to return to his books, but Ellie pushed on. "Yes, well do you believe in them?"

Lucas paused for a moment, studying Ellie's face. Something there must have alerted him to the seriousness of the question because he didn't make any jokes as he answered. "Not the angels from the bible, but I guess I believe there is something out there greater than us. Why not angels? But why are you asking?"

She could tell him; he would believe her. Ellie looked into to Lucas' eyes and opened her mouth.

"Lucas, I'm–"

But the cranky old librarian interrupted her. She was a cliché if there ever was one, half-moon glasses half down her nose, white hair and the worst sense of style, which was saying a lot coming from Ellie.

She hushed Ellie and gave her a stern look before she moved on.

"She is such a cliché," Lucas whispered, mimicking Ellie's thoughts. "Now, what were you saying?"

But the moment had passed.

"Nothing, just ignore me," Ellie said and looked down at her books again. Lucas studied her for a while before he, too, returned to his studies.

THAT NIGHT, ELLIE MADE up her mind. She had tried to ignore what had happened, tried to ignore the rush she had felt when using her power, tried to ignore the need to know, but she couldn't. The dream was ever present in her mind, and she couldn't help but think her lost memories were somehow connected to her powers. She needed to know more.

Her head had barely hit the pillow before she was surrounded by blazing light, and before she could blink, she was back in the meadow.

Hayyel sat in the same spot as before. "You have made your decision?"

"I..." Ellie hesitated. There was no going back from this. She squared her shoulders and took a deep breath. "I want you to teach me how to use my powers."

"You choose wisely. Now sit," Hayyel said and pointed to a spot in front of him.

Ellie did as he asked and looked around. "Why did you bring me here?"

"The reason I brought you here..." Hayyel began, avoiding direct eye contact.

He fixed his gaze on a family of bears crossing the meadow to settle nearby. Ellie should have been terrified – bears so close – but an inexplicable calm enveloped her. She smiled warmly at them, focusing on the largest bear. It lazily lifted its head, meeting her gaze. Ellie could swear she saw a nod of acknowledgment.

"...is because you need to learn control," Hayyel continued, frustration lacing his words. "Are you even listening to me, Eliana?"

She was transfixed by the bear's burning stare, enough to not correct him at the use of her full name. In the depths of the bear's eyes, she glimpsed wisdom and clarity beyond human comprehension.

The bear rose, closing the distance between them. Still, Ellie felt no fear. She knelt, their eyes now level. The bear's nose brushed her cheek, and in that delicate contact, a torrent of images flooded Ellie's mind. Green woods, quiet streams, deep caves. Three bear cubs played in the sun, their joy contagious. After the images, emotions surged: serenity, happiness, utter contentment. It was like drowning, but not in fear like in the street but rather in an ocean of lilies.

Then, a sharp pull shattered the lilies, and Ellie returned to the meadow. Hayyel's glare met her.

"What?"

"This is why you are here. You need to learn control, otherwise your powers are going to consume you," he said while straightening up, never breaking eye contact.

Ellie did the same, holding her breath, suddenly a little afraid of what was about to happen.

"Your first lesson starts now."

CHAPTER FIVE

B*EEP, BEEP, BEEP!*
   Beep, beep, BEEP!
   BE –
"Oh, for god's sake, turn it off! *Turn. It. Off!*"

Ellie groaned and turned to slam her hand onto the alarm clock, its offensive sound quickly becoming her worst enemy. After a few tries without opening her eyes, she finally hit it and the noise stopped. She opened a bloodshot eye cautiously, wincing and closing it quickly when sunlight almost blinded her. Throwing her arm over her eyes, Ellie tried to shut out the world for a few more minutes, but the world had other plans.

Someone cleared their throat and Ellie peeked up from under her arm. She was met by someone no one should ever be faced with this early in the morning. Jen.

"You do realize this was the third time this week your stupid alarm woke me up *two hours* before I actually had to get up?" Jen's angry voice rang in Ellie's ears.

She stood by Ellie's bedside, blocking the sun, which allowed Ellie to glimpse at her dark form. Jen's hair looked like a bird had nested in it and her nightgown appeared more transparent than usual.

As Ellie was about to answer her with an apology, a deep groan drew her attention back to Jen's side of the room. She expected to see an empty bed, but instead she saw a man lying on the covers, a very naked man. Ellie then realized that Jen's nightgown didn't have *less* fabric, she had *no* fabric. None, zip, nada, nothing. There was not a thread on her body.

As the puzzle pieces slowly fell into place, the man in Jen's bed rolled onto his back, giving Ellie another view she most definitely could have done without that morning. Washing her eyes with bleach was not going to do it, she might never lose the mental image.

"Jen! What the hell?" Ellie hissed through clenched teeth.

"What?"

Ellie pointed towards the bed with a glare.

"Oh, Andrew? Yeah, so?"

"Are you kidding me right now? You had sex with him while I was sleeping in the freakin' room? My god, what is wrong with you? And could you put some clothes on?" Ellie barked. She loved Jen, but sometimes she could kill her. "And besides, I thought you dumped him?"

Jen blinked a few times before she answered and held out her arm. "He bought the bracelet, look."

That she kept on, Ellie thought as Jen continued.

"And seriously, Ellie you sleep like the dead these days. Why does it even matter? You didn't even flinch."

"So what? You just skipped the whole 'sex in privacy' part?"

The fact that Ellie hadn't woken up didn't surprise her. Since the night in the meadow, she barely got any sleep at all. The minute her head hit the pillow, she was back there, Hayyel waiting to tell her she was hopeless. If he was supposed to be a teacher, he needed to work on his encouragement skills, because telling someone they sucked all the time really wasn't a good motivation technique.

"Yeah well, Andrew's roommate was sleeping in his dorm—"

"So was I!"

Jen at least had the decency to winch a little, but she still didn't attempt to cover herself. Jen had always been a little too comfortable around her, but it was an argument Ellie had long given up.

"I'm sorry, but you didn't even stir. And we were really quiet."

Ellie gave up. She grabbed a pair of shorts and running shoes and left the room without another word, Puppy close on her heels.

ONCE ELLIE HAD TIED her shoes, she headed towards the park. Within minutes, she was sitting under her tree looking out over the lake. Small waves played on the water, starting out small, then growing larger and smashing against the bank.

After a while, Ellie plunged into a deep mediation without even trying. Her heartbeat slowed and her breathing stilled.

It had taken Ellie a long time to master meditation, which was frustrating because Hayyel wouldn't teach her anything else before she could do it.

"Now, when you reach a place of serenity, look inside yourself. Find your power and master it, don't let it master you."

Ellie tried to do as Hayyel said. Looking inside, she was met with endless walls of glass. Her mind searched its surface for a crack or something to focus on, but she came up empty-handed.

Ellie groaned in frustration and tried to remain focused, but the sounds of the meadow kept breaking through her concentration. Ellie's heart beat louder, and her breathing intensified, becoming fast and loud. She clenched her teeth together and pushed every sound aside, both internal and external. The noise disappeared, but the sound of her heartbeat and breathing only came back louder.

She pushed them aside again, determined to find peace, but they came back only louder. By now Ellie clenched her teeth so hard she practically heard them crack.

Just as she was about to shove them away again, a sharp pain hit Ellie over the head.

Immediately, she shot open her eyes and stared at Hayyel.

"What did you do that for?" she snapped. "I'd almost got it, dammit."

"You were not even close to getting anything, and I'd appreciate if you would try to learn without stopping your own goddamn heart."

Ellie had stared at him with her mouth slightly ajar.

Had I really almost stopped my own heart? she remembered thinking in both fear and wonder.

Hayyel had later explained that everything she did while meditating, she also did in reality. So when Ellie thought she had just calmed her breathing and quietened her heart, she had actually *slowed* her heartbeat.

After a few more nights, Ellie had finally been able to find a tear in the glass wall that appeared to be her mind. Hayyel had seemed baffled as to its origin, claiming the spell to be unbreakable. But after that small victory, she could do nothing right. Hayyel was constantly muttering she was useless under his breath, something Ellie silently registered and worked harder as a result, dead set on proving him wrong. She'd actually been doing rather well at ignoring him, which was surprising given her temper.

Now, sitting in the park, Ellie quickly found the tear in the protection spell. It shimmered, and a delicate fault line etched into existence. Ellie's mind reached out, tendrils of thought curling around the fissure. She could feel the pulse of ancient energy, like a heartbeat echoing through time.

Determined, Ellie focused her mental grasp on the breach. It was a delicate dance – a balance between force and finesse. She had attempted this before countless times, only to stumble at the finish line. But today, something was different. The tear responded, quivering under her touch.

She tore at the seam, unraveling the threads of protection. Her meditation, usually fragile and fleeting, held firm and now she was pulling apart the strands of magic with unwavering determination.

And then, with a surge of will, Ellie pushed through. Before her inner eye, a small ball of what looked like pure fire was pulsating. As soon as Ellie's mind touched it, it flared up and glowed brightly. Instinctively, she pulled back, a strange power coursing through her, but she tentatively neared it again. The moment her mind came in full contact with the fire, it consumed her.

Ellie cried out in pain and bit her lip, a determined scowl on her face. She would not let the power control her.

The taste of coppery blood registered in her brain, but other than that, Ellie's focus lay entirely on the fire. It filled her entire being, sending wave after wave of power coursing through her. The pain slowly subsided and the fire settled down, but it didn't feel the same as before. Ellie realized this must have been what Hayyel had been talking about. The power wasn't controlling her, she was controlling it.

With this new realization, Ellie slowly opened her eyes expecting something to have changed, but to her disappointment, everything looked the same. She closed them again and found the fire, this time without having to look for it. Something had definitely changed, but it wasn't the outside world.

This time, Ellie didn't open her eyes; instead, she tried to open her mind. The effect was instant. Emotions overwhelmed her, and she covered her ears with her hands in an attempt to block them out, but it was useless. Ellie wasn't hearing them with her ears, she was hearing them with her mind.

Hundreds of emotions all screamed in her head, all of them demanding attention. There was joy, anger, sadness, love, fear, hope, despair and hate, all so intense they burned with scorching pain. Ellie's own panic drowned in the chaos.

Just as Ellie thought she was going to pass out, or possibly die, all the emotions suddenly stopped at once. Ellie's eyes shot open, and Puppy stood before her. Any questions she might have still had about him being an ordinary dog were thrown out the window. He was *glowing* as he looked at her with an intense stare.

Ellie slowly gathered herself off the ground and tried to focus when someone caught her off guard.

"You are sitting in my spot," a smooth, velvety voice said from beside her.

Ellie whipped her head round so fast her mind spun.

"Excuse me?" she retorted in disbelief to the man standing in front of her.

"You heard me. I said, you are sitting in my spot."

Ellie couldn't help but gape at him.

He was tall and lean but not at all skinny. The thin cotton of his t-shirt clung to the contours of his chest, revealing the subtle ripple of muscles beneath. His jawline was sharp, a chiseled frame for his mouth. Morning light danced across his hair, turning the brown strands into a tangled halo of gold.

Then he was gone.

In front of Ellie was a woman with raven black hair. There were small crinkles by her kind, brown eyes as she laughed, the sound ringing like small bells in the air. A familiar pull tugged at Ellie, but before she could do anything, the woman was gone, too.

A new memory.

The man was still standing in front of her, his dark brown eyes full of irritation.

Ellie saw his mouth move and realized he'd said something again. She blinked a few times and, still in a daze, asked, "I'm sorry, what?"

Certainly not her most brilliant reply, but it was the best she could muster under the circumstances.

He sighed and looked at her as if she was mentally unstable, which Ellie actually had begun to consider she was, then said very slowly, "My spot. Are you going to move?"

His spot?

"Yes, my spot. God, don't you know who I am?"

Did I say that out loud? Oops, Ellie guessed she had.

A low growl woke her from her daze, and she glanced back to see Puppy standing behind her, his teeth bared. The glow was gone, thankfully, but his growl snapped Ellie back to reality and her calm, or trance or whatever it was, went out the window.

"You can't have a spot. This is a public park," she said with probably a little too much anger in her voice. But who the hell did he think he was? He couldn't just show up here and dazzle her, thinking he could get away with it. "And no, I don't know you. I've never seen you before in my life."

Ellie's pulse quickened, a flutter of unease stirring within her. She couldn't pinpoint the source, but it was there – an echo of forgotten memories, a whisper of something she couldn't place. Yet, she brushed it aside. Too many weird things had unfolded today, and this just added to that list.

The man before her looked like she'd slapped him in the face. He blinked, adjusting to the sudden confrontation, and his tongue found its footing.

"Do you live under a rock or something?" he retorted, his voice edging with irritation. "And this is my spot, so move it."

Ellie boiled with rage, and any attraction she'd felt towards this man was gone. She'd encountered her fair share of haughty college types, but this man took the prize.

"No, I don't live under a rock, you idiot," she shot back, her words as sharp as flint. "But you? You look like you might need to. Perhaps it'll crush some of that ego."

The man opened his mouth as if to say something, but Ellie wasn't done.

"And if this is anyone's spot," Ellie continued, her voice low and steady, "it's mine. Thanks to you, though, I might have to relocate. Minimize the risk of ever running into you again."

With that, she spun on her heel, leaving the man gaping in her wake. Puppy barked once then followed quickly, now wagging his tail. Ellie smiled down at him, wishing she'd be able to let go of a grudge as quickly as he did. This whole day seemed to have something against her, and all Ellie really wanted to do was crawl under her covers and sleep it away.

Ellie was halfway through the park when she heard running steps behind her. She chanced a quick glance over her shoulder and saw the man chasing her. He caught Ellie looking and waved at her.

"Hey, wait up!"

Just keep walking, she thought, quickening her steps a little.

"God, would you just wait, dammit?"

He touched her shoulder in an attempt to stop her, and Ellie spun around, coming face to face with him, a mere inch away. He took a step back in surprise.

"What?" she asked him, her voice laced with venom. He took another step back, letting his hand drop from her shoulder, leaving a warm tingle where his hand had touched her skin.

"You really don't know who I am?" he asked in disbelief.

Ellie rolled her eyes at him and turned to leave again. *Seriously, get over yourself.*

"No, wait. I'm sorry. It's just... that hasn't happened in like, forever. Someone not knowing who I am. It just took me by surprise, I guess." He smiled at Ellie, his brown eyes sparkling. "It's actually kinda nice."

Ellie had no idea what he was going on about, but it didn't matter. She wanted to go home. If it hadn't been for Jen, Ellie wouldn't have left her bed at all. She'd hopefully gone by now, thus allowing Ellie some peace and quiet. She needed time to think.

It had been four years since she'd had a new memory. Ellie had never figured out what had prompted them to appear, but since she learned about her true heritage, everything about them seemed that much more important. So, why would one appear now?

"Fine, I forgive you," Ellie said without much emotion and turned again to leave, but she didn't get very far. This guy could not take a hint.

"Would you stand still for five seconds? Geez!" He shoved his hand in his pockets and looked at Ellie with a small grin. "I was going to ask you if maybe you'd let me buy you a coffee as an apology for being an ass and an idiot and whatever else you called me."

Ellie's gaze sharpened, curiosity pulling her closer. And she allowed herself to look a little more closely at the man in front of her. His nose was slightly crooked and there was a scar that cut through his right eyebrow. Somehow, those small imperfections softened the edges of his arrogance, and Ellie suddenly couldn't help but feel slightly bad.

She huffed and looked at the ground, not able to keep looking at his grin. She really wanted to go to bed, but if Jen was still there, that was never going to happen. Ellie turned her gaze upwards again and he met her with a smile.

That did it. Something shifted within her and her resolve melted away. Before she could stop herself, she nodded in agreement, or perhaps it was defeat. Either way, his whole face lit up like some freaking Christmas tree, and Ellie groaned inwardly, already regretting her decision.

Later, she would wonder what came over her to agree to coffee with a man she'd never met before, but now, she glanced down at Puppy to her left. He eyed the man with his usual unreadable expression.

"Do you live nearby?" the man asked hesitantly.

Ellie's eyes snapped back to his. He better not be some stalker. Although, that would be her luck.

He must have seen her confusion because he cleared his throat and pointed at her clothes.

Shit, Ellie thought, slightly panicked. She was still wearing the clothes she'd grabbed as she fled her dorm, so basically shorts and a sports bra.

"Just thought you might want to change or something. But you know, I'm cool with what you're wearing, so don't feel pressured or anything."

Ellie glared at him, but that only caused his smile to grow.

Without another word, she began to walk back towards campus, silently cursing under her breath. If his hair looked bad, she could only imagine how hers must look. Puppy was running back and forth, circling Ellie as she walked, and his obvious happiness made her smile. Ellie startled as the man's voice broke the silence.

"So, what's your name?"

"Ellie. Or actually it's Eliana, but don't call me that," she added quickly. She had never been too fond of her name; it was girlie, and Ellie didn't do girlie unless forced to.

"Ellie it is then." He smiled and winked.

As in an actual wink.

Kill me.

"Well, I'm Aaron, and feel free to call me that or anything else you find more fitting."

Ellie couldn't help the smile playing on her lips or the blush creeping up her cheeks as Aaron smiled back. *Oh please.*

A comfortable silence fell over them as they kept strolling through the park, side by side with a crazy ass dog running around them.

"So, where exactly do you live? Because I'm guessing that's where we're going."

"Um, I live on campus, UCLA," she answered.

Ellie was amazed at how easily she was sharing things with this man, but then a small scowl on Aaron's face caught her eye. "You don't have to come, you know. I've already accepted your apology. There really isn't any need for coffee."

"Actually, I think there is," Aaron said. "I won't accept your acceptance of my apology until I buy you some. So, lead the way."

Ellie huffed to hide a laugh and once again questioned her sudden ease with this man. Yet, she kept walking, each step a silent protest against the absurdity of the day. The looks they attracted – furtive glances, raised eyebrows – itched at her skin.

As they neared campus, she jerked her head in every other direction, almost jumping at every small sound. Aaron, oblivious to Ellie's small mental breakdown, continued striding forward.

In an attempt to divert her thoughts, Ellie replayed the events in the park. The unlocking of her powers had been both exhilarating and terrifying – a fire of energy threatening to consume her. There was no way she could control that amount of power. She was also pretty sure Puppy was the only reason she was still standing, but she had no idea what he'd done. All Ellie wanted to do was ask Hayyel about it, but she wouldn't see him until that night.

And then there was the woman who appeared in front of her at the park. Who was she? Ellie's mind spun with questions, each thread leading to a dead end.

They were almost at her dorm, weaving their way between buildings when Ellie's gaze flickered to Aaron. Their eyes met. Ellie quickly averted her eyes as heat crept up over her neck. He chuckled at her blush, and the corners of Ellie's mouth turned up into a smile.

Maybe, just maybe, drinking coffee with him wasn't the worst way to pass the time until she could see Hayyel.

When they neared the door to her room, Ellie hesitated, biting her lip. If Jen was still there, there would be questions to answer. Questions Ellie wasn't sure she *could* answer herself yet. Ellie couldn't recall a single time she had brought anyone back to their dorm, least of all a man who wasn't Lucas, and there was no way Jen would just let this one go. Her hand froze at the doorknob.

"Are we just going to stand here all day, or do you intend to invite me in before you hurt your lip even more?" Aaron asked with another chuckle.

Ellie stopped biting her lip and smiled sheepishly. What was the worst thing that could happen, right? She took a deep breath and opened the door. She edged inside but froze in the doorway. Jen was still there, thankfully fully clothed, but Ellie still tensed, really not wanting to deal with her right now.

"Where the hell have you been? You ran out of here like a bat out of hell."

"I was out, didn't feel like sticking around for an encore of last night's show," Ellie said with a glare.

"And here I thought we'd made some progress with opening the door, but perhaps I celebrated too early."

Ellie almost jumped at the sound of Aaron's voice and moved into the room, smiling apologetically at him. He grinned back at her, his gaze intense. Ellie suddenly found she couldn't look away, so she just stood there smiling at him while he did the same.

A gasp followed by a loud bang broke her trance and Ellie looked over at Jen, who in turn was staring at Aaron, who simply raised his eyebrow. Jen had dropped her schoolbooks but made no attempt to pick them up.

"Oh my god. You're Aaron Thompson. Oh my god!" Jen squealed, and Ellie looked at her, tilting her head and frowning with confusion.

"Um, yeah I guess I am. Hi?" Aaron answered, and Ellie looked at him even more puzzled.

He sounded uncomfortable all of a sudden, not a trace of the arrogant ass from the park. He must have sensed her eyes on him because he looked over at Ellie with a sad smile.

"If you don't mind, I'll just wait outside while you change and then we can go."

"No, that's fine, I don't mind. I'll just be a sec."

When the door closed behind him, Ellie turned towards Jen, who was still standing staring at the spot where Aaron had been. "What is your problem all of a sudden?"

"Don't you know who he is?" Jen shrieked as she bent to pick up her books.

"No." Ellie was starting to feel like she was clearly missing something about him. "Why? Who is he?"

But Jen just gave her a wink as she opened the door to leave.

"It'll be more fun to see you figure it out," she said, then left their dorm, ignoring Ellie's calls after her.

Ellie sighed and walked over to her closet instead, looking for something to wear. The closet was alarmingly empty, nothing but a lone green dress on its hanger. Ellie looked at it with disgust, but it was the only thing not in need of a wash.

Jen had bought it for her for their high school graduation, which was also the only time she'd ever worn it, not wanting to hurt Jen's feelings.

She quickly changed out of her shorts and sports bra and slipped into the dress. With a sigh, she looked at herself in the mirror. The dress was a soft green and the skirt flared out at her waist. It was made from some sort of thin material Ellie didn't know by name, and the back was low-cut. Ellie groaned, really not liking it. It was girlie and made her feel uncomfortable, but it was hot outside, and she didn't exactly have the time to wash something else.

Next, she attacked her hair with her brush, letting it fall in soft curls down her back. She slipped on a pair of black ballet flats and headed to the door. She expected to see Aaron just outside, but he wasn't there. She hesitantly moved down the corridor when his voice had her spin around.

"Trying to sneak off I see. Geez, you turn your back for five seconds." Aaron pushed away from the wall he had been leaning on and came over. "That's a nice dress, not that I minded what you were wearing before. Ready to go?"

Ellie nodded, her cheeks heating a little as she followed Aaron.

CHAPTER SIX

Lucas looked at the empty seat beside him and sighed. Ellie was missing yet another class. Something was definitely going on, but every time he thought Ellie was about to open up, something stopped her. He thought she was going to tell him at the library, but then that cliché of a librarian had ruined it.

Dr. Adams was going on about the Victorian era in a monotonous voice, and Lucas glanced down at his notebook with another sigh, paying little attention.

The notebook was filled with research on angels. It had been hard to find anything except the Bible and other religious writings but then, one late night at the library, he had found a book filled with controversial theories to say the least. It had been on one of the shelves at the far back in a section that had nothing to do with religion, but Lucas had still felt drawn to it in a way he couldn't explain.

The book looked old with yellow pages so thin they were almost see-through. While it looked ready to fall apart at the seams, it hadn't torn when he had tried to rip out a page. It was definitely no ordinary book.

In the beginning, angels roamed the world and relished in its beauty. They lived in harmony with every living creature and shared the wonders of their world with all who dwelled in their goddess' creation. For centuries, they walked side by side with men, living in harmony with this growing species.

The book continued to speak of the angel's history, but Lucas caught another interesting paragraph.

Some angels are blessed with the powers of the Creators and act as guardians of the world.

The Protectors of the world are divided into eight orders.

The Water Protectors are tasked with caring for the ocean, seas and streams and all that dwells within. They may use water and bend it to their will to uphold their duty.

The Fire Protectors rule over fire and are skilled warriors who guard those in need of protection.

The Flora Protectors care for the earth itself and all that grows there. They are to keep the balance and help the world grow from bud to flower.

The Mineral Protectors are blessed with the power to bend the earth. Their magic is one of craftsmanship and wonder and their designs are to aid the dwellers of the realm.

The Animal Protectors act as a channel between each species, ensuring every creature's safety in the Creator's blessed world.

The Wind Protectors hold control over the weather, but it is not a power easily wielded. To disturb the Creator's natural order is a great offence and only in the service of others may they wield their power without retribution.

The Corporal Protectors are to heal those in need. They may never turn down someone who is hurt or their powers shall be stripped from them.

The Magic Protectors are to protect the magic of the land. They hold power to create and destroy worlds in their hands but must act according to their beliefs.

The first seven Lucas thought he understood, but the last one was still a mystery. He found it weird that anyone would be granted that kind of power yet still be free to act according to what they believed. What if someone believed in superior races and just wiped out everyone who didn't fit their mold? It was clear the other orders were held by rules, but this last one, and clearly the most powerful one, was just left unchecked.

He had read and re-read the passages about the different orders several times, but the book never dwelled further into the Magic Protectors.

The way Ellie had asked Lucas about angels with genuine fright in her eyes, had woken Lucas' curiosity. Ellie had been many things in the time he'd known her, but frightened was not one of them.

Lucas stared at the name scribbled over the page in his notebook, Raziel Jadon. The name was written in small letters in the corner of the first page in the book, so small Lucas had almost missed it at first, but no number of internet searches had come up with any information about him or the book. There was no page at the front with the usual dates and publication place, either.

"Now, there will be a test at the end of the week on everything you have learned so far, so I expect you to revise as much as possible between now and then," Dr. Adams announced, and Lucas tore his eyes from the notepad to pay attention.

While Lucas had little doubt Ellie already knew everything for the test, he did not. He was more of a 'study the entire course the night before' kind of guy, something Ellie usually gave him grief about.

He turned the page of the notepad and began writing notes for the test, the name Raziel Jadon burning through the pages.

ELLIE LOOKED OVER AT the clock again, impatiently twirling her hair around her middle finger, gnawing at her lip. 5:30 pm. Too early to go to sleep. She stood away from her bed and started to pace the room, trying to think of something that would make time move faster.

Jen had been gone when Ellie had returned from coffee with Aaron, but she had left a note that said: *Planning another club night 'til late tonight. Don't wait up for me. xoxo*

Puppy was sitting at the end of her bed. His eyes danced with amusement as he watched Ellie, his head tipped to the side, looking more like a curious bird than a dog.

All Ellie wanted was to go to sleep and speak with Hayyel about what had happened in the park, but she was wide awake. Each time she tried to close her eyes she practically had to force them to stay closed, and the random thoughts that kept popping into her head made it impossible for Ellie to find any peace.

She thought about her coffee 'date' with Aaron earlier that afternoon. She had actually enjoyed herself, which she didn't expect, Ellie had felt a tug throughout that she had tried to ignore, and when she was finally about to leave it felt like a part of her was ripped away. At first, she had wondered if Aaron had felt it too, but while he had been pleasant enough, he had shown no signs of what Ellie was feeling.

Then there was the woman. Her face was etched in Ellie's mind, the sound of her laughter still ringing in her ears. The more Ellie thought about it, the more she was convinced it was the same woman she had danced with so often before.

Something stirred deep within her; a realization she wasn't ready to face yet. She squeezed her eyes shut, trying to will her thoughts away and her mind to sleep.

It got to the point where she was desperate enough to start counting sheep. The sheep, however, seemed to have other plans as they kept ignoring the hedge Ellie conjured up in her mind. At first, they wouldn't move at all and then, two seconds later, they moved at lightning speed, making it impossible for Ellie to count any of them. When dragons began eating her sheep, she gave up.

Ellie tried watching TV with warm milk, but neither made her sleepy. All Ellie succeeded in doing was burning her tongue on the hot liquid. So, there she was, pacing with a burnt tongue at 5:30 – now 5:35 pm – still wide awake.

With a sigh, she retrieved her running shoes for the second time that day.

While growing up, running always cleared her head and brought perspective, so she hoped that a second run would declutter her mind enough for her to sleep. After an hour's run, exhaustion took hold of Ellie and she dragged her feet back home. She fell on the bed, nearly crushing Puppy in the process, and finally fell asleep.

The light took hold of her, and when she opened her eyes, she was in the meadow, Hayyel sitting in his usual place. Before she sat down herself, Ellie blurted out the events of the day, leaving out the part about Aaron. For some reason, she didn't think Hayyel would approve of that part.

Hayyel sat quietly, listening to everything she had to say before he answered.

"As I have told you before, you are an Empath with the ability to sense and control the emotions of others. What you did today was what I have been trying to teach you to remove the spell put on you when you were six. I have to admit, I am curious, did your memories return as well?"

Brown eyes stared at her as Ellie made a quick decision. She hadn't told Hayyel about her memories. They felt private somehow, not hers to share. But she needed answers.

"Not my memories, but someone else's."

Hayyel raised his eyebrows in a very uncharacteristic way. It was not an expression Ellie was used to seeing, and if it weren't for what she was about to tell him, she would have found great satisfaction in his confusion.

"I am afraid I don't understand what you mean."

Ellie took a deep breath. No turning back now.

"When I was seven, I was put in this awful foster home. The other kids were mean, and the adults neglected us. Once they disappeared and left us alone for an entire week. There was some food in the fridge, but I didn't get much of it. I remember being so hungry I even went through the thrash to find something to eat."

Ellie swallowed the lump in her throat.

"When I thought I would die, a warmth washed over me and suddenly I was somewhere else."

"Somewhere else?"

Ellie nodded. "Yeah. Somewhere else. A small cottage with a fire burning, and for the first time in days my stomach felt full. I wasn't hungry anymore. There was a boy about my age there with his mum and dad and I felt so loved.

"I never wanted to leave but it was gone as quickly as it had come.

But after that, I would get these flashes of the boy and his family whenever life was too much to bear."

"I remember this one time," Ellie said and smiled at the memory, "the boy was at a lake with his parents and the happiness in the memory filled me for days after. The lake was beautiful, too. The sun was glistening in the waves and there was this small island right in the middle of it with a single tree reaching toward the sky."

Hayyel looked at her as she quickly wiped a tear away. If she hadn't been so immersed in her own story, she would've seen his eyes widen at the mention of the lake.

"That lake is in the realm of the angels," was all he said.

Ellie nodded. "Yeah, as I grew older, the memories grew more intense and I realized, or *felt*, they were from another world. But I thought that world was gone, I saw it burn."

"There was a battle," Hayyel mumbled, seemingly more to himself than Ellie.

"I think they are my dad's memories," Ellie said in a quiet voice.

She didn't know how she knew, but she did. Then the woman's brown eyes flashed in her mind again.

"But something happened today."

Hayyel startled at her words, and Ellie finally noticed the paleness of his skin.

"Are you okay? You look... well, pale."

Hayyel grabbed Ellie's upper arms with a sudden urgency in his eyes. "What? What happened today?"

Taken aback by his total change in demeanor, Ellie managed to stammer out, "I don't know exactly, but I got a new memory."

"And that is unusual? You just said you have gotten many of them over the years." Hayyel's voice was strained, and it looked like he was fighting to keep control.

"Yes well, I got the last one like four years ago. And I've never seen this woman before. Or, I think I have, but never this clearly. I think she's my mom. She had these amazing brown eyes and raven black hair. Oh, and her laughter was like–"

"It can't be!" Hayyel gasped and finally let go of the painful grip on her arms.

Ellie rubbed the red marks his hands had left on her skin and glared at him. "What? What can't be?"

It happened so quick that Ellie almost missed it, but she was sure she hadn't imagined it. A single tear fell from Hayyel's eye, then he clamped up like a mussel, his usual detached expression falling like a mask over his face.

"I have asked you once and will not ask you again, do not speak of your mother. As for the visions, it is not something I have heard of before, but I will try to see what I can learn. If you get any more, tell me."

And that was that. The conversation was over, and no amount of nagging or begging would get Hayyel to approach the subject again.

Ellie finally gave up, but only for now. He knew something, something he wasn't telling her. She vowed to find out the truth.

But for now, she asked, "what happened in the park, was that me finding my powers?"

"Yes." Hayyel almost sounded relived she finally changed the subject. "But in the process, you also destroyed the shield the spell had built to protect you. With the shield gone, you have no control over what emotions you hear, and that will eventually kill you."

Yeah, tell me about it, Ellie thought. *Try having the entire city of Los Angeles screaming in your head and then get back to me.*

"But wait, I'm not hearing anything now," Ellie said, confused. "Does that mean I have some sort of control?"

"No, you do not. Your Guardian is shielding you with his powers." It was clear from his tone he had no intention of continuing.

"Yeah, you keep telling me the puppy is my Guardian, but so far, all he has done is glow a little," Ellie prompted. "I mean, there is nothing wrong with glowing, it's just a little underwhelming."

"He is a Guardian. They are rare, almost as rare as Empaths. The last one I had the pleasure to meet was killed almost forty years ago in an attempt to protect her Charge. Guardians are the children of the Creator. She blesses them with her powers and sends them to those in need. They come in many forms, but I suspect yours is a dog because of your father's powers."

At the mention of her father, Ellie sat up a little straighter.

"He was a powerful Animal Protector and his power dwells within you."

"But I thought I was an Empath?"

"You are both. Empaths, like the Guardians, get their powers from the Creator herself, therefore it is dominant. But you are still an Animal Protector."

"But why would I need a… a Guardian?" Ellie asked cautiously, afraid she would not like the answer.

"He is the only reason you are still standing. He is what's protecting you from the feelings of others and keeping you alive."

Ellie looked down at the puppy by her side. Like every night, he had followed her to the meadow and had fallen asleep in the grass, showing little to no interest in what Hayyel and Ellie were doing.

"Are you sure?" she asked in disbelief. "I mean, he looks like any other dog?"

"Shiro."

"What?"

"He says his name is Shiro."

He what? Ellie looked back at the puppy who was now awake, licking his private parts with great vigor, a task he obviously enjoyed.

Returning her gaze to Hayyel, she raised her eyebrows. "He talks?"

"He does," Hayyel answered and looked at the puppy. "You will learn to understand him in time, as he will learn to understand you. Shiro is still a young Guardian and has much to learn, as do you, but for now, he is shielding you until you can build your own defense."

Shiro stopped mid-lick and looked at them. His eyes burned into Ellie's for a few seconds before he returned to his task. Ellie couldn't help but smile at him. He might be a Guardian, but he was still, very much, a puppy.

CHAPTER SEVEN

Ellie groaned as she glanced at the pictures again. There were actually three pictures.

The first one showed Ellie in a green dress, laughing, a coffee in hand with Aaron smiling beside her, his hand at the small of Ellie's back.

In the next one, they were on campus, Aaron leaning forward; Ellie knew he was whispering in her ear, but in the photo, it looked like he was leaning in to kiss her.

But it was the last one that had Ellie wanting to crawl into a corner and die. In the last one, they stood outside her door. She was leaning against it and Aaron had his hand against the wall beside her head. Oh, and then there was the small detail of what she was wearing. A sports bra and shorts, so basically her underwear. It was clear what it looked like they had been doing just looking at the pictures in that order, so there was no need to read the headline.

Ellie hurriedly skimmed through the article.

> Movie star, Aaron Thompson, was seen with a beautiful black-haired girl looking more than a little comfortable. We don't know who this mystery girl is, but by the looks of it, Thompson knows her quite well...

> ...has our long-time single finally settled down or is she simply a source of entertainment – scratching an itch?

Ellie couldn't believe it; the pictures weren't even in the right order. And 'movie star Aaron Thompson?' Ellie guessed that was the one detail he had forgotten to mention.

"Where did you get this?" Ellie asked Jen.

She had thrown the magazine in front of Ellie as soon as she'd entered the room. She hadn't said a word, simply pointed at the pictures with a huge grin on her face.

"It's everywhere! Everyone is reading it. You went on a date with a movie star," Jen squealed, and Ellie rolled her eyes at her.

"It wasn't a date, and I didn't know he was a movie star," Ellie said, more than a little annoyed. "You could have told me you know."

"Seriously, Ellie, you'd have to live under a rock not to know who he is. You need to see him again! Did you get his number?"

Ellie averted her gaze, the corners of her mouth twitching at hearing the same phrase Aaron had used in the park.

Jen interpreted it as something else, however. "You did, didn't you?! Oh my god, you *have* to call him."

Without a word, Ellie grabbed the magazine and her bag that contained the torn-out page with Aaron's number she *had* gotten – Jen didn't need to know everything – then she left, ignoring Jen's shouts after her, Shiro close on her tail.

Ellie had to stop this before it got out of hand any more than it already had. He'd given her his number and told her to call him, which she of course hadn't. Oh god, she hoped he'd at least remember her.

Before she could lose her nerve, she grabbed her phone and dialed the number.

Aaron picked up on the fifth signal and rasped a tired, "hello?" into the phone.

Suddenly, Ellie had no idea what to say. She opened and closed her mouth several times, and when another *hello* reached her ear, Ellie panicked, and words stumbled out her mouth.

"Hi, it's me, eh Ellie. Or Eliana, yeah. I'm sure you don't remember me or anything but I kinda have to talk to you and you gave me your number and told me to call, so I figured you wouldn't mind, but I see now it was a bad idea, so I'll just hang up now..."

Apparently, Ellie's tongue-brain coordination was nothing but a memory because word vomit spewed out of her mouth.

After a few moments of silence, she heard a low chuckle at the other end of the phone line.

"Are you done?" Aaron's amused voice asked.

"Eh, yeah I guess."

"Well, first of all, hi."

Ellie couldn't help it; she smiled like an idiot on crack.

"Hi," she breathed.

"Now that we got that out of the way, I'm glad you called. I've been waiting for days, so I'd like to think it was an excellent idea. So, did you want something, or did you just miss the sound of my voice?"

Ellie could practically hear the smirk in his voice and rolled her eyes.

"I did want something; could we perhaps meet? If that's not too much trouble?"

"Nope, no trouble at all. Just tell me when and where and I'll be there."

Ellie breathed a small sigh of relief.

"Well, actually, I'm on my way to the park right now, so could you maybe meet me there?"

She heard hushed but argumentative voices at the other end of the line.

After a minute that felt like an hour, he finally returned to the phone. "Sorry about that. I'll be there in like, ten minutes. Where in the park by the way? My spot?"

His spot my ass. Ellie huffed. "*My* spot."

His laughter rang out and then he hurriedly said, "Okay, I'll see you in ten, at *our* spot. Bye."

He hung up before she could answer.

Our spot.

ELLIE DIDN'T KNOW EXACTLY how long she sat staring at the grass in front of her, but something suddenly blocked the sun. She looked up and met Aaron's gaze gleaming down at her.

"You beckoned, my queen?" he said with a bow, and his hair fell into his eyes.

Ellie longed to drag her fingers through it.

Not trusting herself to speak, Ellie handed him the magazine. He looked at it, confused, and then it dawned on him. Not only was there an article, but they had made the front page.

"Page twelve," she said, looking down.

Aaron sat down beside her and flipped the magazine open, quickly reading the article, and then frowned.

"So, movie star?" Ellie asked in a low voice, still not lifting her eyes from the ground, but she could feel his gaze burn into the side of her head.

"You never asked," he responded simply.

Ellie snapped her head up and glared at him.

"Oh, I'm sorry. Of course I should have asked. I do make a habit of asking people I've just met if they by any chance happen to be some big ass movie star."

Aaron met her angry eyes with his calm ones. "I'm sure you do, just as I make a habit of *telling* people I've just met I'm a big ass movie star."

A blush crept across Ellie's cheeks. It wasn't like she introduced herself as 'Ellie, half angel, half human.' She really ought to learn some sort of temper control. All it did lately was get her into trouble.

"I'm sorry," she mumbled, feeling ashamed. "I... I, uh. I'm sorry."

Ellie mentally slapped herself at the brilliance of her answer. She studied her lap even more closely, drawing random patterns on her thigh.

After a few moments of silence, during which Ellie wished she could dig another hole to crawl into and die, a hand lightly touched her cheek.

Surprised, she looked up, right into two intense brown eyes. Ellie couldn't look away, afraid to even breathe. She allowed herself to *really* look at him, drinking in his features. There was a small speckle of gold in his eyes she hadn't noticed before. He truly was beautiful. And yet, for all his beauty, he was imperfect. The scar that sliced through his right eyebrow, his nose that curved slightly. But it was precisely these flaws that drew her gaze – the quirks that made him human.

Hayyel, with his carved features, was a different story. He was like a sculpture, each angle and contour meticulously crafted. His skin held an otherworldly luminescence, and his eyes were the color of ancient sapphires. Ellie sometimes wondered if someone had simply sculpted the perfect man out clay and breathed life into him.

Yet, it was the man before her who stirred something deeper, something Ellie desperately tried to ignore. He was a stranger after all. But still, she didn't look away. Every nerve in her body seemed to be oversensitive and her skin hummed with delight beneath his touch. Ellie didn't want to move, and clearly, neither did Aaron.

Then Shiro barked, and the moment was over.

Aaron blinked. The side of his mouth turned up into a lopsided grin, but Ellie noticed a slight tremor in his lower lip. He dropped his hand from Ellie's cheek, and she immediately missed his touch.

"It's okay." His voice sounded loud in her ears, even though it wasn't more than a whisper.

Ellie swallowed and tried to get her emotions in check and think of something, *anything*, to say to break the tension currently suffocating her. She saw the magazine beside her lap and suddenly remembered the reason she was there.

Clearing her throat, Ellie opened her mouth to speak and prayed to God her voice would not fail her.

"So, what do you want to do about that?"

But Aaron dipped his brow, looking like he had no idea what she was talking about, so she gestured towards the magazine.

"Oh. Uh, just leave it. Let them think what they want, it's no big deal."

Ellie scoffed. "It *is* a big deal. What they think isn't true and I don't like lying!"

"Well, if you don't like lying, we could always make it true," Aaron responded with a wink.

It took a couple of seconds for Ellie to realize what he was implying, but when it did – hello instant blush.

"We will do no such thing! This is your fault, you fix it."

"My fault? How is this my fault?"

"You were the one who tricked me into having coffee with you." Ellie knew that wasn't entirely fair, but she was upset. Not only over the article but over the weird emotions still hanging in the air.

"Tricked?"

She could tell he was going to say something else but stopped when he saw her expression.

"Fine, I'll make a statement or something telling them we're only friends. Is that okay with you?"

Ellie nodded and stood up to leave. Class started in fifteen minutes, and she had no intention being late – miracles could still happen.

"So, we're friends?"

"What?" She turned back to him, wondering what he was going on about now.

"You said you didn't want to lie."

Ellie waited, but Aaron said nothing else.

"Yeah, so?"

"So, I'm not lying when I'm saying we're friends." It was a statement rather than a question.

Ellie stood there for a few seconds, then shrugged her shoulders. "I guess you're not. I have to go, see you."

"Ellie, wait," Aaron said, and Ellie turned to look at him. "There is this club on Friday, it's called the Rouge and is supposedly really good."

"Yeah, I know, my friend Jen is in charge of the event that night," Ellie said and then added, "she's a club organizer or whatever."

"Oh, okay. So, you are going then?"

Ellie eyed at Aaron with suspicion. Why did he sound nervous? "Yeah, I usually don't have much of a choice."

Aaron's face radiated as he smiled, and suddenly the word *friend* was not the word Ellie wanted to use to describe their relationship.

"Great, then I'll see you there," was all he said before he turned away, leaving Ellie standing in the park.

Ellie didn't make in on time for her class that afternoon, and after the two-hour lecture, she longed for her bed. As she neared her dorm, she noticed that her door was slightly ajar. She slowed her steps.

Jen's voice sounded through the crack. Ellie reached out to push open the door, but something in her tone made Ellie pause.

"I told you, no. I can't do that, Andrew."

Ellie knew she ought to stop eavesdropping and announce herself, but the defeat in Jen's voice held her fast. Silence fell as Andrew said something on the other end of the line.

"I thought I liked you too," Jen whispered, causing Ellie to strain to hear her.

Ellie waited a few more seconds before pushing the door open. Jen sat at her desk, and if Ellie hadn't been on high alert already, she would've missed the tear she quickly wiped from her face before faking a smile.

"Hi, you're back. How did it go with Aaron?" she said, but the smile on her lips didn't reach Jen's eyes. Ellie eyed her warily.

"It went fine, I guess. He'll make some statement or whatever to shut people up. But Jen, are you okay? You look a little off."

Ellie wasn't about to admit she'd been eavesdropping, but she wanted to be there for Jen if she needed her.

"What? No, I'm great. There's just a lot to fix before Friday."

Ellie narrowed her eyes. "Oh, okay. Are you bringing Andrew?"

The small flash of pain that shot through Jen's eyes was the only inclination that something was amiss. "No, I dumped him actually."

"Oh, are you okay?"

"Yeah, of course. I mean, I can get a new guy tomorrow if I wanted to, I just don't feel like I have the time right now, so I'll just keep things causal," Jen said with her usual cheerfulness. "You know me, Ellie. A new guy every week is just my thing."

Ellie did know her, and she could tell when she was lying, but it was clear Jen didn't want to talk about it, and who was Ellie to demand answers when she was hiding so many secrets of her own? She would just have to hope Jen would come to her if she needed her.

In an attempt to lift Jen's spirits, she changed the subject back to the club event a few days away. "So, what horrors will my poor wardrobe suffer this time?"

"Actually, I don't think I'll have the time to dress you," Jen answered, and Ellie suddenly had hope. "But that doesn't mean I trust you, so wipe that smile off your face. I talked to Isabelle. She'll dress you for me."

Ellie groaned and tried to argue. "But Lucas and Isabelle live so far away, can't you just lay something out for me here? I promise I'll wear it."

"Nope, it's not my fault you befriended a loser who still lives at home. Just be glad he has a sister that's at least helpful."

Ellie took a deep breath and pretended to pout, but in reality, she was relieved that the light had returned to Jen's eyes. She would have traveled to the moon and back to get dressed if that helped her best friend take her mind off whatever had happened with Andrew.

"Fine. But you have to promise to at least try and be nice to Lucas."

"I won't be mean, but that's the best I can do, take it or leave it."

Ellie smiled at her friend. "I'll take it."

CHAPTER EIGHT

Hayyel sat in the meadow and allowed the silence to fill him for an endless time he did not track. Since he no longer breathed, time ceased to hold any power over him. Memories filled his mind, and for once, he did not fight them. The memory of the day by the lake was indeed one filled with happiness, but he had not allowed himself to wander there, not deserving of the comfort it offered. He remembered the feeling of the cool water against his skin and the warmth of the sun beating down from above.

But that was all before. Before his treachery had ripped everything from him. He no longer allowed himself to feel anything. Emotions had to be earned, and his had only ever caused grief and loss. The price he'd had to pay was far too high yet not close to enough.

Eliana's description of the woman she'd seen lingered in his mind only for a few seconds before her beautiful brown eyes turned pained again and her raven black hair became matted with sweat. The image played over and over, forcing him to witness the life leave the woman he loved until nothing but that remained.

Resolve forced his eyes open. He would not let himself drift back to that place of darkness. No matter what, he would help Eliana fulfill the prophecy. It was the promise he had made and the one he had to fulfill.

"Mom! Isabelle hid all my clothes again."

"It's for your own good," Isabelle answered, holding up different items of clothing she apparently could live with Lucas wearing.

Ellie hadn't said much at all, afraid to draw attention to herself.

She failed, yet again, to see what was wrong with jeans and a t-shirt. After all, Lucas was allowed to wear it.

Isabelle held up a dark gray button down and a pair of dark washed jeans. Seemingly satisfied, Isabelle threw them at Lucas.

"Lucas, try those on," she said, then turned her attention to Ellie.

"Ellie, come with me, I have the perfect dress for you," Isabelle said and grabbed Ellie's hand. She was strong for someone so small.

Ellie threw Lucas a look of horror, but he missed Ellie's panicked look, eying his approved clothes with suspicion. With a sigh, she let herself get dragged across the hall and into Isabelle's room.

What Isabelle held up was not a dress. It was a tight skirt with a geometric pattern made out of black, silver and white sequins with a matching crop top.

"I can't wear that," Ellie said and backed away from the clothes like they would burn her if she touched them.

"Yes you can, now go try it." The tone in Isabelle's voice left little to no room for argument, so Ellie sighed and did as she was told.

She locked herself into the bathroom and tried to squeeze herself into the tight fabric of her clothes, if they could even be called that. The skirt ended just above her butt and the top left most of her stomach bare. Ellie made a face as she returned to Isabelle.

"It's perfect, now sit," Isabelle exclaimed and forced Ellie down into a chair, clearly ignoring the look on Ellie's face.

ONE HOUR LATER, ISABELLE declared Lucas and Ellie ready. She had folded the arms of Lucas' shirt to his elbows, leaving the top buttons open, and fixed his hair. Ellie's hair was in a high ponytail, and she wore way more make up than she was comfortable with.

"God, she's ruined you," Lucas said when he saw her. "I'm so sorry, Ellie."

Ellie blushed a little. "Thanks, great confidence builder, Lucas."

"No, I mean you look great, I'd totally do you, you just don't look like you," Lucas backtracked.

Ellie rolled her eyes and firmly grabbed his arm, tugging him outside to hail a cab. She would never admit it, but a small part of her had allowed Isabelle to dress her with the hope of catching another glimpse of Aaron. Despite trying to ignore it, she was impatient to get to the club.

As they reached Club Rouge, a line was already forming. Lucas and Ellie slipped past it, heading straight to the bouncer at the door.

For a fleeting moment, Ellie questioned her decision to not tell Jen that Aaron was coming, but she figured he would hardly have to wait in line anyway.

The bouncer granted them entry, and they checked their jackets before stepping inside. Being only eighteen, Ellie couldn't drink yet – usually not a problem, but tonight, she would have appreciated a shot or two to calm her nerves.

The familiar thump of music greeted them, and the club was already swarming with people. To avoid triggering the memory of dying again – which had an annoying habit of resurfacing in places where she felt out of place – Ellie took a few calming breaths and scanned the crowd for Jen. It didn't take long – Jen spotted them and waved them over. As they neared, Ellie didn't need her powers to feel the stress radiating from her friend.

"Hi, you look great! Will you be alright on your own? We're still waiting for a beer delivery that should have been here hours ago and I need to call them and–"

"Jen, I'll be fine," Ellie interrupted her rambling. "Lucas' here, I'll just hang with him."

Jen looked over Ellie's shoulder where Lucas stood. "Okay, great. I'll see you later then."

Ellie knew Jen was really stressed if she thought it was great that Lucas was anywhere.

Lucas and Ellie made their way onto the dance floor, the pulsating beat of the music enveloping them. But Lucas soon left, telling her he was getting something to drink, not liking to dance much. Ellie nodded and felt the music fill her. The club's neon lights painted the room in electric hues, casting shadows that danced in rhythm with the music.

"This reminds me of last time," a voice said in her ear as an arm snaked around her waist.

Ellie's breath hitched, immediately recognizing the pull and the need to be close. It was the same sensation she'd felt the night Hayyel had first appeared.

She spun around, ready to confront the man, to tell him she wasn't that kind of girl, but Ellie stopped dead in her tracks when she looked right into a *woman's* brown eyes. Kindness radiated from them, but there was more – a depth that transcended mere familiarity. Love, raw and unfiltered, sparkled in those eyes, leaving Ellie breathless. Then she was gone, and Ellie found herself face to face with Aaron.

"You," was all she said before she turned and left, but Aaron quickly caught up with her.

"Ellie, wait."

Ellie spun on her heels. "You knew it was me, didn't you?!"

"Not at first," Aaron said, "but when I realized it was, I figured *you* knew and didn't want to talk about it. So, I didn't say anything."

"Well, I didn't." They were standing in the middle of the mostly empty dance floor, but it was quickly filling up as more and more people entered the club.

"I'm sorry, okay?" Aaron pleaded with her.

Ellie's heart twinged with guilt and empathy, making it difficult to stay mad at him. She didn't *want* to stay mad at him. Not if he smiled at her again. He did and her anger dispersed. A small part of herself was disgusted at how easy he could manipulate her, but just for tonight, she didn't want to fight whatever it was between them.

"Will you dance with me?" Aaron tentatively asked. "Please?"

Ellie nodded, but this time she kept her distance from Aaron. He was a good dancer and she quickly began to enjoy herself. Until someone bumped into Ellie's back, causing her to fall towards Aaron. He steadied her with both hands on her waist and his touch burned on Ellie's bare skin. Then the crowd crushed against them and suddenly, they were pressed against each other.

She could smell him everywhere, sweat and man and something entirely Aaron.

Ellie swallowed hard and quickly pushed against his chest. "I need some air!"

Aaron nodded and guided her through the crowd, ignoring the stares he was receiving.

"I met Jen again," Aaron said once they stepped outside the club. "I think she's mad at you for not telling her I was coming."

Ellie sighed. "I'm sure she is."

Even though the fresh air had cleared Ellie's head a little, she still kept a little distance from Aaron.

"You know, she isn't exactly who I thought you'd be friends with," Aaron said carefully.

"I'm friends with you."

Aaron laughed. "I guess that's a good point."

Ellie smiled at him. He looked good. His clothes were similar to Lucas', but his shirt was white instead of gray. It looked like he was about to say something but a knock on his shoulder had him turn instead.

It was three not entirely unattractive girls who managed to ask for his autograph through their giggles. Aaron only smiled and obediently signed their arms.

At least it was only their arms, Ellie thought with a tinge of jealousy.

But that was ridiculous, she told herself. They were only friends and nothing more. And yet she couldn't ignore that Aaron's hand lingered on one of their arms a little longer than Ellie thought necessary.

When Aaron turned back towards Ellie, she thought she saw a blush on his cheeks, but Ellie wrote it off as the cold wind blowing.

"Occupational hazard?" Ellie asked, trying to keep her voice light. She almost succeeded.

"Yeah," Aaron answered, "something like that."

It looked like he was struggling with himself for a minute, then said, "Ellie, I just want you to know that–"

"Ellie!" Lucas shouted, interrupting Aaron. "I've been looking everywhere for you... oh, who's this?" Lucas had stopped and stared at Aaron, then turned back towards Ellie. "Is this *the guy?*"

Ellie wanted to slap him. Instead, she glared at him and said, "This is Aaron, Aaron this is Lucas."

Aaron greeted him, but Lucas looked at him with suspicion. "Seeing as Ellie does not have a father, it falls on me to learn your intentions with the young lady," Lucas said, making his voice darker and, for some reason, British.

"Lucas," Ellie groaned, but Aaron only laughed.

"No need to worry, we're just friends. My intentions are completely harmless."

"Ah, good," Lucas said, and a wide grin spread across his face. "Now that's settled, would you like to be my wingman for the night? You know the average woman goes on at least four disaster dates and have two heartbreaks before finding the man of her dreams, you and I can be that heartbreak."

Aaron laughed again and said something Ellie didn't hear. *Just friends*, Aaron's words echoed in her mind and, not for the first time, Ellie wasn't sure she wanted his intentions to be completely harmless.

Aaron and Lucas were almost at the door to the club when Aaron realized Ellie hadn't followed them. "Ellie, are you coming?"

Trying to push the thoughts aside, Ellie forced a smile and went to join them.

CHAPTER

NINE

THE MEADOW LAY BATHED in moonlight, its dew-kissed grasses shimmering like silver threads. Ellie sat in its center, her heart racing as the shimmering glow slowly surrounded her.

At first, Ellie had been terrified she would hurt Hayyel or Shiro as the later lowered his shield around her, but Shiro had shielded himself from her and Hayyel was dead, which apparently meant he didn't feel anymore.

The first few times she had tried to create her shield, nothing had happened.

"You need to see the shield with your inner eye, to feel it surround you," Hayyel had said with much more patience than he usually showed during her lessons.

"How am I supposed to see or feel something I don't know?" Ellie had complained as she tried to imagine herself in a proactive bubble, failing miserably once again.

Now, she breathed deep, fingers trembling. The meadow blurred as she reached inward. She'd had an idea after her previous failure that she was eager to try out. Carefully, she began to weave threads of intention as delicate as spider silk in her mind. She envisioned a cocoon, a sanctuary of light. It began as a whisper, a shimmering veil around her. She wove threads into existence, each strand a promise of safety. The cocoon thickened, its glow matching the stars above.

And when her concentration wavered, the glow held steady. It clung to her like a second skin, defying the darkness.

"I did it!" Ellie exclaimed and looked over at Hayyel.

He was wearing his usual attire of leather pants and a loose white shirt. The clothes never appeared to wrinkle or stain, but Ellie hadn't felt like going into how a dead man's outfit worked, so she had refrained from asking.

"You will need to strengthen your shield. It is still weak, but emotions should no longer overpower your mind. Shiro," Hayyel said with a nod at Shiro who sat beside Ellie in the grass.

This was the ultimate test to see whether or not the shield would hold. As Shiro completely removed his shield, Ellie only felt a whisper of emotion from him, and she smiled triumphantly.

"It worked. I can barely hear him at all."

"Good, now focus on hearing him and only him," Hayyel said, not sounding all that impressed.

Ellie did as he asked and focused the fire forever burning within her on Shiro. At first, nothing happened, but then she started to feel a pride that was not her own.

"What is he feeling?" Hayyel asked.

"Pride. He's proud of me." Ellie smiled and broke the connection to scratch Shiro behind his ear.

"Very good. While you most likely will be fine in most situations, Shiro must remain by your side. Your shield feeds on your power, so should you be overcome by emotions, it will first drain your powers and then use your life energy to keep itself sustained. It is part of who you are now and will do whatever it takes to survive, even if it means killing you."

Well, that was probably something he should have told her before she linked a deathtrap to herself. Ellie opened her mouth to ask Hayyel a million questions, but he raised his hand, silencing her.

"You will be able to lower your shield, thus allowing you greater access to the emotions around you, but once the bond you have just created is sealed, it can never be undone. The shield is forever a part of you."

"You're just all gloom and doom today," Ellie said, proud that she had finally succeeded in something concerning her magic despite the shield being connected to her mortality. "But I have been meaning to ask you – if Shiro can shield himself from me, can't others do it, too?"

"The Guardians have been blessed with the Creator's power, which allows them to portal between worlds and use the magic in the land. He can use that magic to shield himself from you. Apart from Shiro, only the Magic Protectors have that kind of power. I hope you remember what I've told you about the different orders, Eliana?"

Ellie quickly answered.

"There are eight orders. The Animal Protectors care for everything that breathes, the Water Protectors look out for the oceans, seas, rivers and streams and everything in them, the Fire Protectors have control over fire and are warriors, and the Mineral Protectors bend all minerals to their will. Then there are the Flora Protectors who oversee plants, and the Wind Proctors who control the weather. And lastly, the Magic Protectors who protect all the magic in the lands and also cast spells, which is really cool," Ellie gloated. "See I pay attention!"

"That was only seven," Hayyel said, sitting down in the grass.

Crap. But which one had she forgotten? Animal, water, fire, mineral, flora, wind, magic and... "The Corporal Protectors! They use their powers to heal angels."

"Yes, angels *and* humans," Hayyel corrected her. "The Magic Protectors are the only order who can shield themselves, and sometimes others, from your power. You will need to learn how to break their shields, but for now, let us work on strengthening your shield and then you can start to learn how to speak with Shiro."

Ellie didn't allow herself to linger on the fact that she didn't want to break anything, and instead paid close attention to Hayyel, the promise of being able to speak to Shiro the only motivator she needed.

THE PHONE ON THE table buzzed; Ellie had received a text from Lucas. Isabelle was forcing him to go shopping with her and he was requesting backup.

With a smile and glad to have an excuse if asked, Ellie replied: *Sorry but you're on your own for this one.*

Shopping with Isabelle was almost as bad as learning about different plants with Hayyel. Although, it was hard to argue with Hayyel when he kept telling her that her knowledge in the land and its magic would one day save her life.

She was sitting at a small café waiting for Aaron. She had chosen a table at the back, hoping to avoid at least some of the annoying fan girls who followed Aaron anywhere he went. The café was really cozy, *and* it allowed dogs, something Ellie had learned to appreciate as of late. Of course, it appeared Shiro could follow her anywhere he wanted without being seen, so if someone had an objection to dogs, they simply wouldn't notice him.

Shiro was now asleep under the table, happy to be out of the rain. Plush chairs, their upholstery worn by countless conversations, huddled around small tables. At the room's heart stood a small stage, its wooden surface scarred by years of performances. Ellie had initially pegged it for poetry nights, but then her gaze shifted, and the walls revealed their hidden treasures: a mosaic of old LP records. Their faded covers bore legends – rock anthems, jazz ballads, forgotten symphonies. Open mic night then, she decided.

The rain was still falling heavy outside, and while everyone always said the rainy season began in November, Ellie hadn't believed them until now.

The bell at the door chimed and Ellie looked up only to be disappointed. The man spotted whoever it was he was meeting and hung his dripping coat at a rack in the corner before he went to sit down.

When Ellie had gotten Aaron's text asking her to meet him at the café, she'd had to force herself to wait five minutes before replying. She didn't want him to think she spent all day staring at her phone, hoping he would be in touch, even though it was the embarrassing truth on some days.

As Ellie glanced at the clock on her phone again, she noticed that he was late. Ten minutes.

Ellie impatiently tapped her fingers against the table when the doorbell chimed again. This time it was Aaron.

He looked soaked and miserable, his hair dark from the rain and dropping down in his eyes. Ellie's fingers twitched with the desire to run her hands through it. He spotted Ellie at the back and made his way over to the table.

"I know, I'm late. Sorry, but it started to pour. Who in LA is prepared for rain?" Aaron said as he shrugged his jacket off and draped it over his chair. He caught Ellie's glance at the umbrella leaning against the side of the table and grinned. "Well, I guess that answers my question."

"It's the rainy season," Ellie defended herself with a smile on her lips.

Whenever she was near Aaron, her entire body relaxed and the past weeks' tension left her. It struck Ellie as odd that she got sore muscles from using her mind when she'd never gotten them from running, but Hayyel claimed it was normal.

"I ordered coffee for you," Ellie said as a waitress came over to their table with two mugs, steam raising from them.

Aaron sank into his chair with a sigh of relief and a small smile played on his lips. The waitress lingered at their table for a little longer than necessary, then headed back to the counter.

Cradling the cup in his hands, Aaron took a sip and smiled at Ellie. "Cappuccino with a little sugar, my favorite. We're like best friends already."

Every time he said the word *friend*, it felt like a stab to Ellie's heart, and he'd been saying it a lot lately. Ellie feared he could see straight through her and was trying to let her down gently, not wanting to hurt her feelings. Ellie guessed she should at least appreciate the gesture.

"Yeah well, it's a lot easier to remember than Jen's caramel ribbon crunch crème Frappuccino," Ellie said, hoping she sounded casual.

Aaron's eyes widened with horror. "That's a real thing?"

"It is at Starbucks," Ellie said with a shrug.

Aaron nodded like that made perfect sense and focused his attention on Ellie. "So, you said you studied but never what?"

"I'm a history major," Ellie answered and sipped at her own cappuccino, without any extra sugar.

"That's cool. I actually have a degree in mechanical engineering."

Ellie almost choked on her coffee and looked at him with round eyes.

"Don't look so surprised," he laughed. "My dad never wanted me to become an actor. Obviously, we don't talk much anymore."

"Oh, I'm sorry."

"Don't be, at least this year I got invited to Thanksgiving, so I'd say we're making some progress." Aaron downed his coffee and put the cup down on the table. "What about your parents, happy about your chosen subject?"

It would have been easy enough to lie – Ellie had fantasied about her parents enough times – but when she opened her mouth, it was the truth that came out.

"My parents died in a car accident when I was six." Well, almost the truth.

"Sorry, you don't have to tell me about it if you don't want to," Aaron said with sadness in his voice. Ellie waved his worries away.

"No, it's fine, it was a long time ago." No need to tell him her dead angel father keeps sending her flashes of memories from another world.

Aaron reached across the table and took her hand. "What happened after that? Foster care?"

Ellie swallowed and nodded, trying not to stare at their intertwined hands. Aaron mistook Ellie's tensing as a reaction to her story and squeezed her hand in a reassuring gesture.

Before she could say anything, the waitress returned to clear away Aaron's now-empty cup, and she stared at their intertwined hands with cold eyes. When she turned her glare at Ellie, Ellie glared right back and thought, *that's right, he's mine,* ignoring the tiny voice saying he wasn't.

"Can I get you anything else?" the waitress asked and turned her attention back to Aaron again.

He looked a little startled at her question, as if he had forgotten she was even there. "Uh, no thanks. We're fine for now."

Ellie smiled at Aaron, but the waitress could not take a hint.

"Are you sure there isn't *anything* I can do for you?"

That was it. Ellie couldn't take it any longer.

"He said we're *fine.*" Ellie filled the last word with her power, willing the waitress to leave.

The waitress blinked and smiled. "Okay, great."

Ellie looked at the waitress retreating, a little scared of herself. Aaron squeezed her hand a little more and she pushed her fear aside, resuming her story.

"Yeah, I was with one family for a few years in a town called Bellingham in Washington, that's where I met Jen, but they couldn't keep me. After that, I was bounced around to a few different homes, but at least I got to stay in the same city. I don't know what I would have done if I'd had to move. Jen was about the only thing keeping me sane."

"She's a really good friend, huh?"

"The best." Ellie replied with a warm smile. "I guess we were both pretty lonely growing up. Jen's parents had all that money, so some of the other kids thought Jen was a snob because of it, and others wanted to be her friend for all the wrong reasons."

"Kids can be cruel."

"Yeah, in so many creative ways as well." Ellie grimaced at the old memories. "But we had each other and that was more than enough."

Aaron held on to her hand for a few seconds longer before he untangled himself, claiming he needed more coffee to get warm. He went over to the counter and the waitress flirted shamelessly with him. To Ellie's delight, Aaron didn't even seem to notice. Her hand was still warm from his touch and she missed it already.

He is just your friend, nothing else.

The next hour passed quickly, and both Ellie and Aaron were startled when his phone rang. After he'd hung up, he stood and put his jacket on.

"That was my agent, apparently, I'm late for something. But we should do this again, I'll call you."

And then he was out the door. Ellie looked after him with longing eyes.

He is just your friend.

CHAPTER TEN

THE NEXT FEW DAYS passed uneventfully. During the days Ellie worked hard in school and during the nights she worked even harder with Hayyel. Building her shield was actually going quite well, but when it came to Shiro, they were at a standstill.

It was not because of lack of trying, Ellie really wanted to be able to speak to him, she just couldn't understand *how*.

Ellie sat crossed legged in the grass and stared intently at Shiro. She had no trouble sensing his emotions anymore, but she was starting to fear that her Empathic powers had suppressed her father's powers altogether.

Ellie was deep in meditation, surrounded by the fire, and tried to make Shiro hear her somehow. Just one tiny word.

"This isn't working," Ellie said, breaking free from the meditation. "It's pointless."

Hayyel looked up from the scroll in his lap and simply said, "try again."

"I don't want to," Ellie whined.

Hayyel sighed and set the scroll down beside him.

"Eliana. You must learn this, it is crucial. Once you have control of your power, all of your powers, you will be able to access it without being in meditation. It is something only the strongest of the Protectors can manage, and you must, too. Now, try again."

Ellie took a deep breath. As she let the air out, she closed her eyes and fell back into meditation.

Shiro was gone. So was Hayyel and the meadow. A horse stood before her, happily eating at the moist grass at its feet. Then she looked inside. Where she expected to see her own flame, there was a green orb pulsating. This was her father's memory, she reminded herself, as she let the light fill her.

When she opened her eyes again, the horse shone with the same green light, and as the scene around her disappeared, Ellie finally knew what to do.

With this new realization, Ellie let her own fire fill her completely as her father's had filled him. She opened her eyes to locate Shiro. He burned with a bright light to the right of her.

She closed her eyes again and opened her inner eye; suddenly, the entire meadow shone with light. Every living thing in the meadow glowed with its own light and they were all bound together by the magic in the land.

That's what she needed to do, she needed to ground herself and connect to the land itself. Before, she had always directed her magic at Shiro, but now, she focused her powers into the ground. She let her power become a part of the river of magic flowing beneath her.

Then she was everywhere, she was everything. Her magic pulled her into the land itself until she *was* the magic. With a gasp, she let go of her power and opened her eyes again. This time when she sent a tendril of power towards Shiro, his head jerked up and his eyes met hers.

Hayyel had told her that once she had connected with Shiro, she needed to make that link permanent, but before Ellie could even begin contemplating how to do that, Shiro started to glow. White light flowed from him into the thread, and when it reached Ellie, it crystallized. *You don't have to do everything yourself, you know.*

The shock of the strange voice in her mind caused Ellie to widen her eyes at Shiro. *He talked.*

I have been talking for some time now, but it's nice to heard.

Ellie looked at Hayyel and then back at Shiro. "I – I can hear him. And I'm not even in meditation."

For what might have been the first time ever, Hayyel smiled at her. "You are connected. Everything you feel and think, Shiro will know as you will know him. You are of one mind and two bodies."

Ellie had thought it would scare her to share herself that intimately with anyone, but Shiro's presence in her mind only gave her comfort. Shiro trotted over to her, and Ellie buried her face into his soft fur. As a response, he put his cold, wet nose in her ear, making her giggle.

I think we'll be just fine, you and I, Ellie thought with warmth.

We might not be, Shiro thought back, *if you don't start paying attention to the fascinating lesson on the different types of leaves.*

Ellie groaned as she realized Shiro was right. Hayyel had already moved on to yet another lesson on different plants. How knowing which root could stop bleeding could one day save her life, Ellie understood. How learning what different rocks and stones were called would, Ellie did not understand.

Well, at least I won't have to suffer alone anymore.

I don't need to learn this, you do. I am going to take a nap. Wake me when we are going back.

Traitor, Ellie thought, but Shiro was already closing his eyes.

Before Ellie let her focus shift back to Hayyel and his lesson, she sent one thought soaring through the sky, hoping it would be heard.

Thank you, Dad.

You're going to be *late again.*

Ellie jumped at the sound of Shiro's voice ringing in her mind. It had been almost a week since he first spoke to her with words, but his voice still surprised her. Ellie looked down at her watch and realized he was right.

Crap, Lucas is going to kill me if I'm late again. Ellie threw the phone she'd been staring at for the past fifteen minutes into her bag along with her books.

She had been trying to decide whether or not to call Aaron when Shiro had reminded her of her plans with Lucas. She and Aaron hadn't seen each other since the café, but he kept sending texts. Actually, they were mostly pictures of him promoting his new movie, usually with the words 'kill me' attached. Aaron liked acting, just not the fame that came with it.

Ellie glanced in the mirror and cringed. She had dark circles under her eyes and her hair was a mess. But there was no time. She grabbed a rubber band from Jen's desk and pulled her hair up in a messy bun. There was nothing she could do about the circles.

She grabbed her bag from her bed and ran out into the corridor, Shiro close behind. He was with her less and less now that Ellie had her shield under control and her connection with Shiro established, but he always followed when she went to see Lucas. That was something Ellie had been meaning to ask him about.

You don't have to come you know, she thought, racing through the campus grounds.

I know.

And yet, here you are.

They were almost at the library when Shiro came to a sudden halt. Ellie backtracked a few steps and looked at him. His usual ice blue eyes looked more like a stormy sky and Ellie felt his alarm.

Maybe I simply like your company.

I think we both know there is something else going on here, just spit it out already.

Shiro made a noise sounding a lot like a sigh and lowered his head. *There is something going on with Lucas. I can't explain, but his presence feels wrong.*

What do you mean 'wrong'? Ellie asked, a small knot of anxiety forming in the pit of her stomach.

I don't know exactly, which is why I'm coming. I need to be near you to protect you.

At that Ellie almost laughed. *Lucas would never hurt me, that's ridiculous.*

He knows there is something special about me, Shiro prompted, but Ellie waved him off.

That's because you act special. Try doing some ordinary dog stuff every once in a while, then maybe he wouldn't be suspicious.

Shiro didn't say anything else, but Ellie still felt his worry.

With a sigh, she continued to the library. They had a test coming up and while Lucas was capable of learning an entire semester in one night, she was not. She needed to study.

LUCAS WAS PRETTY SURE he was on the verge of a nervous breakdown.

It would at least explain a lot of the things happening at the moment. He was in the library waiting for Ellie, but he didn't feel the usual calm he always felt at the smell of books. Instead, he tugged his hair as he stared at the book in front of him. It was changing again.

The first time it had changed was after he noticed it was missing in the description of the Magic Protectors, but the next morning, a whole chapter on them had appeared. A chapter Lucas could have sworn wasn't there the day before.

New paragraphs on the First Four were appearing as Lucas stared at the page in front of him now, as if the book was writing itself. He closed it with a thud and pushed it aside, covering it with other books.

Not that it mattered much. The words writing themselves whispered to him, fluttering in and out of his mind. Then he heard a familiar voice.

He remembered the first time Ellie had spoken to him in her light singsong voice. He'd thought it was one of the most beautiful voices he had ever heard.

"I know, I'm late, again. I'm so, *so* sorry," Ellie said and sat down at the table.

Lucas had chosen a table at the back, hoping to avoid the librarian, thus giving them more freedom to speak. Even with dark circles under her eyes and her hair a complete mess, Ellie was beautiful. Her eyes were bright and her cheeks a little flushed, probably from running there.

Something white at the corner of his eyes caught Lucas' attention; Shiro slip under the table. He was sure Shiro was no ordinary dog, but every time he tried to talk to Ellie about it, she laughed it away, claiming Lucas was being paranoid.

He forced a smile and opened the books in front of him. "No worries. I actually just got here."

Lucas wanted to talk to Ellie about what he had discovered in the book, but every time he tried, something stopped him. He couldn't explain it, but it felt like the book was *keeping* him from sharing its secrets.

Nervous breakdown, next stop.

"I guess 'white' was a fitting name," Lucas said, glancing under the table at Shiro.

Ellie looked up from her textbook about the alliance between Sweden and the United Kingdom against Napoleon. "Huh?"

"Shiro. It means 'white' in Japanese." Ellie still looked like she had no idea what he was talking about, and Lucas' suspicion grew. "Wasn't that why you named him that?"

"Eh yeah, sure." Ellie sounded nervous and she resumed reading again, but Lucas didn't miss the look of suspicion she gave him.

When Ellie noticed he was still looking at her, she sighed and closed the book. "Are you okay? You've been acting a little weird lately, and you look exhausted."

"I'm fine, Isabelle's just been giving me grief lately," Lucas said in a rushed tone. He could see in Ellie's eyes she didn't believe him.

In an attempt to act normal, Lucas said the first thing that popped into his head. "Seriously, I'm fine. You know, I saw this kid today with an iPhone. Seriously, when I was his age, I used to put glue all over my hands, wait for it to dry and then peel it off."

Ellie laughed and some of the tension left her, but when Lucas bent down to retrieve a pen he'd dropped, Shiro glared at him with caution. He was definitely *not* an ordinary dog.

STILL A LITTLE ANNOYED with Shiro for insisting there was something wrong with Lucas, even causing her to doubt him, Ellie had left for the park alone, giving him stern orders not to follow her. She'd finally found the courage to text Aaron and ask if they could meet, which he had agreed to almost immediately after she'd hit send.

When she arrived at the park, she found no signs of Aaron. She checked her phone to see if he had called her, but then realized that she was early for once. Not minding a little quiet time, Ellie strolled over to the big oak and sat down, her head resting against the bole.

Closing her eyes. she thought back to her study session with Lucas. He had looked even worse than she did, and it hadn't escaped her notice that he had hidden a book when she had entered the library, but it felt unfair to ask him to share his secrets when she had so many of them herself.

Ellie hated the little seed Shiro had planted in her mind, but only someone blind could ignore that something was going on with him. Even his attempt at joking felt halfhearted at best, but Ellie hadn't had it in her to confront him.

Sighing, she opened her eyes and watched the pond instead, trying to shake the mental image of Lucas slamming a book shut with a look of panic in his eyes.

A family of ducks slowly made their way around the pond, gliding through the water without disturbing it. Without warning, one of them ducked below the water, its tail sticking up in the air, and Ellie smiled. As she watched them, an idea formed in her mind. One she'd been thinking about quite a bit lately but hadn't had the opportunity to try out.

She closed her eyes and cleared her thoughts. At once, Ellie's heartbeat and breathing slowed, and she felt the power consume her. Like she had done with Shiro, she sent out a small thread of power towards the duck closest to her, then waited.

The thread had barely made contact when a strange emotion filled her, and Ellie realized she was linked to the duck. Carefully, she sent feelings of safety and comfort through the link, silently telling him not to fear her. The duck stopped in the middle of the lake and looked in Ellie's direction.

It had actually worked! Ellie wanted to break out into a happy dance complete with jazz hands, but she stayed calm, not wanting to break the connection. She tried to think of something to ask him and finally settled on his name. She pondered for a while how best to ask him until she assumed it would just be best to ask him with words.

At first, nothing happened, filling Ellie with disappointment. Perhaps she hadn't made as much progress as she thought. But then she felt something pushing though their connection. It wasn't words like with Shiro, but images. Images of different rocks, all brown. Ellie tried to understand what the duck could mean by them, but after a while, she noticed that the images were of the same rock, reappearing over and over.

For the first time, Ellie was glad that Hayyel had tortured her with hours upon hours, teaching her the names of everything in nature. The stone was called Aragonite, and when she sent the name back to him, the duck answered with a feeling of happiness.

Ellie smiled to herself and broke the connection.

"Aragonite," she whispered to the wind, liking the way it rolled off her tongue.

She'd done it! Ellie had successfully communicated with an animal without any help from either Hayyel or Shiro.

Slipping back into meditation, Ellie wondered if she could connect with all of them. This time, it took her a while longer to fill herself with the flame forever burning inside her. It was smaller than Ellie was used to, but once she touched it with her mind, it willingly followed her command.

I guess I'm just tired, she thought without worrying, arguing that she could take a nap after she had tried this.

This time, she sent out not one, but seven strings of power, one for each duck in Aragonite's family, but, to Ellie's disappointment, they died out before even making it halfway across the lake. Ellie poured more of her power into them and tried again. A small alarm in the back of her mind rang, warning her about using so much power when she was already tired, but Ellie pushed it aside and focused solely on the task at hand.

Slowly, very slowly, Ellie's threads made their way over the lake. Once they were a few feet away from the family, they stopped but didn't disappear. Ellie used one last push of her power and let it flow into the threads, and she finally connected with all seven ducks.

The second her power came into contact with them, seven different sets of emotions overflowed Ellie, and she instinctively poured more power into her shield. But her powers were gone, and the shield was rapidly feeding on her life energy, like Hayyel had told her it would.

Ellie fought to keep her eyes open and slumped against the tree, no longer having the power to sit upright. Her shield was weakening as her strength left her, and as it did, she began hearing all the emotions of the people in the park.

In a final attempt to sustain itself, the shield used the last of her energy before it collapsed and left Ellie exposed.

I probably shouldn't have done this without Shiro after all, was Ellie's last thought before she lost consciousness.

CHAPTER ELEVEN

"Okay, guys, great job. See you tomorrow."
Aaron groaned as he tried to work out the kinks in his back. These settings were really killing him, and he was starting to regret the decision to do his own stunts.

He headed back to his dressing room, hurrying his steps to avoid anyone talking to him. He had been in a bad mood all day and it hadn't gotten any better when he messed up take after take. He glanced down at his watch and saw he was late. Fishing his phone out of his pocket, Aaron expected to see a text or missed call from Ellie – patience wasn't exactly her strong suit – but there was nothing. Great, she'd probably left the park by now, and if her previous temper was any indication, she would be pissed.

Aaron reached his dressing room and quickly shut the door behind him. Gathering his stuff, he decided to go to the park anyway.

Maybe by some chance of luck Ellie was still there, but even if she wasn't, he'd still enjoy spending time there on his own.

He'd found the park while running away from the media. His career had just taken off and the paparazzi were relentless. The spot under the big oak tree quickly became his favorite place and he used to sit and watch the lake for hours. Imagine his surprise when the girl from the club had been there, sitting in the grass and staring at a white puppy.

When Aaron got a phone call telling him his address had leaked over the internet, he rushed to the park in under fifteen minutes. Not only would there be fans and paparazzi everywhere, but Aaron would have to move. This had happened once before, but Aaron had refused to move at first. He didn't want his profession to control his life, but after a few weeks of fans screaming at him and camera flashes going off around him, Aaron had reconsidered.

If his address was out, it was only a matter of time before people would start showing up at his door. Aaron's agent had already sent people to move his stuff, so all he really had to do was stay out of the way.

He had reached the gate to the park and pushed it open. It was made entirely of iron that had once been white, but nature had left it rusty, giving it character, and it had decorative flowers and vines winding around the bars. As he walked through it, Aaron's phone had started to ring and his agent's number had flashed the screen.

"Yes, Mark?"

"Did you get out?"

"Yes, I got out," he'd sighed. Mark was a good agent and everything but sometimes he got on Aaron's nerves. "Now what I would like to know is *why* I had to get out of there? There being *my* apartment. How the hell did they get my address?"

"I have no idea; someone must have leaked it. But you know, this wouldn't happen if you would just listen to me."

"You know I'm not going to move to one of those Hollywood mansions with gates and security just so you won't have to worry about someone leaking my address. I'm just not that guy," Aaron had said in frustration. This was a discussion he had not wanted to have again. Aaron wanted to live in a normal apartment like a normal guy and if that meant more work for Mark, well, that was Mark's problem. After all, that was what Aaron paid him for.

Aaron had heard Mark mumbling something under his breath on the other end of the line and if he knew Mark it was all the curses he could think of, both in English and any other language he knew. Mark had been his agent for two years now and with time Aaron had learned to handle his personality. He was pushy and could be quite mean if he didn't get his way. In the beginning he hadn't liked Aaron much, especially since he didn't do what he was told, but the more famous Aaron got, the nicer Mark became.

Marks rambling had finally come to an end when Aaron neared the oak. "Fine, I'll get you a new apartment similar to the one you had. I'll text you the address when I have one. It might take a few weeks to sell the other one."

"Thank you, Mark. I appreciate it, but now I have to go."

"Yeah okay, I'll let you go. Just don't be late," Mark said with a sigh.

"I never am." And with that, Aaron had hung up, ready to throw himself down in the grass and continue his interrupted sleep.

Aaron was almost at the park now and parked his car a few blocks away, smiling at the thought of Ellie.

Ellie was everything he wanted in a girl. Her tall, lithe frame held curves in all the right places. Long, ebony hair cascaded in soft waves down her back, each strand a silken promise. But it was her eyes that captured him – their shade a mesmerizing green, framed by lashes as thick as secrets. She was, without a doubt, the most beautiful girl he'd ever seen in his life.

Yet, Ellie's allure transcended mere aesthetics. She moved through life with an unconscious grace, unaware of her own beauty, which only amplified its effect. She was smart and funny and didn't take any of his crap.

Unfortunately, Ellie had made it clear she wanted nothing more from him than friendship. Aaron found he had to keep reminding himself that's what they were, so he said it as often as he could to convince himself of that fact. But during the conversation about Ellie's parents, she didn't pull away when he took her hands, so a little hope had glowed inside of him.

Quickening his steps across the grass, Aaron made up his mind. If Ellie was still in the park, he would tell her how he felt. Even if she didn't feel the same way, at least he would know.

But when Aaron neared the oak, he realized something was wrong. People were crowding around something and a few police cars were parked on the other side of the fence. Then he spotted Shiro, who sprinted towards him, the crowd parting for him like the Red Sea parted for Moses.

"Hey, boy, what are you doing here?" Aaron asked, not really caring that he was talking to a dog. "Is Ellie here with you?"

At the mention of Ellie's name, Shiro's eyes saddened and he whined. It sounded like he was in pain, but giving him a quick look, Aaron concluded he wasn't hurt.

Shiro pivoted, retracing his steps toward the bustling crowd. His gaze swept back, making sure Aaron was following him. A knot tightened in the pit of Aaron's stomach and the emotions he'd dismissed as a foul mood now clawed at his insides, demanding attention.

Something was terribly wrong.

Aaron pushed through the crowd, deaf to the calls of his name. He'd lost sight of Shiro in the crowd, but the oak tree loomed ahead, its ancient branches a beacon. He jostled past the last strangers, their protests fading to the buzzing in his ears.

Then, an authoritative grip seized his arm. A police officer, stern-faced, blocked his path. "I'm sorry, sir, but you can't go there."

But the feeling of wrongness only grew, and Aaron yanked at the officer's arm, staring blindly ahead of him. Where was Ellie?

The officer's explanation blurred – something about a collapsed girl and thirty wild animals. But that was absurd, and either way, Aaron just wanted to find Ellie.

Aaron shook his head, desperate to clear the fog, when Shiro bolted towards him again. But Shiro wasn't alone this time. Three stray dogs trailed him, their eyes feral, teeth bared. The crowd gasped and the police officer took a step back.

Shiro stopped about ten feet away from Aaron and the police. His single bark echoed, and the pack mirrored him – growls rumbling from their throats. Aaron's heart raced. Ellie's absence gnawed at him, a void he couldn't ignore.

He stepped forward, heedless of the danger. Shiro's eyes locked onto his, and in that charged moment, Aaron didn't care that he was a dog, he *needed* to find Ellie.

"No, you can't go over there!" The police officer reached to grab Aaron's arm but jerked back at the sight of the dogs advancing towards him, barking.

Aaron moved forward again and, once he reached the dogs, Shiro left his post and joined him, leaving the others behind. He stumbled forward, propelled by fear and a gnawing dread. The ancient oak that usually gave him comfort now loomed over him, its gnarled roots like fingers clawing at the earth.

As he circled the tree, the scene that unfolded before him defied reason. Creatures of all kinds – ducks, squirrels, stray cats, and dogs with collars – stood in a solemn ring. Even two police horses and a handful of police dogs had joined the peculiar congregation. Their collective gaze was fixed on whatever it was in the middle of the circle.

Shiro threaded his way through that circle, each animal parting to allow his passage. Aaron followed hesitantly. Then the heart of the circle revealed itself – a heap on the ground, obscured by a curtain of damp, black hair.

Ellie.

Her chest lay still, a fragile silence that echoed through Aaron's bones. Panic surged, a cold hand clasping his heart. Air abandoned his lungs, and a sob tore from his throat, raw and unbidden.

He moved again, knees sinking into wet grass, forgetting when he'd stopped. Ellie's face emerged from the tangle of hair – pale, fragile, and too still. Very carefully, as if she was made of glass, Aaron took her small hand into his, gently squeezing it. But her hand was cold, and as he looked down, a small drop of water landed on it. That was when Aaron realized he was crying.

Ellie's hand lay lifeless in Aaron's, and he could hear his own heart break. She was gone. He had been too late. She would never know how much he loved her.

"Please... you have to wake up," he whispered helplessly in her ear.

Then, like a miracle, her fingers slowly curled around his. Aaron sat up with a jerk, staring at their now entwined hands.

"Ellie?"

Her chest rose and fell as warmth was returning to her hand. The color on her cheeks turned from white to a light pink and her eyelids fluttered.

She opened her eyes with a heart-breaking scream, and Aaron was torn between relief and panic. He held her in his arms and whispered calming words in her ear. Ellie stopped screaming, but her shrill panic was replaced with silent tears streaming down her face.

A broken whisper sounded from her lips. *"No."*

CHAPTER TWELVE

ELLIE GAZED DOWN UPON the scene below as if standing on a cloud, yet every detail etched itself into her consciousness.

"Am I dead?" she whispered.

Hayyel turned toward her, but Ellie couldn't tear her eyes from the unfolding drama.

"Yes, you are. But not lost."

I'm dead.

This couldn't be how her life was meant to end. One reckless mistake, and everything had been snatched away. No second chances. Just one irreversible error.

"What do you mean 'not lost?' Everything is lost." Ellie's voice trembled.

"I mean exactly what I say. You may be dead, but you are not lost – not yet."

"Please, Hayyel, could you just answer this one question, and *actually answer* it?" she pleaded. Her irritation helped Ellie whip her eyes from her dead body to glower at him.

"Your body lies dead, but your soul lingers. Thus, you cannot truly die."

"Why hasn't my soul moved on?" It struck Ellie that maybe she should shut up and be happy about not being a complete goner, but her curiosity had a mind of its own.

"Something, or someone, anchors it here," Hayyel replied.

He turned back to the clearing where her body rested. Ellie waited, but he remained silent. With a sigh, she faced forward again

She was no longer alone.

Aragonite and his family stood a few feet away from her body. Soon, dogs and cats joined them – not just strays, but pets too, their collars of varied colors and quality. Squirrels, mice, frogs, and birds followed, filling the sky. Their silent descent onto the ancient oak tree was like a celestial ballet.

"What is this?" Ellie's voice barely carried.

"This is what is keeping you earthbound." But they were only animals. Hayyel must have seen the confusion in her eyes, because for once, he actually tried to explain something. "They offer you their life energy in order to save you."

They were sacrificing themselves for her? Ellie's mind reeled. She wouldn't allow it.

"Tell them to stop."

Hayyel's gaze bore into her, unyielding. "If they cease, you will die. Besides, I cannot tell them what to do. They chose for themselves. Look."

"I *am* looking."

The animals were all staring at Ellie's body, not moving. But other than that, there was nothing to see.

"You are not. Look." She *was* looking, maybe it was *him* who wasn't. Ellie opened her mouth to protest, but Hayyel silenced her. "Just look."

And so, Ellie looked.

Her body lay sprawled in the grass, shadows from the oak tree stretching across the clearing. The sun blazed overhead. The animals were slowly circling her, all eyes focused on her body. A horse entered the circle and there was something about it that felt familiar. Ellie narrowed her eyes, trying to remember what it was when she noticed the word 'police' written on the side of its saddle.

Not long after, a police officer followed and froze mid-step and moved carefully when he laid eyes on the animals. Then he saw Ellie's body in the middle of them. He gasped and ran towards her, but no other than Shiro stopped him. He stood in front of the police officer, growling, and the man slowly backed away, casting worried glances between her body and Shiro.

Finally, he made up his mind and turned to leave, speaking into some sort of radio as he went.

Although Ellie saw all of this, she did not *see*, but it didn't take her long to figure out that Hayyel meant for her to look with her mind, not her eyes. But Ellie didn't know how without meditating.

Ellie hovered on the edge of existence, suspended between realms. How could she still her nonexistent breath and silent a heart that no longer beat?

Still, she closed her eyes and tried to find the fire, but as Ellie gazed inside herself, she found nothing. Her consciousness flickered like a dying ember, memories slipping through her ethereal grasp.

Hayyel touched her cheek with his cold hand, and Ellie met his gaze with hers. She dared not breathe – not that she needed to anymore, but perhaps it was safest not to risk it.

In all these weeks, he had never touched her.

Hayyel slowly lowered his hand over Ellie's eyes, closing them in the process, and a flicker of a memory filled her mind. Ellie tried to grasp it, but it slithered through her fingers like water.

Hayyel's voice pierced the silence. "Let go and breathe." His breath ghosted across her face, intimate and otherworldly. "Your memories will return when the time is right. But now, you must see."

Ellie did as he said, letting the memory slip between her fingers. She focused everything on her breathing. Soon, she was mimicking Hayyel's even inhales, and the place where their skin touched burned.

It wasn't long before Ellie felt a similar sensation to the one she had experienced when connecting with her own power. Hayyel lifted his hand from her forehead and Ellie slowly opened her eyes. And then, she *saw*.

The clearing teemed with animals, each tethered to her lifeless body by threads of energy. They were all connected to her, feeding her their life energy in order to save hers. But Ellie couldn't bear it. She didn't want their lives forfeit for her mistake.

Some smaller creatures faltered, their energy waning. A silent tear slipped down her cheek.

"Why?" Ellie's voice trembled, almost dissolving into the ether.

"Because you are important," Hayyel replied. "More than you comprehend now. They know it and are willing to give their lives for it."

The police officer returned, accompanied by a growing crowd. Soon, the park had filled with humans, their attention on Ellie's body. Some of the paramedics and police officers were trying to get past the animals without any luck, but Ellie didn't pay them much attention. All of her focus lay on the animals.

"But why haven't I woken up?" Ellie's confusion swirled. The torrent of power should have been enough.

"I do not know." Hayyel's admission surprised her. For once, he lacked answers. "Ah, Shiro. I wondered where he'd gone. And he brings someone – perhaps he knows something I do not."

Ellie looked back to see the animals making way for a figure. She recognized him immediately. Aaron.

Her heart broke at the sight of devastation radiating from his entire being as he knelt by her body with tears tracing his cheeks. He ignored everyone calling after him and gently took Ellie's hand.

Somewhere in the far distance, his voice floated to her ears, thick with pain. Ellie fixed her pleading gaze on Hayyel. "Please, I'm not done. This can't be it."

"I am sorry, but there is nothing I can do, and the animals' energy does not seem to be enough."

Ellie knew he was right. More animals had fallen and the ones remaining weakened, their legs struggling to support their weight and their eyes drooping as if ready to close for good.

I'm going to die, Ellie thought as a tear slid down her cheek. Her shoulders slumped in defeat, and just as she was about to lower her eyes, Aragonite waddled to the inner circle with his family. They were bathing in blinding light, and Ellie looked down, puzzled as to why.

Then, without any warning, the light intensified, blinding Ellie for a few seconds, only to shoot straight up in the air. Aragonite and his entire family fell to the ground as the light returned and entered her body. Ellie felt a tug deep within her core, something pulling at the very essence that was her, then she woke up with a scream, wrapped in Aaron's arms.

A BROKEN WHISPER ESCAPED Ellie's lips, barely audible as the truth slammed into her. Aragonite was dead. He and his family had given Ellie all of their life energy to save her.

Ellie trembled, clinging to Aaron with a desperation that obliterated the world around her. In that moment, Ellie's chest tightened with pure devastation as a hollow ache gnawed at her soul.

She had wanted to live, but not like this.

Aaron's arms encircled her, soft murmurs brushing against her ear. His soothing words were a lifeline, an attempt to anchor her unraveling soul. Time blurred as they sat there – hours or seconds, it didn't matter.

Aaron shifted under her as he started to get up, still holding onto her in a tight grip. But Ellie couldn't let go, not yet.

"You need to let go of her and let us have a look," a gentle voice said, and Aaron made as if to release her.

Ellie shook her head, clinging tighter to his body.

"I think she's okay, could you just give us a few minutes?" he answered the paramedics who stood waiting.

"We really need to check her out, sir," the man persisted, but the woman next to him nodded back towards their ambulance.

"I'm sure we can give them a few minutes," she said in the same gentle voice as before, then tugged at her partner's arm to get him to move.

As they backed away, Ellie buried her head into Aaron's chest and tried to still her breathing.

Soon, Aaron shifted again and tried to untangle them.

"Wait," she whispered, and Aaron halted instantly.

"You need to go to the hospital," he urged, concern etched in his voice and mirrored in his eyes as he gently eased her down.

The ground beneath her was solid, yet her legs wavered.

"I'll go, but I need to do something first," Ellie said as she moved towards the dead bodies.

All of the wild animals were gone, and the tame ones sat, patiently waiting for their owners to come and collect them. She took a faltering step toward them, but her strength waned. Aaron caught her in his arms, protective and worried. Ellie tried to give him a reassuring smile, but pain twisted her lips into a grimace.

Still, Aaron gave her a small smile back as Ellie carefully moved again. She slowly sank to her knees, lifting Aragonite's lifeless body in her hands. Ellie had only wanted to learn how to talk to him; how could it have gone so wrong?

They did it because they loved you. Because they believe you will set them free. The voice rang in Ellie's mind as clear as Aaron's voice in her ears.

Ellie looked up and into Shiro's icy blue eyes, staring into them for a while before burying her face into his soft fur. He said nothing more, but nothing more was needed right now.

Silent tears trickled down Ellie's cheeks and she tried to speak. "I... I ca–"

"What, what is it?"

"I need for them to be buried," Ellie said in a low voice, and when Aaron looked like he was about to argue, she added, "please."

Aaron nodded at her desperation and said, "Okay, I'll go see what I can do, but then we really need to get to a hospital, okay?"

"Okay," Ellie whispered, nodding in agreement.

Aaron walked away and talked to someone Ellie didn't recognize, then she realized they were surrounded by people. A few policemen were breaking up a crowd of people while another team were pushing back a crowd of paparazzi. Everywhere Ellie looked, phones flashed alongside the paparazzi's cameras, and her chest tightened.

Where was Aaron?

Her breaths had turned into short gasps by the time he finally returned. He crouched beside her and said, "I asked them to bury the ducks under the oak, if that's okay with you."

"Thank you," she said, meaning it from the bottom of her heart.

With Aaron by her side again, her shoulders relaxed and she released a breath she didn't know she'd been holding.

Ellie had no idea how he had convinced them to bury seven ducks, but in that moment, she didn't care. He had been so patient and kind, and Ellie didn't know what she'd done to deserve it. *He's just your friend.*

Sighing, Ellie placed Aragonite back down onto the ground with his family and stood up slowly. But Aaron didn't let her take more than two steps before lifting her off the ground, cradling her into his chest.

Ellie was too tired to ask questions or protest, so she rested her head on his shoulder and closed her eyes. But people shouting and camera flashes caused them to fly back open. While the crowd had dispersed, the reporters had not.

"Who is she?"

"Is she your girlfriend?"

"What happened to her?"

Aaron hurried past them all, not bothering with a single answer. He continued to the ambulance, where a glowing Shiro waited unnoticed, and sat Ellie down. Ellie realized that Shiro was shielding her; her own powers must be next to non-existent.

The paramedics felt for her pulse, flashed a light in her eyes, and listened to her heartbeat, but they couldn't find anything physically wrong with her.

"We need you to come back to the hospital with us for further checks, just to be on the safe side," the female paramedic said.

Ellie nodded again, and as they loaded her into the ambulance a sudden fear of being alone ripped through her. She wondered if Aaron could sense her fear, because he climbed in beside her and took her hand in his, stroking her skin with his thumb.

AFTER THE DOCTORS FOUND nothing wrong with Ellie, Aaron arranged for someone to pick them up from the hospital and escorted her back to her dorm.

Jen wasn't there when they entered, and Ellie didn't know if she was happy about it or not. A part of her wanted to throw herself in Jen's arm and tell her everything, but another part feared how Jen might react if she knew.

"I'll stay with you until Jen gets back," Aaron offered, and Ellie allowed herself to relax a little.

She knew he was doing it because of who he was, not because he had feelings for her, but for a few moments, it felt nice to pretend.

Ellie laid down on her bed and closed her eyes. Shiro, who hadn't left her side since the park, lay down on the floor by the foot of her bed. His eyes were drooping, and he rested his head on his paws, seeming to lack the strength to hold it up any longer. He looked as exhausted as Ellie felt.

The bed shifted, and Ellie opened her eyes again. Aaron lay down facing her, but she couldn't meet his eyes, not without risking ruining the illusion she had created in her mind, so she stared past him and out the window. He gently touched her arm, slowly stroking it, but Ellie didn't know how to respond. She felt like she had nothing left. No tears, no hurt, no fear, nothing. She was empty.

"Please look at me," came a quiet whisper filled with pain. She slowly, very slowly, shifted her eyes and finally met his. Ellie hadn't expected to see *that* emotion on his face. Aaron moved his hand from Ellie's arm up to her cheek and sighed. "Do you want to talk about what happened?"

Ellie closed her eyes and shook her head, not ready to face any of it yet and wondering if she ever would be. Aaron nodded with understanding, and nothing more was said. Silence filled the room for so long that Ellie wondered if Aaron had fallen asleep, but she didn't dare open her eyes and find out. Instead, she remained still, waiting for sleep she knew wouldn't come.

"You scared me." Aaron's voice startled her, and she opened her eyes. "Don't you ever scare me like that again, you hear me?"

Ellie didn't know what to say or do, so she ended up just staring right into Aaron's brown eyes. His face was closer to hers than before, so close that Ellie could smell his sweet, minty breath as it fanned across her face.

"So beautiful," he whispered, more to himself than Ellie, she thought.

After everything Ellie had been through that day, she couldn't bring herself to move away, and to be honest, she wasn't sure if she wanted to. Perhaps this was what she needed, to help her forget if only for a minute or two, even if she knew it wasn't real.

Ellie focused all of her attention on Aaron, pushing everything else to the back of her mind. He inched closer until their bodies were pressed against each other's, his face barely an inch away. Their noses touched and he tilted his head ever so slightly, getting even closer if that was possible.

And just before his lips gently brushed against hers, he whispered three words Ellie would never forget.

"Last first kiss."

CHAPTER THIRTEEN

Ellie waved the bartender over to order another drink to replace her empty glass.

Jen sat next to her, her concern pressing on Ellie's shield. "Maybe you should slow down a little?"

"I'm fine, *mom*," Ellie retorted, rolling her eyes.

Jen had squealed when Ellie told her she wanted to go out drinking – she would finally be able to use the fake ID's she'd gotten for them during first week of college. But as Ellie downed drink after drink, that excitement quickly faded and turned into concern.

Aaron hadn't told Jen about what had happened to Ellie, something Ellie was grateful for, but it would take an idiot not to realize there was something wrong with her, and Jen was not an idiot.

Ellie had made her peace with the deaths of Aragonite and his family through working harder than before with Hayvel, adamant that their deaths would not be in vain. But she had not heard from Aaron since he'd left her sleeping in her dorm.

Ellie had texted him once, and when he hadn't replied, she'd freaked out. That was over a week ago, and now she wanted to get drunk and forget.

Jen didn't say anything else for the next two drinks.

The night Aaron had kissed her felt like a dream to Ellie; she wasn't even sure it had happened. But if he had kissed her, why wouldn't he call or text her back? Could it be that her powers had forced her own feelings onto him, creating feelings he didn't have?

Most likely he kissed her out of pity and couldn't find a way to let her down gently.

Ellie took another sip as Jen finally broke the silence. "Ellie, I wish you would just tell me what happened. Maybe I could help."

Ellie looked at her over the rim of her glass. A part of her told her she was drunk and should probably stop drinking – that part was currently seeing two Jens in front of her – but Ellie told that part to shut up.

"Am I, like, unlikeable?"

Jen wrinkled her face, confused. "What? No, why?"

"Well, clearly I'm not because *everyone* wants to be my friend, I am Ellie *the friend*." She laughed at her own wit while Jen's eyes widened with alarm. "I mean, Lucas hit on me, but he like, gave up after one try. Lucas does not give up after one try."

"Wait, I'm confused. You *want* Lucas to hit on you? I thought you liked Aaron," Jen said, sounding relieved that Ellie was finally talking to her.

"*No*," Ellie said, dragging out the o. "I want him to *want* to hit on me. All the guys just wanna be friends, I am officially the definition of friend-zoned."

Ellie groaned.

Then she registered the other part of Jen's sentence. "How do you know I like Aaron?"

Jen rolled her eyes and Ellie giggled, finding the gesture surprisingly funny. "It's obvious to anyone with eyes that you like each other. I just can't figure out why you don't do anything about it."

"Aaron doesn't like me. He only sees me as a friend," Ellie said, her smile dissipating.

"He does not want to be your friend, believe me. The way he looks at you is not the way you look at a friend."

Ellie, who had been studying a circle left by a glass on the bar, snapped her eyes to Jen and groaned a little when the world started to spin.

"But he tells me we're friends," Ellie said, making a wide gesture that caused her to tip over a glass on the counter. Luckily, it didn't break. "Like, all the time."

"God, you are a mess. He probably does that because he thinks that's what *you* want," Jen said in a tired voice.

Ellie's head was spinning, and not only from the alcohol. "What? Why would he think that?"

Jen sighed. "Well, knowing you, you probably didn't invite much else. I bet you even told him you were just friends?"

"I did not!"

"You sure?" Jen asked, a small smile playing on her lips.

If Ellie hadn't been drunk, she would have been annoyed at how well Jen knew her, sometimes better than she knew herself. As it was now, realization suddenly hit her. She *had* told Aaron they were friends when they had talked about the article. Maybe he had thought that was what she wanted all along.

Ellie stood, her chair falling behind her, and turned towards Jen. "You're right, I'm gonna go see him."

Jen held up her hands with alarm. "Maybe now is not the best time, Ellie..."

But Ellie was already moving towards the door.

"Now is the perfect time. I will see you later," Ellie said.

She promptly stumbled into a man and grabbed his shirt to stop herself from falling.

"Ellie!" Jen hurried towards her while Ellie smoothed down the guy's shirt, her eyes transfixed on his chest. Thankfully, he only laughed at her and told her to take it easy on the drinks.

"I'm fine, just lost my balance!" Ellie shouted to Jen, and then she was gone, pushing through the crowd.

As Ellie made her way down the street, focusing on walking straight, her annoyance at herself transformed into anger at Aaron. She took each step with more purpose while her mind raced. If he liked her, he should have just told her, but she conveniently forgot she hadn't told him either.

Luckily, the club wasn't far from where Aaron had told her he lived, and she was soon pounding on his door. It took a few minutes before a light turned on inside and someone shuffled around.

Aaron finally opened the door, and Ellie realized how late it was. He was only wearing pajama bottoms, and Ellie stared a little too long at his bare chest.

"Ellie?" Aaron said, confused. "What are you doing here? It's the middle of the night."

Tearing her gaze from his chest, Ellie looked up into his eyes. "What am I doing here? What are *you* doing here?"

"I live here," Aaron said and blinked a few times. "You're drunk."

He sighed and beckoned her inside.

Ellie staggered past him with her head held high. "I'm not. I threw up on the way over here *and* held my own hair. Does that sound like the sort of multitasking a drunk person would do?"

Aaron laughed a little. "No, but the throwing up part does. Come on, you can sleep it off here."

He put his hand at the small of Ellie's back and suddenly she forgot why she was mad at him. He steered her through his apartment until he came to the bedroom. Everything from the furniture to the bedspreads had been decorated all white. It could have looked like a hospital room, but the shade of white he had chosen made it work.

"Oh, the bedroom. I see where this is going," Ellie said.

Aaron groaned. "This is going nowhere; I like my women conscious. Would you please stop taking off your clothes!"

Ellie had managed to get her tank top off and was working on her pants, but the stupid button wouldn't work.

With another sigh, Aaron led Ellie to his enormous bed and lifted her up, laying her down in the middle of it. Ellie was facing what she'd at first thought was a mural, but now realized were windows. They covered the entire wall and overlooked the city below.

The room was spinning, and suddenly, all Ellie wanted to do was sleep.

Seeing her struggle with her pants, Aaron took pity on her and undid the button. Ellie then managed to squirm out of the tight fabric.

"I'll be on the couch if you need me," Aaron whispered and made as if to leave but Ellie grabbed his arm.

"You can't just kiss a girl and leave while she sleeps." Ellie's eyes were closed, and she started to drift off to sleep. "And I don't want to be your friend."

OPENING HER EYES, ELLIE was faced with a ceiling she did not recognize. The sun shining through the huge windows hurt her eyes, so she clamped them shut.

Thinking back to the night before, she tried to remember where she was. Then the memories came crashing back. Ellie groaned and covered her face. Had she been talking about throwing up with Aaron?

Carefully opening her eyes this time, she looked around. She remembered the white bedroom now and spotted a picture of Aaron and an unfamiliar woman on the dresser.

There was no denying it, Ellie was in Aaron's bed, admittedly not in the way she would have hoped it would happen.

Ellie groaned again as she sat up, cradling her throbbing head between her hands. She glanced to her side and spotted a little white pill and a glass of water on the bedside table. There was a note with, hopefully, Aaron's hand-writing beside it. *Take this,* was all it said, and Ellie did, not bothering to question what it was.

After a short while, the worst of the headache was gone, and Ellie was able to stand. Looking down at herself, she realized she was in her underwear, and she prayed she hadn't made a complete fool out of herself.

A sudden smell distracted her from her train of thought. She sniffed a few times, trying to place the all too familiar aroma. Her stomach answered with a growl. Waffles.

Ellie pulled a white t-shirt from the dresser, relieved when it covered most of her, then tip-toed her way to the door, slowly pushing it open. As she made her way through the apartment towards the kitchen, she was amazed at the beauty of the apartment.

The ceiling was high, and like in the bedroom, the wall facing the city was made entirely out of glass. A black couch sat in front of a large TV with a lot of electronic things Ellie would never dare touch. All things technical despised her, but the feeling was more than mutual.

The rest of the room was elegant and clean. There were a few frames on a bookshelf and one or two paintings hanging on the walls. There were no plants in sight. Ellie wondered why that was.

Ellie made her way through a short corridor, passing a closed door, and finally rounded a corner into the kitchen. Everything had been decked with stainless steel and top-of-the-line equipment. There was an island in the middle with a big stove, pans and pots hanging above it. And then there was *him*.

Standing in front of a waffle iron was Aaron. He wore a pair of low hung jeans and a white t-shirt, his hair a perfect mess.

"That smells amazing," Ellie said.

The sound of her voice must have startled him because he spun around, dropping the plate in his hand. She cringed at the sound of it smashing on the floor. "Oh, hi, you're awake."

"Yeah," Ellie said a little hesitantly. Then she decided to just ask. "Did you take off my clothes?"

"No, you did that all on your own after bragging about your awesome multitasking skills," Aaron said with a laugh, and Ellie flushed. *Crap.*

"I can't believe Jen let me leave the bar," Ellie complained and looked down at the floor, hoping it would somehow open up and swallow her whole.

"I think you ran off, actually. She called a few times, so I picked up and told her you were fine, but you should probably call her yourself." Ellie only nodded and lifted her eyes to meet Aaron's. "And I'm sorry I haven't called, but I lost my phone and Mark has been taking forever to replace it. Apparently, I'm not allowed to simply buy a new one."

He lost his phone. The explanation was almost too mundane. He lost his phone.

"Anyway," Aaron continued. "I guessed you might be hungry, so I made waffles."

He glanced down at the ground. Ellie followed his gaze at the smashed plate by his feet.

"I'm so sorry, wait, I'll clean it up, don't move," Ellie said. Aaron wasn't wearing any shoes and was surrounded by tiny pieces of porcelain.

"I actually think that might be a good idea," he answered with a laugh, looking at his feet. "There's a broom underneath the sink."

She darted over to the sink, avoiding the area of smashed porcelain, and quickly gathered all the fragments into the scoop. She tossed them into the garbage and Aaron could move freely again.

"Thank you," Aaron said as he finished the last waffle. "I was just trying to make you breakfast, but you surprised me. You should really make some noise when you enter a room. A person could have a heart attack."

Ellie smiled and looked over at the set table. Atop the table was a pile of waffles, a can of whipped cream, and fresh berries.

"You did all this? You really didn't have to." She didn't want to be a burden – not more than she already was, that is.

"I wanted to. Besides, I have to eat too, you know. So, dig in before it gets cold."

Ellie headed for the table when she realized Aaron wasn't beside her. Instead, she could almost feel his eyes on her.

"Quit staring at my ass, you douche," she said without turning around. The white t-shirt she'd pulled form his drawer didn't leave much to the imagination.

"I wasn't staring at it, *it* was staring at me," came the answer.

I'm sure it was, Ellie thought, realizing he was making fun of her. Her eyes fell upon the can with whipped cream on the table, and a mischievous grin spread across Ellie's face. It was hardly fair he got to look as good as he did when she felt like crap.

Aaron was almost at the table when she grabbed the can and turned to face him. Aaron gaped, startled, and he started to back away, holding his hands up in mock horror. "You wouldn't."

"Oh, but I would," Ellie said with a wink, then sprayed his face until cream covered his features. Ellie stopped spraying only to see Aaron's expression and almost fell to the floor laughing, tears blurring her vision.

"Oh, so you think this is funny, huh?"

Ellie could only nod her head. It felt like it had been forever since she'd last laughed.

"Well then, two can play this game."

With that, Aaron threw a handful of blueberries at her, all of them hitting her square in the face. That stopped Ellie mid-laugh, and before she knew it, they were having a full-on war, food flying everywhere.

Ellie tried to escape, but Aaron caught her, an arm encircling her waist as she turned the corner of the kitchen counter.

"Do you give up?" he asked, holding her firm against his chest.

She shook her head and he began to tickle her relentlessly. Ellie laughed even harder, but she still refused to give up, at least until she had to pee.

"Okay, okay, I give up!" she cried.

Aaron laughed as he sat her down and turned Ellie around to face him, their faces inches apart.

His eyes danced with laughter, his hands still on her hips. Ellie's breath caught, the air thick, vibrating with emotions that went unspoken.

Ellie lowered her eyes, and the moment was broken.

Aaron released her hips and averted his gaze. He grabbed a towel and wiped his face before handing it to Ellie, who continued to look away.

Ellie grabbed it, careful not to touch him. "Aaron, I –"

She needed to say something, anything.

"Last night, I –" she tried again, but Aaron stopped her before she could even finish the thought in her head.

"No, Ellie it's fine. You were drunk." He turned his back towards her and moved to the table. "Come on, let's eat whatever's left. I'm starving."

Friend.

She could just go to the table and sit down, agree with Aaron's explanation. God, he must think she was such a mess just showing up at his door in the middle of the night. But he had *kissed* her. Even though she had just returned from the dead, she knew she hadn't imagined it.

Friend.

But then he had never mentioned it again. It could have been out of pity. No, she knew what he felt, it was something real.

A pair of brown eyes looked into Ellie's. A smile of pure bliss played at the woman's lips, and with the memory, warm emotions followed. The love filled Ellie until she thought she would burst. It was gone in an instant, but it was enough.

Friend.

"I meant it."

Aaron turned towards her, and at last, his eyes met hers again. There was a question written there, and this time, Ellie would answer it.

"I don't want to be your friend."

With those words, Ellie closed the distant between them and pressed her lips against Aaron's.

At first, nothing happened, but then he slowly wrapped his arms around her and pulled her closer. When his lips finally moved against hers, something inside of Ellie broke. All of the hope, longing and desire she had not allowed herself to feel seized her entire being and she could not pull away, even if her life had depended on it.

Aaron's lips were gentle and warm against hers, his sweet breath mingling with hers. Ellie's breathing intensified as she explored Aaron's muscular back, feeling every twitch as Aaron's did the same, making her feel *alive*.

They drew back from each other, both of them trying to catch their breath. Aarons' eyes were hooded, and Ellie could only imagine she looked much the same. A small smile played at Aaron's lips as his hand reached up to cup her cheek.

"So..." He smiled and let his thumb gently brush her cheekbone, "...not friends then."

Ellie mimicked his smile, and just before their lips touched again, she whispered, "no, definitely not friends."

The kiss started sweet but soon turned hungry. Aaron's tongue brushed against her lips, seeking entrance, which she eagerly granted. He gave her a gentle push and led her towards the bedroom, lips never leaving hers, hands never letting go of her body. But it was hard to move fast enough when consumed by the man in her arms and Ellie wrapped her legs around Aaron, thanked god he caught her, and let him carry her the rest of the way.

She hit the bed with a *thud* and pulled Aaron with her. Their teeth knocked together, still not breaking their kiss, and Ellie snickered into his mouth.

"Sorry," he mumbled as he drew back a little, their eyes locking.

Ellie caressed his cheek and a sudden calm washed over them, but her body continued to ignite with fire at his every touch. Somewhere between the kitchen and the bedroom, they both had discarded their shirts, but she still needed more. Not letting her eyes leave his, she let her hands travel down his body until she reached the button of his jeans.

"Are you sure?" his voice trembled, and Ellie knew he would stop if she wanted him to, even if it killed him.

But she only smiled and pushed his pants bellow his hips, the button finally undone. Aaron was quick to help her, pulling back only long enough to peel away the last layer of fabric from his body.

They finally became one, and Ellie lost herself in the bliss that was Aaron.

Laying encircled in Aaron's arms was like nothing Ellie had ever experienced before. Her head rested on his chest, falling and rising with Aaron's every peaceful breath. Her arm was flung over his torso and their legs were tangled together with the sheets.

Everything about this was new to Ellie. While there had been one or two boys, it had never been like this.

The walls disappeared and a night sky full of stars twinkled at Ellie. Although the woman's eyes were closed, there was no mistaking it. It was the same, brown-eyed woman from before. But her father's feelings could just as well have been her own in that moment.

Aaron shifted under Ellie and started to stir. She smiled, still not moving, feeling him wake up.

"Hello, beautiful," he croaked.

Ellie realized he probably didn't get much sleep last night either; a small blush crept up her cheeks.

"Hi." Ellie smiled.

Nothing more was said for a few minutes. They simply lay there, Aaron stroking her hair, and Ellie drawing lazy circles on his stomach.

The silence was comfortable, but it didn't last, courtesy of Ellie's stomach. A loud growl almost echoed through the room, causing Aaron to laugh, Ellie's whole body vibrating from his laughter.

"I think you need to actually eat some food, not just throw it," he said, trying to get up from under Ellie.

But she didn't want the moment to end. No matter how complete she felt, there was always a small voice at the back of her mind reminding her of her powers. A tiny voice whispering that Aaron might have just mirrored Ellie's desire. She was desperate to ignore it, but Ellie felt certain the voice would win if they left the bed.

"I'm not that hungry, and throwing the food was simply more fun than eating it."

Sadly, Ellie's stomach betrayed her with another growl.

"Well, apparently your stomach does not agree with you," Aaron chuckled. "Come on, there might still be something left in the kitchen."

"No," Ellie said stubbornly. "I'm not going."

She knew it was childish, but she didn't care. Ellie wasn't ready.

Aaron shifted under her, and suddenly, he was standing by the bedside, naked, with a grin on his face.

The voice grew a little louder.

"If you won't go to the food, well then, the food will just have to come to you," he said with a wink, then turned and walked out of the bedroom, not caring to put anything on.

Ellie was left slightly dazed, the voice a little further back in her mind again. No one should be allowed to look that good, with or without clothes.

She wrapped the sheet around her and scooted up so her back rested against the headboard. She leaned her head back and closed her eyes. *Please let it be real.*

It felt like an eternity before Ellie dared to open her eyes. Before her stood Aaron with a tray of fruit and, to Ellie's dismay, a pair of boxers on. He placed the tray onto the bed and captured Ellie in a fiery kiss that left her both speechless and breathless.

"You need to eat," he said with a smirk, nodding towards the tray.

Ellie couldn't believe he was teasing her. She gave him a glare and shook her head.

Aaron pouted and looked at Ellie with puppy eyes. "Please?"

Ellie shook her head again but with a smile on her lips this time.

"Pretty please, with a cherry on top? No whipped cream though. I'm out."

She couldn't help but laugh. "Fine! Give me the damn food."

Aaron's smile was gorgeous as he handed Ellie a strawberry. She reached her hand out to take it from him, but he moved away.

Ellie tilted her head and frowned. "First you want me to eat and now you won't give me the food?"

He gave her a smug smile as he held up the strawberry, moving it towards her lips. He was going to feed her, she realized, and began laughing again.

"Oh my god, that is so cheesy. Are you serious?"

"I was going for romantic, but I'll take cheesy. Now, open up."

"Oh, I'm not eating that unless I'm the one putting it in my mouth."

Again, with the smirk, like he knew everything.

"I think you will," he answered, his smirk turning into a grin.

"And why is that?"

"Because if you don't, then this," he said, gesturing towards his body, "is off limits."

Ellie's mouth dropped open in shock.

"You wouldn't," she managed to stammer out.

"Oh, but I would," he said, mimicking Ellie's words from earlier.

He didn't need to say any more. Ellie opened her mouth and let him feed her. He didn't let her have the damn strawberry until he'd 'missed' a few times first, though, and Ellie was sure her laughing didn't help when he actually tried to give her the cursed thing.

Now he had gotten what he wanted, Ellie figured it was fair that she did, too. She needed to quieten the voice in her head before it couldn't be ignored.

She grabbed a strawberry from the tray, smiling sweetly at him. He obediently opened his mouth, but Ellie shook her head. She put half the strawberry in her mouth, daring him with her eyes to come and get it. Then she slowly let the sheet drop from her body, hoping it would help. She didn't know where her confidence came from, but she liked it.

Aaron gave her a smoldering look, then more or less pounced

on her. He quickly ate the strawberry, causing Ellie to giggle at his sudden urgency, then flipped her so fast that Ellie didn't have time to register what happened.

She was now on top, straddling his waist. She smiled down at him, loving the way he made her feel. He made her feel eighteen. Not like an Empath or half-angel and not like someone with the entire world on her shoulders.

As Ellie looked down at him, a sudden need to explain her feelings overwhelmed her. She could always *show* him how she felt, but that would most likely freak Aaron out, and if that wouldn't ruin the mood, then nothing would. She wasn't ready to say 'I love you' yet either. Those were three words she had never said to anyone but Jen.

Instead, Ellie lowered her lips to kiss his cheek and moved to graze his ear.

"*Last first kiss,*" she whispered, and when she lifted her head again, Aaron's smile was so wide it looked like it hurt.

"Last first kiss," he agreed, then pinned Ellie down on the bed, kissing her with all the passion she felt.

And right then, nothing else mattered. Hayyel, the angels, her powers, or the mystery woman. Whatever *this* was made everything else fade away and left her feeling nothing but happiness.

For Ellie knew, in that moment, that Aaron was indeed her last first kiss.

CHAPTER FOURTEEN

"**O**H MY GOD!" Jen exclaimed the moment the door closed. "I'm so happy for you."

Ellie had finally returned to her dorm and the vague answers she had given Jen over the phone had apparently done little to hide what had happened with Aaron.

She bent down to scratch Shiro behind the ear when a shoe hit her in the shoulder.

"What the hell?"

"You could have told me what was going on when you called," Jen whined, her eyes sparkling at the same time.

"I'm sorry, I–"

"Yeah, yeah. Apology accepted, now tell me everything," Jen interrupted her. "Have you slept with him?"

The blush rising on Ellie's cheeks seemed to be answer enough because Jen squealed again. "Oh my god you did, didn't you? How was he?"

Thankfully, Aaron arrived from the car with his bag, sparing her from answering.

When Ellie had said she was going back to her dorm, she secretly hoped he would stop her. She'd tried to hide her disappointment as she packed her things when she found a bag waiting by the door.

"They've been bugging me for weeks about some renovation that needs doing in the kitchen, so I figured I could crash at your place for a few nights?" he had said.

Ellie hadn't called him out on the reason he'd clearly made up.

While Ellie wasn't sure what they were just yet, she was glad she could stay in their happy little bubble for a while longer at least.

Aaron walked across the room and reached out his hand for Jen to shake. "Hi, we haven't been formally introduced. I'm –"

He dropped his bag to awkwardly catch Jen, who threw her arms around his neck. "Aaron, I know. I'm Jen, but you should know that, too."

Aaron looked over Jen's shoulder at Ellie, searching her eyes for what to do next, but Ellie just shrugged with a small smile.

With a final squeeze, Jen took pity on him and let him go.

"Well, I think I'll sleep at Collin's for a night or two. We'll have all the time in the world to get to know each other later."

"Oh, you don't have to do that. I don't want to push you out of your home," Aaron hurriedly said, but Jen looked past him at Ellie, who was giving her a look of gratitude.

"Nah, it's fine. I haven't seen him in a while anyway, so. I'm just gonna grab a bag and then you two can get back to whatever it is you do," Jen answered with a wink and disappeared into the bathroom.

Ellie didn't linger on the fact that Jen had never mentioned Collin before, but she was happy that she had gotten over Andrew. Despite her tough exterior, Ellie knew the breakup hurt more than Jen was willing to admit.

Aaron looked over at Ellie and picked up his bag from the floor. "So, where should I put my things?"

LATER THAT NIGHT WHEN both Aaron and Ellie were getting ready for bed, a piece of paper slipped under the door.

"What's that?" Aaron asked as he walked towards the door. He was only wearing a pair of pajama bottoms, so it took Ellie a real effort to tear her eyes away from his chest and answer his question.

"Oh, um, it's probably just some takeout menu, throw it in the trash."

Aaron started towards the bin but stopped halfway there, reading the piece of paper more carefully.

"What? What is it?" Ellie's interest was piqued, so she got up from the bed and stood on her tiptoes to read over his shoulder, resting her chin against him.

It wasn't a takeout menu like Ellie had first thought, but an invite to the university's annual ball. There was a mask at the top right corner and some swirly text below she didn't bother to read.

"It's probably for Jen," Ellie dismissed, having no interest in a ball. "She's on the committee organizing it."

But Aaron simply ignored her and continued to read. "It says that it's for both of you and you can both bring a plus one. *And* it's a masquerade."

Something about his tone made Ellie back away from him, allowing him to turn and face her. A huge grin spread on his face, and Ellie knew that could only mean trouble.

"We should go!" he exclaimed.

"Eh, let me think. No, we shouldn't."

"Yes, we should."

"No, we shouldn't!"

"Why not?" he asked, and Ellie could tell he was preparing to bring out the puppy eyes any minute.

"Because it's a bad idea. I mean, how could we go? We wouldn't make it past campus without you being attacked by media and screaming girls. Also, I don't dance, *and* I don't have a dress. So, there you see, we can't go."

Ellie thought she'd put up a pretty convincing argument, but as she moved towards the bathroom, Aaron's voice stopped her.

"Well, first of all, it's a masquerade, meaning there will be masks, so no one will know it's me. As for the dress, I'll get you one. I'm sure my stylist would love to dress you for the night. Now, the dancing. I *know* you dance," he said with a wink, and Ellie's cheeks heated. "And luckily for you, dancing is all about the lead, and believe me when I say, I can lead. So there really isn't any reason why we couldn't go."

He finished his speech with a satisfied look on his face. Ellie's temper started to flare, but she did her best to keep it in check. He just had all the answers, didn't he? Well, he forgot about one important thing.

"I don't *want* to go," Ellie said.

Aaron looked at her with an amused look on his face, no doubt hearing the strain in her voice as she tried to keep her calm. He closed the distance between them with two long strides and lazily rested his hands on Ellie's hips. He lowered his head towards hers until his lips were so close, they tickled Ellie as he spoke seductively.

"Are you sure there isn't *any* way I can change your mind?"

As she shook her head, Ellie knew she'd already lost. And seeing as Jen was not sleeping there tonight, she allowed herself to become lost in Aaron.

THE NEXT COUPLE OF days flew by in a blur.

Aaron stayed for two nights before he had to leave for work, and the voice in Ellie's mind telling her that his feelings weren't real finally hushed.

Something between them had crystallized the night she finally let him in, and their bond felt as strong as hers with Shiro. There was no way she had created all of it with her power. Especially since she still wasn't able to control most of it anyway. She still preferred to have him around though, but she couldn't escape reality forever.

A nagging feeling in the pit of Ellie's stomach had only grown stronger with time and it was getting harder to ignore it. Hayyel had been careful not to mention much about the angels' history after their first meeting, but the fact that he called her *the* Empath still bugged her.

And while she loved Shiro, he was definitely a source of concern. From what little she had learned about Guardians, it was clear they didn't exactly grow on trees, so why had she been blessed with one? She feared the answers to her questions, but knew she had no choice but to ask them. Ellie hadn't been to the spirit world since her first night with Aaron, but she needed to see to Hayyel.

I need to speak with Hayyel, do you know a way to contact him?

Shiro raised his head, and his blue eyes met hers. He lay at her feet by the desk near the pile of books she should have been reading. She'd had a hard time focusing on anything except her past for the last few days, least of all her studies.

Yes, he is quite mad you haven't gone to see him in a while.

What? But... Ellie trailed off and looked at Shiro. *You are the reason I haven't been, aren't you?*

I just thought you needed some time alone.

Ellie couldn't help but smile. *Thank you. But now I really need to speak with him. I feel like there is something wrong, I can't really tell you what though. It's this feeling and I can't shake it.*

Shiro's eyes turned pained. *I know, that's why I wanted you to have this time with Aaron. I fear everything is about to change.*

Can you take me to Hayyel?

Ellie tried to hide her fear at Shiro's words. She didn't want things to change, not now. But the feeling of urgency couldn't be ignored.

While she loved parts of her powers, like the ability to speak with Shiro, other aspects frightened her. It felt intimate to feel what someone else was feeling. Your emotions should be yours and yours alone, but not only could Ellie feel the emotions of others, she could change and manipulate them. It was one thing hearing Shiro's emotions, especially since he had given his permission, but Hayyel was teaching her how to penetrate the minds of those unwilling. The way the waitress in the café had given up flashed through Ellie's mind.

Yes, luckily, he hasn't closed his sanctuary to you. I couldn't bring you otherwise.

I know, Ellie answered.

Hayyel had told her what happened after an angel died. Their spirit was either set free to return to the Creator or they stayed behind, like he had. Those who stayed were bound to their own sanctuary where they waited to fulfill whatever task kept them earthbound. A sanctuary, like the meadow, was the spirit's home and no one could visit unless invited. Well, if you weren't a Guardian, of course. Guardians were usually the exception to the rules.

We will go tonight.

CHAPTER FIFTEEN

"Hayyel, just tell me."

Hayyel had been in a foul mood since they arrived, going on and on about the importance of Ellie's training.

"Why, Hayyel?" she asked. "I know there's more you're not telling me."

"There is nothing more to tell," came his answer.

"Yes, there is. You keep calling me *the* Empath, and why do I still need Shiro when I have control over my powers? What is he protecting me from?"

It hurt to say the last part, and Ellie couldn't look at Shiro as she said it. It felt like she didn't want him around.

After a silence that spanned a lifetime, Hayyel finally sighed and nodded. "I will tell you."

Ellie suppressed a squeal and locked eyes with him. "Everything?"

"Everything."

As Ellie sat in the grass across from Hayyel, Shiro lay beside her, resting his head in her lap. His presence gave her comfort, and she steeled herself for answers she really wasn't sure she wanted.

"I have told you about the Archangels, how they have enslaved the angels as they seek world supremacy. There is a resistance, sworn to stop them, but they have been losing for a long time. Hope started dying when Archangel Uriel was sent a prophecy regarding an Empath who would end their rule and restore peace to both realms."

Shiro kept sending tendrils of calm through their connection, which was the only thing keeping Ellie still.

No, no, *no*.

"The Archangels' betrayal was so great the Creator left this world and has not been seen since. She separated the two worlds with an unbreakable barrier to protect the humans from the Archangels' wrath. Only the Guardians, who are born from her power, can travel between the realms, which is how you were left there. A Guardian is a being of pure light and can never be corrupted. Your father thought you safe in the human realm, but the Archangels are close to breaking free of their prison, and they believe you are what stands between them and total control."

Hayyel's eyes bore into hers, and Ellie's panic threatened to take over. "You are the last Empath, Eliana. You must stop the Archangels' rule and restore peace. It is the will of the Creator."

"NO!" The word rang out in the meadow, startling the animals nearby. "Are you insane? Just no. No way. That is why you've been teaching me to fight and – and… no!"

"Eliana, please. This is much greater than you –"

"I don't care! I live here, in the human realm. Why should I have to sacrifice everything for a world I never even knew? It's not fair."

The meadow started to disappear from around her, but for the first time, Ellie refused to let her father's memories take hold of her.

No, she thought with anger. *You can't do this to me. It is not my world.*

The meadow came back into focus.

"They are your father's people; therefore, they are yours. Please let me show you."

Ellie blinked a few times in wonder. She had never had any control of the memories, and suddenly, what had once offered her such solace now felt like manipulation. For the first time since meeting Hayyel, the temptations of her past didn't feel worth sacrificing her future for. Sacrificing Aaron for.

"I won't do it, and I doubt there is anything you could ever show me that would change my mind. Shiro, take me back."

I think you should let him explain, Ellie. Please.

Ellie was about to argue, but the pleading tone in Shiro's thoughts had her relent.

"Fine, show me. But then take me back and leave me alone."

"Of course, you will never see me again if that is your wish."

THE DEAD BODY ON the ground was no longer recognizable. What had once been a lovely face with soft features was now a hideous mask of pain. Signs of the torture she had endured before her death were displayed all over her body, her fair skin a canvas painted with blood.

Hayyel sighed as he closed the angel's eyes. "Such a waste."

He said it to no one in particular, but a black eye bore into the side of his face.

I don't think 'waste' is a word I would use to describe what can only be called a massacre.

Hayyel lifted his gaze from the girl at his feet and looked out over the field.

It had once been home to poppies, their brilliant red like out of a painting. Now a different red filled the field.

Everywhere Hayyel looked, bodies like the girl in front of him were sprawled on the ground. Their limbs lay twisted in unnatural angles, making them look like broken puppets cut from their strings. There were both angels and humans there but with one important difference. While the humans were all adults and warriors, whole families of angels had perished there.

The girl at Hayyel's feet was no more than fifteen. A life put out all too soon.

"You are right." Hayyel sighed and turned from the girl to face his horse. In his mind, he continued. *I am afraid I am turning numb being surrounded by so much death. It no longer bothers me the way it should.*

Starlight tossed his silver mane as his nostrils flared. *It is hard not to build walls around your heart when death is a close companion. That is why I will always be here to remind you that you do have a soul, and a gentle one at that.*

And I thank you for it. Hayyel smiled at his old friend and scratched him between those black eyes. They were quite the pair, the angel and the horse. The man's dark skin and black hair was a stark contrast to the horse's silver mane and white coat.

Hayyel had raised Starlight from a foal. Of course, back then he hadn't known Starlight was his Guardian.

He looked at him now, really looked. Starlight's coat was matted, and his mane no longer held its old shine. He looked tired. They both were.

For three years they had traveled the land on the council's orders, and they were nowhere nearer to learning why and how the humans were slaughtering angels. To the council, the *how* was more important than the *why*, something Hayyel had a hard time accepting. He couldn't understand why the humans, who were such gentle creatures, would suddenly be the cause of such massacres like the one before him.

Starlight followed his train of thought as Hayyel gazed out over the sea of bodies with a shudder.

They are acting desperate. Like a cornered animal.

No animal would ever do this, Hayyel thought back. *Sacrificing their own kind in such great numbers.*

This was indeed a battlefield, but no battle had taken place. Hayyel's company weaved through the bodies, looking for survivors they knew they wouldn't find. Their armors were clean, as were their swords; no one there had died at the blade of an angel.

Hayyel had gotten word from one of his falcons that another village, only a two days' ride away, had been burned. The angels in the village had been taken by humans, all of them.

That was what bothered Hayyel the most. That not even one of the angels from the village had died defending their home. They were all taken.

It was the fourth message Hayyel had received about villages being burned and emptied, but it had never been so close to their position. He had been determined to not let the angels suffer the same fate as those before them and immediately ordered his company to prepare for departure. But they had been too late.

Without warning, the sky turned dark. Hayyel looked up expecting to see clouds covering the sun, but he was met with darkness. The sun was gone and ripples of color shot across the sky.

What is going on? Is it a Weather Protector? Hayyel thought and looked over at Starlight. He was dancing in place, nostrils flared.

No, this is something else, was all he had a chance to think when a pure, blinding light replaced the blackness. Pained screams sounded, and Hayyel closed his eyes, but the light pierced through everything.

It was gone as fast as it had come, and when Hayyel could finally see again, he didn't know what he was looking at. The black spots still danced across his eyes, but there was no denying it, the humans were gone.

What – what happened? Starlight's voice sounded small in Hayyel's mind. Fear, it was not something Hayyel was used to hearing in his companion's voice, and it helped little to keep his own panic at bay.

He allowed himself exactly three minutes of shear and utter panic before he began barking orders at his men, his military training taking over.

Search the nearby woods, ten angels scurried away.

Go back to the village, another ten gathered their horses.

Search all the remaining bodies again, the rest of the angels went to work.

As twilight settled over the battlefield, the reports started to come. The village was gone. There was no sign of it ever being there. The humans were gone, too. And even more troubling, all of the human villages they had passed had vanished.

When word from the animal kingdom made its way back to Hayyel, there was no time to spare.

We need to get this news to the Council.

Yes, was all Starlight answered. He'd been strangely quiet the past hours, but to be honest, Hayyel had barely noticed until then.

The nearest portal is only an hour away. I say we go now. We cannot wait until morning.

His bags were already packed and on Starlight's back when the sun finally set. As he rode out of camp, he only stopped once to tell his second in command to take charge of the troops, and then he was off. The cool night air rushed past him as Starlight galloped at full speed to reach the portal.

Hayyel had no idea what he was going to say when he reached the capitol, he could barely make sense of the news himself.

It was not only the humans in the battlefield.

All of the humans were gone.

Thanks to Starlight's speed, they reached the portal in under forty minutes. It was well hidden and meant for emergencies only. The Magic Protector's had them all over the world so one could travel fast when needed, but it took much power to use them. If one was not careful, the Magic Protector connected to it might die, drained of their magic.

Hayyel had only used them a few times before, and then he'd had orders from the Council allowing him access, therefore the Magic Protector had been ready. But this was not a luxury he could afford right now.

He needed to go, and he needed to go now.

The guards recognized him and let him and Starlight pass without much being said. Hayyel's rank was clear by his uniform, and it seemed they were not the only ones who were shaken by what had transpired earlier. A few mumbled words and they were left alone in front of the portal.

Its shimmering surface spanned between two old birches. On the other side was a great hall, empty on most days except for the guards who patrolled it. It was the meeting point of all portals, which led to the capitol.

But something was happening on the other side. Angels were running in and out of the room, some gesturing widely while arguing about something Hayyel couldn't hear.

He sighed and steadied himself for the journey. He didn't like the portals much. They usually left him queasy, but he liked going to the capitol even less. While he had a hard time admitting it even to himself, there was something about the palace that felt wrong, and the feeling had only been growing over the past years.

He had been a captain in the Archangels' army for over forty years now, and before that, a solider for even longer. It was his life, what he knew, so to question that made him feel uneasy to say the least.

But this was hardly the time for such thoughts. With one glance at Starlight, knowing he knew his deepest, darkest thoughts, Hayyel went through the portal.

But nothing happened.

Instead of entering the hall, he stood in the grass behind the portal, the canopy of leaves blocking the stars from view. He turned and saw Starlight still in the spot before the portal.

What was that? What is going on? Has something happened to the Magic Protector?

No, came a quiet answer. *She has closed them.*

Who?

The Creator.

The Creator. She had disappeared a few years ago. The Archangels' claimed she was creating new worlds, leaving this one in their hands, but Hayyel had always wondered. Starlight would sometimes disappear in thought, still being able to communicate with his mother if she wished, but he never told Hayyel what was said.

He had the same look now.

What do you mean, closed them?

She will no longer stand for the magic of this land being corrupted. She said nothing more and nothing less than this. Starlight's light returned to his eyes, and he focused his mind on Hayyel. *We must hurry.*

The feeling of wrongness grew in Hayyel's stomach.

But how if the portals are closed? The capitol was several days away even with Starlight's speed.

Step back.

Hayyel took a quick step to the side at the tone of Starlight's thoughts. He didn't have a chance to ask what was going on before Starlight pulsed with light and the portal shimmered with a new intensity.

Go. I cannot hold it for long.

But how?

Later, just go. I am right behind you. Starlight gently nudged Hayyel's shoulder, urging him forward.

In a haze, Hayyel stepped through the portal and the familiar sensation sent shivers down his spine. Almost before it had begun, it was over, and Hayyel stepped out into the great hall.

He was met by blinking eyes, then utter chaos erupted. The guards quickly ushered him out of the hall and down familiar corridors, taking him straight to the Archangels.

This was when it truly hit him. The portals were gone. It was the only explanation as to why he was being offered an audience right away. The Archangels loved to make their subjects wait, and Hayyel had always thought it a childish display of power. Something must have truly been amiss for them to meet with him straight away.

Hayyel turned another corner, and the sound of Starlight's hooves echoing against the stone walls soothed him.

Then they were before the council.

The throne room was impressive to say the least. Stories made from mosaic covered the ceiling, depicting the angels' history and how the Creator gave life to the first angel, Michael. His cold eyes stared at Hayyel, both from the ceiling and from the throne towering in the middle of the massive hall. The rest of the council sat in a half-moon slightly behind him, talking amongst themselves in hushed voices, but as Michael cleared his throat, silence fell over the room.

"Hayyel."

Hayyel knew what was expected of him and quickly bowed, begrudging every second of it.

"Archangel."

The silence stretched on and Hayyel gritted his teeth, but he didn't move a muscle. The Archangels' loved these types of small displays, and Hayyel would not give them the satisfaction of failing.

"You may rise," came a cool voice from the half-moon.

Hayyel thought he recognized it as Raphael, but he cared little. He couldn't help the small grimace that flashed across his face as he straightened his aching back.

"The portals are closed and yet here you are, care to explain?" The calm of Michael's voice scared Hayyel more than if he had shouted. Suddenly, he wondered if going there had been the best choice, after all.

Michael eyed Starlight with hungry eyes, and Hayyel heard himself lie.

"I do not know. I must have made it just as the portal collapsed."

Careful, came a quiet whisper in his mind.

Michael finally released Starlight from under his gaze and turned his full attention to Hayyel. "I see."

Michael's light hair was tied back, and his blue eyes were piercing. He was the only one who wore his black hood down while the rest of the council hid their faces in darkness.

That was too easy, came Starlight's warning whisper, but there was no need to tell him that. It was entirely too easy, and it didn't escape Hayyel's notice that the guards were slowly filtering in behind him and Starlight.

"Archangel Michael. The humans, they are all gone." Hayyel kept his voice steady as he spoke.

"Ah, yes. It seems they are."

Hayyel waited for any type of reaction, but Michael's face was calm.

"We need to investigate. I would like to take a couple of men –" Michael raised his hand, cutting him short and silencing him.

"The humans are not to be prioritized. What matters now is the portals. Say, Hayyel, I have never heard the story of how you got your Guardian. Would you care to share it with us?"

"I don't see how that is helpful," Hayyel said, prickles of sweat forming on his forehead. Something was wrong.

"Please, indulge me."

Hayyel swallowed and cast a quick glance sideways. Starlight was nervously tossing with his mane. He didn't like it either, but Hayyel failed to see how he could deny Michael's request.

Hayyel heard himself tell the story of how he found Starlight as a foal and how they grew up together. Silence once again filled the room when he finished, and Hayyel found himself searching for ways to leave quickly if need be. But there were no escape routes.

"Remarkable, isn't it? Why some are chosen, and some are not. Who is to make such a decision?"

"The Creator," Hayyel answered before he could stop himself, and he immediately realized his mistake when Michael's eyes lit up.

"Yes, the Creator. But she is gone. She left us when we most needed her. Some even say she has abandoned us, so how can we follow someone capable of such cruelty?"

It was clear that Michael didn't expect an answer, but Hayyel's skin turned cold with dread, guessing the outcome.

"Angels have been slaughtered at the hands of humans, and still, she protects them. Her own children killed for their powers, and she saves their killers. Now that is not something we can stand by and watch."

The guards in the room were slowly closing in on Starlight, and Hayyel drew his sword, not believing what was happening.

"What are you doing? I have always served you without question!"

Hayyel screamed at the council as the guards closed their circle around him and Starlight.

"Indeed, you have, and I hope you will continue to do so in this time of need. But the Guardians are a part of her, and they cannot be trusted."

The guards surrounded Starlight. Hayyel readied himself for the fight, but as he tried to swing his sword, the air felt like syrup. It wasn't long before he couldn't move at all.

The same thing could not be said about Starlight, who fought with everything he had, but he was quickly losing as rope after rope found their way around his body. With a pained shriek Hayyel would remember forever, the guards brought Starlight to the ground, then bound and dragged him out of the hall.

Hayyel cried out for him with both mind and voice, but nothing happened. Nothing he could say changed his Guardian's fate.

"I hope you will see that this was necessary with time. You are a great solider and the angels keep you in high regard. It would be a shame to lose you. We will give you time."

With a flick of Michael's hand, the guards grabbed Hayyel and hauled him out of the hall. Right before the doors closed, Hayyel saw how the hooded figures continued with their whispering as if nothing had happened.

HAYYEL SPENT WEEKS DOWN in the deepest part of the castle with nothing keeping him sane but Starlight's presence in his mind. Even though they couldn't communicate, it still gave him comfort when he was left without food for days and forgot how the sun felt on his skin.

Hayyel, came a faint voice in his head, so faint that Hayyel wasn't sure whether or not he was dreaming. But then a faint light filled the hole that was his prison.

"Starlight!" Relief overwhelmed him, and tears poured from his eyes. He was okay.

But as the light faded, only the shadow of Starlight remained.

Starlight, what's wrong? What did they do to you? His thoughts were filled with panic, and he scrambled to his knees, trying to bury his face in Starlight's mane. Instead, he fell on all fours.

Hayyel, please. Pain filled Starlight's voice. *I don't have long. The Creator is calling me home, but first, you need to listen to me.*

Hayyel would later wonder where he found the strength to not fall apart as he realized Starlight was dead, but somehow, he managed to clear his mind and focus.

They are desperate. The Creator has locked them in this world to save the humans from them, so they are now out of their reach unless they find a way to reopen the portals. That is why they took me, because the Guardians still hold the power to the portal.

But the humans killed us, we both saw it. Michael's words rang in his mind.

Yes, I know, but there is more to it than I can tell you now. You must trust me on this. The Guardians who are still alive are in hiding, and the rest of them have died before betraying our mother. They will never use our power against her will.

Then let me die, too. Please. Hayyel was nothing of his former self. He was all skin and bones, and the last piece of sanity was slipping away as Starlight began to fade.

No. You must keep fighting. They are slaughtering the angels. Anyone who questions them is killed along with their families. A resistance is forming, but they need angels on the inside. You are still of value to the council, you and your brother. Please, help them.

The last thought was a whisper, and then Starlight was gone.

A FEW DAYS LATER, Hayyel made up his mind. Guards came to collect him, but he was too weak to even stand, so they had to carry him to the hall in which he had seen Starlight for the last time.

He forced the pain away and tried to focus on what was in front of him, and only that.

"This is *not* the will of the Creator! We are to protect life, not destroy it. I will never support you. You have no right to the throne you sit upon."

"I am sorry you feel this way, Sablo. You have served long and well, but it seems your mind is corrupt and we cannot let you infect anyone else with your poison."

Hayyel managed to focus on the scene in front of him. No more than four guards held Sablo down on the ground.

Hayyel knew Sablo. He was a giant and a great fighter, but he had the kindest heart. It didn't surprise Hayyel that he refused to turn on the Creator.

"I don't care what you do to me, you will never win. I have faith."

Hayyel looked over at the Archangels and saw that only the first four were there, hoods back. Uriel was staring into the distance, his pale eyes glazed over. His skin was so light it almost looked transparent, but he was anything but frail. Like all Archangels, he had clearly defined muscles and looked no older than twenty. To his left sat Gabriel who towered even Sablo. His black hair and beard stood out against his pale skin, and unlike Uriel, his eyes were focused on the scene in front of him. To Michael's right sat Raphael. The sun had tainted his skin, and he was the only one who looked over thirty.

"Your blind faith will get you nowhere," Raphael said. "The Creator is gone, and she stole something from us. If you will not help us get it back then you are of no use to us. Bring them out."

Up until that point, Sablo had looked mildly bored by his speech, but now his eyes turned wild and he thrashed against the guards. A woman and two young girls were dragged inside screaming.

"Stop! Let them go!" Sablo cried. Hayyel instantly recognized the angels, it was Sablo's wife and two daughters.

"Father!" they screamed, filled with fear.

Hayyel had to fight to hide his feelings. He could do nothing for them.

"This is your last chance, Sablo. Either you are with us or you are against us." Michael had left his throne and walked over to Sablo's wife, grabbing her chin and forcing her to face him. "She is truly lovely, it would be such a waste."

"Don't touch her!" Sablo bellowed, and two more guards rushed forward to keep him restrained.

Without warning, roots shot from the ground. They broke the stone floor and snaked around Michael and the guards. They didn't hold for long, but it was enough time for Sablo to reunite with his family. When the roots shattered, they stood as one.

"You'll have to kill us before we help you." It was Sablo's wife. She was as sweet as they came and a Flora Protector, the roots must have been her doing. She now stood tall by her husband's side.

Michael's eyes were wild, but it was Gabriel who spoke. "Your wish is our command."

He rose from his chair, and before Hayyel could react, Gabriel drew his sword and beheaded the two girls. Sablo roared, the only sound he could release, then both he and his wife joined their children in the afterlife.

Gabriel turned to return to his seat. As he passed Michael, he put a hand on his shoulder and whispered something in his ear. Michael nodded and turned, his temper well hidden under a mask of fake delight.

"Ah, Hayyel. Please, come forward."

Hayyel took a deep breath, sent a quick prayer to the Creator, then closed the distance between them.

CHAPTER SIXTEEN

A FEW DAYS LATER, A quiet knock on Ellie's door drew her from her musings. Ever since she had returned from Hayyel's memories, thoughts had been swirling around her head non-stop. She was making decisions and regretting them quicker than most people blinked.

What she had learned from Hayyel that night changed everything, but no matter what was said, Ellie found it impossible to make a decision and stick with it. Time was running out and she knew it all too well. It didn't help that Shiro kept reminding her that *'time is running out'* every chance he got.

Hayyel wanted her to leave the human realm to join the resistance and fight the Archangels. But how could she leave? She had a life here, friends, Aaron. Hayyel had made it perfectly clear she had to leave everything behind in order to fulfill her destiny, a destiny Ellie had never asked for.

But the pain Ellie had felt in Hayyel's memories caused a constant ache in her heart. Not only had she seen the memories, but she had also *felt* the pain of losing Starlight, a pain almost too much to bear. When Sablo and his family had been killed, her heart had shattered to pieces.

After they had returned to the meadow, Hayyel had told her that he swore allegiance to the Archangels and worked with his brother to feed the resistance with information. But they were eventually, inevitability, found out. He omitted to say what happened after that, and Ellie wasn't even sure she wanted to know. The more she learned, the harder it was to say no, which she had done, a lot.

Ellie sighed as she rose from her chair to open the door. There wasn't a single answer to her problems no matter how much she needed one. Whatever Ellie decided would end up hurting *someone*, but without deciding, she was hurting everyone instead.

The woman on the other side of the door waited patiently for Ellie to take notice of her before she spoke.

"Hi, my name is Charlotte. Aaron sent me her to help you get ready," she said in a pleasant voice, smiling at Ellie with kindness.

Ellie's dumbfounded expression must have been obvious because the woman continued to explain.

"For the masquerade. Aaron told you he was sending you a dress, yes? Well, here it is. He mentioned you probably needed help with your hair and make-up as well, so I volunteered to go with the dress to help you. He also warned me you most likely had forgotten all about it and to tell you to play nice or else, his words not mine. Although I'm sure we'll get along just fine," she finished with another smile, then pushed past Ellie and entered her room, leaving Ellie in the doorway looking like the idiot she felt.

The masquerade... but that wasn't for another week, right? Ellie moved to her desk and searched for the invitation.

In the meantime, Charlotte unpacked her bags full of make-up and things Ellie didn't recognize. A chill surged down her spine at the sheer amount of stuff Charlotte had with her. It didn't make Ellie feel any better that Charlotte most likely planned on using them all on her.

Ellie finally found the invite, and it dawned on her that there was no mistake, the masquerade was *tonight*. How could she have been so wrong? Of course, given that her thoughts had been occupied by life-or-death decisions lately, maybe it wasn't the most surprising thing in the world.

"Look, I'm sure you mean well and you're only doing what Aaron told you to, but–" Ellie stopped dead in her tracks.

"Beautiful, isn't it?" Charlotte looked at Ellie with a knowing smile. "I'm so glad I finally had a reason to use this dress. Not that many people can wear it and get away with it."

Ellie stared with her mouth agape.

The dress unfolded like a dream spun from moonlight. White as winter frost, its bodice bore a delicate tapestry of silver threads, weaving constellations across the chest.

But it was the skirt that stole her breath. An otherworldly flare, it cascaded like stardust, each layer a symphony of feathers. Thousands of them, iridescent and soft, mimicking a swan's plumage. Floor-length, the gown swept the ground, its hem trailing in an elegant train.

Ellie's fingers trembled as she reached out, almost afraid to touch such perfection. The fabric yielded like moonbeams, cool and silken.

Ellie stared at the dress in awe, taking longer to find her tongue than she dared to admit. "It's beautiful. But I can't wear that, I'll ruin it or spill something or –"

"Nonsense. You can and you will wear it. Now please sit down and I'll start with your hair, what do you think? Up?" Charlotte gathered Ellie's hair into a messy bun, then let it down again. "Or down?"

After that, it was all a blur. Charlotte rolled, curled and sprayed Ellie's hair until her scalp was numb, and when she finally finished, she moved on to her face, studying it closely.

Ellie feared her face would suffer the same fate her hair had, but Charlotte surprised her by only using some pink blush, a light eye shadow, and a light pink lip gloss.

"Your beauty doesn't need any help from make-up, sweetheart, just a touch to make you glow. Now come on, and let's get this dress on you, shall we?"

Ellie blushed and nodded. She stripped in the bathroom after promising she wouldn't look in the mirror – Charlotte wanted Ellie to get the full picture, not just part of it. She slipped into the underwear Charlotte had given her, the white, lace garments feeling like a soft caress on Ellie's skin.

When she stepped out of the bathroom, Charlotte held the dress in front of her. She motioned for Ellie to step into the middle of it and then pulled it up, lacing it up the back.

"Now you can look," she said.

Ellie turned towards the mirror, afraid she would look like her average self in a stunning dress, which would not be a pretty sight, but instead she saw a stranger.

Ellie stood before the mirror, her hair cascading in voluminous curls down her back. Some strands were artfully pulled back, tiny braids woven into the dark waves. Soft tendrils framed her face, a delicate frame for eyes that held entire constellations within their green depths. The dress clung to her curves and the skirt fell from her body like a waterfall of feathers.

"This is not me," Ellie whispered in awe.

"It sure is, sweetie. Now the finishing touch," Charlotte said and removed a mask from a box at Ellie's desk.

It was made of delicate silver wire, woven in a complex pattern with tiny crystals sprinkled over it. She lowered the mask over Ellie's eyes and tied the black silk band in a bow to hold it in place.

"Now, go find your prince."

They'd decided to meet at the ball rather than arriving together. Or perhaps, it had been Ellie deciding and Aaron having no in say in the matter.

But as Ellie stepped outside her dorm building, trying desperately not to step on the hem of her delicate skirt, a black limousine met her outside, its door held open by none other than Aaron.

Ellie's breath hitched at the sight of him. He was wearing a dark gray suit with a crisp white shirt underneath, the top two buttons open with no tie, a small glimpse of his chiseled chest peeking from underneath. His hair was its usual perfect mess and looked even more golden. Ellie could barely keep herself from running her fingers through his silky strands.

But it was his flaws that drew her gaze. Aaron's imperfections made him human, and Ellie loved the way his lips quirked when he smiled and the warmth in his gaze when he looked at her.

Aaron was looking at her now, and the love and happiness in his eyes made them glow. It was almost enough to make Ellie forget their previous plans and throw herself into his arms.

Almost.

"We were supposed to meet at the entrance," she said with a scowl. "And how is this keeping a low profile?"

The small smile that had been playing at Aaron's lips widened.

"Well, first of all, it was not as much us deciding as it was you telling. Second, this is our first real date, so I should be allowed to pick you up. And third, you can hardly walk across campus in that dress."

The satisfied look on Aaron's face told Ellie he thought he'd made a bulletproof case. And despite the fact that he was mostly right, Ellie wouldn't give him the satisfaction of knowing it.

She gathered her skirt as carefully and gracefully as humanly possible and turned on her heels. "Watch me."

As she stormed away, all of her focus lay on not tripping and making a fool of herself. Well, more of a fool than she already looked with her skirt fabric bundled up in her arms, her legs bare. There was no need to add fuel to the fire.

Ellie heard a car door slam shut and then hurried steps closing in on her.

"You're really stubborn, you know that, right?"

"I do."

Nothing more was said for a while as they made their way across campus. As Ellie's temper cooled, she sneaked a sideway glance at Aaron, then accidentally met his eyes. She quickly averted her gaze, and his laughter rang out through the disappearing sunlight.

"I'm glad I amuse you," Ellie said in a grumpy voice. "Where is your mask, anyway?"

She hadn't noticed Aaron wasn't wearing a mask until now. As they neared the hall where the masquerade was being held, people started to gather around them. Some, Ellie could see, were already whispering and shooting curious looks their way. Something Ellie had wanted to avoid.

"Oh, yeah, right. I've got it right... here." Aaron pulled something black out of his jacket pocket and slid it over his eyes.

They came to a halt outside the entrance and faced each other. His mask was made from plain black velvet and sat askew on his face.

Ellie shyly raised her hand to fix it. "You have no idea what 'keeping a low profile' means, do you?"

As her fingers connected with Aaron's face, a spark shot through them. She was surprised the smallest of touches were still able to send that kind of electric current through her given their level of intimacy, but they were the ones she most appreciated.

Aaron swallowed whatever retort he'd been about to say, making Ellie wonder if he'd felt it, too. He let out a shaky breath and lay his hand over Ellie's, which still rested on his cheek. As he lowered their intertwined hands, he gazed into Ellie's eyes with that same intensity they had held at the limousine. An intensity that both excited and scared Ellie, yet she couldn't look away. Those eyes wove a spell around her, making her forget everything else.

"You look like an angel."

The words were innocent and meant as a compliment, but to Ellie, it was a slap in the face. She jerked her hand back and just like that, the spell was broken.

Ellie's ears caught the grating tones of annoyance, and soon the accompanying emotions flooded her mind. It was an inexplicable sensation – like a hum at the edge of her consciousness, murmuring like a persistent echo.

Ellie had honed her abilities to some degree, allowing her to selectively tune in to these emotional currents. But there were moments, like now, when the feelings demanded attention, leaving her little choice.

Ellie noticed that they were blocking the entrance and the people behind them wanted to get in as fast as possible, probably because of the few droplets of water that were beginning to fall from the sky. Aaron wasn't the only one unprepared for the rainy season.

Ellie dragged a confused Aaron behind her and got the tickets out of his jacket pocket. Once inside, Aaron made as if to stop and Ellie reluctantly turned to face him.

"What was that about back there?" The confusion in his voice was as clear as the hurt in his eyes.

"Nothing, let's just go inside, okay?" Ellie said hurriedly, trying to drag him inside.

A determined look took over Aaron's features, and Ellie realized he was not letting it go. He removed his hand from her grip and crossed his arms over his chest. Aaron was not moving until he got some answers.

But what could she tell him? *I'm sorry, but you calling me an angel just hit a little too close to home. You know, seeing as I'm half-angel. Oh, and did I forget to mention that I am what stands between the angels and them killing every human on earth?* Yeah, that wouldn't sound crazy at all.

He must already question her mental health, if not because of the incident in the park then because of her going hot and cold on him every five minutes. There was nothing she could do about that though. Her emotions were all in a tangle and being an Empath apparently did nothing to help her with her own feelings. Imagine being given the power to control emotions but you can't even decide what you feel about *one* boy.

Story of my life, Ellie thought with a sigh.

She did love him, that much she knew. But that wasn't the problem. The problem was whether or not she *could* love him. The decisions that had been gnawing away at her this past week weighed on her like a ton of bricks, but she was no closer to an answer.

Aaron was still waiting for just that, an answer. An answer Ellie didn't have.

"Just don't call me that, okay?" she finally said in a small voice. It sounded bleak even to her own ears, but she didn't know what else to say.

"Call you what? Angel? Why not?"

"Just don't. Please."

For a second, it looked like he would continue to push for answers, but then his face softened, and he nodded. "Okay, I won't."

Ellie didn't know if it was her pleading tone or the small amount of power she infused with her words that made him drop it, but in that moment, she didn't care.

Still, a small voice in the back of her mind reminded her of the promise to never use her powers on Aaron, but Ellie told it to shut up.

CHAPTER SEVENTEEN

When they stepped into the hall where the masquerade was being held, Ellie and Aaron were met with an enchanting transformation. Gone was the drab, neglected lecture hall; in its place stood a vibrant Italian piazza.

The room now boasted a central fountain, its waters cascading gracefully from the mouth of a mermaid sculpted in stone. Cobblestones covered the floor, their irregular surfaces adding to the illusion of an outdoor plaza.

Against one wall, faux gondolas sat moored, behind them the wall was painted to resemble the winding streets and picturesque canals of Venice. The colors were rich and inviting, as if beckoning guests to step aboard and explore this magical realm.

Yet it was the ceiling that stole Ellie's breath away. Thousands of fairy lights hung there, suspended like celestial constellations. Their soft glow bathed the room in a warm, golden radiance, turning the hall into a starlit haven. Jen had done a beautiful job.

Ellie dared not move too quickly, fearing that any sudden motion might shatter the illusion.

"It's beautiful," she whispered to Aaron, her voice barely audible over the music and laughter.

"Is it? I haven't noticed."

She turned towards Aaron, about to ask him how he couldn't have noticed, when his lips caught hers in a kiss. His lips were both gentle and insistent, pulling her into a moment that transcended time and place. Just as she was about to lose herself in the kiss, he stepped back.

He smiled down at her and said, "As I said. I haven't noticed."

As they descended the stairs toward the indoor plaza, Ellie's heart raced. One wrong step and she feared she would rip her skirt to shreds, but once they reached the bottom of the stairs, she relaxed a little. The dress was still in one piece, and she hadn't tripped. It was a lot easier to walk in the dress on even ground, easier than she would have thought, and she was grateful for that, at least.

All around them people were dancing to music Ellie assumed she ought to know. People crowded in front of the bar at the far back, and Ellie spotted both Lucas and Jen there. Not together, of course. At least Ellie thought it was Jen and Lucas. It was hard to tell with masks in different colors and designs covering everyone's faces.

A new song started to play, its soft tunes filling the room. Most of the people left the dance floor, leaving couples behind to embrace each other and sway slowly to the music.

Suddenly, Ellie was overwhelmed by a need to be like them – to be one of those couples who didn't have the weight of the world on their shoulders. Whose love hurt no one and who never needed to ask the questions Ellie was asking.

Aaron was looking expectantly at her, and she realized he had said something. "I'm sorry, what?"

"I asked you if you wanted something to drink."

She shook her head no and gazed out over the dance floor. "Could we... could we maybe dance?"

Aaron nodded and held out his hand. She let him lead her out onto the dance floor and into the middle of the small crowd of people.

He placed his hand at the small of her back. She wasn't sure where she was supposed to put her own hands and regretted her idea immediately. Aaron must have seen her discomfort; he gently took her left hand and placed it on his shoulder and pulled her close.

Aaron hadn't lied when he'd told her he was a good dancer. It felt like her feet were barely touching the ground as they swept across the room, whirling as they went.

"How come you're such a good dancer? I figured you were exaggerating to get me to go, but obviously I was wrong," Ellie said.

Aaron smiled at her and spun her around. "This is actually a dance from a movie I was in. It's probably the only dance I know, so don't get your hopes up too high."

He spun her again and she came face to face with him once again. Laughter danced in his eyes and a smile played on his lips. He looked happy, Ellie decided. Happy and content. As if he could spend the rest of his days like this and never ask himself what could have been, something she would never be able to feel no matter her decision.

Pushing the thoughts aside, Ellie asked, "last first kiss, why did you say that? What does it mean?"

It was a question she'd been meaning to ask for a while now, but it always slipped her mind.

"I don't know really, it was this song I heard." Aaron whispered in Ellie's ear as they continued to sway to the music.

The meaning behind them filled Ellie's eyes with tears.

"I thought it reminded me of how I felt about you, I never wanted that moment to end. And it's not like I want to kiss anyone else so, yeah. Cheesy, right?"

Ellie shook her head. She didn't know what to say. Nothing was enough. She pulled herself closer to Aaron, resting her head against his shoulder. He held her close with such confidence it made her shiver.

Slowly, Ellie raised her head until her mouth was at his ear, and she whispered, "Aaron, I lo –"

Something was wrong. Aaron had suddenly stopped moving and the music was gone.

"Aaron, what's wrong?"

Ellie drew back to look at him but his hand on her waist didn't budge. She pushed his chest and freed herself, falling to the ground in the process.

"Ouch, why didn't you let go of me when I –" her voice trailed off.

Aaron still hadn't moved, neither had anyone else. What was going on?

Sometime during their dance, a small space had cleared to give them room. Ellie could see both awe and envy in the frozen faces around her, staring at the spot where Aaron still stood. If it hadn't been for the situation at hand, Ellie would have been embarrassed. As it was now, she had other things to worry about.

As Ellie rose from the floor, she caught sight of something from the corner of her eye. Something had moved. She quickly got to her feet and turned to face whatever it was.

It turned out to be a *who*. A tall figure made its way through the frozen crowd, soon joined by others. Ellie was surrounded. There were fifteen of them in total. Dark figures in long, black robes. The hoods of their robes covered their faces, making it impossible to see their identities.

"What do you want from me?"

They moved towards her, circling her and closing off her escape routes. A cold laughter rang through the circle, sending cold chills down Ellie's spine.

"I would have thought Hayyel had told you about your true identity by now, but perhaps I overestimated him."

The voice tore through Ellie's ears and mind like a blade. Ellie bit her lip and she could soon taste the coppery tang of blood in her mouth. She would not give them the satisfaction of witnessing her pain.

"You're the Archangels."

While a Magic Protector could block her powers, they were not powerful enough to freeze an entire room of people.

"Perhaps I spoke too soon. You are not entirely uninformed, but I wonder if you know everything." The Archangel's voice no longer held the same intensity, but it still hurt to listen to him.

"I know enough," Ellie snapped and spat blood onto the floor.

"Tsk tsk, now that is not very ladylike of you, Eliana. I doubt you know as much as you think. I have observed a tendency among people who want something from you; they only seem to tell you the things that will get them what they want. Have you ever noticed that?"

Ellie said nothing, deciding it was the best approach with who she could only assume was Michael.

"For instance, I am sure you have been told about the prophecy, correct?" he asked in an almost pleasant voice. Ellie expected her silence to irritate him, but it appeared to amuse him instead. "Come now, how are we to help each other if you will not speak with me?"

"You have nothing I want, Michael."

At this, Michael laughed again and drew his hood back. As soon as the hood dropped, Michael bathed in light that tumbled off him in waves too bright to look at. Ellie snapped her eyes shut.

"Ah, I see my reputation precedes me. It is safe to open your eyes now, Eliana, I won't hurt you."

Ellie peeled open one eyelid, and then the next. The light was gone, and she was now able to make out his features. She immediately recognized him from Hayyel's memory.

His fair hair sat at his shoulders in waves, framing his face perfectly, but his blue eyes were full of cruelty and his smile was unpleasant. They twisted Michael's features into a hideous mask and his beauty was lost on Ellie.

His eyes bore into hers and the smile he wore on his lips widened. "See, nothing happened."

Yet, Ellie thought gingerly.

"What have you done?" she asked as her eyes swept across the room.

"Oh, this is nothing. No need to worry." He said it almost cheerfully, sending chills down Ellie's spine

"Okay," Ellie spoke carefully, "then I'll ask you one more time. What is it that you want? And how are you here?"

The human realm was supposed to be safe from them since all the portals closed, and yet, there they stood.

"Why, you, of course."

"Me?" The word almost got stuck in Ellie's throat.

"Yes. You. Well, your powers actually." Ellie's head was spinning. "All we want from you is your power. Then you can go back to your life and never trouble yourself with this again. You can have it all: love, a family, anything you want."

"But the prophecy," she managed. He was promising her everything Hayyel had told her she would have to give up.

"Ah, yes. The prophecy. There is more to it than you know. It will claim your life in the end, did Hayyel tell you that? Of course, he did not. Would he have gotten what he wanted from you if he had?"

Michael said all of this as if he was talking about what they were going to have for dinner.

Ellie could only stare at him. *She would die?* If she fulfilled the prophecy, she would die. On some level, Ellie had always suspected as much, but it was one thing to suspect and another to know. She had never asked for this burden, but at the same time, could she ignore it? If she gave up her powers willingly, maybe she would survive.

Ellie's conflicting emotions must have been written all over her face. Michael's smile widened as he watched her. Ellie might not know what she wanted, but she refused to give Michael the satisfaction of being right.

She squared her shoulders and met his gaze, hoping her voice would hold. "Then so be it."

Michael frowned with surprise for a split second, but he quickly composed himself. His smile though, was gone.

"I see, Hayyel has filled your head with lies. He has told you we are evil, no doubt. But is it not he who is evil, wanting you to give up your life for a destiny you never asked for? Is it not he who is evil, wanting you to surrender your one true love?"

Michael's eyes flickered towards Aaron.

A sudden surge of anger ripped through her. "You leave him out of this. He has nothing to do with any of it!"

"But he does. And you are the one who brought him into it, simply by loving him."

His words rang true in her ears. Words she had lay sleepless over on many nights, trying to ignore. Now, she couldn't ignore them anymore. Her resolution wavered slightly, and Michael pounced on her weakness like a lion going for the kill.

"If you gave up your powers, you could live a normal life with Aaron. Can you honestly say you do not resent them? That you have not been tempted to manipulate feelings to suit your own goals?

Can you ever be really sure that you did not make him love you?" His tone was soft, and even though she wanted to scream 'no' at the top of her lungs, she couldn't. "Would your life not be easier without them?"

She remembered the way Aaron had let go of their argument earlier. She knew it was because of her, because of her powers. She also knew he would always be in danger when he was with her. But the death of Starlight and the stupor in the eyes of the two girls as they lay unblinking in a puddle of blood would haunt her forever like a fresh wound.

Before she could get lost in her thoughts, Michael spoke again. "I understand what you must think of me, of us. But we truly want to help you. You were never meant to have these powers; they are a curse, not the blessing some might have you think. We will give you seven days, no more and no less, to surrender them to us. Think of your loved ones. Seven days, Eliana, seven days."

And with that, he was gone. They were all gone, and music played again.

ELLIE WAS TRULY BEAUTIFUL as she glided down the stairs. Her raven hair a stark contrast to the white dress she wore.

Lucas had always known she was beautiful, and it always surprised him that she couldn't see it. But as of late, something had changed. There was more warmth to her smile and a spark in her eyes that had always been missing before. It didn't take a genius to know the man walking beside her was the reason.

In all honesty, Lucas had been a bit jealous when Ellie started seeing Aaron. Not because he was interested in Ellie, but because he feared they would lose what they had. Their sibling-like bond.

But even though Ellie was certainly distracted by Aaron, there was something else weighing on her that had been driving her further and further away from Lucas.

One night, the book had written a paragraph about a prophecy. Something called an Empath would overthrow the Archangels and bring peace back to the lands of humans and angels alike. At first, Lucas hadn't understood why the book was telling him about it, but then a picture had appeared. It had been a woman. Her raven black hair and emerald eyes had screamed at him from the page.

There was no mistaking it, it was Ellie.

Since then, Lucas had tried to get hold of her, but she had been impossible to reach. Lucas wouldn't even be at the masquerade if he hadn't known Ellie was going.

He hadn't been able to find out anything about the author of the book either; Raziel Jadon. No amount of internet searches or late nights at the libraries offered any results, and Lucas was at loss of what to do. But he would warn Ellie. That he could do.

He pushed his way through the crowd in an attempt to reach Ellie.

Lucas needed answers. A lot of them, and he needed to know he wasn't going crazy. If Ellie truly was the woman in the book, she needed to tell him.

As he was about to call out to her, Ellie and Aaron moved out onto the dance floor and started to sway to the sweet melody. They looked beautiful together and their happiness and love for one another was clear to anyone who looked. As they swirled around on the dance floor, an audience formed. Apparently, Lucas wasn't the only one impressed by their dance. Ellie and Aaron were oblivious as they swirled together, Aaron catching her before she could lose her balance.

Deciding to wait for the song to end, Lucas gazed passed the dancing couple and focused on the crowd instead. That's when he saw it. A hooded figure was moving through the crowd like running water, but no one else noticed its presence.

When Lucas tried to move closer, he found he couldn't. He tried to scream out for Ellie, but he had no voice. The entire room was frozen except for Ellie and fifteen figures in black cloaks.

Lucas listened in horror as they threatened Ellie and those she loved. But while Lucas was terrified, both for himself and Ellie, he couldn't help but marvel at her strength. She looked deadly in her white dress and her eyes burned with rage.

Come to me. She is the chosen one and she will need your help to fulfill her destiny. Come to me. The voice rang in Lucas' mind, and he would have jumped in surprised if he had been able to move. The male voice had been dark and powerful.

Voices and music filtered back through his mind and Lucas realized the room had returned to normal. Pushing the voice aside, he searched for Ellie, but both she and Aaron were gone.

Ellie blinked several times, trying to comprehend what had happened. Seven days, and then what? If they wanted to kill her, she assumed she would already be dead. This was something else. And the question as to how they were even there still weighed heavy on her mind.

The sound of her name drew her out of her musings. She turned towards the sound, but it took several seconds to properly register anything in front of her.

"Ellie, what happened? How are you all the way over there?" Concern laced Aaron's tone, and she could hardly blame him. To him, it looked like she had moved a few feet away in the blink of an eye.

"Why do you always ask the questions I can't answer?" she whispered, barely audible.

"Ellie, what's wrong?"

He hadn't heard her, she realized, and perhaps it was for the best. There was nothing he could do to make it better, so why worry him?

"Can we please just go? I don't feel well."

Aaron only nodded and led her towards the door, not saying anything else.

He was quiet in the car that picked them up and when he helped her up the stairs to his apartment. He was *not* quiet after he'd shut the door.

"Ellie, you have to tell me what's wrong. Maybe I can help you."

He couldn't. No one could, at least not in this world. And finally, after days of trying to make up her mind, she had.

She stared out through the windows in the living room, watching the traffic and people go by.

Ordinary people with ordinary problems and ordinary lives, she thought with longing. Perhaps some of them were having problems at work, going through a divorce or buying a present for their new baby. Perhaps the boy crossing the street had failed a test and worried about telling his parents when he got home.

How Ellie wished she was one of those people.

But she wasn't. She knew that.

She slowly turned to face Aaron. Now that her decision was made, a weight had been lifted from her shoulders.

"I love you." She said it without any doubt or fear.

Aaron looked at her with an unreadable expression. "If you're only saying that so you won't have to tell me what's wrong–"

"I'll tell you everything, I promise," she said. "Tomorrow. Can't we please just have this night?"

Ellie closed the distance between them, and Aaron's resolve

melted away with every step. When she pressed her body against his, he pulled her even closer and said, "tomorrow?"

"Tomorrow," Ellie agreed.

"And, I love –"

Ellie quickly pressed her lips against his, the last part of Aaron's sentence stifled by her mouth.

"Tomorrow," she said again as she drew back.

Aaron looked into her eyes and captured her lips with his, their kiss desperate. They clung to each other as if they both knew there would be no tomorrow and they slid down onto the floor.

Ellie let her shield down just enough to bask in Aaron's love one last time.

CHAPTER EIGHTEEN

Pain shot up through Ellie's right arm as she returned to consciousness. The agony was enough to clear the last fogginess from her mind and she managed to open her eyes. Blinking against the harsh light, her vision cleared and she took in her surroundings.

She was at the back of some sort of camp, a fire burning in the distance. Three dark shadows sat with their backs towards her, sharing something between them. Food, no doubt.

Her stomach growled when the scent reached her nose. She tried to sit up, but her wrists were bound tightly behind her back, the coarse rope digging into her skin. A foreign fabric pressed against her tongue, muffling her cries. She glanced down at her right arm, the sleeve of her shirt soaked in blood.

Panic consumed her. She started to thrash around, screaming

through the cloth in her mouth.

This must be a mistake, she thought and begged for the men at the fire to hear her.

Her stifled sounds successfully attracted the attention of her captors and one of the men stood up and walked towards her.

"Wasn't sure you were going to survive the night. A knife in the shoulder could end badly." The man's voice was light and a little squeaky. Not at all pleasant to listen to. Then the word registered in her mind, *knife*. Ellie figured that was the explanation for the blood and pain in her right arm. But she had no memory of how it had happened.

She tried speaking through the cloth again, her cries coming out as a tangle of sounds.

Without warning, the man in front of her kicked her hard in the ribs. "Oh, would you shut up? You are lucky I didn't let Malik kill you."

Ellie's vision darkened and the pain stole her breath. She gagged on the blood in her mouth and throat as it dawned on her; there was no mistake.

"Imagine our surprise when we stumbled upon such a beauty as you, lying all alone in the grass. Didn't even put up a fight when Malik stabbed you." The man was leaning closer to her now, the stench of his breath washing over her face. "He would have killed you, but we have orders to take every stranger straight to the Council. Alive."

Ellie turned cold with fear. The Council could only mean one thing. They were taking her to the Archangels.

She yanked hard at the ropes tying her hands together, and something broke in her right hand. She screamed in pain through the gag, and the man in front of her laughed. Breathing became more and more difficult, and the blood in her mouth had started to dribble down her chin.

He bent his face even closer to hers and sniffed her hair, causing Ellie to shrink back as far as her binds would let her.

"No one said we couldn't play though. That's what really stopped Malik, you know. Just think of all the fun we could have with you."

He lowered his hand to the hem of her shirt and his rough fingers rasped over her tender flesh. Fear crippled her, making it impossible to move. His hand continued to travel upward, towards her ribs, and another surge of pain ripped through her as he touched them.

Then, like a miracle, his hand was gone. He stood up and yelled something at the men back at the campfire. There was an answer, and then he was gone.

Ellie closed her eyes and tried to think. The last thing she remembered was sneaking out of Aaron's apartment, leaving him sleeping on the floor. Shiro had been at her side as she had made her way back to her dorm.

Once there, she'd packed everything she thought she might need, which wasn't much in the end.

What do you pack when you intend to leave life as you know it? A few pieces of clothing, her favorite book and a few pictures of her with Jen, Lucas and Aaron.

Once she had finished, Shiro had pulsed with light and they entered the maze of light together, not looking back.

Something must have gone terribly wrong, Ellie thought as she lay on the ground, desperately trying to breathe and wondering where Shiro was. The fact that the man had told her they'd found her alone gave Ellie some hope that Shiro might be safe.

She tried to look around the camp, but the throbbing in her chest and arm limited her ability to move. She knew the amount of blood filling her mouth ought to worry her, but her mind began to fog. She was stuck facing the campfire where the three men were fighting over something she couldn't hear.

She slipped in and out of consciousness again and her ragged breaths were coming further and further apart, hurting with every intake of air.

She yanked at the ropes again, and the pain shooting up her arm momentarily cleared her head.

Desperately trying to come up with a plan, Ellie called out for Shiro.

Shiro, help! Silence was the only reply, and she pushed down the rising panic. She tried to slip into mediation, but the pain in her chest was all she could think about. She pushed it away, again and again, ignoring Hayyel's warning of stopping her heart. She was dead either way, at least this gave her a chance.

Slowly, the fire filled her, the familiar sensations flowing through her. The bond she shared with Shiro was there, but her powers were draining to support her shields, making the connection dangerously thin.

A sudden shuffle caught her attention, and she opened her eyes in time to see the angel making his way back towards her.

There was no time left to think. Ellie let her shields fall and was immediately overcome with emotions, but she fought them with everything she had. She would only be able to hold them off for a moment or two, but that was all she needed.

Ellie took everything she was feeling, the terror his hand on her body had caused, the agony when the bone in her hand had snapped, the hurt of leaving Aaron, and threw it towards the advancing angel.

The angel stopped and reached to cover his ears.

That won't do you any good, Ellie thought as the man sank to his knees, screaming in agony. When his companions heard his screams, they came running, dragging the angel back to the campfire while shooting terrified glances towards Ellie's slumped body. They were shouting something Ellie couldn't hear, but she hoped their fear would keep them at bay.

As her vision went dark, she poured the last of her power into her connection with Shiro. It blazed up, and before Ellie's shield could drain the last of her life energy and the emotions she'd been fighting could drown her, she let one word soar through the night.

Shiro!

Something wet on her face brought Ellie back to consciousness. Two ice blue eyes met hers and relief filled her entire being.

However, the relief was short-lived when Ellie looked past Shiro. She was still at the camp. Three dark figures lay around the slowly dying fire, seemingly asleep. The sun was starting to rise at the horizon and Ellie feared they would soon wake.

Something cold pressed against Ellie's hand and the broken bone caused her to cry out in agony, the gag muffling the sound.

"Shh, you need to be quiet," a strange voice whispered in her ear as a surge of energy filled her body.

The cold metal cut into the rope binding her, and Ellie bit down on her lip, determination in her eyes. With the newfound strength, she managed to nod. If Shiro was there, surely there was nothing to be alarmed about.

With a final tug at the rope, her hands were free. Ellie slowly moved them and winced. Her wrists were covered in dried blood, scraped raw from the rope, and something was definitely broken.

"Can you stand?" the same voice asked her.

Ellie shook her head.

Her breaths escaped in short gasps and her strength tried to slip away from her.

After several attempts, she managed to rasp out, "I can't... I can't breathe."

"Yeah, I think you might have a punctured lung. We really need to move."

Punctured lung, that doesn't sound too good, Ellie thought before she slipped back into oblivion.

"Shiro, help me with this," was the last thing Ellie heard as darkness overwhelmed her.

A sob broke through the fog in Ellie's mind. Then another and another, followed by words she couldn't quite make out. There was something familiar about the voice. A pair of piercing brown eyes called for her, but a haunting song pulled her in the opposite direction.

"I think she's waking up."

"Run and get Israfel. Tell him she is waking up."

The voices sounded far away, and Ellie fought towards the sound. Her eyelids fluttered open, and several faces came into focus. When Ellie's vision cleared, she saw they were children, all seven of them. Their eyes shone with eagerness and their faces were open and honest.

"Don't you all have chores to do?" a voice asked, causing them to jump in surprise.

Once they saw the man who stood in the doorway, they hurried past him, mumbling apologies. Only one of them remained; a woman in her early twenties. She was short and thin, and her light red hair fell in soft waves down her back. She had eyes the color of the ocean, clear and intent, and freckles on her small nose.

She smiled at Ellie as the man made his way inside the small room. "Sorry about the children, we don't exactly get a lot of guests around here. You can't really blame them for being curious."

Ellie thought there was something familiar about the girl's voice. "You're the one who saved me, aren't you?"

"Saved you? More like risked her own life as well as everyone else's in this village. Lacey should know better," the man said.

The girl named Lacey rolled her eyes at the old man. He was leaning over something but when he turned, Ellie could see his face more clearly. His beard and hair were so gray they almost looked silver. His small eyes were black, and as Ellie watched him, he pushed a pair of round glasses up his nose; a movement seemingly well-rehearsed. He was tall and dressed in what looked like an old-fashioned robe.

"Don't be so grumpy, Israfel. Should I have left her there? Not that she needed much help. You should have heard that angel scream, seemed like he was ready to cut his own wrist to save himself from her."

At that, the man Lacey called Israfel turned to look at Ellie like this was the first time he actually saw her.

"What is your name?"

"Eliana, sir," Ellie answered. Israfel's eyes widened.

"You're the Empath." Lacey's head snapped towards Ellie, her mouth agape.

Ellie tried to sit up in the bed, feeling more than a little uncomfortable that they knew who she was, but a sharp pain in her ribs made her lie back again.

"Empath or not, you need to rest. You have three broken ribs, one of which punctured your lung. Your shoulder should heal fine as long as you don't use your arm for a while."

Ellie listened carefully as Israfel spoke. Her ribs must have been broken when the angel had kicked her, which also explained the blood in her mouth.

Ellie finally allowed herself to feel her body for the first time since she had woken up. A dull ache pounded in her shoulder and soreness burned across her chest. She was still having trouble breathing, and she could only imagine how she must look. What Ellie didn't feel though was any pain from her broken hand.

Looking down, Ellie realized there wasn't a mark on them. "What happened to my hands? I mean, I'm sure I broke something, and the skin was scraped raw. I saw it."

"Israfel healed them." Lacey had found her tongue again, but something in her tone had changed.

"Healed them?"

"Yes, he uses music." *Music?* He must be a Corporal Protector, although Ellie had never heard of them using music.

"That's enough, Lacey," Israfel said in a stern voice.

Lacey shot a glance towards him. Something passed between them, but Ellie was too tired to pay it much attention. A sudden weariness washed over her, and her eyelids felt heavy.

Israfel shooed Lacey out and said, "You need to rest. I have put a spell on you that allows your body to heal itself faster. Such spells use a lot more of your energy than normal healing would, but I imagined you would appreciate being back on your feet as soon as possible."

His words were drifting further and further away, but Ellie managed to nod her head. "Thank you."

CHAPTER NINETEEN

AARON SCREAMED IN AGONY.

"Ellie, please!" The pain made his voice thick, and Ellie fought against her binds. "Help. Please, save me."

Ellie opened her mouth to scream, but no sound left her throat. She tugged at her invisible bindings as a hooded figure emerged from behind Aaron's limp body. Nothing but a cold smile was visible under the hood, but Ellie fought harder against the hold on her.

"Leave him alone." Her voice finally returned, but neither Aaron nor the Archangel heard her.

The Archangel circled Aaron and stood before him. Aaron continued to thrash against his chains, but it was useless. Then the Archangel turned, and his eyes fell upon Ellie. His cold stare never left hers. He lifted his hand and pure fire flew from his fingers, engulfing Aaron in its flames.

Aaron's heartbreaking screams jolted Ellie awake.

The room was dark. Ellie concentrated on taking slow, even breaths as the last remnants of the nightmare left her. Her body ached where the invisible bounds had held her, and Aaron's scream echoed vividly in her mind.

It was just a dream, she thought as she let her eyes wander the dark room. Someone sat slumped in a chair in the corner, a book at their feet. It looked like whoever it was had fallen asleep reading.

Ellie sat up in the bed, scooting back until she could rest her back against the headboard. *It was just a dream,* she told herself over and over until at least a small part of her believed it. She did her best to ignore the pull on her broken heart that told her otherwise.

Her head was spinning, but thankfully, the worst of the pain across her chest was gone and her breathing was effortless. In the quiet, Ellie scanned the room.

The ceiling was low and lanterns were strewn around the room, emitting a soft light. There was no furniture except for the bed, and the chair, the floor, the walls and ceiling were all made out of dark wood.

Something told Ellie she didn't need to fear these people, but she was still wary. She closed her eyes and evened her breathing.

Letting her power fill her, she let her mind wander in search of Shiro. Dozens of animal voices sounded in her mind, almost as clear as Shiro's. Their presence was soothing, and they were curious about who she was. Ellie stumbled out an apology at a loss for what else to do and promised she would come and say hi later.

I hear them, she thought and let herself marvel at the thought before searching for Shiro.

She found him sound asleep in a stable. She gently touched his mind with her own. *Shiro, are you awake?*

I am now, came a grumpy reply.

What happened?

I don't know.

He didn't know? The fear Ellie had felt in the camp combined with the loss of Aaron finally became too much. Rage engulfed her.

You left me! Ellie screamed in her mind. *You just left me with those men! Do you know what they were planning on doing to me? They were going to rape me, and you left me there!*

Ellie knew her anger wasn't fair, but her heart had been ripped apart, and she doubted she could ever piece it back together again.

I didn't leave you, at least not on purpose. Something hit me and I landed miles from you. I ran for hours tracking you. I might never have found you if it wasn't for your call.

Some of Ellie's anger dispersed, but the pain was still there. *What do you mean, something hit you?*

When we were in between the worlds, something came out of nowhere, it went straight through you and smashed into me. Someone didn't want you to arrive here with your Guardian.

The rage left her as fast as it had arrived, and Ellie felt empty.

Not hard to guess who that might be, Ellie replied, her mind tired. *Look, Shiro, I'm sorry I yelled at you. It's just...*

When words failed her, Ellie sent her emotions through their connection. Nothing more was needed, and Ellie wasn't sure Shiro was ever mad at her.

What I don't understand is how they knew when we were going to make the transition between worlds, Shiro mused, eager to change the subject.

That might have been my fault, Ellie said, embarrassed that she hadn't mentioned the Archangels' little visit to Shiro. Shiro stayed quiet while she told him what the Archangels had told her.

That would do it, he replied. No lecture and no yelling. She didn't even know why she hadn't told him.

What I don't understand is how they even got there. I mean, I thought it was only the Guardians who could travel between realms?

I don't think they were there, at least not in both body and mind.

As Ellie was about to ask what he meant, a soft mumble drew her attention back to the room.

I need to go, Ellie said as she started to withdraw from Shiro's mind.

Great, then I can finish the nap you so rudely interrupted.

When Ellie opened her eyes again, a face came into her line of sight. Lacey smiled down at her.

"Great, you're up. Israfel told me you should drink this." Lacey held out a mug that held a green, clumpy, liquid. Not only did it look disgusting, but its burnt, rotting scent assaulted her nostrils.

Ellie took the mug, holding it out in front of her. "Couldn't you just tell him I drank it?"

Lacey gave her a sympathetic look and shook her head. "Sorry, but no. It will help with your healing."

"But I feel much better," Ellie tried again, but Lacey shook her head. "Okay, fine. I'll drink the green goo, but it better not taste as bad as it looks."

It did.

Ellie almost gagged as she quickly swallowed the liquid. The taste was like nothing she had ever tasted before, but she imagined that if someone had left rotting meat out in the sun it would taste something similar to this.

"He really doesn't like me much, does he?" Ellie managed as she swallowed the last of the offensive beverage. Lacey opened her mouth as if to answer, but Ellie cut her off. "No, don't answer that."

Lacey smiled at her, and Ellie found it hard not to smile back. But she was still on edge. "How did Israfel know I was an Empath?"

At that, Lacey's smile disappeared, and squirmed a little in her seat. "I don't know really, sometimes Israfel just kind of knows stuff like that."

Ellie could tell Lacey wasn't telling her the whole truth. "Lacey."

"No, really. It's true. Once, he found this little girl who got lost in the forest, and that was before anyone knew she was missing. And then there was that time when..." Lacey rambled on and finally, Ellie decided to put the girl out of her misery.

"Fine, you don't want to tell me. Tell me where I am instead."

Lacey looked relieved at the change of subject and smiled again. "You're in Stonebridge village. It's one of the old villages, so you'll have to forgive it for being a little old-fashioned. If you feel up for it, I can give you the tour."

"I didn't drink the goo for nothing. Lead the way."

"You might want some other clothes though; it's slightly chilly outside." Ellie looked down at her own stained and torn clothes.

"I guess you didn't find my bag by any chance," she asked, dreading the clothes they might give her. Judging by what Israfel had been wearing, they couldn't be very practical.

"Sorry, no, but I borrowed these from a girl in the village. You look about the same size," Lacey said and handed Ellie a bundle of fabric.

Looking over the clothes, Ellie was pleasantly surprised. It was a pair of dark leggings and a knitted sweater.

When she took a closer at Lacey, she noticed she was wearing something similar. Lacey gave Ellie a knowing smile. "Israfel is as old as this village, probably older. He hasn't exactly stayed in tune with fashion. Most of the younger generation choose to wear more of what's in style."

While the clothes were far better than Ellie had dared hope, she wasn't sure she would call them *in style*. Although, in this realm, they probably were.

She gave Lacey a sheepish grin and quickly changed her clothes while Lacey waited for her outside. Ellie awkwardly pulled on the sweater, wishing it was longer and the leggings not so tight.

"Ah, they fit perfectly," Lacey exclaimed and started to walk. "Shall we begin?"

The village was smaller than Ellie would have thought. It consisted of fifty or so small cabins, much like the one Ellie had just left. There was a small square at the center of the village and the houses there were bigger. These were stores, a small inn and the homes of the wealthy, Lacey told her.

Everywhere Ellie looked she could see the evidence of what Lacey had told her about clothes. The angels wore everything from robes that looked medieval to dresses and pants that were far more practical. The people they met were all friendly, but Ellie sensed an underlying nervousness she couldn't explain.

After two women practically ran away after talking to them, Ellie decided to ask Lacey about it.

"You're the Empath. Everyone here knows what that means. This village has served the resistance for as long as I can remember, and the people here finally see an end to the suffering and pain in this world."

Great, no pressure. "Then why do they keep running away from me like I have the plague?"

Lacey gave her an apologetic smile. "While they support the resistance, it is still dangerous for you to be here. They fear you will bring the wrath of the Council upon them."

An old, fragile lady made her way towards them, leaning heavily on a cane, her frame thin and her back hunched over. Ellie could tell she had once been strong and proud.

"What's wrong with her?" Ellie whispered to Lacey as the lady stopped to talk to another angel in the street. "I thought angels didn't grow old?"

Lacey looked at the woman with warmth in her eyes. "We don't really, but with some magic, there is a price to pay."

She didn't have time to say anything else before the angel stopped in front of them. Lacey gave her a quick hug before making the introductions. "Ellie, this is Shekinah. It's her house you've been staying in. Shekinah, this is Eliana. She's the –"

"I know who she is, child. Welcome to our village. I hope you will enjoy it however long or short your stay may be." The woman's eyes shone with kindness. Ellie smiled back.

"Thank you. And thank you for letting me stay at your house. I hope it's no inconvenience."

"No inconvenience at all, I am simply happy to help. Besides, it is Lacey's bed you are staying in, so it affects me little," Shekinah answered with a small smirk. "After all, she is the one who dragged you here, so she is the one to sleep on the floor."

Ellie looked over at Lacey, about to apologize, but laughter danced in her eyes.

"Yeah, yeah whatever. You love having the Empath in your home and you know it. Now stop with the innocent act and help me start dinner. Ellie still needs her rest." Lacey took a hold of the old lady's arm and started to lead her away.

Ellie looked at their retreating backs. Everyone had so much faith in her and her abilities as an Empath. How was she supposed to tell them she could barely control her powers enough to function, much less defeat the Archangels?

"Come on, Israfel probably has some more of that delicious green goo for you when we get back. You wouldn't want to miss that now, would you?"

Lacey's words drew Ellie from her musings.

She smiled at the older girl and hurried to catch up. But she couldn't shake the nagging feeling at the back of her mind that she was not who they all believed her to be.

CHAPTER TWENTY

During the next few days, Ellie found herself falling into the easy rhythm of life in the village. By the third the day, she had mostly recovered, most likely thanks to the goo Israfel still forced her to drink each day. The taste did not improve.

Lacey was always there to show her around and help her when they allowed her to leave her bed. They hadn't had much time on their own though as there was always someone who wanted to talk to Ellie or touch her hand.

These encounters left an uneasy feeling in Ellie's stomach. It wasn't *Ellie* they wanted to touch, it was the *Empath*. A role Ellie still could not make her peace with.

Today, Lacey had decided to show her the fields outside of the village once Israfel had deemed her recovered and no longer on bedrest

TEMPTATIONS OF THE PAST

"What did you mean the other day when you said magic had a price," Ellie finally asked once they had left the village, leaving all the prying ears behind them.

"Huh?" Lacey's eyebrows rose as she turned to face Ellie.

"You said Shekinah had paid a price," Ellie prompted.

"Ah, yes," Lacey sighed. "You told me a little about Hayyel, so I assume you know that some magic has sort of conditions attached to them. For instance, a Corporal Protector can't deny someone in need of healing or else they lose their power."

Ellie nodded in agreement. At the mention of Hayyel's name, Ellie couldn't help but wonder why he hadn't visited her yet. Each night, she expected to travel to the meadow, but nightmares of Aaron filled her mind instead, leaving her feeling drained the next day.

Shiro had tried to travel there as well but had been met by a wall not even he could penetrate.

"Shekinah was a Wind Protector," Lacey said. "She used her powers to create a storm that sunk several of the Fallen's ships."

The Fallen, Ellie remebered Hayyel telling her, was the Archangels' army.

"But how could that have earned her such a punishment?"

"The ships were at anchor outside of a harbor city where Israfel and Shekinah lived. They had spent several years smuggling children from the Fallen and set up an orphanage in the city. There were hundreds of saved angels who sought the shelter they provided.

When the Fallen's navy closed in, Shekinah feared for their safety. Israfel tried to talk her out of it. You see, the navy had made no threats, shown no signs of aggressions, therefore a Wind Protector could not use their powers as they can only be used in the service of others. But Shekinah didn't dare wait. So, she created a storm that sunk the ships, but in doing so, the Creator stripped her of her powers and imprisoned her in a broken body."

Ellie didn't know what to say. They sat in the grass and for a long while, Ellie just plucked straw after straw. Shekinah had sacrificed everything, knowing the price she would have to pay and paid it, nonetheless. How Ellie longed for the kind of conviction.

"But the kids, they were safe, right?"

"The kids?" Lacey had gotten lost in her own thoughts.

"Yeah, the orphanage."

As Lacey's eyes turned sad, Ellie regretted asking that question in the first place.

"No, it was a trap. Once Shekinah had been stripped of her powers, the Fallen's Wind Protectors rained lightning down on the city. Since they had been attacked first, they could use their powers without fear of retribution. Shekinah was the only Wind Protector who had been strong enough to stop them, but she was left powerless as the city burned. Not many made it out."

Ellie swallowed and lowered her gaze. "How can you still put your faith in the Creator when she is so cruel?"

"But she is not," Lacey replied softly. "She is fair. Shekinah knew the rules and the punishment for breaking them. She did so willingly. The Creator could not let the transgressions go unnoticed. But as the city burned, it was the Creator's tears that finally extinguished the flames."

Ellie wanted to say more of what she thought of this so-called Creator, but she held her tongue. Getting into an argument with Lacey would do her no good.

"What did they do? After, I mean," Ellie asked instead.

"They traveled for a while before settling here," Lacey said with a shrug. "Israfel doesn't talk about it much, but I know it pains him to see Shekinah so weak."

Ellie wanted to ask more, but Lacey had gotten up from the ground.

"Anyway, let's head back. It'll be getting dark out soon, and I'll never hear the end of it if I keep you out after nightfall."

Ellie rolled her eyes but rose from the ground. One minute, she was an almighty Empath, and the next, she couldn't even be trusted to be out after dark.

As they neared the village, something felt off. There was a feverish activity, and no one would meet her eye. She shared a concern look with Lacey and it was clear from her drawn brows and hastened steps, she felt it too.

They hurried together towards Shekinah's small house and pushed through the door.

"Lacey, gear up. We're leaving." It took a few seconds for Ellie's eyes to adjust to the dim light inside of the house, but she knew Israfel's voice without seeing him.

"Wait, what's going on?"

"Someone must have told the Council you were here," Shekinah answered in Israfel's stead as he left after Lacey. "They've sent out part of the Fallen to bring you to the capitol."

She cast a worried glance behind her.

"But how? Who?" Ellie was at a loss for words as unease grew in her stomach.

"It doesn't matter, pack your bag and make haste." Shekinah pushed her through the door to the small bedroom she had occupied. "You must leave for the resistance; they will keep you safe."

Ellie nodded. Shekinah left her as she started to push things into a bag. But what does one pack when fleeing for your life?

Ellie slumped onto the bed and put her head in her hands. No place was safe and everywhere she went, someone seemed to get hurt because of her.

A quiet knock on the doorframe had her look up. Lacey stood in the doorway, and Ellie's mouth dropped open.

Gone was the sweet girl who had shown her around the village, and in her place stood a warrior. Lacey was dressed in tight leather pants with a matching shirt, and weapons covered her entire body. A variation of knives were strapped to her thighs and two more blades poked up out of her boots. Only when Lacey turned did Ellie notice the sword strapped around her torso, a large emerald embedded in the hilt, making it look expensive. Not that Ellie would know – it was the first real sword she'd ever seen.

"Come on, we need to leave before the army gets here," she said, then left the room.

Ellie scrambled to her feet and followed her, clutching her bag. "Wait, army?"

"Yes, army." Shekinah answered as she came back out into the main room "You need to leave, now. Lacey and Israfel will take you to the resistance."

Ellie looked over at Lacey, about to argue when the door flew open.

Israfel filled the doorway, casting a dark shadow across the room. Unlike Lacey, he was still in his robes and wore no visible weapons.

"We are leaving." That was the end of the discussion and Ellie hurriedly got dressed while Israfel and Shekinah had some sort of heated discussion in the other room.

"But what about the rest of the villagers?" Ellie asked. "They will get hurt."

Most of them have already left. There are secret tunnels under the village leading to the forest. They will be safe. Just do what you are told for once. Shiro walked into the room, his tail held high.

"They are leaving through –"

"– the tunnels. Yeah, Shiro told me," Ellie interrupted Lacey.

"You really do speak to him? I mean, Israfel told me you were an Animal Protector as well, but I thought maybe it was a rumor getting out of control."

And just like that, despite the weapons and the severity of the situation, Lacey was back to being a carefree twenty-year-old girl.

"I do. Well, not only with him. Since I came here, I can hear other animals' voices clearer as well."

It was true. Before she left the human realm, it was only Shiro's voice she could hear clearly. With other animals, she still used emotions to communicate, and the deaths of Aragonite and his family still lay heavy on her mind. But here, everything was crisper and took less strength than she was used to.

The argument in the kitchen simmered, and Israfel returned to the room as Lacey handed Ellie a knife. "Take this, just in case."

In case of what? Ellie wanted to ask, but she bit her tongue. She wasn't sure she would like the answer. Instead, she put it into her backpack and walked out the door.

Whatever Ellie had expected, it wasn't what met her outside Shekinah's cottage. Flames rising towards the sky disrupted the darkness of the night. The houses on the outskirts of the village were already burning, and the fire quickly closed in.

She heard Israfel curse behind her. "They were closer than I thought. Lacey we're going, NOW!"

Lacey grabbed Ellie's arm and dragged her in the opposite direction of the fire. She didn't need to use much force; Ellie had no intentions of sticking around.

When they neared the edge of the forest, Lacey released Ellie's arm. Apparently, she could be trusted to walk on her own again.

As they were about to walk through the first line of trees, a whisper fluttered through Ellie's mind. It was so weak that Ellie almost failed to notice it, but it was soon followed by another... then another. Ellie stopped and closed her eyes, lowering her shield by an inch. At once, emotions rushed towards her, but Ellie had been practicing how to sort through them without letting them overwhelm her. She discarded those belonging to the village people leaving and those with minds hard as iron until she found the one demanding her attention. She held onto to it and raised her shields again, shutting everything else out.

Focusing her energy, Ellie broke the connection to the terror and panic with a gasp and sprinted back towards the burning houses. The fire had spread to the town square, but that didn't stop Ellie.

An arm around her waist did, however.

"What do you think you are doing? We need to go!" Lacey's scared whisper was close to Ellie's ear.

"Someone is still in there. There is still someone in the village."

Lacey's arm loosened, but she didn't let go of Ellie.

"Eliana." It was Israfel. "Everyone in this village knew the risks and everyone took it willingly. Whoever is left out there knew them as well and would want you to run, to survive."

"But they are so afraid," Ellie pleaded. "How can you be so cruel?"

Every fiber in her demanded to save whoever it was screaming in her head.

"Don't you think I want to save them, too? That Lacey does not want to? They are our family, our friends. But we both know what is important and it is time you learn, too. We are going." Israfel's words cut through her like a knife and all energy left her body.

"You can let go. I won't try to go again. I'm sorry." But Lacey didn't let go of her grip. If anything, she squeezed tighter.

"Seriously, let go, Lacey. What are you –" Ellie's words were cut short as she followed Lacey's gaze.

Angels were pouring out from between the houses, quickly closing the distance between them. It was too dark to see how many there were, but given the almost suffocating pressure on her shields, Ellie guessed there must have been dozens, if not hundreds of them.

"Too late to run now," Israfel muttered under his breath. "Shiro, take Eliana and run. A few miles from here there is another camp.

They will help you get to the resistance. Lacey and I will hold them off for as long as we can to give you a head start."

No, Shiro. We are not leaving them to die. Lacey had finally let go of her and Ellie turned to look into Shiro's blue eyes. *Please, we have to help.*

The inner war that raged within Shiro was not lost on Ellie. She felt every conflicting emotion. He wanted to keep her safe, but at the same time, his instincts were to stay and fight.

When he finally made up his mind, Ellie let go of the breath she'd been holding.

"Thank you," she said.

Shiro didn't bother with a reply. Instead, he walked up to her side, preparing to defend her from whatever it was coming towards them. The small puppy who had found her passed out in an alley was gone. Youthful playfulness now gave way to a predator's intensity. His muscles coiled, ready to strike, and his teeth, once gentle nippers, were now bared – a silent warning to any threat that dared approach.

"No, you cannot stay. Do you hear me?" Israfel said, still trying to convince them to leave. Lacey, however, had unsheathed her sword and taken a stance slightly in front of Ellie and Shiro.

Ellie turned to face Israfel, shaping some of her power into three words. *"We are staying."*

Nothing more was said after that. They stood together, waiting until they could see the endless faces of the angels who soon surrounded them. Ellie retrieved the knife Lacey had given her from her bag and gripped it so tight her knuckles turned white. Nothing Hayyel had taught her could have prepared her for this.

Blank, beautiful faces surrounded her, their cold expressions frightening her more than their swords ever could. Without any warning, the pressure on her shields lifted and Ellie could finally breathe again. But after the quick relief she felt, Ellie feared the reason for the sudden reprieve. Hesitantly, she lowered her shield and was met with nothing.

Their lack of emotions felt like an empty hole inside of Ellie's mind, and she realized how much she'd come to rely on her power.

Why can't I sense them? I could before.

She didn't ask Israfel because she didn't want him and Lacey to know how untrained and vulnerable she really was.

A Magic Protector must be shielding them. Try looking for where there is nothing.

But there is nothing everywhere.

No, relax and concentrate.

Ellie closed her eyes and tried to breathe. Eventually, she slipped into meditation. At first, she felt nothing, not even the emotions from Lacey, Israfel and Shiro, but slowly, tiny bolts of light appeared before her inner eye.

First it was Shiro; he shone brightly by her side.

Next came Lacey and Israfel, and soon, dozens of lights shone around her. Ellie quickly counted to around fifty, but there, in the middle of the sea of light, was nothing.

"I did it."

But the glee in her voice quickly disappeared when she opened her eyes. They were fully surrounded, and Shiro, Lacey and Israfel stood in a protective circle around her.

A woman stood before them. There was something familiar about her that Ellie couldn't place.

The torches the angels carried glowed with an uncanny light, casting a cold glow over the scene.

"Lacey, don't be stupid. Hand over the Empath and no one else will get hurt." Lacey froze, paralyzed, gripping her sword so tight it was shaking.

"No." It was quiet, but the power in that single word forced the woman back a step.

"No? NO?! You dare defy me, your own mother?"

Her *mother*? So that was why Ellie thought she recognized her. The same red hair fell over Lacey's mother's shoulder and their eyes were the same. No, not the same, Ellie decided. Lacey's eyes shone with kindness, her mother's only with cruelty.

"You are not my mother," Lacey whispered through clenched teeth. A little louder, she added, "If you want her, you'll have to go through me first."

"Ah, well. We shall see about that."

Lacey's mother had composed herself again and waved her hand as if beckoning someone. A man strode forward, pushing something in front of him. Ellie couldn't see what it was in the darkness until it was pushed into the light.

A young girl from the village stood before them with tears streaming down her face. A cold hand grasped Ellie's heart. This must be the one they left behind. Before anyone could react, the woman grabbed the girl and held a knife to her throat.

"Now, let us try this again. Give me the Empath or this child dies."

The detachment in her voice sent chills down Ellie's spine. This girl meant nothing to Lacey's mother.

But before Ellie could say anything, Lacey spoke. "No."

Ellie looked at Lacey in disbelief and tears swamped her freckly face. Her sword shook so much that Ellie was sure she'd drop it, and yet she stood fast. Ellie opened her mouth to say something, anything.

"Oh, well. We'll do it the hard way then."

The knife cut into the girl's flesh with sickening ease and left a gaping wound in its wake.

"NO!" Ellie roared, but the voice that escaped her wasn't her own.

Lacey gasped and Shiro barked, but Ellie didn't hear any of it. She felt like she'd lost control over her own body. A strange power filled her, feeding on her emotions.

I am here. Let go. The voice sounded in Ellie's mind, and it felt oddly comforting. Not questioning it, Ellie dove into the fire within her, letting it fill her entire being. The energy left her like an arrow of light and stabbed right into the nothingness Ellie had felt earlier.

The woman behind the shield fell dead, but before she had even touched the ground, the energy exploded, bathing everything in its light. Ellie felt Shiro raise his shields around them, but Ellie was too far gone to care. The amount of energy running through her created a blinding pain, causing blood to run from her nose. But the presence in her mind gave her comfort.

All around her, angels screamed and dropped to the ground, either dead or unconscious. Soon, only Lacey's mother still stood, fear in her eyes.

That is right, Eliana. Trust in your powers.

With the last of Ellie's strength, she let her power soar through the darkness, piercing the woman with light. A strangled cry filled the skies for a second before Lacey's mother collapsed onto the grass, still pulsating with light.

Whatever had taken hold of Ellie finally let her go, and everything fell into darkness once again.

A flickering light drew Ellie towards it, and she sank to her knees beside the young girl. She was somehow still alive, trembling with terror, but the ground beneath the girl had pooled with blood. For a split second, the girl's eyes were replaced with those of Sablo's daughters. Ellie let out a strangled cry and fought back a wave of nausea.

She placed her hands on either side of the girl's head and closed her eyes. Carefully, she replaced the girl's fears with feelings of love and happiness, letting them fill her entire being before the girl finally slipped away.

When Ellie opened her eyes again, the girl had a peaceful smile on her lips.

"I'm sorry."

She walked back to Israfel and Lacey, covered in the girl's blood. Fear radiated from them in waves. Ellie's shield was dangerously thin, but she didn't care. Shiro licked her hand, giving her all the comfort she needed.

"I want to clean myself up," she said without looking up from her hands. "Then take me to the resistance."

CHAPTER TWENTY-ONE

ELLIE CAUGHT LACEY STARING at her... *again*.

"Oh, would you stop looking at me like that?" Ellie snapped at Lacey, the constant stares getting on her last nerve. "It's not like everyone I look at drops dead to the ground you know, so just stop!"

Lacey dropped the firewood she'd been gathering. "S-sorry... um, sorry, sorry."

Ellie let out an exaggerated sigh and went to help her.

"I know I'm being silly, I'm sorry. It's just that even though Shiro shielded us, I *felt* it. All that pain, it was crippling. I can't even imagine what the Fallen outside the shield must have felt," Lacey said.

She finally looked up and met Ellie's eyes. They were not filled with fear anymore, but sadness. Ellie didn't know what was worse.

"Well, if it's any consolation, I scared myself," Ellie muttered, trying to suppress the doubts and fears that were always close to the surface.

Ellie didn't dare to admit it hadn't been her who had defeated the army – she was still unsure what had happened. She couldn't even tell how many had died.

Ellie and Lacey had entered the small clearing where they'd sat up camp. The trees were tall, reaching towards the sky like a dark ominous wall. Ellie could feel a presence lurking in the shadows, watching their every move. The whole forest felt *wrong*. There was a sickness spreading deep into the roots, twisting the trees into something from a nightmare. Even the animals had fled long ago, making food scarce.

Israfel was sitting by a small fire, his robes draped around him. Shiro, who felt even more apprehensive than Ellie, was curled up in a tight ball to his left. The forest had taken its toll on him and his nerves were on edge, his ears twitching at every sound.

"I know I shouldn't ask, but–" Lacey's voice broke the silence, and Ellie dropped her firewood by Israfel, turning to face her.

"But what?" Ellie already knew what Lacey was going to ask, but she didn't know how to answer.

"My mother, Mithra, did you... is she dead?" Lacey cast her eyes downward, unable to face Ellie. "I know I shouldn't care, but she is still my mother."

"I didn't," Ellie said, trying to keep her voice steady. "Kill her, that is."

The glimmer of hope that lit in Lacey's eyes almost sent Ellie over the edge. Breathing in and out, she tried to get her anger under control.

"I wanted to; I should have."

Tears welled up in Lacey's eyes, then she averted her them again.

Turning to leave, she whispered, "You're right, sorry."

Then she was gone.

"What is she crying about?" Ellie cried, throwing her hands up in the air. "Mithra is a horrible, *horrible* person, angel or whatever.

I mean, I get that it's her mom, but she killed that girl. Like it was nothing."

Shiro opened one eye as Ellie paced back and forth in the small clearing.

"You shouldn't be so hard on her." Israfel's voice drew Ellie to a halt.

"I'm not hard on her, I'm hard on Mithra."

"Eliana, you need to start controlling your temper. I can feel your anger from here and I would appreciate if you would pull it back and into yourself."

Shiro opened both his eyes and stared intently at Ellie. Ellie felt his energy sweep over her, then he lowered his head back down on his paws and yawned.

He is wrong, your shields are fine.

"Shiro says you're wrong, my shield is working."

Israfel eyed the dog to his left with raised eyebrows, something seemingly out of character for him. His glasses fell down his nose and he quickly pushed them back in that well-rehearsed motion.

A small smile played on Ellie's lips. She wondered what her tic was.

You do that when you're nervous; bite your lip, a man's voice whispered in her mind.

Her dreams of Aaron were only getting worse, and Ellie could no longer shake the feeling that something was terribly wrong. But Shiro kept reassuring her he was safe, so what else could Ellie do but believe him?

"Did he now?" Israfel said, interrupting her thoughts. "Well, I suppose I should not be surprised. Shiro is still a young Guardian." A low growl sounded from the back of Shiro's throat. Apparently, he did not appreciate being questioned. "Easy, easy. Her shields are up and protecting her from those around her. However, there is no shield protecting us from her. She is projecting."

"I'm doing what?" Ellie asked.

Shiro's interest was piqued. He sat up and stared at Israfel. This wasn't something he seemed to have heard of before either.

"Sit down, Eliana."

Shiro curled himself around Ellie as she sat on the opposite side of the fire, facing Israfel. In the flickering light of the fire, she could've sworn it was Hayyel sitting on the other side. Both Hayyel and Israfel had the same unearthly presence about them. Israfel must have been beautiful once; his eyes still shone brightly, and his features, now softened with old age, had once been sharp.

"Now, I thought you said you had a teacher, no?"

"Yes, I do," Ellie answered quickly.

But do you? Shiro asked. Ellie gave him a little shove, but his question lingered in her mind. Did she? Hayyel hadn't shown himself since he'd shared his memories with her, and she had no idea when he would decide to grace her with his presence again.

"Ah well, you seem to be lacking in your training, perhaps you need a new one."

The tone in Israfel's voice had Ellie narrowing her eyes at him. It was an obvious stab at Hayyel, but Ellie kept quiet. She wanted to learn more about her power, and since Hayyel wasn't going to help, maybe it was time to find someone who would.

"Okay, so teach me. What's projecting?"

"When learning to control one's gift, you must first learn how to shield yourself and others. This is not unique for Empaths; Lacey, too, has learned this as well as any other angel with a gift.

"You have only learned to use half of that shield, the shield protecting you. It is understandable considering your powers, but it does not give you the right to keep projecting your powers onto others."

Ellie listened carefully. Lacey had powers? She wondered what they were. Perhaps they were more alike than Ellie first thought.

She cast a glance at the edge of the clearing into the suffocating darkness. Maybe she should go after her.

"Lacey will be fine. But you will not be unless you learn to pay attention."

Ellie was quickly discovering that as far as angelic teachers went, there wasn't much of a difference. They all seemed to have the ability to make her feel like she was five years old.

"I was," she muttered under her breath, but either Israfel didn't hear her or he chose to ignore her.

"Now, focus your power and find your shield."

Closing her eyes, Ellie stilled her breathing and found the fire forever burning inside of her. She turned her focus to her shield. It felt like a soft caress against her skin, whispers of power brushing against her.

She opened her eyes and the faint shimmer surrounding her made her smile; her shield was working.

"Good, now find the flaws and repair them. You need to build a second shield within the first one. This shield is not to keep anything out, but to keep you in."

Ellie wanted to tell him there were no flaws in her shield, but she bit her tongue instead. She would *show* him.

Pouring more of her power into the shield, the shimmer started to glow stronger and stronger until Ellie couldn't see past it. When it almost blinded her, Ellie was about to cry out in triumph when a small tremor went through the shield, revealing a small hole by her left hand. It was tiny, but it was there.

Re-focusing her energy on the hole, she discovered a small tendril of power flowing through it, like a thread through a needle.

Israfel had been right.

Ellie found more and more holes as she searched the shield, making it look like a leaking sieve. Her power and her emotions were spilling through everywhere.

Make a shield within the shield was what he had said.

When Ellie had created the first shield, she'd woven her power into a cocoon surrounding her. Now, she weaved her power through the already existing shield. It was tiresome, but Ellie was determined to make it work. She wanted to be in control, so her powers would bend to her will.

One by one, the holes were closed, and finally, Ellie withdrew most of her power from it. The shield swiftly dimmed to a shimmer again, and Ellie closed her eyes.

Well done, that is as good of a shield as I could ever make.

"Thank you," Ellie whispered, opening her eyes.

"How does it feel?" Israfel had not moved while she worked. He was still watching the fire burn, his robes draped around him.

"Different," Ellie answered carefully.

The silence in her mind was almost deafening at first, but as she gradually adjusted, Ellie realized the alien emotions she always felt were gone. Ellie was all that was left. And for the first in a long time, the tension in her neck eased. Her shoulders dropped, and she breathed deep for the first time since she'd gotten her powers.

"Before, I could always hear whispers of different emotions. Sometimes they were louder and sometimes barely audible. Now, there is only me."

The obvious relief in Ellie's voice caused a small smile to play at Israfel's lips.

"Lovely, is it not? To feel in control."

"So, my first shield was keeping them out and this one is about keeping me in?" she asked for clarity, marveling at the silence.

"A shield without its other half is only half a shield. Your shield needed its sister to be complete and take full effect. Think of it as a sieve; when you pour water into it, the holes allow the water to escape. Your second shield is like putting your sieve into another where the holes are in different places. Together they are strong, apart they leak."

Weirdly enough, Israfel's explanation made perfect sense, and Ellie smiled a little at their shared comparison to the sieve.

She couldn't help but wonder why Hayyel hadn't taught her this. She asked Shiro as much.

Perhaps Hayyel's main focus was to protect you and teach you control to fulfill the prophecy. It is possible that his main concern wasn't your well-being.

Although Ellie hoped it wasn't true, it was hard to argue.

A moment of silence ensued until Israfel spoke again, his eyes shining with curiosity as he leaned toward her. "How did you do it?"

Ellie replied, somewhat startled. "The shield?"

Israfel nodded.

"I wove it like I would a net, then threaded another line of power through the entire thing. Or something like that, it's hard to explain. Why do you ask?"

"The shield is different for everyone. Lacey created hers with water, shaping it like a waterfall. Hiding her inside like the water hides the mountainside it falls from."

Lacey was a Water Protector then, Ellie decided.

Israfel continued. "I played mine, creating a melody to surround me."

Suddenly, a melody filled the air, and Israfel began pulsing with a lilac light. As the melody grew, so did the light until Ellie could barely see him behind it. The notes filling the air were hauntingly beautiful, filled with such sadness and longing that a rogue tear rolled down her cheek. This song was the innermost part of Israfel's soul, and Ellie felt like she was invading on something private.

The song faded and took the light with it, leaving Israfel standing in front of the fire. Ellie hadn't even noticed he had moved.

"That was beautiful," Ellie said in awe, a slight tremor to her voice.

"It is what it is," Israfel cryptically answered. He didn't seem too keen on discussing the subject much further, so Ellie changed the subject.

"You told me not to be too hard on Lacey. Why? Because of Mithra?" Ellie refused to refer to that woman as *Lacey's mother*. Nothing that kind could come from something so evil.

Israfel let out a sigh, sitting back down by the fire. Ellie joined him, throwing another piece of wood onto the flames. Being trapped in the darkness was not an intriguing idea.

"I don't know how much you know about the history of angels, but Mithra, Shekinah and I are of the old world. Mithra chose to serve the Archangels, we did not. Neither did Lacey and her twin brother Chehon's father. It is hard to say why some stayed true to the Creator while some so easily betrayed her."

"Love."

"Sorry?"

"I think those who resisted the Archangels did so with the help of love."

Ellie had thought about it for some time now. Sablo loved his family, Hayyel loved Starlight, and when she'd felt Israfel and Shekinah's love for each other, it only supported her suspicions. She didn't tell Israfel this though; she had a feeling it might embarrass him if he knew she knew.

"Yes, you are not the first to come to this conclusion. But whatever it is, their father felt it and their mother did not. In an attempt to keep them safe, their father smuggled them out of the capitol. The mission was doomed to fail from the start, and everyone involved knew it. He reached out to Shekinah and I, asking us to keep Lacey and Chehon safe. We had left over a hundred years earlier and had made a life for ourselves. But of course, we agreed. I think it gave Shekinah a sense of purpose again, to have something to fight for."

A sadness fell over Israfel's eyes, and Ellie remembered what Lacey had told her about how Shekinah lost her powers. She wanted to ask Israfel more, but his eyes cleared once more, and the moment passed.

"Their father got caught on his way back. Mithra killed him herself."

This story was all too familiar. Ellie wondered how many children had lost their parents in a similar manner because of the Archangels.

"Unfortunately, most children born under the Archangels grow up to be warriors in their army. Around the age of five, they are taken in front of the Council, and after that, they are never the same. Children born outside of their reach grow up as the Creator intended. They use their power for good, trying to keep the balance in this world and yours, but the Archangels' power grows every day. That is what you feel here, in this forest, and it is you who will restore balance again."

There was no moon tonight; the only source of light came from their dwindling fire.

Ellie gazed out into the darkness, feeling her courage sink to the pit of her stomach. There it was again. Children were being corrupted and parents killed in cold blood. The whole world was out of balance, and she was the one who was supposed to fix it.

Getting to her feet, Ellie excused herself and hurried out into the forest.

"Eliana, wait! Heywood forest is not safe to wander alone," Israfel called after her, but Ellie didn't stop.

Before Ellie knew it, she was running deep into the forest. When her lungs felt like they were about to explode, she finally slowed, allowing herself to take in her surroundings.

The trees stood close together, making it hard to move in any direction. There were no sounds, no birds chirping, no wolves howling their tribute to the night, nothing.

Ellie sank to the ground, her back against a tree. She closed her eyes, trying to collect her thoughts. Lacey, Israfel and even Shiro, they all had so much faith in her, never questioning whether she was powerful or not. That blind faith scared her.

The forest pressed on her mind like the weight of everyone's trust pressed on her shoulders.

Slowly, Ellie called for her power, letting it consume her. Her new shield shone brightly around her, and she lowered it just enough to send a stream of power out. A sudden sadness washed over Ellie, a sadness she didn't recognize.

It was the forest itself.

There was so much she couldn't do, but she could do this. She fell deeper into meditation and emerged herself in the sadness, steadily replacing it with hope. Hope of life.

It was tedious work and she used most of her powers, but it was worth it when the trees themselves sighed and instantly sprouted new shoots on their branches. Flowers woke from their long sleep and the grass once again glimmered green and bright.

Sometimes all you needed was hope.

The morning arrived with the chipper of birds and warm rays of sunlight finally able to gleam through the canopy of leaves. A tear slid down Ellie's cheek as she listened to the birds singing in the forest again.

Then she groaned as she stood up, wincing at her sore muscles. She must have been sitting for quite some time, and judging by the sun, several hours must have passed. Her powers felt raw, and she shivered in her damp clothes. The morning dew lay thick around her, making her raven hair cling to her face.

A sudden breeze blew through the trees, carrying a whisper on its wings. *Thank you.*

Ellie smiled. If a forest talked, it would have sounded like that. Ancient but young, wild but tame. *If* a forest could talk.

Finding her way back proved to be less of a challenge than Ellie would have thought. The forest so terrifying the night before now flourished, and a new path guided her back to the camp. It was empty when she reached it, but Ellie was too tired to care. She walked over to her bedroll and collapsed, her eyes closing even before she hit the ground.

While she slept, the same dream played over and over in her mind. Aaron, screaming in pain as a hooded figure tortured him, and Ellie helpless to stop him.

When she finally woke, Shiro lay curled at her side, his body heat warming her.

It's about time.

How long did I sleep? Ellie asked without opening her eyes.

Three days, Shiro answered. *You drained yourself healing the forest. How did you do it?*

Three days. Israfel must be furious if they'd been forced to stay in camp for three days. *What do you mean?*

You are not a Flora Protector or Corporal Protector, but you still healed Heywood forest.

I don't know, there was a sadness. I helped it see hope again.

Before Ellie could say anything else, Israfel said, "We are leaving in five minutes."

Ellie grumbled and sat up, looking for Lacey. She was sitting at the outskirts of the clearing, staring intently at her shoes. She still wore her leather armor, ready for a fight. It made her look somewhat dangerous, but Ellie took a breath and went over to her.

"Lacey, I'm sorry about before."

Lacey looked up into Ellie's green eyes, blinking away the tears that had started to form.

"Thank you. I know I shouldn't care. I know and she is this horrible person, but–"

"She's your mom." Ellie finished her sentence.

Lacey nodded.

Ellie understood her sadness. She could only imagine having a mother who was alive but didn't care about you. That was worse than a mother who had died. At least then you could morn and move on.

"Sometimes I fear I will become like her," Lacey confessed, and Ellie waited for her to continue. "I have this darkness inside and sometimes it feels as if I can't control it. I'm afraid it will consume me."

There was so much Ellie couldn't do, but this, she could try and help Lacey with this.

"Lacey, while I don't have that much experience in this whole Empath thing, I can tell you one thing for sure."

Lacey met her gaze. Ellie hated the pain she saw there. "What?"

"Everyone has darkness."

Lacey's eyes widened slightly. "What do you mean?"

"I don't know exactly what it means, but it gives me comfort to know there is darkness in all of us. I have sensed it in the people around me, no matter how kind or noble they might have been. It is what we chose to do with it that matters."

Lacey pondered for a minute. "So basically, I shouldn't let fear dictate my decisions but instead acknowledge it's there and then act despite of it?"

"Yeah, something like that," Ellie answered haltingly, slightly taken aback. That was far more profound than anything she might have said. She could probably listen to that advice herself, but those were things she wasn't ready to face just yet.

"Thank you, Ellie, I will keep this advice close to my heart," Lacey said and held Ellie's gaze until she had to look away.

"No need for thanks," Ellie mumbled. Then, forcing cheerfulness into her voice, she spoke again. "Come on, let's go help Israfel. He's really old, you know; we wouldn't want him to throw his back."

It felt strained even to her own ears but Lacey smiled, appreciating the gesture.

THE REST OF THE journey through the forest passed uneventfully. Setting up camp quickly became a routine, and everyone had their own role. Israfel started a fire, Lacey and Shiro went to hunt, and Ellie sat on the outskirts feeling miserable.

She hardly slept, and even when she did, she woke up in sweat. Aaron's pleading eyes haunted her every waked moment now.

The fact that Shiro was avoiding her, both physically and mentally, did nothing to lessen her bad mood. She finally managed to corner him when he returned from a hunt.

Shiro, please. Something is wrong, I know there is. What was Aaron doing when you saw him? I can feel you hiding something from me. Please, why won't you tell me?

Shiro dropped the rabbit in his mouth and gave what could only be described as a sigh. *I thought if I waited, the memories would fade away. Obviously, I was wrong.*

Panic ascended inside her, but Ellie tried to keep calm. *Shiro, what was he doing?*

I – I didn't see him.

CHAPTER TWENTY-TWO

Anger blinded Ellie, leaving room for nothing else.
You didn't see him? Then how do you know he is okay?
I thought it was your mind trying to cope with the loss, so I lied.

"How dare you?!" she screamed with both voice and mind.

Shiro laid his ears flat against his head and shrank to the ground. *I didn't want you to be in pain. It hurt you so much to leave him, I didn't want you to have to go through it again, and I knew you would go to him if he was hurting. It's probably nothing.* Shiro's voice sounded small in her mind.

The unmistakable touch of Shiro's power graced her shield. He was, no doubt, trying to soothe her. But Ellie didn't want to be soothed, and for the first time since they'd met, she shut him out.

That was not *for you to decide.*

Shiro shrank back even more, his tail between his legs.

Fury ripped through Ellie like waves crashing against the shore.

I know. I thought about telling you, but then I spoke to Israfel and –

He knew?!

"You knew!"

Spinning to face Israfel, Ellie realized that both he and Lacey were staring at her. Lacey's eyes were filled with concern, Israfel's with cold detachment.

"Yes. You need to focus, Eliana. There cannot be any distractions. The boy was just that, a distraction."

"He was everything!"

Everything.

She needed to go back, to see that he was okay. An aching pain pushed aside the burning rage.

You left him, Ellie. It was your choice.

Well, I changed my mind. The tug at her heart was more than she could bear. How could she have ever thought she could leave him, never to look back?

Take me to him. What if the Archangels have him? Shiro, you owe me at least that. Ellie looked into Shiro's icy blue eyes, showing him her pain. It didn't take long before she could feel him give in to her.

She knew it was wrong using her power to get what she wanted, but she didn't care. All she could think about was Aaron. What if the Archangels had chosen to take their revenge on him because of her refusal to their offer?

"Eliana, do not be stupid. You cannot go to him now. How do you know he ever really loved you? When I first met you, you were projecting onto everything and everyone. What is to say you did not force your own love upon him, leaving him no choice but to love you?" Israfel tried to reason with her. "Emotions are powerful things, Eliana."

"He loved me, I know he did."

She held her chin high, but Israfel's words were eating away at her insides. Did she really know? How many times had she thought Aaron's love was too good to be true? Maybe it had been.

"You sound like a child, not a warrior."

"Well, I never asked to be a warrior, did I?" Ellie's cry released all the pent up fear and frustration that had been building for weeks.

No one had ever once asked her if this was what she wanted. Her previous determination when confronted by the Archangel's was gone. Perhaps she should have accepted their offer. She could have her life back.

Shiro?

I'll take you. Shiro started to pulse with light.

"Eliana, you cannot leave. You are vulnerable in the human realm. Your powers are at their strongest here, where they can feed off the magic in the lands."

"I don't care."

Ellie let Shiro guide her as they left the realm of the angels.

"Eliana!" Israfel's cry was the last thing she heard as she entered the light.

She didn't look back.

TRAVELING BETWEEN THE WORLDS was like walking in a maze of blinding light. Without Shiro, Ellie would have been lost within seconds. He took every turn with confidence, never once faltering in his path.

Before long, Ellie heard the familiar sounds of the city surround them. She hadn't realized it before, but she'd missed the blaring of car horns and screeching tires.

Shiro took a left and the sounds faded. Ellie raised her eyebrows.

She'd thought they were going out into an alley or something, but Shiro continued. A flash of pink alerted her to where they were, but before she could stop him, she tumbled into her dorm.

A smash made her wince, and Ellie slowly turned to find Jen standing in a puddle of coffee and coffee mug. Her left hand covered her mouth, her brown eyes big and heavy with red rims and bags underneath. She wore none of her usual makeup and her hair pulled up in a messy bun.

Ellie almost didn't recognize her.

Jen slowly let her hand fall to her side. "Ellie?"

Ellie didn't move, didn't breathe. *Why did you take me here?*

It takes a lot of energy to open a portal, it takes less to use an old one. It seemed practical.

Practical?

Jen's shaking voice cut her conversation with Shiro short. "Ellie. Ellie, oh god, are you – are you okay?"

"I – yeah, I'm fine." Before Ellie could react, Jen threw herself across the room and embraced her in a tight hug. It lasted a few seconds, then Jen pushed Ellie back and hit her shoulder. Hard. "Ouch, what the hell?"

"You're fine, *fine?!* Now that I know you're not dead, I can kill you myself!" Jen screamed. "Where the hell have you been?! Do you have any idea how worried I've been? I mean, look at me!"

Ellie shrank back as Jen continued her rant.

"I thought you were at Aaron's, but then he showed up here looking like hell, saying he hadn't seen you since the masquerade. That was over a week ago! I called the police, but they didn't take it seriously, told me to call back when you'd been missing for more than a few days. I even called Lucas, *Lucas!*"

Ellie's head was spinning. She backed against the wall and slowly slumped to the ground. She lowered her head into her hands and the tears started to fall. It was too much. Her shoulders shook as sobs ripped through her body.

Then a gentle hand stroked her hair, and Ellie crumpled into Jen's arms. Jen held her and said nothing, like she always did. She had done it when boys at school had teased her about her past or lack thereof, she had done it when the first foster family had kicked her out, and she had done it when she had thought Chris Williams liked her but it had turned out to be a cruel joke.

I'll never leave you. And she never had. Instead, it was Ellie who had left her.

They sat like that for a long time.

Then Ellie's back screamed in pain, forcing her to shift with a wince, breaking the silence.

"Feeling better?" Jen asked, loosening her grip a little but keeping her arms around Ellie.

"A little," Ellie answered. "You really called Lucas?"

Jen threw her hands in the air like the drama queen she was. "Fine, he called me. But I still talked to him. And besides, that's what you took from what I just said?"

"Well, it was the most unlikely." Jen's body quivered with silent laughter, hopefully meaning she no longer intended to kill her.

"Whatever, I'm just glad you're back."

Ellie felt safe in the arms of Jen, but she knew she needed to go. She needed to see Aaron, to see he was okay, and then figure out what the hell she was supposed to do next. She had no idea what she would do if he was being held captive by the Archangels, but it didn't matter.

All of the anger had drained from her body, and now she just wanted to feel whole again. She'd only ever felt whole with Aaron.

She carefully untangled herself from Jen's arms and stood. Ellie looked down at her on the floor and tried to remember her like that. No fancy clothes, no makeup and perfect hair, just Jen.

With a deep breath, she spoke. "I'm not though. Back, I mean. I didn't mean to come here. You need to forget about me and live your life because it will be a brilliant one. I am so sorry I will not be here to see it."

New tears soaked her cheeks as Jen scrambled to her feet. She reached out to grab Ellie's arm as she turned to leave. Jen's fingers dug into her skin, forcing Ellie to stop.

"No."

"Jen, I–"

"I said no. We don't leave, remember? Tell me what's going on."

Ellie looked towards the door with longing. Somewhere on the other side was Aaron.

"Please."

She turned her head and faced Jen. Ellie didn't need her powers to sense her emotions. Confusion, hurt, anger, concern and love, all of them filled Jen's watery eyes.

And then Ellie heard herself tell Jen everything. About her family, the prophecy, and the Archangels. About Hayyel and Shiro and Israfel and Lacey and even Mithra. She talked until she couldn't anymore.

Jen had been quiet throughout her rambling and stayed quiet until Ellie couldn't take the silence anymore. "Please say something."

"Well, if you didn't want to tell me what happened, you could have just said so." Her words were slow and hurt more than Ellie expected.

Jen didn't believe her.

"I want you to know, I just told you. How else do you explain me showing up here?"

"Oh, come on, Ellie! Angels? Really? And you've always had stealth like a cat. You used the door when my back was turned. Now, if you would be so kind as to go and talk to Aaron. He keeps calling me like every five minutes to see if I've heard from you, and it may have been cool at first, but now it's just annoying. I have a life to live, you know, and coffee to clean up."

Jen went over to the desk and started picking up the pieces from the broken mug. Ellie stood frozen in place.

Jen really didn't believe her.

Ellie walked towards the door that felt miles away, then rested her hand on the doorknob for a few seconds. "Goodbye, Jen, I love you. I will always love you."

"Yeah, yeah, love you too," came Jen's reply, but Ellie was already gone.

CHAPTER TWENTY-THREE

Lucas was worried. Ellie had been missing for several days and no one seemed to be able to find her.

Come to me. The words haunted him in his sleep as well as every waking hour and still, he was no closer to figuring out what it meant. He studied the book every chance he got, and the more Lucas read it, the more consumed he became. He barely passed his exams and didn't sleep much anymore.

He was fairly certain that Ellie had left the human realm and entered the world of the angels. The only way to get there, according to the book, was by portals. These portals could only be made by the Creator herself or someone blessed with her power, but from what Lucas gathered, they left shadows behind.

Lucas was sure there must be a way to re-activate one of those portals if he could find one.

Come to me. Come to who? And more importantly, why?

His phone buzzed on the table beside him. He was about to ignore it when Jen's name flashed across the screen. Jen never called him.

"Hello?"

"Hi, I just wanted to tell you I've seen Ellie and she's okay."

Lucas rose from his desk. "When? Where?"

"Relax, she was here like ten minutes ago, but she's gone to see Aaron. I figured she would forget to call, and I thought you would like to know she wasn't dead. Although she was acting a little crazy."

If Lucas hadn't been absorbed with the fact Ellie was back, he would have been surprised Jen had thought of him.

As it was, "Crazy? Crazy how?"

Jen let out an exaggerated sigh. "I don't know, she was babbling about angels and Empaths, claiming she was going to save the world. Clearly, she has been hit over the head. But I have to go now, bye."

"Jen, don't–" There was a click, and the line went dead. "Jen!"

Lucas screamed into the phone, but she was gone. Quickly gathering his stuff, Lucas flew down the stairs, ignoring his mother calling after him. He needed to know everything Ellie had told Jen. If what he had read in the book was true, Ellie was in serious danger, and he needed to help her. He grabbed his bike and rushed towards campus.

PUSHING PEOPLE ASIDE, ELLIE ran through campus, her vision blurring from old and new tears. Everything seemed so final.

Being high on the events of the masquerade had made everything seem so easy, so clear. Now, everything was muddling together. Nothing was as black and white as she had once thought.

She had never asked to be anything special. In fact, she'd spent most her life wishing she was ordinary.

She could go back, of course, back to school and to Jen and Lucas, back to Aaron, but how long would that last? The Archangels had already found her once, and something told Ellie they were likely to do it again.

Perhaps she should take their offer and forget about all of this.

Lacey's face filtered into her mind. What would happen to her if she gave up her powers? Nothing good, that was for sure. No, after all that Ellie had seen in the other realm, from the angel who'd taken her prisoner, to Mithra's cold expression when she slit the girl's throat, she knew she would have to return.

The more she thought about it, the more she questioned her return to the human realm. She wished she could ask Shiro for advice, but she was too embarrassed to talk to him. Besides, Ellie had no idea where he had gone. He was probably mad at her, and with every right.

Ellie had left campus and neared Aaron's apartment, but doubt made her steps falter.

Leaving Aaron was the hardest thing she had ever had to do, and she remembered everything, every little detail. How he had looked lying on his carpet, his face relaxed and happy, his arm stretched across the space where Ellie had been, the cut in his eyebrow, and the gold in his hair.

Could she do it again? Could she leave him a second time?

She stopped, causing the man behind her to crash into her back, but Ellie hardly noticed. A sharp pull at her heart caught her attention. She could sense him, like there was an invisible band tugging at her in the right direction. Closing her eyes, Ellie let the pull guide her.

Ellie didn't know how long she walked, but when she opened her eyes, there he was.

She dashed behind a parked car and stared at Aaron, hidden in plain sight. He laughed with someone Ellie didn't recognize. A tall, broad-shouldered man who looked like he belonged in the army with his head shaved and muscular frame visible through his shirt.

Beside him, Aaron looked happy, happy and safe.

It hurt to be that close to him and not run to him, to touch and kiss him. But now that she was there, Ellie couldn't move. It wouldn't be fair to do that to him, to show up just to leave again. And he was clearly fine, which had been all she had wanted to know; at least that was what she told herself. Ellie didn't want to admit, even to herself, that part of her had hoped to find him curled up in a dark corner, longing for her. Perhaps he never had felt the way she did. Maybe her love had affected him like Israfel said, but suddenly, it didn't matter anymore. She loved him and he was happy, which was all she could ask for. And most importantly, he wasn't being kept in a dungeon and tortured by the Archangels.

Goodbye.

Ellie stood and allowed herself one last glance, but Aaron snapped his head up and met her eyes.

Crap.

Ellie turned and moved down the street, trying hard not to run. Perhaps he hadn't seen her. She could have been anyone.

"Ellie!"

She winced; no such luck. Ellie hurried her steps, desperately looking for a way to escape, but a hand clasped her shoulder. She spun around.

"Ellie?"

Silence, then, "Hi."

To be shut out from Ellie's mind had hurt more than Shiro could have imagined. But then again, he should not have listened to Israfel when he had told him to hide the truth from her. Shiro knew her every thought and feeling, he should have trusted his instinct, knowing that hiding the truth about Aaron would only make it worse.

At first, Shiro hadn't been surprised when Ellie told him about the nightmares, but when they only got worse with time, he began to worry. What if there really was something wrong? He'd decided to ask Israfel for advice.

From the way you describe it, it sounds like he is her true love.

There weren't many who could talk to Shiro, so he had been surprised when Israfel had first touched his mind with his own. Hayyel had been an Animal Protector when he lived, so Shiro took their connections for granted, but he found that he liked talking to Israfel. The angel held much wisdom, and Shiro wanted to learn.

True love?

I forget sometimes that you are still young, even with the wisdom of your people. True love is one of the purest bonds there is. It is often mistaken for infatuation, but it is so much more than that. True love runs deep within you, an unbreakable bond connecting you to another person for the rest of your life, even after death. Those who have experienced it often describe it as if a part of them always missing, even when they had life partners or lovers, they always felt a pull at their heart. A pull towards their true love.

I have never heard of this before.

Shiro was always annoyed when he didn't know things. The fact he had thought Ellie's shields were fine still haunted him. After all, he was her Guardian. He should be able to protect her and teach her these things.

It is not a common thing. I have only ever known two for they are as rare as Empaths. Israfel pushed his glasses up his nose. *If she dreams of him hurting, it is quite possible it is the truth. I am amazed she was able to leave him at all; it might be because of her powers.*

But we must tell her. The fire had long since died, and Shiro had looked over at Ellie's sleeping form with sadness in his eyes.

No. You do not understand. If she thinks he is in danger, she will not be able to stop herself from going back to him. The pull on her heart will torture her until she does. And we need her here, focused.

How Shiro wished he hadn't listened. But it had made sense at the time, and Shiro knew this would've happened either way. *She wouldn't be mad at you if you'd told her*, a small part of him whispered.

He sighed and continued his walk through the campus grounds.

What he had said about the portals were true. It did take a lot of energy to create one and it was much easier to use an old one; once a portal to another world had been opened, they never really closed. Left was a shadow that could be called into the light again at will.

But Shiro had also hoped that seeing Jen would somehow help Ellie. She wouldn't let him in, but perhaps Jen would have better luck.

Shiro strolled around aimlessly, lost without Ellie, but he knew he needed to give her time. Ellie and Jen hadn't even noticed when he had left. He had used unnecessary strength to portal out, but it was worth it if Ellie found some comfort.

Suddenly, shadows fell around him, and towering trees replaced the open grounds, darkness fading out the light. Shiro had been so deep in thought that he hadn't noticed until it was too late.

Coming to an abrupt halt, Shiro realized he was no longer in the human realm. But he had not traveled by portal, either. Sniffing in the air, he could smell the forest around him, and something else. Something unknown but still familiar.

Shiro whipped his head to the right as a twig snapped behind a tree. Baring his teeth, he let out a low growl, daring whoever it was to show themselves.

A tall shadow stepped out from behind the trunks. Shiro had never seen an Archangel, but from Ellie's memories, he recognized the hooded figure immediately. He looked much like Michael with a beautiful face, menacing eyes and black hair that contrasted with his pale skin.

"I am Metatron. I have brought you here, Guardian, because you have broken the law. It is the Council who appoints Guardians, we and no one else. You have acted against our will; therefore, you must be punished."

Shiro folded his ears, trying to shut out his painful voice. But like Ellie had described it, the Archangel's voice was of both mind and mouth.

I was sent here by the Creator herself. I am her child, and I answer only to her.

"Dare not speak to me about the Creator. We are her will and she is ours."

There was such force in Metatron's voice Shiro sank to the ground, his paws desperately trying to cover his ears. He knew he had no chance against Metatron, so he needed to act fast.

He had noticed that angels and humans had the tendency to talk a lot before they made their move, telling their victim their evil plan before they killed them. Now, Shiro was a Guardian, but he was still a dog, and dogs always went for the kill.

Without another word, Shiro lunged at Metatron, his teeth closing around his throat, cutting Metatron's rant short. The Archangel screamed and tried to tear Shiro off his body. It felt like biting into fire; Shiro's mouth burned, but he still held on.

A sharp, stabbing pain in his left side finally caused him to let go. Metatron had embedded a knife into his flesh, and crimson covered his white fur.

But Shiro wasn't the only one who was hurt. What looked like liquid fire gushed from Metatron's throat and his face had turned even paler.

"HOW DARE YOU?!"

Shiro did not bother with an answer. With the last of his strength, he opened a portal. He was too weak to travel to another realm, but he hoped he would be able to use an old portal in this world.

Metatron threw a knife as Shiro moved into the blinding maze, but it was too late. Shiro disappeared, and the knife sunk into a tree on the other side.

CHAPTER TWENTY-FOUR

A ARON'S EYES FIXED ON her face, boring a hole in the side of Ellie's skull.

They were back at his apartment. Ellie had almost stopped dead in the doorway as she'd entered the once neat and tidy home. It was now covered in dirt. Clothes were strewn everywhere, and dishes filled the kitchen sink. It looked like a tornado had crashed through it.

Ellie's heart twitched. She had done this to him.

"Ellie, look at me," Aaron whispered.

But Ellie didn't meet Aaron's gaze; she wasn't sure she was ready to face those eyes yet, scared of what she would find. Hurt and betrayal, without a doubt, but she was even more afraid of what she might not find. Ellie wanted to remember the way he *used* to look at her, full of love. She couldn't bear to lose that image.

"Ellie, please."

"I – I can't," she gasped, her throat closing up.

It had been a bad idea going back there, especially as she couldn't stay. The horrors she'd seen in the angelic realm were etched in her mind, she knew she couldn't leave them.

A hand gently touched her chin, tilting her head up. She closed her eyes.

"Please look at me. You owe me at least that." While sadness laced his tone, there was also a hint of anger.

Ellie swallowed.

She had no right, but she looked inward, letting her fire fill her so she could read his emotions. It wasn't fair to do that to Aaron, but she couldn't face him without knowing if he hated her.

Ellie no longer needed to lower her shield to read people, but an eternity passed before she found the bright light that was Aaron. Everything that made him Aaron pulsated, his kindness, his sense of humor, and his capacity to love unconditionally.

But those feelings were tinted with fear and concern. He felt older to Ellie, like he had aged several years since the last time she'd seen him.

With another deep breath, Ellie focused her power to find the answer she dreaded. But there was nothing there but love. Untainted, unquestioned, unconditional love.

Ellie released her power with a gasp. Finally, she looked into Aaron's eyes.

"You still love me? But I left, I – you should hate me."

At first, Aaron's expression held shock, then love, and then, anger.

"I don't hate you, but I'm still mad at you." His hand dropped from her chin. "Imagine waking up alone on the floor, *naked,* not knowing what the hell happened to you. I thought you were kidnapped or dead."

Ellie's breath hitched, her whisper barely audible. "I'm sorry."

But Aaron wasn't done. He jumped from the couch and passed the room, a fire raged in his eyes as he gazed down on her. "You're *sorry*? Great. You are one of the most selfish people I have ever met!"

At that, something in Ellie snapped. "Selfish?! Leaving you was the hardest thing I have ever had to do, and you call me *selfish*?! I was trying to protect you! You have no idea what is going on, and I don't want you to get hurt."

"Selfish," Aaron said, his features hardened. "There are two people in a relationship, and you don't get to decide what I can and cannot handle!" Suddenly, all the anger appeared to drain from his body. "Don't you think I know there is something different about you? Something you are not telling me?"

Ellie swallowed hard. A part of her had always hoped that Aaron blamed her weirdness on her personality, but how could he not have suspected? She was dead, then she was not, she'd moved like ten feet in the blink of an eye, and she freaked out when he called her an angel. Who wouldn't have suspected something?

"The way you always seem to know what I feel, even before I feel it," Aaron continued, taking no notice of Ellie's inner turmoil. "That day in the park, I know you were dead, I just know it, but then you weren't. And I swear that sometimes you are speaking to Shiro, and if he's an ordinary dog then I am the Queen of England."

Aaron slumped onto the couch and Ellie sat next to him. He took one of her hands into his, and his eyes sparkled with unshed tears as he looked into her eyes.

"But I was okay with that, I was okay with it because I loved you and figured you needed more time to trust me. And then you were gone."

Loved. Past tense. Ellie had to stop herself from flinching. How could her power have been so wrong? Perhaps the longing *she* felt had imprinted onto him.

It took all her strength for Ellie draw her hand out of his grasp. She lowered her eyes and let her hair cover her face. "I'm so sorry I hurt you. I'll leave you alone, I promise, but know that I have always loved you. I think I loved you even before I knew you. Even if you don't feel the same anymore."

"Of course I love you, what are you talking about?" Real surprise sounded in Aaron's voice, enough to make Ellie dare a glance from behind her hair.

"You said *loved*," she whispered.

For a moment, Aaron frowned, but then it dawned on him. "Because I was talking of something in the past. You tend to use past tense then. God, Ellie, of course I *love* you. I love you so much it hurts sometimes."

"You – you do?" She winced at how meek she sounded, but it didn't matter, not if he still loved her.

Aaron pushed the hair out of her eyes and gently lifted her chin. Then Aaron's lips were on hers. Gently at first, but the kiss quickly intensified. She tangled her fingers in his hair, the strands like silk in her hand.

She was about to completely lose herself in Aaron when he drew back, breathing hard.

"Would someone who didn't love you kiss you like that?" he said in a hoarse voice.

Suddenly, Ellie felt more like herself than she had in a long time. Her lips quirked into a grin and she tipped her head to the side.

"That kiss was a declaration of love? Now I understand why everyone keeps looking at me funny afterward. If only I'd had this information before I kissed Dr. Garner. I will never pass my history class now. Or when I think about it, I might get excellent grades–"

"Oh, shut up." Aaron scowled at her, but his eyes danced with laughter, a welcoming sight.

She winked at him and leaned in to kiss him again. It was meant to be a quick peck on the lips, but Aaron moved forward as she did, and their lips clashed together. Ellie's breath caught in her throat, and she tasted blood in her mouth, but she didn't break the kiss.

Aaron's hand reached under her shirt, his fingers tracing the bumps of her spine, and Ellie's hands made quick work of his jeans button, his shirt already gone.

But Aaron pulled back again, his eyes glazed over and his breathing heavy. Ellie made a sound deep in her throat, sounding embarrassingly a lot like a growl. She wanted him, bad.

"We – we need to talk." Aaron struggled to get the words out.

Slowly, and hopefully seductively, Ellie rose herself onto Aaron's lap. The last thing she wanted to do was talk, and as she sank down, she could tell that Aaron, despite his words, didn't want to talk, either.

Aaron gasped and closed his eyes as she pressed her body against his, his head lulled back against the back of the couch.

"We will. But not now," she whispered close to his ear.

Aaron opened his eyes then, and Ellie realized this must feel like last time to him. But Ellie had no intentions of ever leaving him again.

Sitting back, she tried to reassure him. "I promise I won't leave again. I don't think I could even if I wanted to."

His eyes searched hers

"I believe you," he said at last. "But you still owe me answers. What the hell is going on?"

Ellie ached to feel his body against hers, but he was right. She did owe him answers, but where could she even begin? After all, Jen hadn't believed her.

"It's not something I can explain right now."

"Try," Aaron pressed, waiting.

Ellie shook her head. "There's no time. Look, I need to go."

Aaron's whole body tensed, causing him to shift away from her.

With a frown, he said, "You've only just got here? You literally just promised you wouldn't leave again!"

"I know, but I shouldn't have come back. I forced them to bring me here so I could just see that you were okay, but they need me."

A million questions danced across Aaron's face.

"Look, I'm not *leaving* leaving, I promise. But I have things to do, people who are waiting for me. I'll be back, I promise."

Aaron's muscles relaxed against her, but he left some of the distance between them.

"I'm coming with you." He held up a finger to her lips before she'd even opened her mouth. "No, I don't want to hear it. I accept that you won't tell me what's going on, but you're scared. I can see it in your eyes, I can *feel* it. I won't let you leave again. I'm coming with you."

CHAPTER TWENTY-FIVE

There were only a few photographers outside Aaron's apartment, and they avoided them easily; clearly Aaron had done it before. He muttered something under his breath about people being unable to keep secrets, but Ellie didn't pay it much attention. They had to find Shiro, but once they did, she had no idea what she was going to do. Was she allowed to bring Aaron? *Could* she bring him?

Ellie sneaked a glance at Aaron walking beside her, their hands locked together. He hadn't asked her any more questions, and she marveled at the complete and utter trust he had in her.

His long fingers enclosed her small hand as they walked down the streets of LA. Ellie hadn't felt like this since the masquerade. The security of being encircled in Aaron's arms and the love she had felt had been perfect until Michael had shown up and shattered it.

Michael.

The second she thought of his name, a wave of uneasiness washed over her. The hairs on the back of her neck stood on end, and she started to sweat in Aaron's grasp.

Ellie tried to tell herself they were staring at Aaron, but she couldn't shake a feeling of being followed.

Then.

There.

In the crowd, a hooded figure. It was gone before she could blink, but it was enough.

"Aaron, run!"

Ellie dragged a surprised Aaron after her while screaming for Shiro in her mind. But there was no answer. Where was he?

Aaron pulled on her hand, forcing her to stop.

"Ellie, what is going on? Why are we running? Look, if someone is trying to hurt you, I'll stop them, I – "

"Oh god, Aaron, I've made a mistake. I should never have come back. You don't understand, they will kill you without a second thought." She tried to drag him, willing him to move. "Please, Aaron."

They ran.

As they turned a corner, causing surprised people to jump out of their way, Ellie called for Shiro again. But there was still nothing. She desperately tried to think back to when she'd last seen him, but she couldn't remember.

A lump formed in Ellie's gut as they rounded yet another corner, hauling Aaron behind her. What if something had happened?

It was a trap, Ellie realized. Surely someone as powerful as the Archangels could send her a false dream.

Israfel had been right.

How could she have been so stupid? She had led the Archangels straight to Aaron. Instead of protecting him, she was risking his life.

They turned into an alley and came to halt. It was a dead end. The black walls towered towards the sky, almost shutting out the sun.

Ellie turned to go back, but a long shadow cast across the ground. It was too late. Five hooded figures closed in on them, pressing them against the far wall.

"Your time is up, Eliana. It is time to give up your powers."

"No." Ellie breathed, bitter with hatred.

"Ellie, what–"

Ellie stopped breathing as the five hooded figures turned their attention toward Aaron.

"Eliana, he is human. A human will never understand you, never love like you wish. They are only capable of destruction."

"You know nothing of love!" Ellie screamed. "You destroy everything you touch. It is your fault I have to leave all I love behind. It is your fault that little girl is dead, that I never got to know my parents."

Her eyes gleamed with tears, but she refused to let them drop.

"Your father lost his way. We released him with his death to help him find peace. But it is not too late. You can see him. If you come with us."

Ellie wanted to cover her ears and shut out Michael's voice, but it rang in her mind as well as her ears. She knew he was lying, but a part of her desperately wanted to believe him.

Throughout her life, Ellie had only ever wished for one thing, and she wished for it every chance she got. With every birthday candle, every fallen star. And that wish was always a chance to know the man whose memory she shared. To know her father.

"Ellie, what is going on?" Aaron pleaded.

Ellie's heart twisted.

"Why does he call me human like it's an insult? And I thought your parents died in a car accident?"

Ellie looked at Aaron, not remembering when she had moved

to stand in front him, trying to shield him with her body. A ray of sunlight found its way into the alley and lit up his hair like a halo. He was beautiful.

"Aaron, I should have told you everything, I'm sorry."

"I am bored now. You had your chance, Eliana. Either you are with us or against us and that, I cannot allow."

Ellie turned her head to look at the faceless shadows. People were passing by on the street, clueless to what was happening in the alley. In fact, none of them even glanced into the darkness. But having frozen an entire room of people, hiding an alley entrance probably wasn't much of a stretch for the Archangels. Ellie looked at them with longing, willing one of them to see her. But no one did.

"I will come with you, if you let him go. Promise me you'll leave him alone," she said instead.

"You have my word; I swear on the Creator."

Ellie turned back again, her eyes begging Aaron to run, but he shook his head. "No, Ellie. I won't leave you."

She believed him. But the decision wasn't up to him and there was nothing he could say or do that would make Ellie risk his life even more than she already had.

With a sudden urge to be near him, Ellie threw herself into Aaron's arms and touched his lips one last time. Before he could react, she pulled back and tried to smile at him, to reassure him.

"They won't hurt me. But I couldn't live with myself if something happened to you. Don't come looking for me, okay?" She raised her delicate hand and placed it over his heart. "Be happy and remember that I will always be with you, here."

Aaron froze in place as Ellie went to stand with the Archangels. One of them grabbed her arm, his fingers digging into her skin, causing her to winch in pain.

She tried to convince herself that this wasn't the last time she was going to see him, but she doubted she would survive once the Archangels got what they wanted.

"You did the right thing, Eliana," Michael said in a flat tone. He then turned to the angel on his right. "We are leaving. Kill the human."

There was no time to think, no time react. Ellie's eyes widened as a bolt of pure light left one of the Archangel's hands. It traveled through the alley, illuminating it with an uncanny light, and pierced Aaron's body. His scream echoed against the walls, a sound Ellie didn't think she could ever forget. Aaron's pain rolled off him in waves, pressing against her shields.

"NO!"

With strength Ellie didn't know she possessed, she yanked her arm from the Archangel's grip. He reached after her, but she was already running.

The light disappeared, and Aaron stood for a second, looking down at the bleeding hole in his chest. Slowly, he sagged to his knees but before he could hit the ground Ellie caught him. She gently lowered him to her lap, desperately calling his name.

Blood poured from Aaron's chest, soaking Ellie's clothes, but she didn't care.

"You promised! You swore on the Creator!"

"The Creator understands that every once in a while, a lie must be told for the greater good."

There was nothing good in Michael's heart anymore, nothing that could save him.

Ellie cradled Aaron's head in her lap, whispering his name.

"Oh god, please. Aaron, please open your eyes."

Pain made her voice thick, and her heart threatened to break, nothing holding the pieces together anymore. And then there it was, a small flicker of Aaron's eyelids.

"Aaron!" Relief overwhelmed her as Ellie's strength faltered.

"You're alive, thank–"

Aaron's chest shuddered, and blood spluttered from his mouth. Ellie gasped as the red liquid trickled down his chin. He was dying. Ellie could feel his energy slipping away from her. But what could she do?

Without a second thought, she let her shields fall and poured her power into Aaron. But her magic wasn't healing magic, at least not of the body. Ellie's desperate attempt was useless, but she still poured more energy into Aaron as a voice made her seethe.

"You brought this on yourself, Eliana. Let him go, he is dead."

"He is not dead!" she screamed with desperation. "Don't die, please don't die. I've only just found you."

But Aaron rasped with difficulty as his skin turned cold in her arms.

"He will be shortly. But I am afraid we do not have time to wait."

Another bolt of light shot towards her, causing Ellie to react on instinct. Everything she felt, all the pain, hatred, despair, and every ounce of love for Aaron surged out her like liquid gold, creating a sphere around them. Michael's ray of power smashed into it with such force the earth beneath it cracked, but the shield miraculously held.

Michael frowned through the shimmering gold of her shield. There was another shudder in the shield as he tried again, but it stayed intact. Ellie's heart leapt with triumph momentarily, but Aaron's sharp intake of breath, ripped her back to reality.

Aaron's eyes were open and fixed on hers. He was too weak to speak, but with Ellie's walls down, she felt every one of his emotions. The same pure, untainted love from earlier, but also fear. Fear for himself and fear for her. Fear of dying.

Words could never convey the deep love she felt for him, so she filled Aaron with it, baring her innermost feelings to him, showing him her heart. His eyes widened as he stared at her, tears prickling down his face.

Slowly, unbearably so, Aaron's lips curled into a small smile. He shuddered, and then became still. A motionless shell in her arms.

Ellie screamed in pain as Michael launched more force at her shield. Her agony flooded into the shield and made it pulse like a beating heart. But Ellie couldn't find it in her to care. She felt detached as she clutched onto Aaron's now limp hand.

Her shield had started to use her life energy to keep itself sustained, and as the last of her love for Aaron filled the barrier, a sound like thunder boomed.

Something snapped then, deep inside of Ellie. She roared in torment as the shield exploded. Ellie covered her eyes as pure light filled her vision, dropping Aaron's hand in the process. The pain ripped through her like fire, and as she slowly doubled over Aaron's body, she saw five black marks. Five black marks where the Archangels had stood.

Tears and blood soaked her shirt as she lay over the dead body in her lap. Aaron filled her every sense, but memories were slowly slipping away. One by one, they faded before her inner eye, and no matter how much she tried to grasp them, they fell like water between her fingers.

Ellie clung to Aaron's body, desperate to hold on, but soon, only the sound of his laughter remained, and Ellie's grasp loosened. Too soon, the final note rang out and Ellie was left in the silence.

Suddenly, Ellie couldn't remember why she was crying. There was a hole where something had once been, but whatever it was, it was out of her grasp now, even though the pain continued to flow through her veins.

Someone screamed in the far distance, filling the deafening silence that surrounded her. Before Ellie realized it was her own voice, a flash of light blinded her, and she was hurtled through the veil between worlds.

DAMP GRASS TICKLED ELLIE'S cheek as she lay flat on her back, something weighing her down. She pushed herself up onto her elbows to see what held her in place, ignoring every ounce of pain. But to Ellie's surprise, there was nothing there. Nothing more than her shirt and pants covered in blood. She searched her body for injuries in a panic but came up empty.

The blood wasn't hers.

Ellie sank back down in the grass and tried to concentrate on her breathing as she scanned... Hayyel's meadow. There was something different about it. Unlike before, it was silent.

"Get up, Eliana."

Ellie jolted at Hayyel's voice as he stood in her line of vision. He looked like he always did, every feature sharp, his dark green eyes set under straight eyebrows. He stared at her, impatient; nothing new there, either.

"I can't," she stammered.

Ellie's dry lips were cracked, filling her mouth with the coppery taste of blood. She could only imagine how she must look.

"You can and you will. Now get up."

Ellie's chest burned with anger. He was such an arrogant ass. Her sudden rage gave her the strength to lift herself into a seated position. She drew in a sharp intake of breath as her insides screamed in pain.

"See? That wasn't so hard. Now I want to know what you think you are doing?"

"What *I'm* doing? What the hell are *you* doing?" Ellie still couldn't place where all the blood was coming from; actually, she couldn't remember much at all. "You just left me with an impossible choice and then you were gone. I haven't seen you since that night. And whose blood is this?"

Hayyel looked at her with real surprise in his eyes. It wasn't often he let his emotions show, in fact, Ellie could probably count the number of times on one hand.

"You don't know?" Ellie shook her head. "It is Aaron's. He died."

"Who?"

Images flooded back to Ellie: the hooded figures, bolts of light and a dead body on the ground. Something flittered by at the far ends of her consciousness, a whisper of a memory, but it dissolved as she tried to grasp it.

"Are they dead, the Archangels?" she asked with alarm.

"No," Hayyel hesitated, like he was waiting for her to fall apart. He spoke next with unusual softness. "They do not die that easily, but you have certainly shaken them. But Aaron, he is dead."

Ellie wondered why he looked at her like she would break. "Look, I have no idea what you're talking about, and I don't care. I want answers and I want them now. Why don't they just kill me? What do they want with my powers?"

It looked like Hayyel was about to argue, but then the usual hardness returned to his eyes. He nodded. "I am glad you are finally beginning to see what is important. The Archangels fear you."

"Fear me?" Ellie found it hard to believe the Archangels feared anything or anyone.

"Yes, you. But it is more than that. I believe they think they have found a way to break the barrier, but in order to do so, they need the power of an Empath. It is the only reason I can think of that explains their desperate search.

"As for what happened, I believe you projected your shield outside of your body. I've never heard of an Empath being able to do such a thing, but I suppose it could be possible. When you arrive at the resistance, you need to find another Empath and ask them–"

Wait, what?

"But you said there were no other Empaths?"

For a few seconds, Hayyel's eyes flickered with panic, but he suppressed that feeling away. "Eliana, do not be so naive. Did you really think you were the only one who managed to stay hidden from the Council?"

Ellie's mind was spinning. She rose to her feet with a groan. Hayyel had told her she was the *last* one, the *last* chance. But now he stood there, telling her he'd been lying. A small glimmer of hope lit in Ellie's mind, but she was careful not to let it grow too big.

She steadied herself and tried to keep her voice even as her anger boiled beneath the surface.

"But what about the prophecy? You told me I was the last one, that I was the *only* one who could do it. I gave up my life for this, and now you're telling me that there are others like me." Her voice rose with every word and by the end, what little control she had over her emotions were out the window.

"Oh, wake up, Eliana. The prophecy could have been about anyone. I said what I needed to say. You needed to believe it for you to understand what you must do. But all the prophecy actually says is that an Empath will bring down the Archangels, not who, not how and not when. Personally, I do not believe in it, but that is not what matters, they believe in it, and after today, they will be sure it speaks of you and no one else."

Ellie opened her mouth to argue, but Hayyel held up his hand, silencing her.

"I know you, Eliana. I can see the hope in your eyes. But you cannot go back to your old life, not now."

"What do you want me to do then?" she screamed. Every time there was even a glimmer of hope of Ellie having a normal life, bad turned to worse. "You tricked me! You promised I would learn about my past if I learned to control my powers, but I've learned nothing! Then you told me I was the only one, and now you're saying that was a lie. But because of you, everyone believes I'm the one. So basically, I'm screwed!"

"You need to go back." Hayyel looked blank, completely unaffected by her anger. "It was reckless of you to come back to the human realm, and it seems you have paid the price. I hope this will teach you not to do something similar again."

Jen's face flashed before Ellie's eyes, followed by Lucas, but she sensed that Hayyel was referring to something else.

"I can take you to Shiro's last portal. My powers are not what they once were, and I can no longer travel as I please. This journey will drain me, and I will not be able to come to you again should you need me. Not for a long time. Once you reunite with Shiro, he can take you to the resistance."

Then Hayyel bathed in light, leaving little room to argue. Ellie hurtled through the blinding maze, and when she stumbled out, she tried to regain her balance.

"That hurt, you know!" she screamed into the night, but Hayyel was already gone. And he probably wouldn't have cared even if he had heard her.

Ellie grimaced as she stretched her aching body, then scanned her surroundings. She was standing in a field. The stars were the only thing lighting up the night sky, the moon almost completely gone. The wind pulled on her hair and the smell of smoke drifted towards her. A black pillar ascended into the sky in the distance.

Where am I? she thought as her eyes adjusted to the darkness, then she noticed something laying in the grass.

His white fur was a stark contrast against the dark ground.

Shiro, thank god. When you didn't answer, I thought something had happened to you. I'm so sorry about before, you were right.

But Shiro didn't move. In fact, Ellie could barely sense him.

Shiro?

TEMPTATIONS OF THE PAST

Ellie closed the distance between them and sank to her knees. She placed her hand on Shiro's side, but his fur felt sticky and matted. She withdrew her hand and inspected her fingers. They were covered in something.

Blood.

CHAPTER TWENTY-SIX

"I SEE LYING IS STILL a talent you wield with great skill."

Hayyel sighed and sank into the grass of his meadow. "I lie to keep her safe, is that no longer your wish?"

"You and I never saw eye to eye, did we?" the presence spoke, a hint of laughter clinging to his words.

The air pulsated as the presence disappeared from all around him and concreted its power into a shining sphere before him. Hayyel normally had full control of the meadow; his sanctuary, permitting or denying access as he pleased. But there was nothing he could do about the presence before him. He was sure it was another way the Creator had decided to punish him.

"Would you be so kind and tell me why you are leaving Eliana when she needs you the most?" The voice was clearer now that its energy was gathered.

"I have taught her all I can for now. She needs to learn on her own who to trust and what steps to take next, otherwise she will never be the savior we need," Hayyel answered, hoping his companion wouldn't press the matter.

"Is that the only reason?" the voice taunted him. "I would have thought the striking resemblance to her mother would bother you?"

Hayyel bit back his reply. There was truth in those words, and he would only look the fool if he tried to deny them. Both of them knew what he had done. He could not hide there.

"Ah, no reply? Well, let us hope for all our sakes you know what you are doing." The sphere was beginning to fade, the presence once again filtering through the air. "The Creator chose you to guide my daughter, but trust me in this. I will not stand by and watch you fail again."

OH GOD. BLOOD WAS pouring from Shiro's body, and Ellie quickly spotted the source, a knife embedded in his side.

Shiro? Shiro, what happened?

Ellie's mind felt oddly empty. Whether or not she had noticed it before, Shiro was a constant presence in her mind even when he wasn't physically by her side. Even when she'd shut him out, she had still sensed him in the back of her mind. Now there was only a mere whisper.

Then, as fear gripped her, a murmur. *Ellie?*

A wave of relief washed over her as Shiro slowly lifted his head. *Shiro, what happened to you?*

It was Metatron.

Metatron, a member of the Council. He was meant to watch over children and was a Corporal Protector.

Ellie silently thanked Hayyel and his endless lessons on the Council and their powers.

You – you need to find Israfel and Lacey.

I need to help you. Ellie felt useless. She had all of this magic but could do nothing to help Shiro. But thankfully, she knew who could. Israfel's haunting melody played in her mind, and a determined look crossed her features.

Once I've stopped the bleeding, we need to find Israfel. He can heal you.

Ellie, no. I'll slow you down. Shiro tried to sit up but whined as he fell back against the ground.

I won't leave without you, so you can either help or this will take longer. Your choice. Besides, I have no idea where I am.

Shiro seemed to struggle with himself for a while.

Fine. You'll have to pull out the knife.

Ellie immediately reached for the handle.

Wait! Once you do, I will probably lose consciousness from the pain. I think this is the portal I used when I first came here. The village shouldn't be too far; I will show you the way. Then I'll help you track Israfel and Lacey.

Ellie's mind filled with images, and using his thoughts, Shiro guided her across the field, through a small forest, and over creeks and streams until she mentally envisioned the village. But it was not burnt down. It looked like it had when she had first seen it, bathing in sunlight. These were Shiro's memories.

Got it.

Afraid of losing her courage, Ellie gripped the knife and pulled it straight out. Shiro whimpered and thrashed, then became alarmingly still. The only thing keeping the panic at bay was the fact that Ellie could still hear his whisper in her mind. He looked so small, reminding her that he was still only a puppy.

Ellie tore her bloody sweater off and then her shirt, which had faired only slightly better than the sweater, but it was the best she could do. Using her teeth, she tore it to shreds and tied it around Shiro's wound to the best of her abilities.

She put the sweater back on and tried to think. Shiro might be a puppy, but he was almost fully grown and far too heavy for her to carry for any longer periods of time. The village was probably a day away by foot, and that was time Ellie didn't have.

Ellie was still worried about connecting with animals after what had happened in the park, but she had spoken to the animals in the village, and nothing had happened. Besides, her powers were stronger than before.

The chill of the night crept upon her, and a decision had to be made.

Her empathic powers and animal powers were not the same, but they both dwelt in the everlasting fire. Unfortunately for Ellie, Hayyel hadn't spent much time teaching her how to use them.

Closing her eyes, she slipped into meditation. At least that part had gotten easier every time she did it. Calling upon her power took longer than it usually did though. Because of her weariness, she had to coax it, gradually pulling it around herself like a blanket.

Then it became even more difficult.

In the park, she had seen where to send her powers, but now, she had no idea where to even start looking.

I might be of some assistance, two-legger. The sudden voice ringing in her mind, as clear as Shiro's, threw Ellie out of meditation, severing the connection. Bewildered, Ellie looked around to find the speaker, but there was nothing living in the field other than Shiro and herself.

There was of course the real possibility she was going insane, but she didn't have time for that right now. Not when Shiro's breathing shallowed by the second.

A little wearier, she closed her eyes again and let her powers fill her, surround her.

You're a jumpy one, the voice said, sounding female and old. It reminded Ellie of Shekinah, and she smiled.

I'm sorry, I didn't try to contact you, so I was a little surprised. Who are you? Where are you? Ellie thought as she stood up and searched the field again.

I am Seed, and I'm down here. Ellie looked down at her feet and saw a tiny brown forest mouse with its front paws balanced on top of her shoe.

Oh, hi. I didn't see you down there. But I still don't understand how I'm talking to you.

Seed tilted her head to one side, reminding Ellie of how Shiro looked when he didn't understand something. Her heart skipped a beat.

Dear, your thoughts were so loud I couldn't help but hear them.

Oh, I'm sorry. This was by far one of the weirdest conversations Ellie had ever had, and as of late, she'd had a few. A whimper drew her attention back to the task at hand. *You said you could help me?*

Yes, I heard you needed a horse. A lot of the horses from the place where the two-leggers lived ran away when the heartless came. Some of them are sleeping over there – Seed tipped her head to the right, indicating a copse of trees – *and I'm sure they would help if you asked them.*

With her profound thanks, Seed scurried off, melting together with the ground. Ellie sat down again, trying to sense any of the horses. But she was growing tired. Her magic was nowhere near restored from her encounters with Michael, and as she looked inside, the fire was burning dangerously low.

With a sigh, Ellie stood from the crossed-legged position she had taken on the ground.

As carefully as she could, Ellie lifted Shiro's cold body, trying not to cause him any more pain. More than desperate, she started to make her way towards the copse of trees.

Trying to navigate the field turned out to be a much more difficult task than Ellie had first thought. The treacherous ground was full of holes and big tufts of grass, so she kept stumbling and tripping as she hurried, carrying Shiro's body. He was heavier than she expected a puppy to be, and he had lost the fluffy white fur he'd had the first time they'd met, but he was still young, despite all of his wisdom and strength. He had also definitely had too many sweets lately, Ellie would have to watch that in the future.

If he has a future.

Tripping over yet another tuft of grass, she shook her head. No, she refused to lose him. All she had to do was get to him to Israfel and everything would be fine.

She finally neared the trees and stopped. They loomed over her, casting dark shadows in the even darker night. Like the trees in Heywood forest, these felt wrong to her. They twisted unnaturally around her, making her take a step back. She heard the horses before she saw or sensed them. Squaring her shoulders, she stepped forward.

WHEN SHIRO WOKE, HE was laying across the back of a black horse who carefully trotted up a small gravel path. Destruction surrounded them, blackened trees lining the road on either side. Ellie thought it looked like an avenue of death.

The sun was still rising in the east, coloring the sky pink, but the beauty was lost in the eerie landscape. Up ahead, the pillar of smoke Ellie had smelled earlier towered towards the sky, making the air harder and harder to breathe.

Once she had found the horses, it hadn't been hard convincing them to help her. The two horses, one black and one white, tossed their heads and their nostrils flared. Ellie didn't blame them. Her eyes were beginning to water, but not only from the smoke. Something touched her cheek, and she looked up to the sky. White flakes were descending from the sky, reminding Ellie of snow. But the flakes were not cold, they were soot from the burned village.

Or what had once been the village.

They had finally reached the outskirts of the outer town, and if the destruction on the road had been bad, this was a disaster. The small houses that once teemed with life were now charred down to the ground, only blackened skeletons remaining.

You made it, Shiro's strained voice whispered. Ellie only nodded in response.

Something in the ruins had caught her attention, and she slid down from her horse, Pure. She whimpered slightly as she hit the ground. Riding bareback for hours had done nothing to help her sore body.

Shadowrunner halted beside them, Shiro a stark contrast against her black coat. Ellie carefully meandered through the debris until she spotted what had caught her eye. Under what looked like a door, a small doll lay in the dirt. It was scorched at the edges, but somehow, it was mostly intact.

Ellie quickly turned away from it, fighting back nausea. Nothing indicated that the doll had belonged to the girl who had been killed, but that made little difference to Ellie.

Ellie, what is it? We can't stop. Shiro's voice sounded far away.

She swallowed thickly. *I know, but I don't know what to do now. Let me down. I –*

Shiro was slowly drifting back to sleep. With a jerk, he woke again. *I can track them.*

No, Shiro, you need to rest. I'll – I'll figure it out, don't worry. She forced herself to sound confident, but it was hard to hide your fears from someone who was in your mind.

Ellie, you need help, you can't track.

He sounded so weak in her mind. Ellie went over to Shadowrunner and gently stroked Shiro between the ears. *I'll be fine, sleep.*

Maybe, maybe just for a little while.

Shiro went silent in her mind as Ellie stood there, stroking his soft fur. When Ellie was sure he was in deep sleep, she let herself panic. She had no idea how to track things. Hayyel had tried to teach her the basics once, but Ellie had been distracted by something Shiro had done, ignoring him. A mistake she regretted now. She might have been able to use her powers like she had done in the village, but they were next to non-existent. Shiro wasn't the only one who needed to rest.

Deciding, she guided Pure through the ruins, Shadowrunner following close by. Thankfully, the wind blew away from the forest, and once they reached the first trees, the air was easier to breathe.

Ellie continued through the forest until she found a small stream where the horses could drink. She opted out of washing herself, not wanting to pollute the water with the grime that covered her.

Carefully, she lifted Shiro from the horse's back and planned to find some rope to tie him. They couldn't continue at such a slow pace, but Ellie had been afraid he would fall off. Sleep pressed on her like a heavy blanket.

I'll figure it out tomorrow, she thought as she curled around Shiro, trying to use her own body heat to keep him warm.

While the forest offered more protection than the burnt down village, it still wasn't safe to light a fire. Ellie sent a silent prayer to Heywood forest to keep them safe, then let sleep take hold of her.

Pure nudged Ellie's cheek and startled her awake. Ellie groaned and threw her arm over eyes, wishing for just one more minute of sleep.

In her dream, she had been out drinking coffee with Lucas,

discussing the different stars and their meanings. Ellie liked Sirius while Lucas preferred Polaris, arguing its clear sovereignty against all other stars. It was something they'd often done, and a discussion Ellie had never thought she would have longed for with such fierceness.

But she was not in a café with Lucas, so she pushed him to the back of her mind.

"Time to go, huh?" Ellie mumbled, both horses staring at her as the sun's rays warmed her face.

She couldn't hear whether the horse replied. She could still only talk to animals other than Shiro when in meditation. That was something she would have to ask about later. Hayyel was unwilling to train that part of her power, but perhaps Israfel would feel differently. After all, he had helped her with her shield.

Ellie shook her head, trying to clear it. She would not learn anything else from Israfel. As soon as Shiro was well again, she was going home. Clearly, she was not the only who could save the angels, and Ellie wanted her life back. As soon as Shiro had enough strength to portal, they would go. The Archangels could have her powers for all she cared.

A part of her hoped she would still be an Animal Protector even if she renounced her empathic powers. She liked being able to talk to Pure and Shadowrunner, but if that was the price to pay for her life, then she would pay it. Surely her powers couldn't be as strong as Hayyel thought, and another Empath would be able to fulfill the prophecy. At least, that was what Ellie tried to convince herself.

Pure gave her another nudge, making Ellie sit up with a grunt. While the pain was slightly better than the day before, it still hurt. Sleeping on the ground hadn't helped matters, either.

The sun was almost directly above her, so Ellie thought it must be around mid-day. Glancing quickly at Shiro sleeping, Ellie slipped into meditation. While her body may not have been restored, thankfully her power had fared better. The fire stretched toward her, trying to engulf her, but Ellie broke the connection. Pure was still close and he eyed her with curiosity.

"I don't suppose you know where we're going?" Ellie asked.

Pure held eye contact for a few seconds longer, then bent down to munch the damp grass.

"I guess that would have been too easy," Ellie said to no one in particular.

Her clothes were damp, and she shivered despite the sun. It had been late autumn when she left the human realm, but Ellie wasn't sure the season worked the same here. Ellie pulled her sweater closer around her and tried to think.

She had no idea where Israfel and Lacey were, nor had she paid any attention to where they were going when she traveled with them. She had basically been a backseat passenger not bothering with which road they'd taken. She could walk around aimlessly, hoping for the best, but Shiro did not have time for even one misstep.

Feeling miserable and useless, Ellie's eyes welled. Shiro's presence in her mind was even weaker than the day before, even though her shirt had stopped most of the bleeding.

Darkness was clouding her mind, and all Ellie wanted to do was give in to it, but a glance at Shiro had her square her shoulders, determination settling over her. She would save him.

Ellie remembered Hayyel telling her that different elements could strengthen her powers, saying it had something to do with angels being creatures of Earth, therefore connected to the land from which they were born. Unfortunately, her mind had wandered as he described how to tap into that power. Ellie cursed her short attention span once again.

But it was a start and the only idea she had. After all, she was in a forest.

How much earthier could something be? she thought as she closed her eyes and let her powers fill her. She tried to concentrate on finding some sort of power to grab, but every time she thought she had something, it slipped through her fingers like water.

Shiro whimpered and Ellie gritted her teeth, diving deeper into her fire. There had to be a way.

Gathering her strength again, she made as if to grab the tendrils of power running though the ground, but a small caress on her mind shifted her focus. It felt like a whisper of hope. A hope she recognized. A hope Ellie had woven herself and filled with everything she had held dear. A hope now silently asking for permission to guide her.

She took a deep breath and allowed the gentle presence of Heywood forest take hold of her. At once, the tendrils she'd been trying to grab turned into streams of power flowing though the ground and the air around her. After a small nudge from the forest, she emerged into one and gasped as power surged through her.

She clamped down on her lip to keep from screaming and ignored the coppery taste of blood. The force of the raw power threatened to overtake her, and everything in her screamed at her to let go, but she stubbornly held on.

As more power flooded though her, she understood that if she couldn't control it, the power would kill her. But Ellie was done with others trying to control her, so she seized the same hope she'd used for healing the Heywood forest and pushed back against the power.

It felt like moving though syrup at first, but for every step she took in her mind, the resistance decreased until the force that had tried to claim her ebbed away. Left was only power.

Ellie concentrated on Lacey and Israfel, imagining them before her inner eye. Israfel's sense of right, his wisdom and soft heart tinged with sadness, and Lacey's carefree spirit, her kindness and courage.

Find them, she whispered, and her mind flew through the forest.

Ellie sighed in relief at the images before her. Israfel strode with determination as Lacey faltered behind him. It looked like she was trying to get Israfel to turn around.

A small warning raced through Ellie. She needed to let go, but the power felt so good. It whispered of true freedom, free of her mortal shell, free to travel the winds and race along the roots in the ground. And for a second, just one second, she wanted that. To just let go. But something warm pressed against her, and Ellie felt Shiro's faint presence in her mind. With a final surge of magic, she pushed free of the powers of the land and returned to her body.

Ellie's eyes fluttered open and she tried to remember how to move her body. The freedom of the earth still lingered like a forgotten promise, and as she glanced down at her hands, she saw they were covered in green vines. The air smelled heavy of the soil beneath her, and longing filled her heart. She had almost let go.

But somehow, Shiro lay pressed against her on a bed of leaves instead of by the horses where she had left him. Ellie sent a quit thank you to the forest before she stood, snapping the vines that still bound her to the earth.

There would come a day when she would let go and finally rest, but that was not today.

She ambled over to Pure and Shadowrunner and placed her hand on Pure's mane, closing her eyes and steading her breathing.

I'm going back to the village. We need supplies.

We will look after your Guardian, Pure's voice rang in her mind. She still felt a thrill as she heard the deep murmur that was his voice but this was not the time to explore things further.

Thank you, she thought, then took off towards the village.

Hopefully not everything had burned.

And for once, Ellie was in luck. She found the rope she needed for Shiro and something that resembled bread in a small house on the outskirts of the village. She didn't dare venture too far in, the focus of the fire having left nothing but destruction. The smoke still lay heavy in the air and the smell lingered in her nose.

At another house, she found a thick blanket she could use as a saddle. She had hoped for a real one, but the stables had been burnt to the ground, leaving nothing but ashes.

Not wanting to linger any longer than necessary, she ran back to her makeshift camp. Both Pure and Shadowrunner were eating grass when she returned, and Ellie hoped they had regained their strength. They had a long way to go.

Now that Ellie had a clear goal, she fought to stay focused and suppress her worry for Shiro, but when she looked at his fragile body in the grass, her concerns threatened to come crashing back.

Forcing her tears back, she lifted him up onto Pure's back this time, trying to give the horses as much rest as possible, and carefully bound him with the rope. A piece of cloth served as a bag to hold the bread.

Shadowrunner lay in the grass for Ellie to climb onto her back. She slung her leg over her side and grimaced at the way the horse felt between her legs. She kicked the horse's sides and let the forest swallow them.

CHAPTER TWENTY-SEVEN

It had been almost two days since Shiro had been awake and lucid enough to speak. Ellie was trying to help him in any way she knew, but he had only gotten worse. He had been running a fever since last night, and with the fever, the nightmares had started. Shiro had thrashed around, whining until Ellie had used her power to soothe his thoughts, but her mind and body weakened with exhaustion.

They had stopped by a small stream after several hours of riding. Ellie lay on her knees, drinking greedily. Her stomach ached from having nothing but bread for the past days, and that had run out last night as well.

Finally feeling satisfied, she took the damp cloth from Shiro's forehead and went to soak it in the stream. She'd seen in movies that they always put a damp cloth on the sick person's forehead and figured it was as good an idea as any. Of course, she had no idea whether or not that applied to dogs or magical Guardians, but she needed to do something to not feel completely useless.

She barely slept anymore due to the fear of Shiro dying during the night, and with no food, it was getting more and more difficult to regain her strength. Plus, she was sending a steady tendril of power to Pure and Shadowrunner, and they were making quick work of her energy. But she doubted she could keep it up much longer.

Ellie took the damp cloth over to Shiro again and wrung it out, causing small droplets of water to fall into Shiro's half open mouth. He looked so small tied to Shadowrunner's back. Ellie looked over at Pure by the water and sighed.

Despite her efforts, the horses were exhausted too, their heads hanging near the ground. They were drenched in sweat that Ellie did her best to clean off with grass, but they needed to rest, even with the energy she was feeding them.

Ellie hated to drive them this hard, but she didn't have a choice.

Ellie was scared. She had thought she would have caught up with Israfel and Lacey by now, but there was still no sign of them.

A sound drew Ellie from her musings. It was faint, but there. Pure rose his head from the stream, his ears pressed to the back of his head. Whatever it was, it frightened him and Shadowrunner, who had gone stiff under her hands. A murmur of voices reached her ears. They seemed to be moving in their direction.

"Shit," Ellie mumbled as the voices drew nearer.

As quietly as possible, Ellie led the horses away from the stream and into the thicker part of the forest. Whispering for them to stay there, she made her way back towards the stream. There were people there, well, angels, and not the nice kind. Ellie hid behind the bushes and strained to hear what they were saying.

"They stopped here," a dark voice said.

"Yes, and the horses are getting tired, look here. Sweat. I have no idea how they've managed for this long, but it's only a matter of time before we find them."

The second voice was much lighter and a little squeaky, a voice Ellie would recognize anywhere. It was the angel who had almost raped her. She threw her hand over her mouth to stifle the scream that threatened to burst out, but not in time.

Both angels turned towards her hiding place.

"Did you hear that?" the first one asked.

The other angel nodded and advanced towards the bush. But Ellie was already running. She stumbled through the woods, falling but refusing to stop.

"Over here! She's over here," their voices yelled from behind her as Ellie continued to run.

They caught up with her by the horses.

"Well, well, well, look who it is." The first angel smirked at Ellie as he neared her. The second angel gripped his shoulder, holding him back and he looked back in confusion

With some satisfaction, Ellie could see fear shining in the second angel's eyes.

"Don't go near her, she can mess with your head. Make you see things, *feel* things that aren't real." His voice shook slightly as he spoke.

"She's a little girl, how much harm could she do?" the angel answered, clear disbelief in his voice.

"She's not just a girl, she's an Empath. *The* Empath."

Understanding dawned on the first angel, and he smirked even wider. Ellie was terrified. She had no way of fighting them off, and she doubted her powers would be able to cause much damage, either. They didn't know that though.

"Don't come any closer and I won't hurt you," she said in a surprisingly steady voice. The angel who had tried to rape her took a step back, holding up his hands, but his companion didn't move.

"Oh, please, Nathaniel, don't be a coward. She is clearly exhausted; I doubt she could hurt us much more than she could a fly right now."

Ellie turned cold with fear; they were calling her bluff.

"Now be a good boy and help me grab her."

Nathaniel edged towards Ellie, and when nothing happened, he seemed to regain his composure and grinned triumphantly. "Not so cocky now, are you, without your powers and your little friends. He isn't looking all that good over there, maybe we'll leave him here for the wolves."

Ellie's back was pressed against Shadowrunner's side. There was nowhere left for her to run. She thought she heard a low growl behind her, but she didn't dare to turn around.

I'm so sorry, Shiro, she thought and closed her eyes, waiting. But nothing happened.

Carefully, she opened one eye, and then the other. Before her were seven gray wolves. They bared their teeth at the angels who were slowly backing away, cursing.

Nathaniel grabbed his sword as one of the bigger wolves launched at him. He cut at the wolf with his blade, but it skillfully dodged it and bit him in the ankle. Nathaniel screamed and kicked the wolf back.

As the second angel finally found his sword, one of the smaller wolves turned to look at Ellie. It seemed to be pleading for her to run. She only hesitated for a moment. She was scared for the wolves, but she was even more scared for Shiro and herself.

Jumping up onto Pure's back, she let her shields fall and poured her energy into the two horses. They dashed past the two angels with Ellie clinging on for dear life. She could hear the wolves' barks and the angels' screams, but they were far in the distance now. Ellie slumped on the Pure's back, her hands twisted in his mane to keep her from falling off.

Ellie's eyelids felt like lead, and it was almost impossible to keep them open. Once she was certain she couldn't hear the angels anymore, Pure came to a halt and Ellie slid from his back. She crawled over to Shadowrunner, who lay in the grass as Ellie untied Shiro using two stones to cut the rope in half. She was all too aware that she was about to pass out, but they couldn't stop. Ellie only hoped that the horses knew where to go.

Having tied Shiro to Pure's back this time, she crawled onto Shadowrunner and clumsily tied herself to hers. As the horses raced off again, she let sleep overtake her.

"WE HAVE TO GO back. What if she comes back and we aren't there? How will she find us?"

Lacey had to jog beside Israfel to keep up with his long strides.

For someone as old as he, he sure was fast. Lacey of course knew he himself had chosen his appearance, so his age could really be anything. Personally, she didn't understand the angels who chose to age; she for one planned on looking like twenty-five for a long time once she reached it.

"Israfel, are you even listening?"

"Eliana made her decision. She chose the human boy, but the Council doesn't know that yet. We might still have some time, but we need to get to the resistance now."

"What? Time for what? You know as well as I do that we need Ellie," Lacey said as they finally came to a halt. Israfel held up his hand, silencing her. "Don't shush me!"

"Lacey, be quiet."

Lacey opened her mouth to argue, but something about the urgency in Israfel's voice made her close it again.

Gazing into the forest, Lacey tried to see what Israfel was staring at, but she saw nothing. She was tired. Israfel hadn't allowed them much rest and Lacey's feet screamed with pain.

Before she could tell Israfel he was starting to hear things, he dragged her down and behind a tree.

"There, in the trees."

Lacey looked to where he was pointing and realized he was right. Something approached, heading right towards them. She slowly reached for her sword behind her back. If she was going down, she would go down fighting. Israfel's surprisingly strong, bony hand clasped her wrist.

"Not everything is solved with a sword, Lacey," he said, then stood up.

Lacey reached after him, but he had already left their hiding place. With a groan, Lacey went after him, preparing herself for whatever was on the other side of the trees. To her surprise, there was only two tired looking horses, both with something tied to their backs.

"Lacey, help me untie her."

Untie her? What was he talking about? Then Lacey saw who were tied to the horses' backs: Ellie and Shiro.

Almost tripping over herself, Lacey ran up to Israfel who checked Ellie's wrist for a pulse. Ellie was slumped over the horse, who looked about ready to pass out.

The color drained from Lacey's face. "Is she…?"

Israfel shook his head and Lacey let out the breath she'd been holding.

"Now go and help Shiro, he seems to be badly injured."

Shiro was indeed hurt. Actually, Shiro was dying.

ISRAFEL'S MUSIC FILLED THE cave where they had sought shelter, but other than that, it was silent, and dark. Lacey could barely see Israfel across the cave, but the darkness didn't seem to bother him at all.

Ellie lay with her head in Lacey's lap as the music filled her. Israfel had told her to let her sleep, but Lacey was dying to know what had happened.

She gave Ellie a gentle nudge and she started to stir. "Ellie?"

"Shiro. Help Shiro." The words were muffled and desperate.

"Israfel is working on him, but he says he cannot fully heal him, only keep him stable. He needs an Animal Protector." At this, Ellie appeared to relax. "What – what happened? With Aaron?"

Ellie finally managed to focus her eyes on Lacey. "The Archangels happened."

"By the Creator," Lacey whispered. "How did you escape? And Ellie, where is Aaron? What happened?"

Ellie's forehead creased and she seemed to search her mind for something.

"I don't–" she struggled. "Who's Aaron?"

At this, Lacey drew back, her eyes round. "What do you mean *who's Aaron?*"

Ellie's eyes squeezed shut and her face twisted with pain.

"It hurts," she gasped, cradling her head with her hands.

"Shh, it's okay. We're here now," Lacey soothed her until Ellie's face relaxed again and her eyes opened.

Ellie turned her head in Lacey's lap. "Why is it so dark in here?"

"Israfel says it's too dangerous to light a fire, and the clouds are covering the moon. But Ellie, Aaron–"

"Lacey," Israfel's warning tone rang out from somewhere in the darkness. "Eliana needs her rest. I am sure she will tell us what happened when she is feeling better."

Ellie was already drifting back to sleep, and Lacey let her head fall against the cave wall, closing her eyes. Something was definitely wrong, and she would find out what it was.

CHAPTER TWENTY-EIGHT

"Sir, if you would follow me, please." Lucas almost jumped at the sound of the woman's voice.

"Oh, yeah of course, sorry," Lucas said with a smile. "I was lost in thought."

The woman smiled kindly back at him and led Lucas out of the waiting room. They passed several elderly, but none were the one Lucas had come to see.

Ellie had been gone by the time Lucas got to her dorm. He had tried to convince Jen that what Ellie had told her was the truth, but she wanted no part of it. After that, both Ellie and Aaron had disappeared.

Raziel Jadon was his only lead and Lucas had become obsessed. He messed up his exams but couldn't find it in him to care. His soul focus was to find Raziel, the author of the book, who up until now had been helpful.

But when no new passages appeared for several days, Lucas tried a different strategy. He stopped trying to find Raziel Jadon the *person* and searched for Raziel Jadon the *angel* instead. Of course, it wasn't difficult to find information on the angel Raziel.

Raziel was said to be the angel of secrets, and his book, *Sefer Raziel HaMalak,* supposedly contained all secret knowledge, a book currently safely tucked in Lucas' backpack.

He was also referred to as the keeper of all magic, and while Lucas held little faith in the Bible, it was quite possible the stories in it originated in some long-forgotten truth.

"Here we are," the woman said, gesturing into a small room. "She is a sweetheart, but sometimes struggles with her memory, so be gentle."

"Of course," Lucas agreed and entered the room.

It was a small bedroom, painted in soft pink with not much more than a bed and a small table by the window. A woman sat there in a wheelchair, and Lucas tentatively made his way over.

"Uhm, hi. Are you Anabelle?"

One late night at the library, a paper cutout had fallen from one of the books he'd been reading about Raziel and his origins. It was from an old newspaper, so the page had turned yellow over the years. He had been about to discard it when a name caught his eye. *Anabelle Stone, together with mister Jadon.*

That was it. The paper was in such bad shape you couldn't make out the rest of the text or the faces on the picture, but Lucas clung to it like a lifeline.

This was the third Anabelle Stone Lucas had visited, hoping to learn what they knew of the mister Jadon in the picture. But it had been difficult to find this one, since she had married, changing her surname to Rogers.

"Oh, hello dear, do I know you?" It was clear this woman had once been beautiful, her face now soft from old age. But her eyes shone with an intensity Lucas found hard to explain.

"No, but I called earlier. I had a few questions about an old acquaintance of yours," Lucas said tentatively.

"Ah, yes. You wanted to know about Raziel." The woman nodded, and Lucas held his breath. He had only asked about Raziel's last name.

"You – you know him?" It was hard to contain his excitement.

"Why yes of course. We were in love once, you see. But I knew he wasn't mine to keep, he belonged to the heavens."

Lucas had taken a seat by the table, but he was practically bouncing in it now. "Why do you say that?"

"He was an angel, you see. He told me from the start, it was his duty to find a human to love and someone to bear him a child every hundred years. Unfortunately, I was not able to give him what he needed, and while it crushed us both, he had to leave."

Anabelle was looking out the window and her gaze glazed over with sadness.

Lucas was just about to ask her to tell him more when her penetrating stare met his. "You look just like him, you know. I am glad he found someone who could give him a son."

Lucas' mouth fell open and he held up his hands in protest. "I'm sorry, but you are mistaken. My father is very much human, his name is Henry."

"You are Raziel's son. Of this, I am sure. And this," she reached into a pocket and pulled out a small piece of paper, "is yours. Raziel gave it to me should I ever need him, but I can see that it is you who is in need."

She thrust the piece of paper into Lucas' hands and turned back towards the window.

"What is this? Please, you have to tell me more." Lucas' fragile grip of reality was starting to falter.

The woman turned her gaze back towards him and smiled warmly. "Hello, can I help you?"

The clarity that had filled her eyes just seconds ago was gone. Whatever had happened, Lucas was suddenly sure there was nothing left for him here.

"You already have," he replied and made to leave. "Thank you."

As he hurried through the retirement home, thoughts were running around in his head. He couldn't be Raziel's son, that was crazy. He had a very real, very human father. He tried to convince himself of this over and over until he was outside again.

There, he finally glanced down at the small piece of paper that lay crushed in his fist. The black ink was a stark contrast against the creamy white and there was only one line written on it. An address.

CHAPTER TWENTY-NINE

Ellie gazed up as they entered through the enormous gate. The wall encircling the entire city was built of stone and it looked like it had stood there for hundreds of years and would still stand after hundreds more. The city itself was built around and up a hill, the streets circling up towards the castle at the top.

"The city was built long before the resistance got here," Lacey told her as they made their way along the brick road. "The higher up you got, the richer the people who lived there were. So, this was called the Pit, which is where the poor used to live. Now soldiers and those who work at the castle live down here. The scholars and merchants live on the next level, and you have the leaders, knights and knights-in-training up at the castle. We're going to the castle."

Ellie wanted to say it didn't sound like much had changed since before the resistance had taken the city, but she held her tongue.

They entered through the east gate and Ellie marveled at how thick the wall must be. People were coming and going through the city in a steady stream, but thankfully, none paid them much attention. She had been worried people would stare at her like they had in the village.

Lacey, sensing her worry, leaned over Pure's back and whispered, "This is Tamrin. They've seen much weirder things than you."

Ellie threw her a grateful smile as Shadowrunner continued through the streets, avoiding stepping on people with great care. She looked more than happy to follow Israfel's big half-breed, Steadfast, who led the way.

Ellie had called him to her once she'd felt better despite Israfel's protests, arguing they would reach Tamrin much faster on horseback. He had only agreed after they found a large enough village to buy proper saddles, stating that no man his age should be forced to ride bareback.

They were finally though the gate when Pure tried to snatch an apple from a stand nearby.

"Ey, keep that horse off my goods!" the woman behind the counter shouted with a rude hand gesture.

Lacey quickly gathered the reins and bent down, speaking soft words Ellie couldn't hear in Pure's ear until he settled down.

Unlike Shadowrunner, who was timid, Pure had to test every boundary there was. Lacey had fallen in love with the warm-blood immediately, claiming he was a free spirit like herself, supposed to run free. Ellie had not argued; she was content with the much calmer Shadowrunner.

Once they had left the narrow streets of the lower level behind them, the road became wider, and they made faster progress. Unlike the pit, which was made up of small houses almost lying on top of each other, the higher levels were filled with manors. The higher they got, the bigger and more flamboyant the houses were. Ellie had never seen anything like it. Some houses looked ancient, and others looked like they had been taken straight out of the Hollywood hills.

"Are all of these people scholars? And the houses, they look so… different." She had almost said *human*.

Lacey was scowling at Pure, who seemed intent on eating an old man's beard, and answered absently. "Yeah, well some are rich people who fund the resistance. Pure, stop that. We do not eat people."

Pure gave one more defiant tug on the reins before he fell back behind Israfel and Steadfast, next to Shadowrunner and Ellie.

Lacey sighed and looked over at Ellie. "I know I said he was a free spirit and all, but sometimes… And the houses look different because they were built in different times. You see over there…" Lacey pointed to a street turning left before them. "Those are some of the oldest houses in all of Tamrin, except for the castle itself, of course. Then angels have added as the city grew."

"Have you been here before?" Ellie supposed new houses were no weirder than anything else.

"Yeah, once. When we left my brother, Chehon, here to train. He doesn't have a gift like I do, so he stayed here to train to be a knight, and I followed Israfel who taught me to use my powers. That was ten years ago."

Ten years was a long time not to see your only family.

"Do you miss him?" Ellie wondered.

"Of course I miss him, all the time. But we both trust that the Creator has a plan for us and that we are where we are supposed to be. And see, she led me to you."

They had reached the end of the wealthier district now and the road opened up, leading straight up to the castle. Tower after tower reached towards the sky, a lot of them in different designs like the houses below. It seemed the castle had grown with the city. The gates opened up into a stone courtyard, a single tree in the middle. Rows of pillars held the second floor, leaving passages with different doors below it. Ivy clung to the pillars, giving the hard, unyielding rocks warmth.

A man was walking up to them as Israfel came to a stop and dismounted Steadfast, Lacey and Ellie following his example. The man was short and muscular, his hair a disarray of golden locks like he had just woken up. His clothes, blue trousers and a puffy-armed shirt with a golden tunic over it, were wrinkled. He bowed and spoke to Israfel.

"Master Israfel, I have been instructed to tend to your horses. Miss Lacey's brother, Master Chehon, has offered to show you to your rooms." As he said this, a second man crossed the courtyard in long strides.

"Lacey!"

The man, who Ellie assumed must be Chehon, had none of his sister and mothers red hair. Instead, it was a warm blond, cut at his shoulders. His muscles bulged beneath the thin white shirt he wore with black pants. But as he neared, there was no mistaking that they were twins. He had Lacey's eyes and her soft and open features. Right now, his smile lit up his entire face, his eyes sparkling in the sun.

"Chehon!" Lacey was already running towards her brother, throwing her arms around him. Chehon picked her up and spun her around laughing.

Ellie stood back and watched them with a little sadness. She missed Jen and Lucas. They may not share blood, but they were as close to a family she had ever had.

Lacey and Chehon were walking towards them, and Ellie quickly blinked the unexpected tears away. She would not cry.

"Ellie, this is Chehon, my baby brother. Chehon, this is Ellie."

Chehon laughed and looked lovingly at his sister. "You are like three minutes older." He then turned towards Ellie, and to her surprise, he took her hand and kissed it lightly. "I am Chehon, son of Haroth. It is indeed a pleasure to meet you. I hope your journey was pleasant?"

Ellie could describe their journey with many words, but pleasant was not one of them. "Eliana Whitmore. And I am afraid I must ask for your help at once. My dog, sorry, my Guardian, is injured and needs a healer."

Chehon looked past her with a look of concern. Shiro lay over Shadowrunner, sleeping. Israfel had kept him asleep throughout their journey, and while he had not gotten any worse, he hadn't gotten any better, either.

"Of course, Jonathan here will take him to the healers. Jonathan."

The man who had offered to take their horses stepped forward again.

"Of course, right away, Master Chehon."

Jonathan gathered the reins of all three horses and started towards the far end of the courtyard. Ellie tried to follow, but Chehon stopped her.

"There is nothing you can do for him right now. He will be fine in the hands of our healers." When Ellie still hesitated, Chehon gently put his hand at the small of her back, guiding her in the other direction. "Please, you must be tired. Allow me to show you to your rooms."

"If Chehon says Shiro will be alright, he will be, Ellie," Lacey said as she followed her brother and took Ellie's hand. "Now come on, I desperately need to wash up and so do you."

Ellie knew she was right. Shiro needed to heal before they could leave. And while she had changed her clothes, she was still covered in dirt. The cold water from the different small streams hadn't helped much, and Israfel hadn't allowed them to stay in the only village they'd passed long enough to wash.

With a sigh, Ellie let the twins lead her away, casting a worried glance over her shoulder after Shiro.

The door closed behind Lacey and Chehon, leaving Ellie in silence. The twins had chattered non-stop through the castle, recapitulating everything that had happened during their extended time apart in great detail. Lacey would be staying in the same hall as Ellie, a few doors down, but apparently, Israfel had his own rooms where he lived while in Tamrin.

The room was small but nice. There was a four-poster bed in the middle, taking up most of the space. A small vanity table with a mirror was on the wall opposite the bed and there was a closet in the far corner. A door led to a small bathroom where Ellie realized modern plumbing had not made an appearance in this realm.

Walking back into the main room, Ellie headed to the closet where she discovered it was full of clothes obviously meant for her. She closed it, not giving it much thought and walked over to the window. Below was a courtyard, much similar to the one they had entered but with a small fountain in the middle instead of a tree.

Ellie longed to throw herself on the bed, but looking down at herself, she refrained. She didn't want to ruin the beautiful linens.

Hopefully, Shiro would be well enough to portal within a few days. They could portal back and Ellie could return to her life. Perhaps it was enough to convince the Archangel's that she had no interest in their wars and prophecies anymore. Let that be some other Empath's problem.

Chehon had showed them where they could clean up, so Ellie hurried to the women's bathtubs and thanked her lucky stars when she found them empty.

There were three larger tubs that looked like they could hold up to twenty people, but Ellie opted for a smaller one at the far back. She shed her clothes and sank into the hot water with a grateful sigh, letting it rise to her chin.

Ellie washed quickly and was about to close her eyes and let the warm water sooth her sore muscles when murmured voices entered the bathing area. Sinking even farther, she hoped they wouldn't see her.

"She's only a girl, and half *human*." The word sounded like an insult, filled with disgust. "I saw her when Master Chehon was showing them around, she looked dreadful. Master Chehon should really find better company. I wouldn't hold my breath waiting for her to save anyone."

"Well, I heard she can't even control her powers yet."

Ellie sank a little deeper in the water. It didn't take a genius to figure out who they were talking about. The nasty comments continued for a while. The girls in the other tub giggled at her own incompetence. They played at every self-doubt she had ever had, but then the conversation took an ugly turn.

"And oh, did you see her Guardian? Half dead, he must have skipped out of training. If he had had any dignity, he would have died, at least then he wouldn't have to live with the shame of failing."

That was it. Ellie rose from her bathtub and dried herself, dressing fast. She felt the girls' eyes on her but refused to turn around until she was sure all of her clothes were in the right place. Holding her head high, Ellie stalked over to their bigger tub.

There were four of them, all beautiful. Long hair, big eyes and, from what Ellie could see below the water, they weren't exactly fat either. Ellie's cheeks blushed as they stared at her, mouths slightly ajar. They actually looked like guppies in a pond and the mental image gave Ellie the strength to speak.

"Shiro fought Metatron and survived. Not only did he survive, but he hurt Metatron in the process. Have any of you faced and *fought* an Archangel? No? I didn't think so. Well, when you have, you can get back to me and we will discuss whether or not Shiro failed. That is, if you do return, which I very much doubt you would."

Before any of them could think of an answer, Ellie turned on her heals and stalked out of the bathing area, trembling all over. Once she was sure they couldn't see her any longer, she sank to the ground against the cold stone wall.

She felt alone. Jen wasn't there to drag her to her feet and tell her to get a grip. Lucas wasn't there to make her laugh no matter how horrible she felt about herself. And now, not even Shiro could offer her comfort. She supposed she could try and find Lacey, but it wasn't the same. Besides, Ellie wanted Lacey to have time alone with her brother.

Another soothing memory flickered at the far reaches of her mind, but as Ellie tried to seize it, the memory faded, lost.

Collecting herself off the ground, Ellie wandered the halls aimlessly. The castle was huge. Long corridors opened before her with tapestries on the walls and some sort of crystals embedded in the stones at even intervals, lighting the entire castle with a low glow. There were no windows to be seen, so Ellie assumed she must be deep within the castle, lost, but it didn't matter. Every once in a while, voices sounded from somewhere nearby, but they never came close to her, something she was grateful for. If everyone thought of her like the four girls in the bathtub, then Ellie wished to have as little contact with the residents as possible.

She turned another corner and instantly recognized the corridor in front of her. She had entered what Chehon had pointed out as the healing wing. Even if she couldn't talk to Shiro, his mere presence would give her comfort.

Ellie took the next turn with more purpose. *He must be in there somewhere,* she thought as she looked down the corridor of doors stretching before her. She couldn't exactly barge through every one of them, so taking a deep breath, she listened for Shiro. She soon found him at the end of the corridor.

As quietly as possible, she slipped into the dark room and froze. Shiro wasn't alone. There was a woman sitting on the edge of the bed where he lay. The bed was huge, obviously meant for a human, Shiro almost disappeared in the duvet.

Ellie was taken aback but managed to stammer out, "I – I'm sorry. I didn't think anyone would be here."

The woman on the bed stood and smiled kindly at her. She was tall, taller than Ellie, with chestnut brown hair and kind eyes. There was something regal about the way she carried herself.

"You must be Eliana. Shiro has told me a lot about you."

Ellie couldn't hide her excitement. "He talked to you? He's okay?"

"He did. His injuries were grave and had become infected, but I have healed him to the best of my abilities. Now he needs to rest and allow his body to heal itself."

Ellie gazed down at Shiro with a smile, tears of relief pouring down her cheeks. He would be fine. They could go home.

"You should be resting as well. I heard what you did, pouring your energy into your horses. It surprises me that you didn't heal Shiro yourself, you are obviously powerful enough."

"I," Ellie faltered. But there was no mockery in the woman's tone, only kindness. "I can't heal things, animals I mean. I'm just an Empath."

"What you did with the horses was not the power of an Empath. That was from your father." Ellie's interest was piqued. "He was a powerful Animal Protector, having power over not one species, but all of them."

"My father, you knew him?" Ellie asked, but the woman shook her head.

"I've heard *of* him; all Animal Protectors have."

Ellie wanted to ask her a thousand questions, but the woman moved towards the door.

"You should rest. It will take a long time before your powers are restored."

"They're fine, it only took a few days. But my father–" Ellie almost stumbled over the words in her eagerness to ask about her father, but she was interrupted by the woman's surprise.

"Really? That is strange. Usually, when you empty yourself like you did, it takes weeks, sometimes even months, to restore it."

There was something else in the woman's eyes now, respect and fear. Fear of what, Ellie didn't know.

Ellie opened her mouth to ask her what she meant, but the woman swept from the room. "I will see you at dinner, please try and rest."

I didn't even get to thank her, Ellie thought, and the woman hadn't introduced herself, either.

With a sigh, she lay down beside Shiro. His fur was white and shining again, the blood and dirt had been washed away.

Ellie decided to stay with Shiro for the rest of the afternoon, giving him strokes and attention while he slept.

As the hours passed, a million thoughts swirled around in her mind: the sudden fear in the woman's eyes, her father, her own powers. Then there was the same feeling as before. Something that filtered in and out of the far reaches of her mind, but she couldn't grasp it no matter how hard she tried. A sense of wrong filled her, but it was a feeling Ellie couldn't place.

The sound of a bell startled Ellie from her thoughts, and Shiro's ears twitched in his sleep.

"It's okay, Shiro, go back to sleep," Ellie whispered against his fur.

At that moment, Lacey appeared in the doorway of the infirmary. "Ellie, we need to get ready for dinner. Didn't you hear the bell?"

"I did and I ignored it," Ellie mumbled. "I'm not hungry, okay?"

Evidently it was not okay because Lacey dragged her out of Shiro's room, not letting go until they'd reached Ellie's own room.

Pushing Ellie inside, Lacey went straight for her closet where she pulled out a dress. Urging Ellie to hurry, she forced her behind a screen to change, ignoring Ellie's loud complaints.

"No way, I'm not wearing this," Ellie protested when she looked in the mirror.

The floor length dress was a deep green with thin straps holding it up on her shoulders. It could have been fine, but Ellie hated wearing dresses at the best of times, let alone ones that revealed her entire back, cut low enough to barely cover her ass.

"Why can't I wear pants?" Ellie whined.

"Because this is dinner. We might be somewhat caught up with the world outside, but some traditions don't die that easily. Now sit still and let me fix your hair." Lacey was already wearing a beautiful midnight blue dress.

Her dress allows at least a bra, Ellie thought grumpily as Lacey pulled her hair.

Twenty minutes later, they were walking down the stairs into a great hall. Tables filled the room in a complicated pattern with one table at the far end, standing on a small dais.

Oh, please god don't make me sit up there, Ellie thought when she spotted Israfel sitting in the middle of the table, speaking to a man to his left. Ellie couldn't make out his features more than his brown, shoulder length hair and beard.

The high ceiling was full of spectacular chandeliers casting a pleasant light on the scene below. Angels were already sitting at most of the tables, a low chatter filtering through the room.

The chatter stopped though when they entered, and Ellie swallowed as almost everyone turned to stare at them.

Dread heated her chest at the thought of walking through the room, and when Chehon stood and waved for them to join him, she could have kissed him.

Lacey and Ellie hurriedly navigated the room and sat at the bench next to Chehon.

Before anyone could say anything, the man Israfel had been

talking to stood up. "Now that we are all here, let us eat."

Ellie's cheeks flushed. Being late was obviously not an option here.

Two doors at the back of the room opened and angels spilled out, young men and women carrying tray after tray of food. They all wore the same blue and gold clothes that the man who had taken Pure and Shadowrunner had worn.

The chatter had started up again, but Ellie still caught glimpses of people staring at her. It was unnerving to say the least and made it difficult to eat.

"So, Lady Eliana, did you find the rooms to your liking?" Chehon leaned around his sister, catching Ellie's eyes. His smile was contagious, and Ellie found herself smiling back despite herself.

"Yes, they were fine, thank you. And please, call me Ellie."

"Ellie it is. And you call me Chehon."

Ellie was about to say she hadn't planned on calling him anything else, but changed the subject instead. "Who is the man Israfel is talking to?"

"That's Lord Theron, he is the leader of the resistance. And beside him is his wife, Lady Cassiel."

Ellie hadn't noticed that a woman had taken her seat next to the man sometime during the meal. She looked now and laid eyes upon the same woman who had healed Shiro. But why would someone so important help her? She was about to ask when another young man came up with another course.

"How much do you people eat?" Ellie exclaimed.

Laughter rang out around the table and Ellie wanted to disappear. *Me and my stupid mouth.*

"When you have trained all day, you learn to appreciate food in a way you never thought possible," Chehon answered.

He was still leaning over Lacey despite her obvious irritation. Not even her constant poking him with her fork seemed to bother him.

Finally, Lacey threw her hands in the air.

"Seriously, why don't we just switch places so you can talk undisturbed."

It was obvious to Ellie it was meant as a hint to get Chehon to back off, but he blinked in surprise at his sister. It seemed he had forgotten she was even there.

"Oh, thank you, sister dear. That would be great." Standing up, he moved his plate with him as Lacey muttered under her breath. She scooted over the bench nonetheless and immersed herself in her food. "Now, where were we?"

"You were telling me about your training. Lacey said you were training to be a knight?"

"Ah yes. Indeed I am. We all are actually," he said, nodding around the table. "Anyone can become a knight here if they wish to. Not a lot do, however. The training is long and hard. A lot of angels only train to become soldiers, to be part of the army."

"Anyone?" Ellie asked. "Even girls?"

"Of course. There are not as many girls as boys though. But it is allowed."

A third man spoke up then. "Some of the girls are the best in our class."

His muscles flexed under his shirt as he bent forward. Ellie quickly averted her eyes, hoping the dim light would hide her blush. Damn these angels and their perfect bodies.

His blond hair fell into his eyes as he pointed behind Ellie and whispered, "You see that girl over there, she is amazing. Her beauty alone would kill a man, but when she picks up a sword, you don't stand a chance."

Chehon rolled his eyes at him. "Sebastian has it in his head that Lady Eleonore is in love with him, which is apparently why she keeps knocking him over the head in the practicing ring. Personally, I think she just likes to hit things; she is as cruel as she is beautiful."

Ellie looked behind her at the girl Sebastian had pointed out. She was beautiful. Her blonde curls were bundled on top of her head, exposing the delicate skin of her neck. She wore a pale pink dress that clung to her lean body, as if it had been painted onto her. A pendant rested between her breasts, which were spilling out of the dress. Her blue eyes met Ellie's for a second, and she turned cold. It was one of the girls from the bathtub. Ellie quickly returned her attention to her plate and began poking around in her food.

Sebastian was not done, however. "She is not cruel. And you," he said, pointing his fork towards Ellie, "you're the Empath, you can make her fall in love with me."

Chehon shot him a look across the table. "You can't create something from thin air, you know."

A carrot came flying across the table, hitting him in the face.

"Hush you, I am talking to Ellie." Sebastian's blue eyes fixed on her, filled with hope.

Ellie's hands started to sweat and she looked around the table. Everywhere, she was met by a pair of hopeful eyes, even Lacey's. She felt like a dancing monkey, everyone waiting for her to show them her tricks.

"I'm sorry, I can't."

"Oh, come on. Of course you can. At least tell me how she feels, I'm sure she loves me."

"No, you don't understand."

"You're *the* Empath, this is only one tiny favor," Sebastian continued relentlessly.

The color drained from Ellie's face. They all thought of her as either useless or all-powerful. Neither were options she preferred. But none of them understood what it was like to feel someone else's soul, their emotions. It was intimate and draining.

"I need some air," Ellie said and stood up.

She had forgotten she was sitting on a bench, so when it didn't move with her, she fell backwards, hitting the stone floor with a *thud*.

Both Lacey and Chehon moved to help her, but Ellie scrambled to her feet and ran out of the room. Giggles followed her out as the door closed behind her.

The doors she pushed through led out into a garden that had grown wild with no one tending to it; forgotten. The sky above was dark, clouds covering the moon.

Ellie hugged herself when a gust of air ripped at her dress. The rain hung in the air and strands of her hair escaped Lacey's updo. Ellie took a deep breath, letting the cool night air caress her lungs.

"Ellie!"

Running steps were closing in on her, and Ellie thought of running, but really, what was the use? Instead, she turned and faced a slightly out of breath Chehon.

"Damn it, you're fast." Ellie raised her eyebrows and he quickly added, "I mean, not for a girl or anything, but for someone running in high heels and a dress."

Ellie sighed. "What do you want, Chehon?"

"I wanted to make sure you were okay and apologize. Sebastian is the nicest guy, but he doesn't think."

"Apology accepted."

Ellie turned back towards the garden and started to walk. Chehon was at her side almost immediately. Strangely enough, Ellie didn't mind the company, and they walked side by side for a while, going deeper into the gardens wilderness.

"It's hard, huh?" Chehon broke the silence.

"What?"

"To be an Empath," Chehon explained. "To feel what someone

else feels, their deepest secrets. I couldn't do it, and I wouldn't want anyone to do it to me, either. You should have the right to your own emotions."

They had reached what must have been the heart of the garden. An overgrown pond lay in the center of a small round space with benches adorning the sides. The rain that had threatened to fall earlier came down in small droplets, and Chehon swore.

"You must be freezing. Here, take this," he said and gave his green jacket to her.

Beneath it, he wore a thin white shirt with lacing at his chest, tucked into black leather pants. Ellie was cold, so she gratefully slipped it on. It was still warm from his body heat.

"Thank you."

Chehon smiled at her, and she wanted to tell him she would never use her powers on him if he didn't want her to, but a strangled cry in the near distance cut her short.

"What was that?" she asked instead.

Chehon looked concerned. "I don't know. But there shouldn't be anyone here but us. This garden is part of the old castle and isn't used." He crept towards the sound, his hand on the sword hilt Ellie hadn't even notice he was wearing. "Wait here, I'll go check it out."

He had only gotten to the other side of the pond when Ellie caught up with him.

"Don't tell me what to do," she hissed.

It was darker in this part of the garden with no crystals lighting up their path anymore.

Chehon's white teeth flashed as he grinned at her. "Well then, by all means come along."

Then he was off, moving soundlessly through the thickening vegetation. Ellie hurried to follow, doing her best to keep quiet.

Before long, they reached the far end of the garden where a high wall encircled it. Following it, they made their way until Chehon came to a sudden halt, causing Ellie to stumble into him, but he didn't budge. In the bushes before them lay two bodies, guards with their throats slit. Ellie stared at them in fear.

With great caution, Chehon stepped over the bodies and found a small hole in the bushes. Ellie tore her gaze from the dead bodies and joined him. Before them, angels were streaming in through a gate that looked almost destroyed with rust. A man in blue and gold seemed to be guiding them.

"Grayson," Chehon gasped, a name Ellie didn't recognize.

Chehon signaled Ellie to follow him back, and when they were hopefully out of earshot, he ran, Ellie close on his heels.

"Chehon," she gasped between breaths. "Chehon, what's going on? Who were those angels?"

Chehon stopped and turned towards her. Ellie took a step back when she saw his eyes. They were filled with anger and fear.

"They were the Fallen. We've been betrayed, and I bet it is no coincidence it happened on your first night here either."

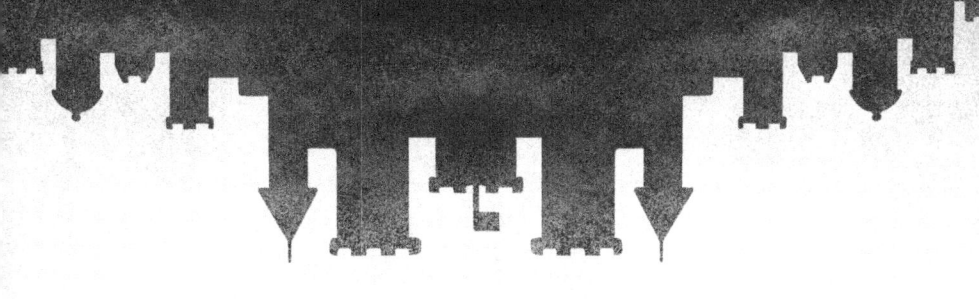

CHAPTER THIRTY

LACEY HAD TRIED TO go after Ellie, but Chehon reassured her she would be fine. Instead, he set off after her and Lacey was left with his idiot friends.

They had been discussing which one of them Lady Eleonore truly loved when the double doors to the great hall had blown open, torn off their hinges. Angels dressed in black were pouring from the opening, swords drawn. A chill ran up her spine as they charged. She was one of the first to react. The angels closest to the doors were still trying to make sense of what was happening, and the black clad angels were almost upon them.

Reaching inside, Lacey found her pond of blue fire. She quickly immersed herself in it, letting it soak her. The burn that had pained her in the beginning of her training was now a welcome tingle.

Opening her eyes, she saw that the first angels had reached the tables. There was no time left to think. Instead, she drew the water from everything around her. Food crumbled as it dried, people's glasses emptied, even the wooden benches and tables dried and cracked. Focusing, she willed the water to do her bidding. It gushed across the floor until it reached the end tables where it rose to the ceiling, creating a wall. It would only last for a few seconds, but it was enough.

Men and women fumbled with their swords, shouting orders to form ranks and to remove the children and old. As the water smashed against the floor, the angels met steel with steel. After that, everything happened at once.

Bolts of fire flew from the entryway, striking angels in their paths and setting tables and benches alight. Lord Theron stood on the dais, sword in hand, shouting orders as lightning crackled around him. A woman near Lacey screamed as the man to her left fell dead to the floor, pierced with arrows.

Lacey darted under the table to reach the fallen man but her legs tangled in her skirt. *Damn this dress,* she thought as she scrambled to her feet. Once beside the man, she unbuckled his sword and cut off most of the fabric of her skirt. Satisfied, she twirled and faced a charging angel.

Not only was he wearing black, but his face had been painted black as well. The man was much larger and slower than Lacey, and she quickly averted his attack, striking him from behind instead, cutting a long gash along his back. That drew a scream from him as he turned and advanced towards her again. Lacey ducked once more, but this time, she attacked before he could regain his balance. With a swift motion of her sword, she pierced his heart.

Immediately, two new angels closed in on her, a man and a woman. But their charge was broken mid-stride when the entire room shook. Lacey wasted no time and struck at the man first, slitting his throat, then turned and let her sword sink into the woman's body until she was close enough to feel the angel's breath on her face. The woman's eyes bulged with surprise as she fell to the floor.

The room quivered again, and Lacey turned in time to see one of the big chandeliers plummet to the ground, crushing angels underneath it. Her temporary distraction earned her a blow to the arm, and she winced in pain. She turned to see Sebastian kill the angel responsible, and she gave him a quick nod before descending on a new target.

"Shit," Chehon swore as they took a sharp left turn.

He held his sword in his right hand, and it was dripping with blood. This was the third time they had been stopped on their way to the great hall, and Ellie could hear screams and the clatter of metal in the distance.

Chehon quickly shoved her behind him as the two angels advanced on him. He was drenched in sweat but still moved with lightness as the first angel attacked him. Chehon dodged the blow and slashed at the angel's side with his sword. The angel got his sword up just in time and Chehon's blade only grazed him. But Chehon was relentless as he attacked again, swiping his sword in a wide arc above his head. This time, the angel dropped to the floor, dead.

"Chehon!" Ellie's warning cry had Chehon turn just as the second angel stormed at him from behind.

A look of surprise crossed Chehon features, almost like he had forgotten he was even there. It lasted only for a second, then Chehon swung his sword, backing the angel up against the wall. Their swords locked and the much larger angel tried to force Chehon to his knees.

Ellie could do nothing but watch as Chehon's muscles trembled with the effort. Then, with what looked like only a small flick of his wrist, Chehon sent the angel's sword soaring though the air. Before it could hit the ground, Chehon buried his own blade in the angel.

"Chehon, are you alright?" Ellie managed, her voice quavering

Chehon still stood bent over the dead body, breathing heavy.

Taking three deep breaths, he stood up and pulled out his sword.

"I hate killing," he said as he wiped his sword the best he could on the clothes of the angel at his feet.

His face was unreadable, and Ellie itched to use her power to hear his emotions, but she refrained. Had she not just thought she would never use them on him?

"Come on, we need to get back to the others," she said instead, then added, "and he would have killed you without a second thought, so yeah."

He smiled a little at that. "Is that your idea of a pep-talk? Because it isn't very good."

Then they sidled down the endless corridors once again. After taking yet another left turn, Ellie realized that Chehon was not taking her back to the great hall the same way they had left. Instead, they skirted around it.

The screams and shouts were closer now and people were fighting in the corridors. Chehon didn't stop unless forced to, fighting his way towards a set of doors.

Conflicting emotions from all around her pressed on Ellie's shields. Hiding in a doorway, she took a moment to strengthen them, pouring more power through the threads.

Someone grabbed her by the arm. Chehon's face entered her field of vision.

"Ellie, we can't stop!" he shouted over the noise.

She nodded and allowed him to drag her to the door. He closed it behind them and Ellie froze when she cast her eyes on the scene below her.

The great hall had transformed into a battlefield. Everywhere angels were fighting, and not only with swords. Two angels at the far wall were engaged in battle with water and fire. Bolts of flames burst from the fingers of one of them and hit a wall of water suddenly surrounding the other angel. Bodies scattered across the room and the floor was red with blood.

The floor beneath her feet shook as a ripple surged through the room, causing a momentary pause in the fighting. A loud *crack* sounded, and Ellie watched in horror as one of the huge chandeliers plummeted towards the ground. Angels scrambled to get out of the way, but not everyone made it.

The crash snapped Ellie out her frozen state, and Chehon screamed her name.

"Ellie, move!"

They were above the dais, and Chehon was running down the stairs to reach the head table. Ellie caught site of Israfel as he wielded a longsword with great skill, cutting anything in his path. Lord Theron and Lady Cassiel were both stained with blood as they fought the angels in front of the table. A small space before them was beginning to clear as the resistance reached their leaders.

As Ellie descended the stairs, she spotted Lacey holding off five angels on her own, almost dancing as she pirouetted with her sword.

Chehon and Ellie reached them as Lady Cassiel screamed, "Let go of me. I am your Lady, and I am ordering you to let me go!"

"Dear, please. They are our guard, let them do their job." Lord Theron looked tired as he pleaded with his wife.

Israfel was examining a cut on his cheek while the angels closed ranks around their leaders. Chehon and Ellie had reached them now, and Ellie looked in disbelief at the once so gentle Lady Cassiel. The front of her white dress was crimson, and there was a gash across her stomach she didn't even seem to have noticed. Instead, she locked eyes with Ellie.

"Oh, thank the heavens, you are safe," she said and made her way over to Ellie.

There was a sickening thud as one of the angels in the ring surrounding them fell. It was a woman, and a steel pitcher morphed into a makeshift spear protruded from her chest.

Lady Cassiel swore under her breath. "Mineral Protectors."

Another angel had already filled the space, and Israfel knelt beside the woman. He sighed and raised his hand to close her eyes; she was dead.

"Listen to me, Eliana!" Ellie tore her eyes from the dead angel and stared at Lady Cassiel. "You cannot stay here. I don't know how long we can hold them off."

"But–" Ellie protested.

Where would she go? Angels continued to swarm the hall, mostly the Fallen dressed all in black, but Ellie also spotted flashes of blue and gold. The soldiers were joining the battle.

"Chehon." Lady Cassiel beckoned him over from Lord Theron. Ellie presumed he had been telling him what had happened in the garden. "You need to get Eliana away from here. You know of the tunnels."

Chehon shook his head. "No, I want to stay here and fight. My friends, my sister..."

"I understand, but they all know what we are fighting for, and if the Council manages to catch Eliana, then it has all been in vain."

Chehon looked like he wanted to argue but nodded instead. As he started to lead Ellie away, she cast a glance over her shoulder.

Lady Cassiel was pulsating in a green light, her eyes closed. A sudden howl broke through the screams and the clanging of metal and a wolf's grin spread across Lady Cassiel's face.

They reached the top of the stairs from which they had come. Before the door closed behind them, Ellie thought she saw dogs and wolves engaging in the battle.

As they raced down the corridors, Chehon took every turn with confidence, something Ellie truly admired because the place was a maze. The farther away they got from the great hall, the fewer angels they met.

Ellie struggled to keep up with Chehon, her dress not helping matters much. She had broken off the heels of her shoes but it only helped a little. "Chehon, stop. Please, where are we going?"

But Chehon kept running.

"Fine! I won't take another step until you tell me where we are going."

And with that, Ellie stopped. It may have been childish and it may have been stupid, but none of that mattered much to Ellie at the moment.

"Ellie," Chehon groaned as he came back, clearly planning on dragging her behind him if he must. "We have to go."

"No. Not until you tell me where you're taking me."

Chehon threw his hands in the air. "Fine. There are secret tunnels under the castle leading out of Tamrin. After that, we will have to find what is left of the resistance."

Ellie didn't understand. "But what about everyone here? They *are* the resistance."

"No, Ellie," Chehon sighed. He looked pained. "They are only a part of it. They are willing to die for what they believe in."

"But the Fallen, there are too many." As she said the words, she understood. "You don't think anyone will make it. But what about Shiro, and Lacey? We have to go back; we have to help!"

Ellie turned to run back but Chehon grabbed her arm.

"Don't you think I don't know that?" he said through clenched teeth. "Don't you think I want to help my sister, my friends? You are more important. You can end all of this. Please, they cannot die in vain."

The pain in his eyes made Ellie turn her head away. Her conversation with Hayyel lay heavy on her conscience. It wasn't even certain that the prophecy was about *her*. It could be about anyone. But how could she tell Chehon that? How did she tell him all of his friends *were* dying in vain because she was nothing more than a fraud? A fraud who planned to leave the first chance she got.

Closing her eyes, she strengthened her shield even more. But there was nothing protecting her from the hope and pain in Chehon's eyes. "Chehon, I–"

Three angels appeared at the end of the hall. Chehon turned to run in the other direction but found another pair of angels closing in on them there as well. In desperation, Chehon started yanking on doors until he found one that wasn't locked. He shoved Ellie inside and slammed the door shut, locking it behind them.

"Hide," he said.

Ellie looked around. The room was empty of almost all furniture and Ellie doubted the old rocking chair in the back corner would offer much of a hiding place.

"Where?" Someone wrenched at the handle.

"Anywhere."

"What's the point? They saw me enter with you. They're not that stupid."

The door shook as someone bashed it over and over. Ellie doubted it would hold much longer.

"Fine, get behind me and stay out of the way."

Chehon focused on the door, his sword in one hand and a knife in the other. The second the door opened, he threw the knife and the blade hit one of the angels, who let out a strangled cry and collapsed into the room. Chehon drew another knife from god knows where and threw that as well, hitting the second angel trying to enter in the shoulder. With a roar, the angel launched himself at Chehon, who stood his ground, swords in both hands now.

They were equally skilled at using their swords, but Chehon was a little faster. With a wide swipe from below and a fast side cut, the angel fell.

The three angels that were left were smarter. They attacked together, forcing Chehon to defend himself blow after blow. Sweat ran down his face, and he blinked furiously to clear his sight.

Ellie watched in horror as Chehon backed up step after step, getting closer to the wall where she stood helpless. He was losing. Ellie wanted to help but she couldn't fight. The closest she'd ever been to fighting was a slap across the face of some guy who had tried to kiss her.

Use their fear. Shiro? No, it wasn't Shiro's whisper in her mind, but the voice still sounded familiar. It was gone as soon as it had come, leaving Ellie uncertain if she'd heard it at all.

Chehon's triumphant yell drew her attention back to the fight in front of her. The female angel to her right had tripped and Chehon pounced on her in a second. With a swift stab from his sword, he killed her.

Chehon was winning ground again, slowly but steadily, but in the middle of a complicated pattern with his sword, he suddenly bellowed in pain, taking Ellie by surprise. She was sure he hadn't been hit, yet his face twisted in agony and he fell to one knee.

"Lacey," he stammered out.

One of the angels raised his sword to deal a killing blow. Ellie shouted for Chehon. He managed to shift out of the way but was hit in the head by the hilt of the other angel's sword. He fell to the ground motionless.

Lacey grimly drew her sword loose from the body it pierced and looked towards the dais. A small group of angels were holding off the attacking force there and she continued towards them.

Lacey thought she had seen Chehon and Ellie there and she was relieved they were safe.

Everywhere angels were fighting. Wolves, dogs, large cats and even a few bears were lashing out with teeth and claws. Before her, a wolf lay motionless on the floor, a long bleeding gash on its side. Without warning, the wound began pulsating with a green glow, healing it.

The wolf rose from the ground and launched back into the battle again. Lacey smiled as she looked over at Lady Cassiel. She glowed with the same green light.

She was almost at the dais when a large black clad woman blocked her path, armed with two knives. She darted toward Lacey with incredible speed. Lacey barely got out of the way in time and one of the knives cut her across the chest. Lacey screamed in pain and charged the woman, blinded by rage, but she was too fast and easily avoided Lacey's sword. They danced around each other, exchanging blows, but Lacey could feel herself losing energy. The cut across her chest wasn't deep but she was losing too much blood.

The woman threw one of her knives at Lacey, who wrenched herself out of the way just in time. Instead of piercing her heart, the knife embedded itself deep in her shoulder.

The pain caused black spots to fill her vision and Lacey sank to her knees. With a scream, she pulled the knife out and threw it back at the woman. It flew straight and true through the air and struck the woman hard. The woman did *not* move in time and the knife landed square in her heart.

CHAPTER
THIRTY-ONE

ELLIE STOOD PROTECTIVELY OVER Chehon's unconscious body with his sword in her shaking hands. The two remaining angels were circling, assessing her. Ellie's knuckles were turning white from clenching the sword, and when one of the angels lunged for her, he sent the sword soaring through the air with a single blow.

Their cold laughter filled the room, sending chills down Ellie's spine. This was it then. The two angels didn't say a word as they gripped her arms, leading her towards the door, Chehon thankfully forgotten. Ellie struggled the best she could, but they were both stronger and bigger than her. They had reached the end of the hall when she heard the voice again.

Use their fear, Eliana. Ellie looked at the dark faces beside her, but if they had heard the voice as well, they didn't show it.

Well, Ellie thought. *When all hope seems lost, why not listen to the crazy voice in your head.*

Unlike what she had done with Nathaniel, where she had basically thrown her own fear in his face, she called on her power, sending out one tendril. It reached for the angel holding her right arm, but they both still appeared oblivious. Once her power came into contact with the angel's mind, she was met with a shield. It felt foreign, so Ellie doubted it had been put there by the angel herself. But with every shield, there was sure to be a crack. Ellie simply had to find it, fast.

Her mind raced across the shield, searching for a fissure of vulnerability. Whoever had put the shield there was good, but then she found a small rip. Ellie poured her power through crack until the shield blew up from the inside.

The grip on her arm didn't falter. It was quite possible the angel didn't know a shield had been put on her, but the Magic Protector who had cast the spell might be able to tell it had been broken. Ellie didn't have much time.

The angel's mind was surprisingly devoid of emotions. It felt off to Ellie, much like the Heywood forest had. Some feelings seemed to be suppressing others. Love, joy and happiness were nowhere to be found while honor, hatred and fear shone brightly.

Ellie's stomach turned as she graced their minds, they were twisted. Not wanting to linger, she singled out the angel's fears. She was afraid of failure, of the Council and of being dishonored. Ellie used her fears and fed them, making them irrational and real.

The angel's grip on her faltered, and Ellie doubled her efforts. Soon, the angel's eyes dashed around the room, nervously looking over her shoulder for enemies that weren't there. Ellie let her mind go.

The angel's eyes bulged as she scanned the area, chasing a non-existing ghost. A clatter nearby was what sent her over the edge. With a hollow scream, she let go of Ellie and ran back into the depths of the castle. Her companion screamed after her, but his cries were in vain. The angel was gone.

Cursing, his grip on Ellie hardened and he dragged her behind him. But now that Ellie knew what to look for, it was easy enough to break through the remaining angel's shield and feed his fears.

His eyes mirrored the woman's, round with terror, almost all black and brimmed with red. He let go of Ellie and put his hands over his ears, shaking his head.

They had reached the outer part of the castle and windows lined the walls. The angel turned from Ellie and bolted.

"No! Stop!" Ellie shouted, realizing where he was going.

But it was too late. With a crash, the window shattered as he threw himself through it. They were at least five or six stories up, and when Ellie reached the gaping hole where the glass had been, she could barely see the lifeless body in the darkness below.

Ellie felt disgusted with herself. It didn't matter that they were going to give her to the Council. She had driven them mad. Her stomach turned and she threw up what little food she'd had at dinner. Dinner – it seemed to have taken place years ago, not hours.

Collecting herself as best she could, she started back towards Chehon, the same voice as before guiding her through the castle's long, winding corridors. The angels had taken her much farther than Ellie realized, and it took her precious time even with the voice's help to return to Chehon, still lying in a heap on the floor.

Ellie rushed over to him and sank to her knees. She placed two shaking fingers on his throat and relief washed over her like water. Under her fingers a strong pulse beat, Chehon was still alive.

Ellie stroked stands of his blond hair out of his face, and Chehon's eyes fluttered open. He groaned, and Ellie noticed the ugly welt at the side of his head.

"That looks like it hurts," she commented as Chehon regained consciousness.

"It does," he groaned. Then he jerked upright. "The Fallen!"

Chehon tried to sit up, but he cringed and slumped back down to the ground, his head no doubt spinning.

Ellie put a hand on his shoulder, holding him down. "They are gone."

No one needed to know what she had done. It was enough of a punishment to live with it herself. For some reason, she didn't think she could bear Chehon looking at her in disgust, or worse, fear. It was one thing to fight with a sword in combat, that was fair. But to drive someone to suicide by messing up their mind, that was something else entirely.

"Gone? Gone where?" More carefully this time, Chehon gingerly lifted himself up. "No, don't bother. It doesn't matter, we need to keep going."

With Ellie's help, he managed to stand, but the second Ellie let him go, he swayed dangerously, looking like he would fall over. Ellie quickly grabbed him again.

Together, they made their way back out into the hall. It was completely empty of angels now and was left in an uncanny silence.

In the beginning, Chehon leaned heavily on Ellie, but the farther they walked, the more his head seemed to clear. By the fifth turn, he was walking on his own again.

Ellie looked at him, puzzled. She'd been sure he at least had a bad concussion, but he appeared totally unaffected by it. The nasty looking mark on his head was also fading.

Chehon noticed her staring. "All of the knights and knights in training have spells put on them. For strength, stealth, agility and healing to name a few."

Ellie didn't respond and they continued.

After a while, Ellie broke the silence and asked, "Why do only knights get them?"

"Huh?"

"The spells, why doesn't everyone get them?" It seemed to Ellie everyone would benefit from having them.

"Oh, well it takes a lot of power for someone to cast the spells. Only the Magic Protectors can do it, and they are rare and secretive. Most are still under the control of the Council. The Fallen have at least one or two spells put on them. Therefore, the knights are the priority since there are so few of us."

Ellie stopped, taken slightly aback. "So, what, your lives are worth more than others?"

"To the resistance, yes," Chehon answered her truthfully. "As is yours."

"Jen would've kicked your ass for saying that."

"Who is Jen?" he asked, looking at her curiously.

Ellie's stomach knotted at the thought of her, and she blinked away the tears.

"Someone I used to know. She hated people who thought they were better than the rest," Ellie replied in a meek voice, hoping he wouldn't press the issue. He didn't, but he looked at her with curiosity.

They walked for a few more feet until Chehon stopped.

"We are here," he exclaimed, but Ellie didn't see anything except a stone wall.

Chehon pulled a small key from beneath his shirt and slid it into a keyhole Ellie never would have found unless she'd known where it was. The wall creaked once, then glided easily to the side.

Chehon produced one of the glowing crystals from his pocket and was about to go inside when Ellie stopped him.

"What now?" Chehon groaned.

"We can't leave."

"By the Creator, not this again. Ellie, I've told you–"

"No, you don't understand," Ellie interrupted him. "If what you say is true, that you are more equipped than most of the people, angels, fighting then I cannot believe you would leave them. Not knowing that you could save so many lives. My friend, your sister, is out there, fighting without any spells, and you're here instead of there, helping. That's wrong."

Ellie might not be the Chosen One, but the Archangels believed she was. She couldn't leave and let angels die because of her. She could end all of this, and no one would need to get hurt. She didn't tell Chehon her plan though.

"But you heard Lady Cassiel. She gave me orders." Chehon looked pained as he answered, but Ellie was relentless.

The sounds from the battle could no longer be heard, but Ellie still felt a pressure on her shields. No emotions passed through, but Ellie didn't need them to know what they were. She didn't want this, any of it. She wanted Jen and Lucas and dusty books about adventures in the past. The promise to learn about her father no longer felt like a promise but a curse and she wanted rid of all of it. But still, she couldn't leave.

She didn't know how, but she had to survive this without anyone else dying, and the best way of doing that seemed to be to give the Archangels her powers. She didn't dwell on what would happen when they did. Everyone was overestimating how powerful she was. Another Empath would fix it. They had to.

"From what I heard, she ordered you to protect me, and I'm going back. It will be hard protecting me from a tunnel on the other side of the castle." A little more gently, she added, "Please, Chehon. I can't fight, I know that. But you can. I promise I'll stay out of the way if you help them."

"I could just hit you in the head and drag you with me," Chehon said as a threat, but it was halfhearted at best.

"You could, but you won't."

CHAPTER THIRTY-TWO

Making their way back to the great hall took an eternity, and once they finally reached it, it was empty. Well, not empty – bodies covered the floor, many of which were alarmingly still.

Ellie spotted Israfel across the room, navigating through the sea of bodies. Every once in a while, he would bend down and either move on or motion for someone to carry away the body on a stretcher. Following one of those stretchers with her gaze, Ellie noticed what looked like a makeshift medical center in one of the corners. Angels were hurrying around putting bandages on the wounded while others glowed with magic.

Since there was no immediate threat to Ellie's life, Chehon left her side and searched for his friends and sister, even after Ellie pointed out that anyone would have spotted Lacey's red hair from a mile away.

Ellie made her way across the room, trying hard not to step on anyone as she caught up with Israfel.

"Eliana! You should not be here. Lady Cassiel told you to leave, and she was right."

"Yeah, yeah spare me the speech. I'm here now and it seems the danger is over."

Ellie was getting really sick of people ordering her around. To her surprise, Israfel shook his head.

"The battle is still raging. We managed to force them out into the courtyard, but it is not over yet."

A man groaned by Israfel's feet, and he immediately bent down, humming a melody until the man's eyes closed.

As two other angels hurried over to carry him away, Ellie realized he wasn't a man at all but a *boy*, no more than twelve-years-old. Ellie looked away.

Standing, Israfel continued. "The fight is not over, which means you are still not safe. Please take Chehon and Bria here and go back to your room."

A young woman looked up when Israfel said her name and came to stand next to him. Like everyone in the room, her dark skin and clothes were covered in blood, and there was a slump to her shoulders Ellie doubted had been there before. She squared them as she stood in front of Israfel, and Ellie realized with a shudder that the blood wasn't hers.

Chehon made his way back to them and shook his head at her questioning look. Lacey wasn't there.

"Escort Eliana back to her room and keep her there. If you think you can manage?"

If Chehon noticed the obvious stab at him, he didn't let it show.

"Of course, Master Israfel," he said and glanced over at the girl called Bria. "I don't acquire any assistance but thank you."

"Well, since you were told to get her out of here and did not, it seems you do. She is just one girl, half human at that, how hard can it be?" Bria asked.

Why did everyone keeping saying *human* like they would when referring to a slimy slug no one wanted to touch? Both Chehon and Ellie started at Bria, but Israfel tiredly held up his hand.

"All of you, be quiet. There are angels dying in here while I waste my time arguing with you three. Just go to your room, Eliana."

Ellie glared at Israfel and spun on her heels. No one had sent her to her room in, well, never. Mostly because she hadn't had her own room in most of her different foster homes, and more importantly, seldom had any adults cared enough to send her there. But still, the feeling was humiliating.

Both Chehon and Bria scrambled to catch up with her as she stalked out through where the double doors had once been. Outside were even more bodies of dying or dead angels. A large bear also lay in a corner, and Ellie's earlier suspicion was confirmed, animals had taken part in the battle.

"So nice of you to join us when the battle is almost over, Chehon. I've said it before and I'll say it again, the spells were wasted on you."

"I'm sorry you cannot handle the fact that I was chosen for a mission beyond your comprehension," Chehon bit back at Bria, and Ellie rolled her eyes at their bickering.

As they continued to walk, Ellie's footsteps wavered. Something felt off.

All of the pressure against her shields was gone. But with the number of hurt and dead angels in the great hall, fear, pain and sorrow should be weighing heavy on her.

Stopping, Ellie closed her eyes and focused her power to hear the emotions around her. It should have been enough for her to hear the emotions of most of the castle, but it was utterly silent. She focused her powers on Chehon, trying to hear his emotions, but was met by a deafening silence.

"You guys, something is wrong."

Bria and Chehon were still arguing, and Ellie got no response.

Taking a deep breath, she shouted, "Oh, will you shut up and listen!"

That, at least, got their attention.

"Ellie, what's wrong? You shouldn't raise your voice like that, we don't want to draw any unnecessary attention to us."

At least he had the decency to blush a little when Ellie glared at him. "You're one to talk."

Bria unsheathed two slender knives, their long, thin blades both beautiful and deadly. An amber crystal was embedded in the top of the hilt of both knives. "What is it?"

"It's just, I don't hear anything," Ellie said, nervously looking around.

"What? Ellie, we're in a deserted hallway, of course you don't–"

"No, I don't *hear* anything. Nothing. It's like all of the emotions are gone. I can't even read you and you are right here."

"And it isn't simply because you are untrained?"

Ellie glowered at Bria. "No, it has only happened three times. Once in the village, there was a Magic Protector there blocking me, but it wasn't like this. It wasn't this deafening..." Ellie trailed off, not wanting to think about what she knew was true.

"And the other times?" Chehon prompted.

Ellie swallowed hard. "The other times were when I met the Archangels."

Chehon paled when he realized what she was saying.

"They're here?" he whispered.

Ellie nodded.

"Archangels, in the castle? By the Creator, we have to tell–"

But Chehon and Ellie never got to know who they had to tell.

Bria gasped and dropped to the ground, an arrow embedded in her eye.

Chehon didn't wait to find out who had fired the arrow. He pushed Ellie behind him. "Run!"

But there was nowhere to run. Black clad angels were blocking both ends of the hallway. Instead, Ellie grabbed Bria's knives, feeling some comfort at their weight in her hands.

"I knew this was too easy," Chehon swore. Another arrow came flying and missed him by mere inches. "Ellie, get behind me."

Ellie shook her head.

"You promised," Chehon prompted, a slight desperation to his voice.

Ellie looked at Chehon, but his eyes were fixed on the angels in front of them. The narrowness of the hallway offered some help at least; they couldn't advance more than two or three at a time. This was of little comfort, though, seeing as they came from both directions. Another arrow came flying, smashing into the wall next to Ellie, who gave a little yelp. She finally resigned and pressed herself against the wall behind Chehon.

Then, the angels were upon him.

He was beautiful as he fought, but even Ellie could see he was slowly losing. For every angel he killed, two more appeared. One man had managed to get behind Chehon's back unnoticed and raised his sword. Without thinking, Ellie plunged a knife into the man's back.

Upon hearing his surprised gasp, Chehon turned and killed him with a swift cut to the throat. The man sagged to the floor, dragging Ellie's knife with him. Chehon gave her a small smile before he turned back to the steady flow of angels.

Chehon was holding off three opponents at the same time when Ellie realized it was the end. As they circled him, they cut him where they had not managed to land blows before.

"Chehon, get up!" Ellie screamed as he fell to one knee, but he didn't move.

A female angel raised her spear and held it just above Chehon's bent head. Then, as if in a dream, the angel dropped the spear and fell to the ground.

There was some sort of commotion to Ellie's right and the remaining angles rushed over, leaving only two who were pointing their swords at Chehon.

Triumphant shouts echoed down the hall and the angels exchanged concerned looks. They didn't see how Chehon's hand closed around his sword. The first angel went down before either of them realized what was happening, and by the time the second angel lashed out with his sword, Chehon had rolled away. Sparks flew from where the angel's sword hit the stone floor.

Members of the resistance filled the hallway, and Ellie thought she saw Sebastian and several of Chehon's other friends, but there was one face in particular she was relieved to see.

Lacey cut the last angel down without a second look and knelt beside her brother.

She looked wild, her hair a mess, the once beautiful blue dress cut haphazardly above her knees with a tear above her chest. Her left shoulder was drenched in dried blood. Ellie figured her wound had also been the cause of Chehon's sudden collapse.

He stood now, linking arms with his friends, and Lacey came over to Ellie. "Are you okay? Your hand, is it bleeding?"

Confused, Ellie looked down at her hand. "No, no it isn't mine."

Ellie couldn't tear her eyes from her blood-covered hand. Memories of the sickening feeling of the knife sinking into flesh came rushing back, and for the second time that night, she threw up.

"How did you know where to find us?" Chehon asked as she wiped her mouth on the back of her clean hand.

"It seemed too easy all of a sudden. One second, we were losing, and next thing I know, we were winning ground, forcing them outside," a man Chehon had called Gareth at dinner answered.

"Sebastian saw you leave with Ellie and Bria and got us from the fight," Lacey said. "And you're lucky he did."

"Figured you might need some help, even if it was just dealing with miss know-it-all." Sebastian smirked and then looked around. "Where is she by the way? I was sure she would be rubbing your failure in your face by now."

Chehon lowered his eyes to Bria's body on the floor. A black clad angel lay across her, hiding most of her from view. "She – she didn't make it."

Sebastian followed Chehon's gaze and swore. "Oh shit, I'm sorry. I didn't realize."

Before anyone could say anything else, a thunderous, booming sound echoed down the hall. Everyone turned to see a row of angels materialize, their boots connecting with the stone floor.

"I think now," Lacey said slowly, watching the angels with hatred, "would be a good time to run."

There were no arguments as all of them dashed through the hallway. Sebastian took the lead, guiding the group, but they met dead end after dead end as more and more angels appeared in the halls. Sebastian pushed a door open and motioned for them to get inside.

The room was huge, with four large tables with chairs around them in the middle of it, making a perfect square. Two chairs stood at the table opposite the large glass windows. They were not bigger than the rest of the chairs, but advanced designs were carved into the wood that the others lacked. The windows were made of colored glass, creating different images of angels, and the walls were covered in maps full of different colored pins. The room, like the rest of the castle, was dimly lit by crystals.

"This is the advice chamber," Gareth panted. "I've been here once with my father."

"Gareth's father is the chief adviser to Lord Theron and second in command of the resistance," Chehon explained.

"Thank you for the information, Chehon, but I think we have a more pressing issue," Lacey said as the thick wooden door shuddered.

"Quickly, help me with the table."

Sebastian and Chehon grabbed one end of the table while two other angels – Ellie thought they were brothers but couldn't remember their names – grabbed the other end. Together, they managed to lift it and place it up against the door.

"That won't hold them," Ellie said in a tired voice. "If the Archangels are really here, nothing will hold them."

Splinters flew from the door as it quaked again. The angels in the room formed a loose half circle around Ellie, weapons at the ready. Not all of them held swords, Ellie noticed.

Gareth carried a long wooden staff ending in a curved blade, and Sebastian and the brothers prepared their bows with arrows, swords dangling from their waists.

As the door trembled for a third time, it broke, leaving a gaping hole in the center. Sebastian let an arrow fly through the hole, and they heard a cry on the other side. Two more arrows flew, and two more cries of pain sounded.

Sebastian had time to fire one more arrow before the Fallen breached the door. Chehon and his friends worked like a well-oiled machine, moving as if they shared one mind.

Lacey stood back with Ellie, watching the scene before them, but when one of the brothers screamed and dropped to the ground, she sprang into action, filling the space. The other brother had tears streaming down his face, but he didn't break formation.

"Is he dead?" The pain made his voice thick, and in that moment,

Ellie was glad her powers were temporarily switched off. "Eliana, is James dead?!"

Ellie crawled over to James and dragged him back towards the end of the room. He was heavy and left a trail of blood after him. Ellie searched him with shaking hands until she found the source of the blood, a small diamond-shaped hole beneath his heart. Ellie ripped up the bottom of her skirt and pressed the cloth against the wound, trying to stop the bleeding.

"I don't – no, wait!" James' chest moved up and down as he took shallow, rasping breaths. "He's breathing but he's losing too much blood!"

Blood soaked the fabric and pooled between Ellie's fingers.

"Focus, Ethan!" Chehon screamed, but too late.

Ethan looked back at his brother as another set of angels pushed through the door and he was cut down on the spot. With tears streaming down Ellie's face, James went still beneath her hands, joining his brother in whatever afterlife there was.

"Ellie, use your powers!" Lacey screamed while fighting a huge man. He towered above her, making Lacey look like a doll.

"I can't." Ellie fell back and crawled away from James' body. "They have shields, I–"

"Yes, you can! Remember the village," Lacey said between gasps.

But how could Ellie tell her that even if it had been like in the village, she still couldn't do anything? That someone else had wielded her power, only using Ellie as a channel?

"Ellie, please!"

Come to me, my child. It was the same voice. Ellie's eyes felt like lead, and she fought to keep them open.

Gareth swung his long staff and cut down two more angels as Sebastian and Chehon fought back-to-back. Now was not the time to pass out but the voice continued to call her. *You cannot save them like this, Eliana. Come to me.*

Against her will, Ellie closed her eyes and watched the fire burning hungrily within her, beckoning for her. Ellie let it surround her, consume her like it always did, but this time, she went deeper into the very heart of the fire. A hand reached out towards her, flames licking its fingers.

Take my hand, Eliana.

Ellie reached out and saw that *she* was the fire now. Somewhere in the distance, she heard Lacey shouting for her alongside the clanging of metal. Ellie knew she ought to go back, to give herself to the Archangels to save her friends, that had been the plan after all, but instead she moved against her own will. Then the hand grasped hers and pulled her through the heart of the fire.

Ellie was bathing in light. There was nothing else as far as she could see. Strangely, it didn't blind her as she stood and looked around. A woman appeared in front of her, causing Ellie to take a startled step back. "Who are you?"

The woman smiled, flashing her white teeth. Her white hair reached the floor, the curls melting together with a simple yet beautiful white dress.

Her silver eyes were fixed on Ellie as she answered, "I am light and I am darkness. I am heaven and I am hell. I am the Creator of life."

Ellie recognized the voice at once. "You."

"Please sit, my daughter." The Creator held her hand out to a couch that had not been there before.

Ellie's legs were shaking, and rather than falling to the ground, she sat down on the plump cushions.

"You may ask me what you like, my daughter," the Creator said as she gracefully perched next to Ellie.

"I'm not your daughter."

Ellie felt like she was about to break. She had accepted magic, talking animals and even angels, but she had been sure the Creator was a story, like humans and their god. But it was hard to keep telling herself that when she was sitting next to her, light radiating from her like a star.

"Ah, but you all are. I am the mother of life itself, therefore every creature, plant and rock are my children. But you are my daughter in a much closer meaning of the word. Like the Guardians, Empaths are born from me and as my children, I bless them with my power."

"You're wrong, my mother was human."

"She was. But while you are her flesh and blood, your soul and spirit are mine." The Creator spoke with nothing but gentle kindness, and Ellie's shoulders dropped with relaxation, the tension suddenly melting away.

"You said I could ask you anything?" The Creator nodded. "Do you help all of the Empaths like you have me?"

The Creator shook her head, a little sadness in her eyes. "No, Eliana. Most Empaths grow cold, the feelings of others causing them to lose their own. But you, Eliana, you shone so bright, like a star in the darkness and I knew you were my best hope."

It did not pass Ellie's attention that she had said "shone," but she wanted to know more. "Is that why you helped me at the village? Why didn't you save that little girl? She had done nothing to deserve a death filled with such horror."

Ellie's anger surfaced as she spoke of the girl and some of the calming fog cleared from her mind. If this was the Creator, if she really existed, then why hadn't she helped the people she called her children? How could she watch as they were slaughtered?

The Creator's silver eyes glistened with unshed tears. "Creating this prison drained my powers, what little I have managed to restore

I couldn't use to save a single girl no matter how much it pained me. And all I did at the village was to guide you to your true potential."

"Then why didn't you do it now? Before James and Ethan died?" Ellie's voice broke a little, but she refused to let the tears fall.

"Something inside of you has broken, Eliana."

"You said 'shone'," Ellie whispered, and the Creator nodded slowly.

"What made you different from all others was your ability to love." The Creator held up her hand, silencing Ellie as she opened her mouth to protest. "I know what you are going to say – a lot of people, angels and humans alike, love. But not deep and pure enough to form a true love's bond. You did."

Ellie didn't understand a word she was saying. If she was that in love with someone, surely she would know it. She said as much.

"I am truly sorry," was all the Creator said, then Ellie doubled over in pain. Images of Aaron flooded her mind, and she couldn't breathe. Ellie screamed in agony and crumpled to the floor. Emotions flooded back to her: love, happiness and then unbelievable pain as she looked down at Aaron's still face.

Aaron was dead. Ellie let the words sink in and curled into a tight ball on the floor. Sobs ripped through her body as her heart shattered all over again.

A feather-light touch helped her uncurl herself and she looked into the Creator's eyes.

"Why?" Ellie whispered. "Why couldn't you just have let me be?"

"A true love's bond is said to be unbreakable, but when Aaron died and yours broke, I was glad for you. If I could spare you the pain of living without your other half, I would have. But your powers..."

"My powers weren't as powerful without the bond," Ellie realized, her voice dangerously low. "So, you took me here and restored it, not caring what it might do to me, is that it?"

"You are the only one who can stop him."

"Maybe I don't want to!" Ellie roared, the last embers of calm leaving her mind. "No one asked me, everyone just decided *for* me and dragged me along the way! I didn't ask you to create me!"

The hurt in the Creator's face was as plain as if Ellie had physically slapped her. Not in a million years had Ellie thought she could hurt a god. But she clearly had, and the Creator shrank away.

"I am sorry. So sorry you have to carry my burden. It is my fault, you see. Everything."

The Creator sank back down onto the couch, staring far into the distance. "I loved him once, Michael. He was everything I had ever asked for and I was delighted to share this world with him. I gave him everything. But he grew jealous, and my love blinded me to his faults. He hated the humans, said they were a lesser race and that I loved them more than the angels, more than him. He began killing them, causing chaos everywhere he went. I could not bear his betrayal and left my living form here on Earth, isolating myself in the great void. But I cannot ignore what he is doing anymore. I need your help."

So, they had been lovers. Ellie found it hard to find anything lovable about Michael, but maybe the Creator had known another man.

Carefully, Ellie sat beside the Creator. Their eyes met and Ellie saw her own pain mirrored in those deep silver eyes. They had both known love and loss.

Nothing was said for a while, then Ellie broke the silence. "Hayyel showed me how the humans killed the angels. The Archangels only claim they were protecting the angels."

"Michael is a master of manipulation. And humans were a young race, they still are, easily led into temptation. Michael cursed the angels, taking away their free will. I created this world as a prison to keep the human race safe, out of reach."

"But they can leave. I mean, they have been in the human realm."

"Guardians are blessed with the power to portal because I know their loyalty can never waver. They cannot be bought nor tortured to give up their secrets."

Starlight's fading form entered Ellie's mind, and she swallowed.

"It is true the Archangels are close to finding a way to pass between worlds but so far, they have only managed to send their spirits. You have not yet seen their full power, Eliana."

Ellie swallowed again, hard this time. If what she and Aaron had fought in the alley had only been a spirit, a shadow of the real Archangels, then things were looking rather dark.

"But can't you stop them, kill them?"

The Creator shook her head. "I am the Creator; I cannot destroy what I create. This is my blessing and my curse."

"So, you created me," Ellie said.

"I created you," the Creator agreed.

"I want them to pay for what they did to Aaron," Ellie determined, and the light came back into the Creator's eyes. "I can't promise you I can do it, but I will try if you promise me something."

"Anything."

Ellie leaned over to whisper her request in the Creator's ear.

She knew she probably had no right to ask the mother of everything for favors, but she didn't care. Ellie sat back while the Creator looked at her.

"Of course, that I can promise. You have my word."

"Thank you," Ellie said while looking around. "Now what?"

"I can lend you my power if you agree to be my conduit. But I must warn you, using that amount of power will drain me and I will no longer be able to take on this mortal form."

"You'll die?" Ellie asked, a slight tremor in her voice.

The Creator of life couldn't possibly die.

"In a sense, yes. But I will not be truly gone, just take on another form, as is always the case with life," the Creator replied with a calm smile. "But you would have to let me in. You cannot hide anything nor hold anything back."

Ellie gulped. All her life, she had never let anyone see all of her. Her memories had always been something she'd hidden, and there were other parts of her she even hid from herself. But suddenly, the idea of finally letting go didn't seem as terrifying. And most of all, Ellie was tired.

She looked straight into the Creator's eyes and nodded.

At first, nothing happened, but then the Creator started to shine more and more brightly. Ellie refused to cover her eyes. Her vision blurred and tears ran down her cheeks, but she still held her gaze. The Creator touched Ellie's cheek with her blazing hand, burning her skin, and then she was everywhere.

Ellie let go.

Everything that was Ellie, the good and the bad, bathed in the Creator's light, but there was no judgment. Her presence caressed her mind, giving equal love to Ellie's strengths as well as her weakness. She saw her rashness and her patience, her pettiness and selflessness, her ability to hate and to love. And then finally, Ellie just existed. Without walls around her, to keep others out and to keep herself in.

The Creator's magic filled her, and when Ellie opened her eyes again, they burned.

The sword to Lacey's throat pressed hard enough to draw blood. Lacey looked into her mother's eyes with hatred. Chehon, Sebastian and Gareth had their arms pinned behind them and several arrows and swords aimed at them.

Lacey had watched in fear when Ellie had collapsed and started to pulse with light. Their line of defense was broken and all of them fought for their lives. Two of the angels had made their way over to Ellie to grab her, but they had burst into flames before they could even touch her. Then, without warning, Lacey hadn't been able to move, and Mithra had entered the room. She had shouted out orders to capture but not kill them.

"Is that any way to look at your mother, Lacey?" she said now, the tip of her sword still digging into Lacey's throat.

It was Chehon who answered. "If you are going to kill us, Mother, would you please get on with it? I would prefer to spend as little time as possible in your company."

"You are your father's son, Chehon, in such a hurry to die. But don't worry, you will join him soon enough. Lacey here will join the Fallen; her gifts are rare indeed."

"Don't you dare touch her!" Chehon shouted, and Lacey turned cold. She would kill herself before helping the Council.

"Now, now. No one will die just yet."

The voice was male and hurt. Lacey tried to turn her head to identify the speaker as a line of hooded figures entered the room. Lacey quickly counted and the color drained from her face: fifteen.

The Archangel who had spoken continued as they spread out in a half circle. "We would not want you to miss us killing the Empath. Witnessing your last hope die along with the pitiful army you call the resistance will give us great pleasure. She will give us her power first, of course, if she values her friends' lives."

"I'd rather die than help you."

"But you won't have a choice," Michael said and smiled almost sweetly at her. "You see, to open a portal to the human realm, we need the power of all Protectors."

"But Ellie is an Empath, not a Protector." It was Chehon who spoke.

"How ignorant you are. The Empaths are the Protectors of the

Creator herself." Michael started to move towards Ellie, a dangerous look of hunger in his eyes.

"Don't touch her!" Lacey screamed.

"How dare you address the Archangel Michael? You are not worthy daughter," Mithra hissed and pressed the sword harder against Lacey's throat as Michael laughed.

"This is your daughter? How delightful."

Lacey was about to say he wouldn't find her that delightful with her sword piercing his heart, but she never got the chance. An explosion knocked everyone to the ground and the room burst with light. Ellie lifted from the floor, white wings spreading behind her. Her black hair and dress blew in a sudden wind, causing the maps on the wall to spring free. Her dress wasn't the same torn, green one she had been wearing but a sheer white, falling behind her in a trail of clouds. In her right hand, she held a sword made of pure light. She was beautiful and terrifying.

Then Ellie opened her eyes. Her emerald irises were gone; instead, they blazed with the same light as the sword. They looked at the figure in front of her and Ellie raised her sword, pointing it at Michael.

"You disappoint me, Michael."

Lacey, along with everyone else in the room, screamed and tried to cover her ears. The voice was Ellie's but layered with someone else's, and the raw force in that voice was excruciating.

"Creator," Michael managed to stammer out. "We have only ever served you."

"Silence!" Michael was pressed to the ground. "You dare claim to serve me? You will pay for your crimes. Now, be gone from this place!"

The light of the sword intensified as Ellie plunged from the air, striking it into the ground. The room filled with light for a few seconds and screams echoed off the walls.

With another explosion, the room fell into darkness.

CHAPTER THIRTY-THREE

There was no other sound in the empty hallway except Ellie's footsteps. She made her way to the great hall where she stood for a moment, looking at the ruins. Only two of the four chandeliers were still working; one had fallen and the other's crystals had shattered. The crystals, Chehon had told her when walking her to her room a few days after the battle, were made by the Mineral Protectors, and no one outside their order knew how.

They had left yet another interrogation where she, Chehon, Lacey, Sebastian and Gareth had once again been asked to go over what had happened the night of the fight. While Ellie told them about her meeting with the Creator, she left out the parts about Aaron and herself and the Creator's relationship with Michael. It felt private and it wasn't Ellie's place to say anything.

Ellie reflected on her conversation with the Creator in her mind, repeating her words over and over. It surprised her how easily she had accepted the answers she had been given. Ellie suspected that the Creator had only told her what she wanted her to know, after all, despite claiming Ellie could ask anything she wanted.

With the exception of the meeting where her presence was demanded, Ellie spent her time crying in her room. She had been robbed of her grief before, so now she was making up for it. But she was never left alone. It seemed Lacey had taken it upon herself to make sure Ellie didn't spend a single waking moment alone; it was most likely some sort of suicide watch.

Chehon seemed to have gotten most of the watches after Lacey herself, but Israfel, Lady Cassiel and even Sebastian had sat by her bedside, trying to comfort her. Despite Ellie's first impression of Sebastian, it turned out he reminded her a lot of Lucas, making it hard for her to dislike him.

On her first visit, Lady Cassiel had brought Shiro with her. He had snuggled close to Ellie and laid there while she cried. While he still wasn't completely healed, Lady Cassiel decided he could rest just as well with Ellie as on his own. While Ellie no longer planned on leaving, it felt good to have Shiro by her side again.

The nights were the only time everyone left Ellie alone, but she didn't sleep even though she was exhausted. Her dreams were haunted by Aaron's face and the Archangels, so she spent her nights talking to Shiro, telling him everything that had happened.

Shiro was guilt-ridden that he had slept through the whole thing no matter how many times Ellie told him there was nothing he could have done. Once he heard about Aaron, he told Ellie what he knew about true love, but it wasn't much.

I think you somehow transferred the bond outside of your body and into the shield. It is a rare talent to be able to project your shield outside of yourself to include others. Perhaps, when it broke, the feelings in it broke, too.

I don't understand how I could use my powers at all, Ellie thought. *Both at the masquerade and at the battle, it was like my power was frozen.*

Shiro thought for a while before he responded. *But did they work? On anyone else other than Aaron?*

Ellie didn't like thinking back to that day; it plagued her dreams enough. But Shiro was right, she realized. *No. Just Aaron.*

Well then, not even the Archangels seem powerful enough to interfere with a bond made of true love. Perhaps that is why the Creator believes you to be the one who can end them.

Ellie hadn't said much after that, there wasn't much to say.

On the fifth day after the battle, Ellie ran out of tears, which seemed to unnerve Lacey even more because she extended the suicide watch to nights as well.

Ellie sighed and went back out into the hallway. It was exactly two weeks since the attack, and everyone were attending the funeral being held outside of Tamrin. Everyone except Ellie and the many guards who were combing the castle for other hidden or forgotten entrances.

The gate the Fallen had used had been long forgotten, no one was even aware of its existence. When Lord Theron had learned of this, he had ordered the entire castle to be searched.

Three angels, two men and a woman, had been identified as the traitors who had led them inside. Ellie hadn't recognized them, but Chehon had told her they were trusted members of the resistance. They had survived the attack, but one of the men died from his injuries and the others were sentenced to death. Ellie had not attended their execution; if it had been up to her, they would have been thrown in jail. There had been enough death. But the laws were apparently clear, and Ellie hadn't had the strength to argue.

Everyone who had taken part in the fight was being buried today. At first, Ellie had wondered why they waited for so long before the funeral, but as the day passed, she realized the bodies didn't decompose. The angels looked as if they were sleeping.

The angels burned their dead, believing it set their spirits free to return to the Creator. They had planned to bury the bodies of the Fallen, thus denying them that journey.

It had been a week after the fight and Ellie had been forced to attend another meeting. She had been staring down at her lap when the voice of Gareth's father, Master Amriel, drew her attention to what was being discussed.

They were in a smaller room than the old advice chamber; no one had been allowed in there after what had happened. Everything about the new room seemed temporary. The original furniture had been pushed to the far back and maps and documents were spread over the big tables that had been moved there.

They were discussing the funeral and where to bury the Fallen when Ellie realized what they were saying. "No."

It was a single word, but it was the only word she had said except when giving testimony. The room fell silent.

"What do you mean 'no,' dear?" Lady Cassiel said, her voice was tentative, making Ellie feel like a deer they would scare off if they spoke too loud or made any sudden movements.

"No. You will burn them all. It is not your right to damn angels or their actions."

Chaos erupted in the room, angels shouting at each other. Some were defending Ellie, saying it was the Creator who passed judgment, while others claimed the Fallen didn't deserve redemption.

Lord Theron sat slumped in his chair and looked at Ellie. His eyes were a deep blue. They reminded Ellie of a stormy sky and stared right into her soul. But Ellie didn't break eye contact or look away. Finally, it was Lord Theron who looked down and with a sigh, he stood up, raising his hand, silencing the angels.

"Eliana is right. What a lot of you seem to have forgotten is that many of you have once been Fallen yourself, including my dear wife. And do any of you deny her the journey to the Creator?" The angels around the table lowered their eyes. "We will burn all who fell at the battle and wish them peace in the next life."

No one had argued after that, but Ellie had gotten a few dirty looks on the way out.

Lacey had tried to convince Ellie to go to the funeral, claiming she needed to say goodbye to Aaron in order to let him go. But Ellie didn't want to let him go.

She had reached her destination and was relieved when she found it empty. She went over to the wall at the back and picked out a sword.

The training area was located behind the castle and looked out over the city. There was a bigger one outside the city wall, but this one was big enough for Ellie's purpose. There was as small area assigned to archery, targets with red dots lined up in a row. Ellie walked past it until she came to the area with dummies made of hay.

She wore soft pants and a t-shirt, clothes to give her as much mobility as possible, and her hair was tied in a ponytail.

Ellie raised the sword and brought it down onto the dummy. It was awkward, nothing like the dance Chehon and Lacey did, but Ellie was determined. She raised the sword over and over, hacking away at the dummy until she was drenched in sweat.

"That sword is too heavy for you." Ellie jumped at the voice. Lady Cassiel stood at the edge of the training area, leaning on the fence that surrounded it. "I think knives are a better choice for you, or perhaps a naginata. You are certainly tall enough."

"A what?" Ellie wiped her forehead at the back of her hand as Lady Cassiel walked over to her.

"A naginata. It is a wooden staff ending with a blade."

She pointed to another wall full of weapons and Ellie recognized the weapon Gareth had wielded the night of the attack. She thought of the ease with which Lacey had moved with her sword with a tinge of jealousy.

"I'll never be as good as Lacey anyway," she said and went to put her sword back.

Lady Cassiel followed her. "Lacey has had years of practice with one of the finest swordsmen who ever lived. She could outmatch even me."

But Lacey had spent her life in the village with... "Israfel?" Lady Cassiel nodded. "But I thought he was teaching her to master her power."

"Indeed, he was, but unfortunately one must learn to fight in this world in order to survive it."

A sudden bitterness in Lady Cassiel's voice made Ellie wonder what she had to do to break free of the Council. But Ellie didn't feel it was her right to pry and she changed the subject instead. If Lady Cassiel wanted her to know, she would tell her.

"I thought you'd be at the funeral."

"I was. But it is... difficult for me. Bad memories." Lady Cassiel offered no more explanation than that and Ellie didn't prompt her. "Would you sit with me? It is such a beautiful day."

It was a beautiful day. The sun was shining, warming Ellie's face. That reminded Ellie of silly thought lost in the madness of reality. "Do you have seasons here? Like in the human realm?"

"Why yes, we do. This is the beginning of spring."

Ellie smiled and followed Lady Cassiel to a bench by the stone wall. She had always loved spring, it felt like a fresh start.

"Why did you heal Shiro? I mean, you must have, like, servants who do that sort of thing." Ellie winced a little at the look Lady Cassiel gave her, but a smile quickly followed.

"First of all, I do not have servants to do my tasks. I see all angels here as equals. Of course, not everyone shares that view. Master Amriel for one."

Ellie nodded. That didn't surprise her at all. During the interrogations and meetings, Master Amriel was one of the angels who seemed more focused on revenge rather than freedom and justice.

"And as to why I healed Shiro, I am a Canine Protector. A sort of sub-order of the Animal Protectors, if you will."

"I know of them. I've had a teacher, he taught me about the different orders," Ellie said, and Lady Cassiel smiled again.

"Yes, well that is also what made me the most equipped to heal Shiro, and a Guardian who protects you deserves the best and nothing else."

Ellie smiled at that, and they sat in silence for a while until Lady Cassiel broke it.

"You may have heard but I felt I should tell you; Lord Theron and I share a true love's bond."

"No, I didn't know."

"Ah well, we do not talk about it much and not many know about it. A true love's bond can be a powerful thing, Eliana, but it can also be dangerous. A weapon an enemy can use against you. I am telling you this because I want you to know that while I don't claim to understand your pain, I can imagine it."

Ellie didn't know if it was exhaustion or the kind look in Lady Cassiel's eyes, but before she could stop them, words were bubbling up and out of her mouth. "I think about him, all the time. It hurts, all the time."

"The man you loved has died, it will take time. You have to allow it to take time."

"But that's just it. I think if it felt like he was dead, I could at least grieve, but it feels like he is in pain, like he is suffering, and I can't do anything to help him."

It was true. Since Ellie had woken from the attack, her insides had been screaming in agony. In all of her dreams, Aaron writhed in pain on a dirt floor, the Archangels standing over him. Ellie would scream, but he didn't hear her, then Michael would turn and smile at her. In many ways it was like the dream she'd had when she first arrived at the angels' realm but yet, it was different. The pain was more intense, the fear more real.

Lady Cassiel looked at Ellie with concern. "I do not know what happens when your other half dies. Perhaps the pain you feel is caused by half of you missing. Or maybe you are right, and something is amiss. You have my word that I will do all in my power to help you find out either way. It is the least I can do."

"Thank you," Ellie said and looked up at the sky. "Do you think they are gone? The Archangels?"

Lady Cassiel sighed beside her. "I wish I could say yes, but no. I do not think they are gone. They are wounded most likely, but not gone."

"I think you're right," Ellie said, still looking at the sky. There was something reassuring in watching the clouds drift by. "The Creator told me she could not kill what she created, but I guess a part of me hoped."

"We all hoped, Eliana."

There had been no trace of the Archangels after Ellie, high on Creator, had blown everything to pieces. Once the Fallen still fighting in the courtyard realized they had been abandoned, they retreated. Some escaped and some were captured. The resistance called it a victory, but Ellie wasn't so sure.

"The Creator told me something," Ellie began, and Lady Cassiel waited for her to continue. "I didn't say anything at the meetings. It's... private."

"I will not tell anyone if that is your wish," Lady Cassiel said kindly, and Ellie breathed a sigh of relief.

"She said that Aaron was the reason she chose me, because I loved him. I even think he was the one who unlocked my powers." It was something Ellie had been thinking about when she had not been crying. It was no coincidence that Hayyel had first appeared on the same night she'd met Aaron in the club.

Lady Cassiel nodded at this. "I am not surprised. It was Theron who saved me from the Council. His love is what freed me so it would make sense that the love you and Aaron shared is what woke your powers."

"Yes, but what if just me isn't enough?" Voicing her fears to someone other than Shiro felt freeing.

"What do you mean?" Lady Cassiel asked.

"What if I can't help you now that Aaron is gone?" Ellie couldn't make herself say dead; she didn't believe it in her heart.

Lady Cassiel was quiet for a long time before she answered. "I believe we are all in this world for a reason. It might be that Aaron's reason was to help you realize your destiny. And your love is not lost. You carry it with you and will be able to draw strength from it when you need to, because Aaron will never leave you. He will always be a part of your heart."

It wasn't the answer Ellie had expected, but perhaps it was the answer she needed.

Before she could say anything, a bell sounded, causing a few birds to lift from their resting place in a nearby tree.

"I think," Lady Cassiel said as she stood up, "the funeral is over. I must go to my husband; he will need me."

She turned to leave, and Ellie jumped to her feet. "I want to learn."

Lady Cassiel stopped and turned to look at Ellie. "Learn what?"

"To fight," Ellie said, and a smile spread across Lady Cassiel's face. "I never want to feel as helpless as I did that night again."

"I will see to it. Your lessons will begin tomorrow."

Sometime during their talk, Shiro had come back from the funeral. He had wanted to attend and give his blessing to the dead in their journey to the Creator. He wagged his tail at Lady Cassiel as she passed and sat next to Ellie.

I like her, he thought as Ellie sat back down on the bench.

You would, she saved your life, Ellie thought, then added, *I like her, too.*

Are you thinking of Aaron? Ellie nodded. She was always thinking of Aaron.

You know I am, but also Jen and Lucas. I never had much growing up, not many friends, but at least I had them. Here, I feel so alone. I don't even have my father's memories.

Since the night she had refused them, Ellie hadn't received a single flash of memory from her father, and a part of her feared they were gone forever.

Ellie looked down at Shiro, giving him a small smile and scratching him behind one ear. *Well, I have you, I guess, and that is good enough.*

Shiro leaned into her touch. His tail thumping against the ground stirred up some of the dry dirt.

You do and you always will, but maybe, he thought and turned his head to the practicing area, *you have more friends here than you think.*

Lacey, Chehon and Sebastian were entering the practice court. They had all changed from their black funeral clothes into clothing similar to her own. Both Chehon and Sebastian had known many of those who had died, including Ethan and James, and had gone to say their goodbyes and pay their respect. And even if Lacey hadn't told her, Ellie was sure she had gone mostly to support her brother.

She was laughing now at something Sebastian had said, reminding Ellie of the carefree girl she had met in the village. Chehon saw her then and called for Ellie to join them. Ellie looked up at the sky once more and smiled. Then she stood up and went over to the small group.

Maybe, just maybe, she wouldn't have to be alone after all.

EPILOGUE

The snow was falling from the sky, covering everything like a blanket. It was a welcome sight after the silver thaw that had been falling since Jen had gotten back from college. She sat looking out a window in her parents' house with Christmas carols playing in the background.

Ellie had been missing for a month now and there were still no leads. Aaron, too, was gone. His agent claimed he was on vacation, but when the police asked, he admitted he had no idea where he was. And that was it. The police wrote it off as an elopement, ignoring Jen when she demanded that Ellie would never leave.

She stared down at the phone in her hand. She had scrolled through her phone book until she had found Lucas' number. She'd only ever called it once before; to tell him Ellie was okay.

She had labeled them both crazy after their strange stories about angels and prophecies, but now, she wasn't so sure anymore.

She gathered her courage and pressed the call button. Four rings before Lucas picked up.

He sounded exhausted as he rasped a tired "hello" into the phone, and Jen found herself actually longing for his quick remarks and rude comments.

"Jen?" Lucas said on the other end of the line, and she made up her mind.

"Lucas, I think maybe you were right. Can we meet?"

ACKNOWLEDGEMENT

I started this book 15 years ago and I honestly didn't think it would ever see the light of day. While there isn't much left of the original manuscript, the idea and heart of the book is still the same.

To finally let this book enter the world is both exciting and terrifying but I am so thankful for all the support I've had along the way.

I would like to start by thanking Chelsea, my amazing editor who managed to take my story and elevate it to become a novel. I'm sorry about the lack of commas though and promise to try and add a few more in the future.

Next, I want to thank the design team at MiblArt who took my sketch of the two cities and turned it into the amazing book cover you now hold in your hands.

And thank you Mariska for the work on both the formatting but also the fantastic interior design. You transformed my old word document into a masterpiece.

A big thank you to my family and friends who has endured years of me going on about this book and for their support once I decided to self-publish.

To the bookstagram community, I was afraid of joining at first but the support and encouragement I've found there is like nothing I've ever experienced before. A special thank you to Carly and Bea who have listen to me babble about plot holes, grammar, creating content and marketing and helped me in ways I can never describe or repay. Thank you for always rooting for me and being there when I need you.

And lastly, thank *you,* the reader. Thank you for picking up a copy of my book and for loving Ellie with all her flaws. Thank you for loving Lucas' banter, Jen's loyalty, Shiro's bravery, Hayyel's sternness and the unbreakable love between Aaron and Ellie.

Thank you.

Made in the USA
Las Vegas, NV
02 May 2025